Acclaim for earlier novels ... pkirk and Eve Pollard:

'Spicy, sharp but sympathetic insider's view' Celia Brayfield

'Flashy, trashy and lots of fun, this book sashays as confidently as its authors through the media circus' *Daily Mail*

'An entertaining account of boardroom battles and family rivalries' *Woman's Journal*

'A page turner . . . great fun' *The Times*

'Enjoyable blockbuster' *Sunday Times*

'Sizzling' *Ideal Home*

'An ebullient airport novel . . . a rattling good yarn by three media high-flyers who have been there, done that and survived to tell an excellent tale' Carmen Callil, *Telegraph*

'The three heroines are indeed a sympathetic trio, swapping love and advice and caustic banter but always caring, sharing and raising a glass to friendship' Lesley White, *Sunday Times*

'Witty, perceptive and warm . . . should not be missed' *Daily Express*

'Sex and shopping with a touch of class' Maureen Freely, *Options*

'The pace is unflagging, the detail spot-on' *Good Housekeeping*

'Fascinating story of sex and power struggles, love and betrayal, ambition and friendship . . . At last, a real insider's view of the media, from the front seat. Glamorous and engrossing, frivolous, fun and deadly serious – exactly what I'd expect from these three top-flight women' Shirley Conran

'Bold, bubbly and deliciously bitchy. From three women who have seen and probably done it all' Michael Dobbs

'Unputdownable' *The Times*

Val Corbett, Joyce Hopkirk and Eve Pollard are also the authors of bestselling SPLASH and BEST OF ENEMIES.

Val Corbett was a newspaper journalist in South Africa and London before switching to television. She produced several acclaimed programmes and became a director of a leading independent television production company. She is married to Robin Corbett MP and has a daughter and two stepchildren.

Joyce Hopkirk has been an editor on *Cosmopolitan*, the *Sun* newspaper, the *Sunday Times*, the *Daily Mirror* and the magazines *She* and *Chic*. She has twice won the Magazine Editor of the Year Award. She is married to Bill Lear, an executive of De Beers; they have a daughter and a son.

Eve Pollard worked on newspapers and magazines before becoming editor of the *Sunday Mirror*, where she won the Editor of the Year Award. She was editor of the *Sunday Express* when it won both the Newspaper of the Year and the Sunday Newspaper of the Year awards. She is a regular broadcaster on television and radio. She is married to Sir Nicholas Lloyd and has a daughter, a son and three stepchildren.

Also by Val Corbett, Joyce Hopkirk and Eve Pollard

Splash
Best of Enemies

Double Trouble

Val Corbett, Joyce Hopkirk
and Eve Pollard

First published in 1997
by HEADLINE BOOK PUBLISHING

First published in paperback in 1998
by HEADLINE BOOK PUBLISHING

10 9 8 7 6 5 4 3 2

ISBN 0 7472 5638 1

Typeset by
Letterpart Limited, Reigate, Surrey

Printed and bound in Great Britain by
Clays Ltd, St Ives plc

HEADLINE BOOK PUBLISHING
A division of Hodder Headline PLC
338 Euston Road
London NW1 3BH

To Polly, Victoria and Claudia

ACKNOWLEDGEMENTS

Thanks to our American contingent: Jerianne Ritchie, Joan Parker, Don Shea, Lucy Purdy, Clare O'Brien, Jinny and Tim Ditzler; and to the British: TV scriptwriter/director Glen Cardno; producer Ann Webber; TV technician Harry McGee; financial whiz John Minshull-Beech; David Webster; Robert Cox, assistant director public affairs (news), New Scotland Yard; Dr Tony Gaze; Ann Dennis, cosmetic surgery consultant; Dr Raj Bharma; Maggie Goodman; Vincent McGarry, Reuters; Judy Wade, *Hello!* magazine; psycho-analyst CM; Veronica Robinson; Sheila Pratt; Sue Thomas; Sue K in France; Linda, Sue, Janine and Irene; Lord Thurso, Gilly Turner and all the staff at Champneys international health resort; Margarita Riera; Vera Ambrose; Nicholas Lear; Oliver Lloyd; Amy Gregson; our editor Marion Donaldson; agent Carole Blake and, as ever, our supportive husbands Robin Corbett, Bill Lear and Nicholas Lloyd.

MAIN CHARACTERS

Katharine Sexton	**Anchor *Here and Now***
Buzz Newbold	her agent
Freddie Hamilton	her escort
George Hemmings	lover extraordinaire
Nina Spenser	her friend
Milo Lomax	her former husband
David Crozier	her accountant
Abbie Lomax	**Anchor *Tonight***
Mateo (Matt) Nicolaides	her agent
Robert Bridges	her boyfriend
Sam Wolfe	Network President (ABN)
Mike O'Brien	Producer *Here and Now*
Ed Dantry	Network President (Globe TV)
Chuck Dempsey	his Rottweiler
Jeri-Ann Hagerty	Producer *Tonight*

Prologue

The two men were hunched down low, shirt-sleeved shoulders touching, crouching over the monitor. Transfixed, they pored over the transparencies, their faces almost touching the computer screen. To any onlooker, it seemed more like pawing. To the editor-in-chief passing through the newsroom, their deep growls, appreciative grunts and excited shiny eyes told him the pictures could be of only one thing. Female flesh. Famous female flesh – naked, with any luck.

'OK, let's see,' he said as he re-directed his path across the newsroom to the art desk of the *National Planet*, the top circulation supermarket tabloid in the US.

At once a magnifying glass was placed in his hand and he homed in over the tiny squares of plastic. His deputy editor and picture editor were gratified to hear his sharp intake of breath.

'Wow.'

What else could describe the sight of America's most famous female television interviewer rubbing suntan lotion into the firm body of a beautiful younger woman? They were lounging beside an aquamarine pool and both women were gloriously, unashamedly topless.

A selection of other shots showed Katharine Sexton and her companion walking in a verdant garden, heads close together, Katharine's mouth whispering into the younger woman's ear.

'I've never heard rumours about Sexton being a dyke,' muttered the editor. 'That so-called man of hers – what's his name?'

'Freddie Hamilton,' said the deputy. 'Owns a shipping line.'

The editor narrowed his eyes. 'Must be just window-dressing.'

'That's not what we're told. He bought her a sensational diamond ring. Huge. The jeweller tipped us off. Apparently this guy wanted to get engaged but she wears it on her right hand.'

'Maybe she was trying to tell him something.'

Once again the three men examined the transparencies.

'Maybe she swings both ways.' The picture editor glanced up. 'She's been divorced for years, no kids. No other guy in her life apart from Freddie.'

The deputy editor nodded. 'And she's very friendly with that New York socialite Nina Spenser, which could be significant. She's also single.' He pointed to one of the pictures. 'So who's this chick?'

The picture editor shrugged. 'Never saw her before. I'll check the agencies.'

'Kate the Great is on our A list of faces that sell copies,' explained the deputy for the benefit of his new editor. 'But she doesn't suffer from Hollywooditis, doesn't have minders, thinks of herself as a journo rather than a celeb. Hell, she doesn't even wear shades.'

'What can we do if she has a cover like this Freddie Hamilton?'

'Let these pictures speak for themselves, boss,' suggested the deputy.

Some of the photographs in the series included the photographer's original target, Hollywood film star Brad Browning, unconcernedly smoking, gazing intently into the eyes of Nina Spenser, also bare-breasted, sipping champagne by the pool.

The three newspapermen paid scant attention to the others in the pictures. Children and wives held little interest; they would be either cropped off or removed with a computer paintbox if these pictures were published.

' "Heart-throb plays away from home?" would be good on an inside page.' The editor prided himself on being able to pluck a headline instantly out of the air and hoped that question mark would keep him out of the courts. A British journalist, he had arrived in Florida from that boulevard of broken dreams, Fleet Street, with his tail between his legs, having been responsible for the publication of a libel against a high-profile British politician. Despite America's more lax laws, Tony Burns was determined not to repeat the mistake. 'Now that Browning is running for Governor of California, I wonder how the no-smoking lobby will react to this pic. Think of all those cancer benefits he's hosted.' He smiled broadly. 'We'll run it big, really crap it up for him.'

'Yeah, he'd be better off trying to get elected in Virginia,' laughed his deputy. Snatched snaps rarely got any better than this.

'Who got them?' asked Tony Burns.

'Gino wired them this morning from Nice.' The picture editor grinned. 'He told me he sat in that olive tree on the edge of the estate in Cap Ferrat for so long he's got them growing out of his ass.'

'Well, he'll be able to sit on it and do nothing for six months with the money he'll earn from this little set.'

'But how far can we go with them, boss?'

'Dunno. We've got eight other writs out so we'd better be careful and there are tough privacy laws in France that could spell trouble. I'll ask the lawyers. The circulation hike may be worth the pay-out but I don't want the proprietor on my back. I'll let you know.'

'Ask him how he'd feel if the enemy got their hands on these,' came the swift response from the picture editor.

'Gino will find a buyer for them real easy if we back off.'

'I know.' Tony straightened. 'Nice work, boys. Do me prints of the best. I'll show them to the lawyers after lunch.'

'OK, boss, and I'll do an extra large close-up for your desk drawer.' The picture editor's forefinger tapped one of the transparencies. 'This one showing all four bazoombas.'

Chapter One

Lightly muscled tanned arms flashed rhythmically in perfect arcs as they scythed through the clear water of the Olympic-sized salt water pool. With the precision of a machine they continued for ten minutes before the swimmer paused. The peaceful sound of the slow roll of the waves below the cliffs was abruptly shattered by the clang of a bell on the veranda.

Katharine Sexton glanced up and spied the diminutive white-robed figure of her hostess enthusiastically semaphoring that lunch was ready. Driven by anticipation of the delights ahead, Katharine's return crawl back to the shallow end broke the week's record.

Emerging from the pool, she tweaked her minuscule bikini bottom to dispel the excess water and pushed her feet into a pair of shiny white mules, revealing square-cut toenails painted iridescent white, a perfect contrast to her slim, tanned legs. She shook out her fuchsia sarong, hanging over a sun lounger, and knotted it round her breasts. It clung to her damp body which, though not model-thin, still fuelled many an erotic fantasy as her fan-mail testified.

How exhilarating it was, she thought, to substitute all those mind-deadening exercises usually done in her gym at home in New York for half an hour of brisk crawl either in the sea or in her host's swimming pool, though she wasn't at all sure that it compensated for eating the temptations offered at each meal. Even from this distance she could smell the roasting loup de mer, the freshly-caught local fish prepared with basil and garlic, a speciality of the villa's chef.

As she hurried through the bougainvillea and honeysuckle-covered pergola, a tendril brushed her damp shoulder, releasing its pungent scent. She inhaled appreciatively, giving a quiver of pleasure, and ran her fingers through her heavy bob to dislodge the droplets of water.

The automatic sprinkler fed by one of several wells in the grounds began sending a fine mist of water across the lawn, catching the sunlight, as she walked up to the ochre-coloured steps towards the turn-of-the-century villa. It was built in the style of a mini chateau, with mellow stone turrets and circular towers in each corner, one of which housed Katharine's bedroom.

Lunch was the first serious decision of the day, with Pierre waiting at the side of the buffet table to take orders. Here on the patio shaded by a vine-covered trellis he and the rest of his staff were ready to satisfy any whim of the guests. He would offer to whip up his special pasta sauce or make a light-as-air omelette filled with any one of a dozen different ingredients. The herbs and spices were artistically arrayed in earthenware dishes in a semi-circle round the heavy cast-iron skillet.

The rest of the villa party was already at the table, sipping at bowls of chilled tomato soup served with a warm crusty loaf.

'Come on, Katie, you're two hundred calories behind,' joked her hostess, Verity Browning, wife of one of the most bankable actors in Hollywood. Katharine had remained friends with the family since a particularly successful interview with them on her show years ago.

'Don't worry, I'll soon catch up. I'm dithering between the pasta or the omelette *fines herbes*.' Katharine, one of the most sought-after dinner guests in New York, revelled in this rare experience of being able to appear in public without the need to maintain an image. She was at her most relaxed with this group. She had known them all for several years and was particularly close to fellow guest Nina Spenser, one of her first neighbours after moving to America. They had met in the lift when Nina was on her way to take her frisky Scottish terrier Angus for a walk in the park.

At the beginning of their friendship it was a coup for Nina to be in the same circle as someone who became as famous as Katharine and it was true that initially she had enjoyed the reflected glory. But as they began to confide their problems and fears to each other, the bond deepened. Both lived alone, and increasingly Katharine had found herself enjoying the generous hospitality of Nina's sprawling estate in the Canopus Valley. It was a bolt hole from her relentless schedule and they spent many leisurely afternoons in the invigorating country air lazing away Katharine's days off, or taking Angus for long, energising walks.

Although her alimony settlement had left her wealthy enough to be a lady of leisure, the glamorous Nina, who had made body-maintenance nearly a full-time hobby, had returned to interior design work after her divorce. Without children or other dependants to care for, she was bored and, as she said to Katharine, some sporadic redesigning of apartments brought her into contact with rich husband potential. A sympathetic ear at a vulnerable time when men were either refurbishing new apartments or throwing out old memories could lead to the altar, she maintained. So far it had not happened.

Katharine was the more serious of the two but Nina was a welcome antidote to the ever-present grind of TV journalism. She kept her eyes and ears open for fascinating New York gossip and as she had never worked in television, Katharine felt safe confiding in her and comfortable enough not to hide behind false bonhomie. Over the years Katharine had learned to appreciate the shrewd mind behind Nina's slightly scatty façade. Surrounded as she was by insincere people for much of her time, Katharine valued Nina's honesty; she could trust Nina to tell her the truth, unpalatable or not.

Katharine watched in admiration as the chef deftly broke the eggs with one hand and folded in the fresh herbs with the other. As she held out her plate expectantly, there was a shout from inside the villa. Brad Browning raced grim-faced on to the patio waving a sheaf of fax papers.

'God damn those bastards,' he yelled. 'How the hell did they manage to take these?'

He shook out the fax and handed it to Katharine. At the top was a copy of the front page of the *National Planet*. Beneath the headline 'Katie And Gal Pal Smooch In The Sun' was a picture of Katharine and a young woman, arms linked, smiling warmly at each other, the bright sunlight catching the gleam of water on their breasts, bare except for the ubiquitous black square over the nipples. This American-style censorship had the effect of making the picture appear more raunchy. Photographs obviously from the same set filled what appeared to be the inside spread of the paper.

Katharine's plate dropped from her hand, shattering across the flagstoned terrace. Nina jumped up and made her way carefully round the fragments of crockery.

'Are you OK, Katie?'

Katharine handed her the fax wordlessly. Nina made a grimace as she scanned the page before handing it over to Brad's wife. The holiday mood vaporised as fast as a Mediterranean shower.

'Shit, they would have to get me smoking.' Like most actors, Brad was more interested in how the publicity affected him than anything else.

Verity scrutinised the fax briefly and said tartly, 'It'll do you more harm to be seen with topless women without your wife than with a cigarette in your mouth.'

'The only time I was lying stretched out sunbathing, you were right next to me,' he replied crossly. 'The shits have cut you out of the picture.'

Just then a tall, slender figure appeared through the French doors wearing a black bikini with a toning filmy shirt.

'What's all the noise about?' asked Abigail Lomax, her eyes wide.

'I was about to come and find you,' answered Katharine. 'You're not going to like this.' She handed over the fax.

'Oh God.' Abbie stared at Katharine. ' "Gal Pal"?' She groaned. 'All over the front page of this rag. What'll people say?'

'They'll say they made it up. Anything to sell papers,' said Verity, an ex-actress, bitterly. She and Brad had been tabloid fodder since their marriage five years earlier and she and their children had been pursued relentlessly.

'Maybe,' said Abbie, 'but there'll always be people who think there's no smoke without fire.'

'We'll have to tell them the truth,' said Katharine slowly. 'We have no choice now.'

'After all the precautions we've taken, the hiding, your careful interviews, all wasted,' sighed Abbie.

'It's unfortunate that it's come out now in the way it has,' said Katharine, 'but we'll learn to cope. I've a nasty feeling that in the end it's going to be worse for me.'

'I'm not sure about that. People are never going to look at me without thinking you helped to pull strings.'

'How come this paper didn't do its homework and realise Abbie's your daughter?' asked Verity. 'I know you've different surnames, but don't they have a cuttings library?'

'They wouldn't think to check. The *Planet*'s published

in Florida, darling,' explained her husband. 'The scum who write this filth wouldn't see Abbie on screen because she appears only on local TV in Chicago.' He frowned. 'What puzzles me is why you wanted to keep your relationship such a secret?'

Verity looked at mother and daughter, her eyes shrewd. 'Is it because of all that fuss a few years ago?' Abbie nodded and Verity noticed her husband's baffled expression. 'You must remember.' Brad shook his head and she laid a slender hand on his arm and whispered, 'Abbie. You know.'

'Know what?'

'Oh, for heaven's sake.' Verity shook her halo of long, dark curls impatiently.

'It's all right,' said Abbie. 'I'm over all that now. It's rather encouraging that you don't remember, Brad, because you were filming in Britain then and there were giant headlines all over the tabloid press. It lasted only a few days but it seemed like weeks to me.'

'It caused a great stir at the time,' said Katharine. 'Abbie and a friend were at one of Britain's most exclusive girls' boarding schools and they went and did a little light shoplifting.'

'Oh, lots of us shoplifted from the local five and dime when we were kids.' Verity laughed. 'We did it for the thrill, not for the value of the stuff we pinched.'

There was a chorus of 'I didn't, I didn't' which was silenced when Abbie went on, 'I was only fifteen, and I wasn't named but I was still hounded by the press. They hung around the school, taking pictures, talking to everybody. It was hell.'

'Yes,' said Katharine, 'the press made a meal of it in Britain because a royal princess was studying there and they were hoping she was involved. Abbie and her friend had a tough time at school.'

Memory stirred in Brad. 'I think I do remember

something – you told me about it, Verity.'

'It was just a couple of pairs of cheap earrings,' said Abbie, 'but I cried myself to sleep for weeks. They kept telling us we were lucky not to be expelled. And we would have been if the Palace hadn't said that they didn't want any more fuss.' She sat down on the swing sofa next to Nina. 'I hated the press because they went on and on offering bribes to the kids. One pupil was promised a thousand pounds if she'd talk. They tried the staff, even the caretaker. Luckily nobody would give them the time of day. The school was really snobby and hated all that. The headmistress cancelled all exeats and everyone blamed us. What made it worse was that the parents of my best friend whisked her away from school pronto. I wasn't allowed to leave.' She threw a steely glance at Katharine.

The incident had exacerbated the existing coolness between mother and daughter. Already upset at being forced to attend a school she hated, Abbie's resentment redoubled. She thought her mother, then working as a broadcaster in London, was using the boarding school to keep her out of the way while she concentrated on a burgeoning career. By then divorced from Abbie's father, a foreign correspondent on a London national newspaper, Katharine bore the brunt of Abbie's distress and confusion over the breakdown of the marriage, and a large part of the blame too.

Even after all these years, the memory of that time never failed to make Katharine feel guilty. Had she used boarding school as a convenient excuse? Had she sacrificed her domestic life to the demands of an absorbing and glamorous career? The nagging doubts had never really left her.

The experience with the press had so scarred Abbie that she had made her parents promise never to mention her in interviews again. Since then the existence of a child had formed no part of Katharine's professional biography, and Abbie, now twenty-six, was never referred to in any press releases.

The evasion grew and fed on itself until it became deception. Katharine refused all requests for interviews or pictures at home and successfully confined media interest to her work, but she had no illusions that the control over publicity that her fame gave her would protect her. All it would take was thorough homework by one journalist and her daughter's existence would be uncovered. It never happened.

When she had arrived in America eight years ago, journalists were far more interested in her love life and the bitchiness among her rival TV stars than her past. Abbie followed a year later to attend college in Boston, but the media, unaware that Katharine's married name was Lomax, did not link them. Katharine parried questions about family with the standard phrase, 'I'm a single woman in America.' When pressed about children, she would comment, 'My life is so hectic, I wouldn't have the time.' She comforted herself that this evasion was not an outright lie, merely a chance to re-invent a little of her history, something it was possible to do when changing countries.

It was Brad and Verity Browning who had suggested that Katharine might ask Abbie to join them on their Cap Ferrat holiday. No one was more surprised than Katharine when, three days before they were due to fly out, her daughter agreed. Katharine rather thought that some other plan of Abbie's had probably been cancelled, but what the hell? She was grateful that they would be together in a relaxed atmosphere and she might start to get to know her grown-up daughter better.

Abbie threw the fax on to the patio in disgust. 'It's outrageous what this paper's done. No way did I want to trade on Mum's name. I'm very low profile in the

Chicago newsroom, just one of the reporters. At least I used to be,' she added ruefully. 'And that's the way I wanted it.'

'I must admit I was happy to go along with that.' Katharine gave a wry smile. 'What TV anchor wants to admit to having such a grown-up daughter, however talented or beautiful?'

'Come on, honey.' Brad attempted to lighten the atmosphere. 'In La-la Land, age isn't important, unless you're a cheese.'

That raised a smile but, like Katharine, the group well understood the way the entertainment industry worked. Ageing, particularly in a woman, was a problem. Even more worrying was a hint of being sexually unorthodox. Everyone realised how damaging the pictures could be for Katharine and her daughter.

Their host began pacing up and down. 'Sue the bastards. I would.'

'We all of us should,' said his wife. 'Reading this, it seems to me that when they're not implying you two are lesbians, they're making out the three of you are here on your own in a *ménage à trois*. There's no hint this is a family holiday with a wife and kids.'

'Sometimes suing does more harm than good,' said Katharine, who was aware of how this kind of action could backfire.

'But we'll have to do something, Mum, and soon,' said Abbie, her face troubled. 'The people who run my station aren't exactly cosmopolitan. They worry if any of their reporters come over on air one cent less wholesome than homemade apple pie. It might upset their precious advertisers.'

'Your lot?' Katharine's eyebrows rose. 'My big players are not exactly liberal about these things either. This is likely to give my boss another heart attack. I bet he's already been on to my agent. At least Buzz knows all about you, Abbie. He'll handle it right.' She examined her watch. 'What's the time in New York? Yes, he'll be awake.'

As if on cue, the phone shrilled. Katharine picked it up and everyone on the patio could hear the excited shout from the other side of the Atlantic. Her agent, Buzz Newbold, was in full flow.

'Katie, you got 'em by the balls. I've never seen three lemons come up at once but I'm certainly seeing them now.'

Katharine frowned. 'What's so funny? It doesn't seem such a laugh to me and Abbie.'

'C'mon, your relationship was bound to come out sooner or later,' he replied. 'And this way it has a multimillion-dollar libel tag on it.'

'If you can tear your mind away from calculating your ten per cent, can I tell you how we see it from this side? You know we wanted to tell the public about us when we were ready, when Abbie was more established.'

'Listen, kid, take it from someone who's been in the business for more than twenty years, this ain't gonna do her any harm.'

'What's everybody saying?'

'Nothing, yet. That was my advance copy I faxed you but all hell'll break out once it hits the news stands this morning. But don't worry, nobody important takes any notice of that rag.' He paused. 'Of course, that doesn't mean we ignore it. If you don't nail lies, the others will run with it. I'll talk to Sam. He knows about Abbie so he'll be cool. And I'll get him to have the network lawyers work on it so you won't have any bills.'

'That's reassuring.' Katharine felt calmer now. As ever, Buzz had switched immediately to damage-limitation mode.

'I imagine Sam's people will also want to draft a press statement,' he went on. 'Station boss he may be but I want to run my eye over it and if I think it's good enough,

I'll fax it to you when it's ready. Give me the word and I'll send it out on the wires.'

Katharine put her hand over the receiver and went over what was planned.

'Can I have a word with him, Mum?'

Katharine held out the phone.

'Buzz, could you keep my agent up to speed? He doesn't know much about my background.'

'Sure thing, kiddo. We need to speak with one voice. I'll fax this to his home.'

When Abbie put down the phone, Brad instantly reached for it. 'I'd better get on to my agent too. He likes to be warned if we look like falling into the manure,' he said, well aware that a squeaky clean image was vital in present-day American politics. He often bemoaned the fact that he was not running during the Kennedy era when the press was more reverential.

Abbie's agent was soon on the line. Matt Nicolaides had been representing Abbie for only a few months and she had a more formal relationship with him than her mother had with Buzz Newbold who was practically family. Matt and his wife ran one of the big independent agencies in Chicago and Abbie had been given their name by several colleagues at the station as a go-getting firm.

He sounded downcast. 'Buzz Newbold's just faxed me the *Planet* stuff. I've been trying to get back to him but his line's permanently engaged.' Over three thousand miles, Abbie heard a sigh. 'Baby, I wish you'd told me.'

'Told you what?'

'That you're gay. Don't you think that's something you should've mentioned?'

There was a short pause.

'I'm not gay. Katharine Sexton is my mother.'

There was a silence across the Atlantic then a startled whistle. 'Kate the Great? Your mom? If only I'd know that when you started—'

'Yes, yes,' Abbie interrupted sharply. 'That's the very reason I didn't tell you.'

Matt sounded excited now. 'Hell, I could've got you acres of space.'

'Yes, but for the wrong reasons. I didn't want to use nepotism to get any job.'

'I can understand that. But now it's out, don't worry. You're good, so they'll say it's in the genes.'

'It's not just from my mother, you know. My father's a great journalist, really talented. I've always thought I take after him.'

Katharine gave no sign that she was upset by her daughter's words. She had heard this refrain many times over the years. Abbie had put her father on a pedestal. She had always been Daddy's girl and although he had worked abroad for much of her childhood, she never blamed him for his lengthy absences. Katharine did not tell her daughter until much later that it was her father's repeated infidelity that had caused the marriage to fail. Even with this knowledge, Abbie excused him, saying he must have needed to search for affection from other women as her mother was too busy with her career to care for him. The implication was clear. She, Abbie, had been neglected too.

The separation from her beloved father when she went to boarding school was another bone of contention between them. To Katharine's fury, when Milo spoke about this decision to Abbie he always managed to sound ambivalent, as if Katharine had been the driving force behind it, when in fact it had been a joint decision.

Over the years Katharine lost confidence in how to say the right thing, do the right thing or be the right mother. She learned to tread on eggshells where Abbie was concerned because she would take umbrage for the oddest reasons. Often Katharine could not fathom how she had upset her daughter. She longed for the easy jocularity that existed between Abbie and Milo, even at long distance. Maybe it was a male-female thing, although discussing this with her friends she found they did not have her problem. She envied their ability to behave like sisters or friends with their female offspring. What was hardest to bear was that Abbie seemed to avoid any physical contact. She rebuffed all attempts at affection, disliked being hugged, and kisses were pecks on the cheek, reserved for birthdays and Christmas.

Katharine often thought that Abbie's coldness was a continuing punishment for concentrating on her career. Her move to New York from London was a career development she had not expected. When the offer came, she was already a highly-regarded presenter at the London bureau of the American Broadcasting Network. Her expertise was the Middle East. She had cultivated invaluable contacts in the region who had given her several top scoops which caused the world to tune in to ABN. This had made her bosses in New York decide there could be a role for her over the water at the head office. She declined ABN's first offer of a top anchor job in New York because Abbie was in the middle of her A-levels. US networks did not usually ask twice but ABN needed a high-profile woman interviewer, and when the next offer came a year later from Sam Wolfe himself, the head honcho in New York, Katharine made up her mind to accept.

The move made sense. Her ex-husband was as likely to be found covering the United Nations for his newspaper as he was fulfilling his custodial duties with Abbie round the duck pond at Kensington Gardens. As he told Abbie himself, he would probably see more of her in America. The memory of the two previous Christmases when his fatherly presence had been limited to a stream of emotional faxes, one from Afghanistan and one from Beirut plus a large, late, delivery from Harrods helped make up

Katharine's mind. As did the fact that the money on offer was more than four times her London salary.

Katharine went on ahead to New York to rent an apartment for them but found herself caught up in work when a series of terrorist attacks, unprecedented in number, occurred in the city. The perpetrators were alleged to be from a little-known sect from the Middle East, and her expertise and far-reaching contacts ensured that she was featured on many of the news bulletins. She also contributed authoritative background pieces for widely read newspaper and magazine articles.

Katharine had already signed the lease of a Fifth Avenue apartment when Abbie changed her mind and announced that she wanted to stay in Britain. Katharine had been devastated but then reality dawned. Her daughter was now eighteen. If she made the sacrifice to return to Britain, Abbie would not appreciate it and she doubted if it would change much between them. So she accepted the inevitable and said she would make herself available for Abbie's holidays. But when Abbie suffered her first romantic setback ten months later, she decided to leave her father's home to start a new life far away from London. She would go to university in America but with three conditions: she wanted driving lessons, a car of her own, and she would not, under any circumstances, be known as Katharine Sexton's daughter.

'How was I to know you'd become twenty times more famous than any telly person in Britain?' she complained. 'The minute you arrive on campus it'll blow my cover. I'll be followed and spied on, just like at boarding school. So I think it's best that you stay away.'

Katharine stared out towards the swimming pool, remembering how hurt she had been by those words. Somewhere in the welter of work, the divorce, boarding school and the move to America she had lost the thread that bound her to Abbie. Abbie had become self-reliant, something her independent-minded mother welcomed while at the same time mourning the loss of that loveable little girl of yesteryear.

After Abbie entered TV journalism, they had more in common and their edgy relationship had improved, so much so that Abbie had agreed to spend her precious holiday with her, the first since she had left college. Over the past few days they had been able to relax and even laugh together. Katharine had allowed herself to hope that they might be able to begin again. Now these damned pictures threatened to spoil everything. And the irony of it was that she had consciously taken her daughter's arm in an effort to bridge the gap between them. It had been years since they had been so comfortable with each other and that brief contact, only a few seconds of rubbing suntan lotion into Abbie's shoulders, a whisper about a bird perched in the laurel bush, those had to be the moments captured by that bloody photographer.

Katharine was drawn back to the present when Brad rapped on the table with a spoon.

'Attention, everyone. Life, or rather lunch, must go on. As your host, I apologise that this has happened to you all under my roof.'

Katharine had been so preoccupied that only now did she notice that a new plate with a fresh omelette had been placed before her.

'Brad, we don't blame you. Much,' Nina assured him. 'Those reptiles wouldn't be interested in you if you weren't so damn rich, famous, talented and good-looking.'

Brad grinned. 'More, more. You forgot sensitive, retiring, modest, presidential potential.'

'I'll drink to that.' Verity smiled. 'Is it time to open another bottle of champagne?'

There was a loud chorus of agreement as she beckoned to the chef.

'In case we're photographed again, Brad, do you think that it should be Californian champagne?' asked Nina with a cheeky smile.

Brad took the comment seriously. 'You have a point. I don't want any more sneaked pictures. Where the hell was the pap hiding anyway?'

Verity peered at the fax then said slowly, 'From the angle of the picture I think he must've climbed up one of those trees over there.' She pointed at dense rows of olive and cypress at the far end of the lawn.

Brad stood up.

'Sit down, Brad,' said Verity. 'Let's enjoy lunch and forget all about this.'

'And hope we're not being spied on,' added her husband as he obediently sat down again.

'This patio's OK, honey,' said Verity. 'But we'll need to plant a lot more cover by the pool. I'll find out how soon we can move in some fully-grown trees and put in more hedging down there.'

'Good idea. See when the garden people can do it. Today would be good.'

Verity winked at Nina. In LA, Brad's legendary impatience was easier to satisfy than in the laid-back Provençal atmosphere of the south of France where there was a more leisurely approach to work.

As the group pondered the huge expense involved in this instant garden growing, Nina asked mischievously, 'Won't you miss your movie star salary when you switch to politics?'

'Well, we may not be able to keep this villa if I get elected,' responded Brad. 'Still, that's tomorrow. Today I want to buy an air gun and binoculars. I'd like to shoot the snapper next time. Katharine and Abbie in particular have had their holiday spoiled and, believe me, it hasn't started yet. By this evening we'll be under siege and the phone will be overheating.'

His gaze shifted to the pair, one so fair, the other dark. They were not at all alike and he could understand why no one had guessed at their relationship. Katharine was neat and small-boned, with long legs out of proportion to her height. She was blessed with wavy chestnut-coloured hair, which curved below her ears.

Countless profiles had remarked on her lavender-blue eyes which, unknown to the journalists, had to be enhanced with darker-hued contact lenses because they did not film well. Her classic features reminded him of Catherine Deneuve in her younger days, with an expression in repose that could be classed as aloof. But it was Katharine's smile that captured the hearts of viewers and in frequent research data this featured strongly as the reason why they switched on to her programme rather than to that of her rivals. 'She makes me feel good,' was the often-quoted comment at focus groups.

Brad had never met Milo Lomax, Katharine's ex-husband, some Brit journalist who had virtually disappeared from her life. He supposed Abbie had inherited her looks from her father. He could detect little of Katharine in that heart-shaped face with greenish almond-shaped eyes, its lashes long enough to sunbathe under, and pert nose framed by chin-length sun-streaked fair hair. Even the shape of their bodies was different, although they were practically the same height, at least 5 feet 8 inches, he guessed.

Abbie, although larger boned, had a spare frame, with each vertebra visible through her shirt, the hollows above her hips well defined above long, tapering legs. If she had been two inches taller she could have made a fortune as a supermodel rather than as a local television reporter. And, as he was well aware, she had remarkably large breasts for such a slender woman.

'This couldn't be worse,' Abbie was saying to her mother, her voice rising in anger. 'Perhaps I should go and work in London. At least I wouldn't be in Dad's shadow over there.'

Katharine adopted the neutral tone which she had found most helpful in dealing with her sometimes volatile child.

'Don't take it this way, Abbie. It'd be crazy to throw away what you've got. You've worked hard to get this far.' Katharine smiled. 'And if you're not around, who else would tell me the truth about my performance? I wouldn't want to rely on the "oink machine".' The 'oink machine' was what Katharine called the coterie of sycophants at her TV station who agreed with her every suggestion. They reminded her of seals in a circus applauding with mindless flapping of flippers and oinking noises.

'Well, if I can't make it on my own, perhaps I should get out of the business, do something else completely.' Abbie's voice was defiant.

Katharine shook her head. 'That would be a terrible waste. Chicago's reckoned to be one step away from the big time and remember you did get there by your own efforts. Didn't your boss send you a hero-gram the other day? You can't say that was anything to do with me. It's obvious they think you're good. They've asked you to do more interviewing on screen so this is not the time to consider leaving.'

Abbie looked mutinous. 'I'm going to be pigeon-holed as Katharine the Second. It's going to take some getting used to.'

'And I hope it won't cause you hassle but you know something? I'm pleased it's come out. In spite of the jokes about my age, I hated having to keep you in the background. I think you'll find it won't be half so difficult as you imagine. I'll probably take more flak than you. They'll say I kept you a secret because I didn't want the competition, and my age will suddenly become a focus of unfriendly interest.'

'No, Mum. You're still the best.'

Touched by this unexpected compliment, Katharine looked affectionately at her daughter. She dearly wanted to give her a comforting hug but, knowing Abbie's reserve, she held back. For a moment she remembered how it once was, when she had held an adorable infant chortling in her arms, burying her head in Abbie's soft neck, gripping her chubby hands with warmth and love. Now, despite the holiday atmosphere, she was still nervous of showing her affection for fear of a rebuff.

The second bottle of champagne had already been opened and the two children belonging to their hosts, sensing something unusual had disturbed the atmosphere, were clamouring for attention, showing off by attempting cartwheels over the lawn.

The sun was dappling through the vine leaves, highlighting Abbie's gleaming blonde hair. One of the youngsters had perched on her knee and she was bending her head to listen to the childish prattle.

I wonder if she has any idea of what's about to hit us, thought Katharine. Brad was right. In a few hours the paparazzi would be circling the villa like hyenas, wrecking the easy-going holiday atmosphere they had so enjoyed.

As she lay on the lounger beside the pool after lunch, Katharine supposed she ought to phone Freddie, he'd worry when the story broke. They had been together for several years and he was a dear man but from the start she had resisted all his pleas for them to live together or to marry. Was she being fair to him? It was a question she asked increasingly often these days. Freddie must have guessed something was different but since he never questioned her, she did not provide answers. She ought to say goodbye to him but did not want to hurt this kind, loyal man.

She toyed with the idea of phoning her new lover. If

George had enjoyed their last sensuous night together as much as she had, the idea of her being a lesbian would certainly make him laugh. Before the *Planet* hit the streets, she wanted to tell him about Abbie herself. How would he react to the news that she had a 26-year-old daughter? It was an uncomfortable thought. George was in his early forties, a few years younger than she was, but age had not been a factor in their affair. So far.

Katharine rarely rang him, recognising early on that he was someone who needed to be the pursuer, but this was different. She stretched languorously then wandered into the villa to use the phone in her bedroom. But George's mobile was not ringing out and the answering machine was switched on. It was still early morning in New York and he was not in his bed. Where on earth was he?

As she rejoined the rest of the house party, none of the others could have guessed from her expression how disconcerted she was. A lifetime of disciplining her face not to reveal on screen what she could hear from the director upstairs meant she was adept at concealing her feelings. Successive studio directors marvelled that whatever information they hurled down her earpiece, Katharine's demeanour did not alter.

Her ability to mask her reactions, so that while she acted carefree, laughing and chatting, her mood was in sharp contrast, carried her through the day.

Until now she had never been out of touch with George for longer than three days and she was irritated to find herself waiting for his calls like a lovesick puppy. He was a secret from everyone except Nina who had introduced them seven weeks, three days and four hours ago.

The attraction had been instant. The steady eye contact, the quickening pulse as if a magnet was stirring shadows in long-dead corners of her body. The affair was so new that after each meeting she found herself smiling the next day at sweet, remembered moments. Once, she had even doodled his name on a camera script.

This was the first time she had deceived Freddie and she felt enormous guilt. Since her experience with her errant husband, loyalty and fidelity had been her credo. Milo Lomax, eight years older, well-read and well-travelled, had been her mentor as well as her lover. For the first two years of their marriage Katharine had lived in a state of euphoria and initially Milo had found her adoration and enthusiasm for learning beguiling. But this had obviously palled since her devoted admiration was not enough to keep him faithful. She forgave him the first affair when he vowed it would never happen again. But it had, many times.

Since her divorce she had fled from anyone who might again arouse that intensity of feeling that had led to such heartbreak and was practised in dousing possible infatuations before they could develop.

With Freddie she felt secure. She had met him at a charity lunch. He had been widowed many years ago and had two grown-up children with whom he enjoyed good relations. He had wooed her determinedly, sending flowers to her office every day, accompanying her to the finest restaurants, first-nights and showbiz parties which he so enjoyed. She liked his company, appreciated his qualities but was aware from the beginning that fondness for Freddie would never transmute into the kind of love she associated with marriage.

After a few months Freddie realised it too but was happy with what she was able to give. Or so he told her. If he was irritated when she needed to go home early after functions, he never showed it. If she indicated that sometimes she wished to spend her leisure time without him, he did not complain. He was content to fit in with her timetable. His shipping company was successful enough for him to take time off work when it suited her. He very much enjoyed being part of a glittering partnership and she occasionally had the rueful thought that her fame was her most important asset for him. Certainly, sex with Freddie had soon become a secondary aspect of their relationship.

But the giving was not all one way. She needed Freddie's calm reassurance and trusted his judgement. He was also completely faithful. His crinkly-eyed charm and confident manner made him an object of some interest to other women but he assured Katharine that there was no one else for him and she instinctively knew this to be true, which was why she felt so bad now.

She had noticed George, towering over the woman he was talking to, as soon as she had entered the room at Nina's country house in Connecticut. He looked as though he might be in his early forties and he had the affluent, assured stance of a confident man. Katharine could hear his deep attractive voice across the room as he held court, the small crowd around him laughing at some joke. She was suddenly glad she had worn the blue softly-clinging crepe shift dress that always turned heads. She assumed that the vibrant woman he was being so attentive towards was his wife and she was ridiculously pleased when Nina told her she was mistaken.

'Who is he? I've not seen him at one of your parties before.'

'No. Lyle brought him along,' Nina said, referring to a mutual friend, an antique dealer. 'His name's George Hemmings and he's in hotels. Lives in New York.'

'Interesting.'

'Divorced.'

'Hmmm?'

'Dangerous.'

'Oh?' it was a description that could never, ever, be given to Freddie.

'Apparently he has a formidable reputation with women and Lyle said I should beware of him but I don't need to worry, he hasn't given me so much as a glance.'

Nina wagged a finger jokingly at Katharine. 'But I've spotted the vibes between you two. Be careful.'

Katharine had tried to be. During lunch she avoided looking in his direction but once caught his dark, mischievous eyes on her, a half-smile on his tanned face. He had stared at her a fraction longer than was polite and before turning away she felt the first curlings of lust.

She was not surprised when after lunch he ambled over and manoeuvred them into a corner, putting an elbow up against the wall and using his broad shoulders as a shield against the rest of the guests. Ordinarily Katharine would have fled from such proprietorial behaviour but she found she rather liked it in him. He was disarming, not the least bit in awe of Kate the Great, and treated her without the deference she was used to from most strangers.

'Thank God, you don't appear to be as clever as you are on the box,' he said, deadpan. She was about to freeze him out when she noticed his mouth curling upwards, on the verge of laughter. 'I suppose you haven't been briefed about me.'

'Oh yes I have.'

'What have you heard?'

She wondered how far she should go. 'Apparently you're the playboy of the Western world.'

He threw back his head and laughed. 'Infamous exaggeration.'

'So why have you got this reputation?'

'People like to gossip. You know what the poets say, "A little love and good company improves a woman." '

'Which poet said that?' she challenged.

'George Farquhar in the seventeenth century,' he said, surprising her.

'And I suppose you've improved many a good woman.'

He gave an exaggerated sigh. 'I wish I had the time but I'm too busy improving my business.'

For the next few minutes he gave her an eloquent rundown of the economics of running a small hotel chain. He explained that he was in the area to inspect a mansion he was thinking of converting into a hotel.

'What an exciting project,' said Katharine, 'to see something dilapidated being transformed.'

'It's one of the most magical things in the world,' he said enthusiastically, 'to give new life to a building which has been written off. And then to see it, particularly at night, all lit up, filled with people enjoying themselves, having fun, making love – it's a tremendous feeling.' He touched her arm in what appeared to be an impulsive gesture. 'Why don't you come with me and see the mansion? It's not far and I could do with some ideas.' He looked at his watch. 'I'm due there now.'

Katharine hesitated. After journalism, interior design was her great love as guests to her apartment could testify. They had spread the word of its elegance and increasingly Katharine received requests from the *Architectural Digest* or *Elle Decoration* to photograph her home. She turned them all down with the excuse that she was not a collector of the rare or the splendid but simply bought pieces she wanted to live with. So what harm could there be in accompanying this man to view a property in broad daylight?

When she said her goodbyes to Nina, her friend threw up her hands in mock horror.

'You're not going off with him, are you? Is that wise?'

'Nina, it's nothing like that. We're off to see one of his properties.'

'Oh yes?'

'It's his business. He wants my advice.'

'Katie, how can you fall for that one?'

'You know how much I love renovating rooms. Besides, he hasn't said one flirty thing or made any pass at all.'

'Not yet,' said Nina to Katharine's retreating back.

The day was crisp and bright. George unbuttoned his shirt, loosened his tie and tossed his jacket on to the back seat of his convertible. After checking with her, he slid open the hood at the press of a button. Katharine was relieved to discover that the car was so well designed, the wind travelled in a slipstream well above her head, hardly ruffling her hair.

As the road snaked along the Hudson River to Putnam Valley, Katharine could hardly concentrate on the scenery, so conscious was she of her inner excitement, a feeling she had not experienced since . . . well, since Milo.

George seemed oblivious of the effect he was having on her as he animatedly pointed out places of interest. She quickly discovered they had a number of acquaintances in common and many minor obsessions. Like her, he spent most of his spare time in antique shops and confessed to preferring the cosmetic side of hotels to administration and financial affairs. Refurbishing hotels meant he was always on the lookout for the unusual.

He told her he found it more convenient to be looked after in the penthouse of his hotel in New York than to maintain a home of his own. He had been married, to an Italian woman, but the marriage had floundered. 'She was too jealous, too temperamental, too Italian. Thank God we didn't have children.' Since then there had been a couple of live-in relationships. 'But I travel such a lot and it was difficult. I guess I've become too self-centred.'

'Too self-centred? A man? I can hardly believe it.'

He tapped her smartly on the knee and let out the laugh that had captured her attention.

'My problem is my age. I'm forty-two and most of the women I'm attracted to are already married. I'm not in tune with younger ones. After the first couple of dates I find we've nothing much to talk about.' He gave her a sideways glance. He gave no hint there was anyone special in his life and for reasons Katharine at that stage did not want to analyse, this pleased her.

It was the perfect moment to tell him about Freddie. But she did not. Instead she steered the conversation back to his business.

The Hemmings Hotel chain was a small group but George had plans for expansion. Currently he was having trouble with environmentalists because he was in the process of gutting one of New York's oldest buildings. 'I don't have any choice, it needs a complete overhaul.' Then he gave her a roguish look. 'I see your game, you're interviewing me. Now let's change the subject because I want to know about you.'

For the first time for ages she talked about what she really felt about doing her job, the work, the competition, the fame, and he responded with questions that were perceptive rather than the 'What's President Clinton really like?' approach. And while he expressed admiration for her achievements, there was no sense of his being in awe, which she found refreshing. Katharine began to relax. This man was on her wavelength. She liked him.

George collected the key from the realtor, refusing the man's offer to show him around. As he told the doubtful salesman, he had viewed the large house and surrounding gardens several times before and was quite confident he could manage without help. He had already made an offer on the property so the agent seemed content. Had he known that the famous Katharine Sexton was waiting in the car he might have insisted on accompanying them.

The partly furnished turn-of-the-century mansion had been empty for six months. Built in the style of a rambling English manor house, it was unmodernised and dusty, but signs of its recent splendour, parquet floors, perfectly moulded cornices, almost unscratched gilt paint and mahogany balustrades, were still apparent.

They wandered through the ground floor, pausing to admire the grand reception rooms which were bare apart from a twenty-foot refectory table marooned, Katharine suspected, because it could not easily be taken in and out of the doorway with its elaborate architraves.

He gave her the guided tour, talking knowledgeably about the families that had lived here and his plans for renovation. Katharine made a few suggestions which he appeared to welcome and she explained that unlike most of New York, she had not used an interior designer for her apartment, preferring to seek out the fabrics, furniture and accessories herself.

'My friends thought I was mad but it was my only recreation in those days. I was married when I was twenty and hard up so I learned how to decorate with one can of paint and a metre of gingham.'

'I know what you mean. My first hotel could have been a terrible mistake. It used to be a brothel and they were very fond of the colour pink and mirrors. The place was covered with them.'

Katharine laughed when she heard that his master-stroke had been to take the mirrors off the ceilings and reposition them on the walls.

Telling her that he wanted her to see the spectacular view over the Hudson, George steered her gently by the elbow up the curved staircase.

They entered what was apparently the main bedroom, a Chesterfield sofa lining one wall. Katharine walked over to the casement window and exclaimed with pleasure at the sight of thousands of beech trees covering the park surrounding the mansion. George came quietly up behind her and put his hands on her shoulders. Katharine felt her heart quicken. They remained standing, silent and motionless. If she wanted to break away, this was the time but she could not move, did not want to move.

George turned her round, pulled her towards him and stared at her. As if in a trance, she watched his face coming closer and as his lips gently touched the side of her mouth she gave a slight shiver. She had forgotten what it was like to feel this surge of adrenaline, a fear mixed with excitement. Half-heartedly she gave him a slight push but he began moving his lips across her jawline, travelling slowly, softly, sensuously across to her ear, down towards the base of her neck. She gave a low groan and George's hands cupped her face, turning it towards him as he kissed her, the pressure becoming stronger, more urgent.

Katharine found her body responding as his muscular frame enveloped hers and with what seemed no pressure at all, he guided her towards the Chesterfield. Slowly and deliberately he unbuttoned her dress, punctuating each opening with soft, gentle kisses. She felt no hint of embarrassment realising that by this time she wanted him to make love to her as much as he did.

Katharine was aware that she was breaking all her own rules, she was naked and enjoying being taken by a man who only a few hours earlier had been a stranger. What had happened to a lifetime's discipline, her fabled self-control? This was madness, but she did not want him to stop. She had gone well beyond the limits of her usual behaviour. She was supposed to be someone important, not a bitch on heat. And she was breaking her self-imposed code of never two-timing Freddie.

But this sex was more exciting, more unnerving, more wonderful than anything she had experienced. What was worse, if she was being honest, she did not want him to stop.

If the realtor had chosen that moment to walk through the door, she would not have been able to prevent the wave upon wave of pleasure that rendered her helpless. It had been so long since she had experienced an intense orgasm that she had begun to think that she was no longer capable of experiencing such emotion.

As he withdrew gently and their breathing subsided, she

supposed he had always intended this to happen. But she did not know or even care now and surprisingly she had not felt any inhibitions. There had been passion but gentleness too and he had been a considerate lover, making sure she was as aroused as he.

'God, you're a handsome chap,' whispered Katharine.

' "Chap"?' he said, mimicking her British accent. 'How very cucumber-sandwich.'

He took her hand and led her across to the four-poster which dominated the room.

This time, though the lovemaking was as erotic as before, it took longer. Much longer.

It had been some years since Katharine had felt such a carnal *frisson* that gave her the confidence to take the sexual lead, kissing and caressing her lover and running her fingers through his thick mane of greying hair. He groaned, turned on his back and she lowered her breasts on to his chest then trailed her tongue slowly down the centre of his body, down, down. He lay quiet, his breathing getting shorter . . .

Later, when he held her close against him, she felt for the first time in years a yearning for some emotional meaning in her life, something Freddie could not offer.

George suggested they stay the night at a nearby hotel but she reluctantly decided she had to return to New York, having arranged to see Freddie that evening. But she would meet George Hemmings again.

That had been nearly two months ago. Gazing into the clear water of the swimming pool, Katharine wondered again why he was still not answering his phone. Then mentally she shook herself. This was ridiculous. She had enough to worry about without getting herself all wound up over nothing like an adolescent schoolgirl.

Pushing George, and Freddie, to the back of her mind, Katharine got up and dived into the pool, which was warmed to perfection by the Mediterranean sun.

Chapter Two

Abbie halted in front of the frosted swing doors leading to *Globe*'s Chicago newsroom. She guessed that the first few minutes back from her holiday would give a good indication as to what the station felt about the press conference she had given with her mother in front of the villa in the south of France.

She was the same reporter her colleagues had known for over two years but few could resist an overt glance as she walked swiftly through the open-plan office, revealed now as the famous Katharine Sexton's daughter. This kind of notoriety was exactly what she had been trying to avoid.

The fitted dress with its matching tight-cropped jacket in fuchsia crepe which she had bought at a little boutique in the Place Lice in St Tropez seemed out of place in the crammed Chicago newsroom. Abbie had decided she would be upfront and wear it on her first day back at the office but five minutes in she regretted her bravado.

Walking to her corner of the newsroom, she tried to catch a friendly eye but the weather woman appeared transfixed by her computer, the sports correspondents were apparently immersed in newspaper clippings, while the political and financial guys were on the end of a phone. In her work pool, the general reporters were as usual too preoccupied with gathering stories to acknowledge the arrival of a colleague, though Alice, at the desk next to hers, raised a casual hand in greeting while continuing her conversation.

At last, a friendly voice. 'Saw the reports about you and your mom. Everyone covered it big time. If you're going to go on TV on your vacation, hon, and doing it without pay, you'll get all of us a bad name.'

Thank God for Blanche Casey. As the station's number one anchor, if she was friendly, the rest would follow. Abbie understood that none of her colleagues was actually hostile but finding out about her mother and, she supposed, the way she had kept it secret, made them embarrassed. The *National Planet*'s mistake had been publicly corrected the following day but perhaps there was an element of guilt too. How many of them had, however fleetingly, believed she was on holiday with her lesbian lover?

'I saw the film clips of the press mob round your villa.' Blanche's crisp voice carried across the newsroom. 'It looked pretty noisy out there.'

'It was,' said Abbie, grateful for this opportunity to address the room. 'They stayed there all day until our statement came out. But of course they wouldn't be fobbed off with that. They wanted to hear directly from us that Katharine is my mum. Sorry.' She smiled. 'I can't get used to calling her "Mom".'

'I think you both handled yourselves very well.'

'Thanks. That European pack don't have any inhibitions. They smell a story and they go for it, no holds barred, so we tried to buy them off by agreeing to a short interview.'

'I saw that too.' Blanche's face showed concern.

'But they weren't satisfied with the interview, it started a feeding frenzy. The phone didn't stop for two days after the British papers latched on to it.' Abbie rolled her eyes.

Blanche leaned over the desk. 'Abbie, I wish you'd told me about your mother. What a strange childhood you must have had, not being able to be with your mom in public. Must've been a strain for you keeping that to yourself.'

Abbie was loath to discuss this with an outsider but it was rare that Blanche took such an interest in anyone, let alone a comparative newcomer. 'It's complicated,' she said with a shrug. 'It was my decision to keep it quiet as much as anyone's.'

Blanche gave a little laugh. 'Of course, as you got older, I guess your mom might've found it easier to keep schtum about having a grown-up daughter.'

Abbie did not reply. It was easy to understand why Blanche was unpopular in the office. And was there also a hint of jealousy? Katharine, only ten years older than Blanche, had achieved national success by her age.

Blanche had echoed exactly what her mother had said, but Abbie would not give her the satisfaction of knowing that. She and her mother might not see eye to eye on many things but she would always be loyal to her in public.

'Don't worry about these people.' Blanche indicated the rest of the newsroom. 'Things will soon be back to normal.'

'I guess. But I didn't want anyone, especially in here, to think I landed this job because of my mother's contacts. I wanted to make it on my own.'

'And you will, my dear. I've been watching you. You're young, sassy, smart. You have a spark that's all your own. With more experience under your belt I think you'll be really special. If I was to look round this newsroom and say who would follow me one day, I'd point to you.'

Abbie was overwhelmed. Approbation from Blanche, star of the newsroom? Then she immediately had an unworthy thought. Had this approval anything to do with her new status? Quickly she chastised herself for her cynicism.

Blanche's exquisite Eurasian features came closer, her thick black hair swinging over her face. 'There's a lot of jealousy here,' she said conspiratorially. 'Believe me, I know. Keep your head down, dear, it'll pass. And if things do get rough, be sure to give me a call. Here or at home.'

'I appreciate what you're saying. Thanks,' said Abbie, aware that this was the longest conversation she and the station's number one had ever had.

Blanche walked away, swaying her narrow hips, and Abbie sat down to face the heap of mail on her desk and sighed. Ever since John Logie Baird had perfected the cathode ray tube viewers had felt they had the right to communicate with those who regularly appeared in their living rooms.

Early in her career Abbie was advised by her colleagues that there was no point in reading missives which were abusive, over-critical or from sickos, and her mother who received hundreds of letters a week had also told her, 'The public feels it has a right to make comments and at first you're amazed that people take the trouble to write. Then you feel flattered that the letters keep on coming. The trouble is that after a while it becomes too time-consuming.' Her mother had been right.

Most TV stations employed specialist staff to deal with the many complaints, the competition entries, the fan letters and the rare compliment. These hired hands were a cross between the fans themselves and an agony aunt. Often fans would write about the milestones in their lives, weddings, birthdays, anniversaries, and such was the warm, interested response that never once would the recipients guess that the star had no contact at all with the letter. The mature women who replied to this mail took great pride in their work. Their longevity in a business which was proud of its macho hire-and-fire attitude was a testament to how important the studios thought these fan-maidens were.

By now Abbie was appearing as a news reporter several times a week and was beginning to be noticed by viewers but she was still too junior to be included in the sift-and-reply service. Her letters were often left unanswered for weeks before a secretary would get round to sorting through the requests for signed photographs or sending formula letters responding to the most frequently asked questions: 'What are your hobbies? What make-up do you use? Where do you buy your clothes and have you a steady date?' The story of her relationship with America's most famous TV interviewer emblazoned on front pages of the nation's press and on TV bulletins had nearly doubled her mail, bringing out the inevitable crazies, cranks and the "I-knew-you-whens".

The first letter Abbie opened was in a small blue envelope, on lined paper. It was direct. 'You were sending me a message today from the television. And my answer is yes. You are my destiny. I will call every day until I get you.'

She was about to throw it into the wastepaper basket when she hesitated. Better to let security have the name so the switchboard could be alerted.

The next missive was from an amateur iridologist. 'I see from the outer ring of your iris that you could be prone to a heart attack. Avoid this by eating carrots, as many as you can, thirty every day, as I have for the past eighteen years. My heart is still sound.'

Abbie decided to send this one to her father. It would appeal to his sense of humour.

She then turned to some expensive-looking cream notepaper from a man who claimed they had had a close friendship at college. With a puzzled frown she re-read the words. For the life of her she could not recall the name so she scribbled 'Please send the "I remember" letter' on it and put it aside for the secretary who typed her mail. The 'I remember' letter was a friendly response that gave no hint that the sender had not the slightest idea who they were writing to.

She put the rest of her mail to one side and scrolled down the computer list of that day's news jobs, frowning when she saw that her name had not been assigned to any story. Maybe her boss had forgotten she was back today. She was about to go and see him and joke about not wasting her Mediterranean tan off air when the phone flashed. It was an internal call.

The honeyed tones of her boss's PA came on the line. 'Miss Lomax, there's a meeting in Mr Svenson's office. He wondered if you could be kind enough to join him.' There was only the slightest of pauses. 'Now.'

Abbie quickly pushed the rest of the letters, without looking at them, into her out tray for answering later. Omitting to read one particular letter in that pile would prove to be a big mistake.

As she hurried to the elevator Abbie put aside her first thought, that she was about to be fired. She had seen enough people coming out of the news editor's office whey-faced to know that the twentieth floor did not bother itself with such minor matters.

She tugged at her skirt, checked her stockings and composed her face, trying to ignore the internal tremors. What on earth was this about? Were they angry about the *Planet* story? Were they upset that she had not told them about her mother and that she had left her agent to contact them?

The instant she was shown into the room her fears were allayed. Taking her cue from the three smiling men waiting to greet her, she relaxed her guard, slightly.

First to greet her was Paul Svenson, head of news and her immediate boss. Sadly, the head of the Chicago station, who would gnash his teeth at missing this meeting, was on vacation. Next to Paul was Chuck Dempsey, someone so remote she had only exchanged pleasantries with him once, when he had paid a brief visit to the office Christmas party. She had heard rumours about the third man at the gathering.

'Come in, Abbie.' Her boss was welcoming. 'Sit down. You know our vice president, of course. Ed Dantry.' His voice lowered with respect as he made the introduction.

Abbie suppressed a nervous smile and nodded. In an industry renowned for ruthless ambition both in front of and behind the camera, Ed Dantry's vulpine qualities were infamous. Dantry was in his early forties but was already on his third marriage, his second having ended abruptly when his wife choked on a fish bone while dining on their yacht the previous summer. Abbie had heard there had been a considerable delay in alerting the rescue services but rumours that another woman had been on board when the boat docked next day were never confirmed. Neither were suspicions that money had changed hands to quieten witnesses at the inquest.

During his short reign over *Globe*'s eight regional stations Dantry had cleared out one-third of what he called the time-servers. Now there were rumours that he was organising the ultimate putsch, to take over the presidency. He was admired in the industry for his dynamism and had a reputation for talent-spotting new stars – his God-given instinct, he called it.

Ed Dantry sat ramrod straight looking directly at her. His enemies said this posture and intent expression took attention away from the shortness of his frame. 'His stare is like a searchlight, you daren't look anywhere else,' was how one sacked employee put it. It was true, for Abbie found herself unable to turn away from his deep-set, hooded eyes.

Dantry was first to drop his gaze and Abbie saw Svenson gesture to a chair set centre stage, obviously meant for her. The huge room was an endless surface of black and pale grey; even the September sunshine was filtered through a grey metallic curtain. The only concession to softness was a pale stone urn set on a marble table, containing an abundance of white lilies. A large glass and chrome desk dominated the room.

'I think you've met Chuck Dempsey, head of our factual news division.' Svenson indicated a thick-set man to Dantry's right.

What was unfactual news? The irreverent thought caught Abbie off guard and involuntarily she smiled at Dantry, who was staring at her impassively. Like many men who had reached the pinnacle of their profession, he went straight to the point. 'I've interrupted my schedule in New York to meet you because—' he paused, his eyes going slowly up and down her body – 'we're creating a new show for the national network.'

The men were staring at her so intently now that Abbie felt supremely self-conscious and wished she had worn anything other than this brightly-coloured outfit. It was fine on camera but not serious enough for this interview. Still, it was great that they were crewing up for a new show in New York and no doubt were going to offer her a job. However important Chicago was, going national was a major step up. But why did it need the vice president of the network to tell her that?

The overhead spotlight reflected Ed Dantry's bald dome. His face widened in what his wary staff called a smile although to Abbie it seemed more like a leer.

'I've chosen you to anchor our new programme.' Dantry was silent for a few seconds, allowing his announcement to have its desired effect.

Abbie fought hard not to show her shock. Her mouth moved but no sound came out.

'You'll front a series that's going to put our station on America's television map.' Dantry jabbed a stocky finger in her direction. 'From all the people we could have chosen, we want you. Are you up for it?'

Abbie was astounded. Front a series? It was so unexpected, so off the wall, she had nothing prepared. Frantically she ransacked her mind for something smart to say, something adroit, but enthusiasm was such an essential commodity in the television industry that even in her shocked state she was aware she would have committed professional suicide had the acceptance not been instant.

'Yes, I certainly am.'

'That was what we hoped you'd say,' said Dantry smoothly. 'Congratulations.' He rose and shook her hand fiercely. 'You're going to be great. I can always tell. You have the talent, you're a happening person. You have that look which says, now!'

Abbie was uncomfortably aware of her increasing breathlessness and was irritated to feel her ears start to burn, her usual sign of agitation. Soon they would redden. She gave her smooth bob a slight flick so that her hair swung forward to cover her ears.

As Dantry returned to his seat, she tried to push aside the unwelcome thoughts that began to crowd in. Maybe it was just a coincidence that this amazing opportunity was being offered on the first day she was known as Kate the Great's kid.

Get real, as the cynics on the news floor were fond of saying.

Since college Abbie had worked her way up from newsroom gofer to cadet reporter and finally she had made it on screen despite tough competition. For every on-screen reporter's job there were twelve internal applicants and hundreds trying to get in from outside.

'Can you tell me what kind of programme you're planning?' she asked, sounding cooler than she felt.

'Sure.' Dantry was beaming broadly. 'Chuck, this is your baby, take us through it.'

'OK, chief. Straight after our new sitcom, so the ratings

will start high, high, we'll come to . . .' Dempsey raised his hands, outlining imaginary opening credits, '*Tonight*, a new current affairs-based magazine programme. You'll be in the studio, Abbie, or up a tree or in a rocket,' he paused for Svenson's too-effusive laughter, 'interviewing people making the news.'

'The people who *are* the news,' interjected Dantry.

'And of course, Abbie, you'll be talking to celebrities, the big stars from the movies, the stage, all of those.'

Like my mother, thought Abbie.

'The programme will be going out in the evenings prime time,' Dempsey continued.

Like my mother's.

'It's scheduled for Sundays . . .'

Like my mother's.

'. . . An hour from seven p.m.'

'Exactly like my mother's.' She found she was saying the words out loud as her initial excitement evaporated. Capped teeth gleaming in the morning sunshine, the men were still smiling at her, confidently expecting her to enthuse over their plan to pit her against her mother. So cold-blooded, so cynical. 'Aren't you offering this to me because of who my mother is?' Abbie's disappointment outweighed her discretion.

'See, I knew that was what you'd think.' Her boss's voice was instantly placatory. 'I warned you guys this was how she'd feel. Didn't I?' He glanced across at Dempsey who gave a perfunctory nod.

'How can I help feeling like that?' Abbie's voice was quiet. 'Of course I want to anchor a show, who wouldn't? But I want to get there on my own merits, not because I'm someone's daughter.'

Svenson laughed. 'No, you have it all wrong. I was talking to New York about you long before I knew who your mother was. Chuck, tell her what I said.'

Without missing a beat, Dempsey said smoothly, 'Paul

here really did give you a great build-up a couple of months ago.'

'I said I had a reporter in the newsroom who had what it takes, didn't I?' Svenson tapped the table for emphasis. The others nodded assent in unison.

'Didn't I predict she'd get to the very top? And quickly? I told them we have to look after you well or somebody'd come and filch you off us.'

No man in that room would have volunteered to take a lie detector test at that precise second but their reassuring façades did not alter.

'To back up my hunch about you I followed up my phone call by sending your show reel to New York,' Svenson continued. 'Right, Chuck?'

'Right.'

In fact the show reel had never travelled further than ten floors up from the Chicago newsroom and now lay in a desk five feet away from where it had first been viewed not an hour before Abbie had been summoned.

'I'd no idea,' said Abbie, still hesitant but wanting to believe him. Not by a flicker of facial activity did either Svenson or Dempsey communicate Ed Dantry's initial reaction after they had watched the tape of Abbie's most recent broadcasts.

'We're taking one helluva chance here. Are we sure this one can do it?'

'Look, chief, I reckon she's OK and the truth is this new show has to be better than what we've got now. For Chrissakes, we've tried everything for early Sunday evening, goddamned wildlife programmes, movies. Hell, you know we get slaughtered by the other three networks, particularly by that Sexton show. So now we luck in. We find out we've got the Sexton daughter already working for us. Great. We create a new show just like her mother's and put them head to head. Think of the publicity. Everyone'll tune in. I can already see the slogan: "You watched the mother for years, now catch the daughter." '

'What's the worst that can happen? So it's a bummer. So she's lousy. We get rid of her. What have we got to lose?' was Dempsey's verdict. Globe's vice president had nodded slowly.

Dantry lit a cigar with great deliberation, his eyes never leaving Abbie's face. 'Believe me, this was a hard commercial decision. No favours. No patronage.'

'It looks so obvious,' Abbie muttered.

'Don't worry about what others might think.' It was Dempsey's turn to reassure her. 'I'm telling you, we don't give a shit about who your mother is.' As he finished he had the grace to glance away and examine his fingernails.

'It's your talent and only your talent we're interested in,' said Dantry forcefully. 'We need younger viewers. That's why we chose someone your age. We're very happy to have you on board in New York.'

Abbie's eyes turned to her newsroom boss. She respected Svenson as a hard-nosed, experienced reporter and she raised her eyebrows questioningly. Maybe she would get the truth from him.

'OK, yeah, it's a plus that you're Sexton's daughter. I wouldn't deny it,' said Svenson. 'But that alone wouldn't make us want to give you this chance. The whole world knows you tried to make it your way, Abbie. You have the talent, you got this far against a lot of opposition. All this has done is hurry things up for you. Don't you see that?'

He sounded sincere and Abbie was keen to be convinced. Surely they would not want to make fools of themselves by putting a useless unknown on screen? They, as well as she, would be finished if she bombed. Maybe, just maybe, they were telling the truth. She was not unduly modest about her abilities. She had done some good work and had confidence she could do the new job. It would be great to be working in New York, the capital of all the television action.

Ed Dantry leaned forward. 'Come and make television history with your own show,' he growled.

His words triggered a pulse of excitement. How many people of her age were offered this opportunity? Not more than dozen in a lifetime but here she was being handed it on a plate. No auditions. No nerve-racking interviews with competing candidates.

Her own show.

The thought of a starring role on a network series would make any broadcaster salivate. In that instant she made the decision.

There was hardly a pause for congratulations before ideas for the show, staffing arrangements and promotional plans were tossed to and fro. Management and her agent would wrestle with the contract, which they gave Abbie to understand would have quite a number of noughts.

Dantry admitted that recruiting for the new show had already begun and Abbie would be given two days to sort out her life before being required to fly east to attend the first staff briefing in New York. The show would go on air three weeks from Sunday.

At last Ed Dantry stood up. 'Let's go and tell the troops.'

Abbie was not looking forward to meeting her ambitious comrades-in-arms downstairs. Whenever anything big happened at the station, a folksy announcement would be made on the newsroom floor. It could cover extra-high ratings, the start-up of a new series, a new appointment; everything possible was done to bond staff into one family in this rapidly developing company. This jump of a tadpole into the shark tank would certainly merit a newsroom blast.

Abbie had been present at previous announcements of promotion and had seen the resentment and jealousy they aroused. None of the other jobs had been in this league and Abbie could guess at the hostility her news would cause. In this building at least she would be about as popular as Chicago's most infamous son, Al Capone.

The paperweight hurtled through the air towards the large television set, crashing into it mid-screen and shattering the inch-thick toughened glass.

As splinters flew outwards, the vacuum behind the glass punctured with a sharp hiss, the tube imploded and the acrid smell of phosphorus-coated tubing permeated the apartment.

But that face, that self-satisfied face filling the screen, that patronising simper had been obliterated. It was a good feeling to inflict damage on that perfection even at a distance.

Abbie Lomax had cast her shadow over their past. Since appearing on screen as a TV news reporter she had become an intrusive, unacceptable presence invoking memories of shared passion that had eventually destroyed hopes, dreams and, finally, love.

Like the television set, Abbie's career had to be smashed. It would take guile and ingenuity but it could be done. This woman had to be taught how much harm she had done. How much she was to blame.

'Abbie Lomax, you bitch, it's pay-back time.'

For the second time that morning Abbie nervously entered the newsroom. This time, no one ignored her. Instead, a frisson went around the office as the journalists recognised Ed Dantry, a rare visitor to their planet.

Abbie found she was avoiding Blanche's gaze as Ed Dantry put his arm round his new star's shoulder and called for quiet. He barely had to raise his voice to achieve this. There was an immediate, expectant hush.

'I wanted all of you in our little family to be the first to know the news.' He paused theatrically. 'The company has decided to launch an exciting new talk show on

Sunday nights. And guess who's gonna head up the team as anchor?'

There was a low murmur around the room.

His smile could not have stretched any wider as he lifted Abbie's arm into the air in a victory salute.

The murmur expanded into a few calls of 'Congratulations, Abbie' from some of her less inhibited colleagues. But there was no doubting the atmosphere of shocked surprise.

For a fleeting second Abbie saw Blanche's face register a jigsaw of emotions, disbelief, anger, jealousy and hurt, before a mask of politeness was yanked into place. What a difference an hour made. Abbie risked a glance across the crowded newsroom. The faces were impassive.

After the two executives left, several of the reporters crowded round her and one or two of the younger ones who could afford to be more generous offered congratulations. A few made sure she had their home phone numbers in case, they said, trying to make a joke of it, 'you miss me so much you want me on your show'.

Abbie walked to her desk and tried to catch Blanche's eye but the star was talking rapidly into the phone.

'You won't think I'm sucking up to you if I bring you a cup of coffee?' asked a friendly voice.

It was Robert, a reporter on a nearby desk. Thankfully Abbie sipped the hot liquid. The two of them had been flirting across the newsroom for weeks, making eye contact over the computers and enjoying repartee around the coffee machine. She liked the look of him but their exchanges had never, so far, extended beyond banter about work.

'They'll get over it,' he said, jerking his head towards the rest of the reporters. 'You'll do great, you'll see.'

The enormity of it all hit her. She was going to have to start again and could vividly remember the gut-wrenching fear of her first days at the station. How much worse it would be in New York where the rewards were phenomenal but the back-stabbing was legendary.

As if reading her mind, Robert leaned forward and said quietly, 'Don't you go thinking they've given you this plum because of your mom. Those guys play hardball and they know you can do it. Remember your air crash story? That was top quality.'

In common with most news reporters, Robert was not in the habit of tossing out undeserved compliments so Abbie was encouraged.

'And when you step off into the stratosphere and leave the rest of the human race behind, remember who was nice to you in the beginning.'

'Remind me how nice you've been,' she said innocently.

He grinned impudently. 'Give me half a chance, I could be a whole lot nicer.'

He held eye contact long enough to make her feel embarrassed but she was saved from having to respond by a call for him from the news editor's assistant. Watching his confident stride across the room, she felt a brief pang for what might have been.

She had had only one long-term relationship since coming to America, and that had been at college in Boston. It had ended, without rancour, on either side, when she moved to Chicago. Since then, a bruising affair with the station's predator when she had first arrived had made her wary. She had ignored the coded warnings from female colleagues about the office Lothario's reputation and when, after three whirlwind months, she was unceremoniously dropped in favour of a newer recruit, it came as a devastating blow. More than eighteen months later she was still suffering from the after-effects of being so publicly dumped. He had eventually moved to another network and she had channelled her energies into her career.

She looked at her watch. It was late afternoon in

London. She was a little apprehensive about her mother's reaction to her new job so breaking the news to her father was top of her list. She picked up the phone and dialled his office number.

As luck would have it Milo Lomax was sitting at his desk. He let out a great guffaw when she told him about her promotion. 'I knew you'd get there. It's my genes. You couldn't fail.'

She laughed. 'Self-reflected glory, that's typical. Just what I'd expect.'

He turned serious. 'You've done well, Abbie. That's fantastic. I'm proud of you and it would have been almost impossible to get that kind of job over here. I can only think of people like Michael Buerk and Jeremy Paxman and virtually no women. The TV stations here allow women to read the news, not comment on it.'

'But Dad, Britain doesn't have the same kind of infotainment programmes we do. It's a mix of news and showbiz. We'll deal with three, sometimes even four different subjects within the hour. An anchor is the opposite of a news reader. One minute I'll be interviewing a rock star, the next someone whose baby's been kidnapped.'

'Sounds great.'

'Apparently audiences are responding more now to female interviewers.'

'Well, people like Barbara Walters and your mother have played their part in that.'

It was true. Increasingly, audiences in America were reacting to female interviewers, not least because of her mother's efforts.

'Yes, Mum's been a role model, women tend to be better at making people feel comfortable and relaxed once the cameras are on them. And we're more successful in netting the "gets".'

'What the hell is a "get"?'

'It's the people I was talking about, like the woman with the kidnapped baby, remember? The people who are at the centre of what we call the hot button issues of the week. Networks fight each other and bribe people with small gifts to get them on their programme. You can't offer money.'

'That sounds like a tough world you're getting into there, Abbs.'

'Tell me about it. Television here is completely advertising-led. If I don't deliver the ratings quickly, I'm out.'

'Surely you get some time to establish yourself?'

'Not really. You see, Dad, the number of people who watch the show fixes the price the network can charge for advertising time. If we don't attract the promised number of viewers, the network ends up owing the advertisers.'

Her father whistled. 'It's not like that here although I can see signs it's moving in that direction. Brutal business.'

'It's much worse than that because it's such a crowded marketplace. We have three other news magazine programmes crowding the prime time schedule, not to mention all the syndicated stuff that's broadcast around the clock.'

'Beats me why you want to put all this pressure on yourself.'

'I'm just beginning to think I'm crazy. I guess it's that old corny thing, the challenge. I want to prove I can do it.' Abbie laughed. 'Besides, as you pointed out, I have the right genes.'

'Ah yes, talking about that, what does your mother think about your new job?'

'I haven't told her yet.' Abbie hesitated. 'Dad, I'm worried about how she'll react.'

'Why?'

'My show's going to have the same format as hers.'

'Well, she can't complain about that.'

'No, but it's going out at exactly the same time, on Sunday evenings.'

There was a pause. 'Ah,' said her father. 'That's a bit tricky.'

'How d'you think she'll take it?'

Her father's voice sounded too hearty. 'I'm sure she's going to be fine, pumpkin. You're not exactly a rival to her, are you? You're just starting and she's one of the best-known women in America.'

'That's true, but won't she feel I'm being disloyal taking this job?'

'Well, you've no control over the timing of your programme. And Katharine of all people will appreciate that.'

Abbie was not convinced. The twentieth floor had done its best to persuade her that the job, its format and timing had been in the pipeline before they knew of her connections but Abbie was too level-headed to believe them entirely. And if she was sceptical about their motives, how much more so would Katharine be after her long experience with such manipulators?

Abbie could well imagine the publicity that would be generated for the new show when the press was told about it. Although her mother would be pleased for her, Abbie was sure Katharine did not need this extra complication in her life.

She said her goodbyes to her father and promised to send him a video of her first show converted from the NTSC American system so he could view it in Britain.

'See you soon, darling,' he said cheerily. 'I'm hoping for a nice escalation to that White House story so that I can get back to Washington.'

Abbie put off phoning Katharine and instead made a few calls to her close friends, telling them the good news. Then she began the Herculean task of sorting out her desk. It contained two years' accumulation of out-of-date invitations, video tapes, long-forgotten post-it messages, bank statements, spare pairs of tights, make-up, crumpled magazine clippings which had seemed so essential at the time, shopping catalogues, fan mail and a pair of Styrofoam arcs meant to give her bosom even more of an uplift but which she had never used.

She handed the most recent *Chicago Restaurant Guide* to the office bon viveur and gave the town map to the news desk as a spare. Then she came across gold dust, a pair of tickets for next season's games of the Chicago Bears. If it was true, as Blanche often claimed, that she had been promised the next promotion to New York, Abbie could understand her silence. She would offer the tickets as a peace overture.

But Blanche had already gone down to make-up to get ready for her noon spot. Abbie, in search of her, finally caught up with her in the corridor. Tentatively she held out the tickets.

'I thought you might like these for your nephews,' she said.

Blanche's head reared up, her eyes glittering harshly. She ignored the proffered hand. 'I'll be watching you,' she said quietly. 'Every step of the way.'

Abbie took a step back as if she had been slapped. Professional jealousy was one thing, but Blanche seemed almost to be threatening her. Shaken, she went back to her desk.

After a moment she took a deep breath and reached for the phone. Now for her mother.

She was put through immediately. 'Mum, you'll never guess what's happened. I've been promoted. I've got a new job.'

'Tell me. Tell me,' said Katharine.

Abbie outlined the great package she had been offered.

'You see, I said you were good.' Katharine sounded delighted. 'Believe me, they wouldn't have given you the job only because you're my daughter. What's the show going to be called?'

Abbie hesitated. '*Tonight*.'

'Simple. Nice.'

'Mum, there's only one thing. I don't think you're going to be too pleased about it. I wasn't.'

Her mother was silent.

'They're keen to do the same format as your show.'

'Oh?' Katharine's voice was guarded.

'Yes, I'm going to be interviewing people in the news, celebrities, that kind of thing.'

'Ah, the same as me.'

'Yes.'

'Do you have to do this every day? It'll be killing.'

'No, once a week. On Sundays.'

'Don't tell me. At seven.'

'Yes.'

There was a pause. 'You realise they've done this on purpose.'

'Of course I do. But they went to enormous trouble to convince me that they wouldn't have considered me for the job if they didn't think I could do it. Do you mind very much?'

'If I'm honest, yes, I do.'

'Do you want me to turn them down?' asked Abbie, reasonably confident that her offer would be refused.

'No. Of course not. I'm not blaming you for accepting the job. It's a great opportunity. You couldn't do anything else. If it wasn't you, it'd be someone else. But these bastards know what they're starting even if you don't.'

'What do you mean?'

'Whether we like it or not, you and I are going to make news. And some of the stories are not going to be like *Life With The Waltons*, I can promise you that. They'll be full of nasty, bitchy stuff and some downright lies. These people are masters at twisting anything we say. We'll need to be very careful.'

'You sound annoyed.'

'Not on my behalf. I think your damn station is manipulating you.'

'Mum, give me some credit. I have been a journalist for a few years. I realise I'm not in your league but I can handle myself.'

'Fine.' Katherine's voice became warmer. 'And I wish you luck. It's very exciting for you and I'm sure you'll do well.'

'Thanks, I appreciate that.'

'I suppose it was inevitable. They've tried movies, sport, sitcoms, the only thing left was to try a clone of my show.'

Abbie winced. Thanks, Mum, she thought. Nice choice of words. 'I'd better get off the phone,' she said, keeping her tone light; Globe's newsroom was not the place to voice her resentment at her mother's sour note. 'I finish here today and then I have just two days to pack up my apartment and get myself to New York.'

Just two days, Abbie repeated to herself as she put the phone down. For the first time her thoughts turned to what she would be leaving rather than what lay ahead. She looked around the large, untidy, noisy newsroom. She would miss this place. The job had been tough, a real challenge sometimes and very competitive but it was made bearable by the humour and shared laughs.

She had beaten five other candidates on the shortlist and still shuddered recalling the dry-mouthed terror she had felt at the audition. After a false start she was allowed to try again. The tape of that nervous beginning had been shown at her first Christmas office party. At least she had got the job under her own steam – and her own name. She shook herself. Really, she had to stop this kind of thinking.

'This is my last free evening,' she said to the room at large. 'Anyone want to come to the Wine Tavern? My treat.'

There was a slight pause.

'Sorry, Abbie, I wish I'd known, it's too late to cancel my plans,' said Robert.

Abbie found herself childishly disappointed but put on a brave face. 'Not to worry, I didn't know myself that this would be happening. Alice?'

Alice shook her head regretfully. 'Heavy date.'

None of the others were free though one or two said they 'might be able to come for just one drink', but they sounded unenthusiastic.

Abbie went back to packing up her things. In their place, hell, she would have come for a drink. Several. Oh well. Jealousy was not a companion she hankered after, it was their loss. In any case, she had to start clearing out her stuff at home so it was just as well.

The goodbyes on the executive floor took longer than anticipated and it was nearly two hours later when a slightly deflated Abbie let herself into the apartment. Loaded down with belongings from her office and a bottle of champagne she fully intended to open and drink all by herself, she pushed the door shut behind her with her foot. As she switched on the hall light, the apartment erupted with hoots and cheers. It was crammed with her friends from the newsroom.

'Surprise, surprise,' they yelled, laughing at her stunned look. Someone relieved her of the packages and handed her a glass of champagne.

'Quiet,' yelled Robert. 'Abbie Lomax, did you really think we'd let you go off to a wicked city like New York without giving you a big Chicago send-off?'

'No. No,' came from a dozen throats as they toasted 'the next star of American television'. Abbie beamed with delight.

Her colleagues had brought food and, knowing about the ill-fated romance with the Lothario, a framed cartoon showing an irritated-looking woman staring up at the ceiling in bed next to her sleeping partner.

The caption read:

> When you do finally meet the only man in the world who's courageous, humane, witty, intelligent, sensitive, charming, sexy, imaginative, independent, single, filthy rich*, your hormones will make you say . . .
>
> 'I can't BEAR his snoring
> 'I can't BEAR his BREATHING
> 'I can't BEAR the way he SLEEPS lying DOWN.'
>
> **this character is purely fictitious and any resemblance to any living person is highly unlikely.*

Amid laughter from the women and groans from the men, Abbie promised she would cherish it for ever. Then they sat her down in front of the television set to watch a special video containing messages of good luck they had recorded in a hurry only an hour before, performed with such warmth and humour that Abbie had to gulp furiously to hold back her emotions.

Alice pressed the freeze frame on the video. 'Now for the *pièce de résistance*,' she said. 'On the way over here we called in at a famous clairvoyant.'

'Oh my God,' laughed Abbie.

'We gave her one of your scarves to get your vibes.'

'I hope you got it back.'

'Yes, but listen to what she said.'

A neat, grey woman of mature years with grey hair, grey face and dressed in a floral dress and faded grey cardigan sat on a worn sofa staring nervously at the camera.

Alice pressed the remote again. 'I admit she doesn't look famous—'

'That's because she isn't,' someone called out.

'OK, but she's all we could get in the time. Abbie, we merely told her that the scarf belonged to a young woman who was leaving. That's all.'

The woman began speaking in a quavery voice. 'This person . . .' She peered beyond the camera. 'You did say she was young? Yes, thought so. She's nice. Tougher than you think but nice. And pretty. Yes, definitely pretty. Good hair.'

'Wow,' laughed Robert. 'So accurate.'

'Within three months she will travel to a different country and in the air she will find romance . . .'

'You're gonna marry an air steward,' came a voice.

'If that's what it takes to get an upgrade.' Abbie raised her glass.

'. . . But she won't find happiness with him, she should look much nearer home for that . . .'

Robert leaned forward and gazed into Abbie's eyes, a serious expression on his face. The moment lasted only a few seconds and Abbie wondered if she had misunderstood it. But before she could dwell on it further her attention was caught by the clairvoyant's last few words.

'I foresee great changes here . . .'

'Yeah, we told you, lady, a new job.'

'. . . It will be an exciting time but,' her voice dropped, 'it will also be dangerous.'

'Definitely. Working in the same building as Ed Dantry, brrr.' Alice raised her two index fingers in the shape of a cross.

'Fame, fortune, yes, she will have these but the price will be high. She must beware of a name beginning with C.' A frown wrinkled her forehead. 'Or B.'

'Or D or P or W,' someone shouted.

'Only another fifty letters to go, lady,' said another.

The woman leaned towards the camera. 'Money will not be a problem and the owner of this scarf will live to old age.' There was only the briefest of pauses before she said, 'That'll be twenty dollars.'

'Twenty bucks? You were robbed,' laughed Abbie, but delighted that they had taken such trouble.

Soon after midnight the party broke up because many of them had to be on duty early. Alice gave Abbie a hug then struggled unsteadily towards the front door where a cab was waiting.

'Robert? Lift?'

'I'll help Abbie clear up, you go ahead.'

'No, really,' said Abbie, 'I have all tomorrow and you have a job at six.'

He sighed. 'You're right but . . .'

'I'll wait downstairs,' said Alice. ''Bye, Abbie, phone you tomorrow – oops, today.'

Abbie closed the door, turned round and found Robert waiting for her, arms outstretched. His lips were firm and dry as he kissed her and he smelled of musk. The kiss went on for many enjoyable minutes before, rather reluctantly, she pulled away.

'This isn't goodbye,' Robert told her. And kissed her again.

'What is it then?' whispered Abbie.

He nuzzled the tip of her nose.

'This is just hello.' He gave her a grin and left.

Abbie smiled to herself as she turned off the light and went into the bedroom. What was it that ditzy clairvoyant had said? Something about true happiness being found nearer home?

A new job and a new man all in one day. Who would have thought it? Robert Bridges. She had always liked him. But there were logistical problems. He was in Chicago and she was about to up sticks for New York. She sighed. Wasn't that the story of her life?

Chapter Three

Katharine was pleased that Abbie had phoned her about her new job so quickly, not least because it would be embarrassing to hear the news from someone else. Mike O'Brien, her producer, had rushed into her office bursting to tell her just after Abbie had hung up. He had seemed disappointed when Katherine told him Abbie had informed her already. She had immediately felt apprehensive. Unless she and Abbie presented a united front they could be torn apart by vultures ready to exploit weakness. They had been back from holiday for such a short time, but already she feared that this new job of Abbie's could jeopardise the bond they had been able to build between them. God knew it was fragile enough, but Katharine wanted it to grow stronger. She would have to be careful. For both of them.

Her anxieties were confirmed when media interest in the mother and daughter TV stars intensified during the next feverish few days.

The focus of interest was not the nepotistic angle of the new appointment, however. Americans were realistic enough to understand that sometimes this was how the system worked. But they did criticise the appointment on nationalistic grounds.

The lead story in the industry's trade magazine – 'Another Brit Snaffles Top TV Job' – started the trend. Other writers quickly climbed on the Stars and Stripes bandwagon and lamented the lack of imagination of US TV bosses for pushing yet another British-born presenter out front.

'After the launch of *Elle* when they brought a London editor over specially, US media moguls seem to think these stiff upper lips are best,' was the line they took. 'Our top magazines, *Vogue*, *Vanity Fair*, *The New Yorker* and *Harpers Bazaar*, and many newspapers throughout the country rely on talent from the UK. Now it's the turn of television. Why?'

These articles had their effect. The Television Guild brought out a statement indicating they would be investigating the employment of foreigners taking jobs in the US media.

By refusing to comment, Katharine and Abbie stayed as far away as they could from the commotion caused by this patriotic fervour. Although Katharine issued a statement in which she was careful to acclaim her daughter's ability, welcoming her projection to stardom, some of the critics could not resist malicious speculation about the ratings war to come.

The publicity supremos of both stations claimed daily victory in the exposure battle. The hype was enormous. Thousands of inches of space were devoted to the minutiae of Abbie's life, what she ate for breakfast, where she shopped, her hairdresser, the false plait she wore at parties, her favourite designers and of course her love life. Who was the man in her life? They all wanted to know. The official line was that there was no one special. Robert was assiduous at keeping in touch by telephone but her schedule was so packed that so far she had not been able to fix a time to see him.

Katharine and Abbie were pursued by the videorazzi, cameramen with hand-held videocams, who earned their lucrative daily bread by selling unflattering footage of celebrities to the tabloid American television shows.

These were described by their loftier brethren as 'the wallpaper of the early evening airwaves'. But they were unlucky with the footage of these two. Katharine had warned her daughter to stay cool whatever was shouted. 'They'll try to provoke you by saying terrible personal things, complete lies, to get a violent reaction. Shots of you spitting with rage or trying to hit them will be news headlines. Keep smiling and the scumerazzi won't be able to use a thing.'

What the media also failed to get, despite repeated and inventive pleading, was a picture or interview with Katharine and Abbie together. Neither woman wanted to be part of a double act.

Katharine found it disconcerting to be asked, several times a week, what advice she would give her daughter about her new job and how she would cope with a daughter presenting a show identical to hers. Abbie was constantly interrogated about whether she was trading on her mother's fame, whether she was nervous of doing a head-to-head with her. Who would not be? Katharine was a television icon. Photographers followed them everywhere; flash bulbs popped when one or other went to lunch or did some shopping or attended a function. Most of the pictures were not published but cameramen were dispatched by their editors to get that day's shot in case there was a news development.

Abbie hated the feeling of being constantly watched, of being the topic of late-night talk shows where the respective hosts competed with each other with the latest Katie and Abbie jokes.

Katharine, who had prided herself on being scrupulously polite and charming to interviewers, found herself wishing, for once, that she could be brutally frank and tell them the truth: that she wished to God Abbie had not gone into the high-stake world of TV journalism in the first place.

When Abbie told her mother she had not had time to

find somewhere to stay, Katharine found herself offering her a home in her spacious five-bedroomed apartment. It overlooked Central Park in one of the most prestigious blocks on Fifth Avenue with neighbours who kept their front door triple-locked to guard their valuable collection of Cubist paintings despite the presence of two doormen on 24-hour duty downstairs.

Abbie had gratefully accepted her mother's offer. 'It's been so hectic, what with meetings, planning schedules, discussions on wardrobe, press calls and photo shoots, I haven't had a minute to read the suggestions Matt's office has come up with, let alone visit them.' She paused. 'I promise I won't get in your way. And I won't bring any dates back here.'

'That's not necessary,' said Katharine. 'It's your home.'

'Yes, but you know how people often like to come in and nose around, see how a celebrity really lives. You need your privacy, so unless there's someone really special, I won't do it. OK?'

'That's very sensitive of you, Abbie. I appreciate it.'

'You know what they say,' Abbie smiled, 'an Englishman's home is his castle – even in America.'

But Katharine, who was pleased to have Abbie living with her at first, soon found it inconvenient having someone else in her apartment. She had forgotten how untidy Abbie was. After she moved in with all her paraphernalia, her clothes soon spread out of the bedroom, jamming the closets in Katharine's gym. Her files and copious cuttings were spread all over the spare room desk and often littered the hall table. Her daughter was so messy that making a simple cup of coffee would untidy four separate surfaces of the kitchen. And within three days of Abbie moving into her bedroom, it was impossible to detect the pale grey Wilton under the welter of tried-on and discarded clothes. Although her housekeeper, Conchita Suarez, valiantly tried to keep some sort of order, it was virtually impossible.

Suspecting how nervous Abbie was about starting her new job, Katharine exercised great self-control and did not criticise her messy habits. Instead she used Freddie as her release valve.

'Guess what I'm growing in my house? It used to be daisies, impatiens, geraniums. Now it's penicillin. Honestly, Freddie, that young woman doesn't lift a finger and it gets really gross when Conchita's away at the weekend. Last week, as I was leaving for the studio, Conchita found this collection of bread covered in green mould in Abbie's bedroom and cups that were ingrained with tea stains. If Abbie eats toast in her room on Friday night the crumbs stay there until Conchita sweeps them up on Monday.'

'Poor darling, it's grisly living with the zoo animals,' said Freddie soothingly. 'My son was like that.'

'But she's twenty-six years old, for God's sake. When is she going to develop some neatness genes? When did your daughter change?'

'Lisa was such a tidy child,' he replied, 'it was never an issue.'

Freddie had brought up his two children alone since his wife had died of cancer fifteen years earlier. Katharine had seen a great deal of his son Charles and even more of his daughter Lisa who lived and worked in New York as a computer programmer. She tried hard not to compare the friendly, easy-going relationship they enjoyed with their father with the one she had with Abbie, but she couldn't help envying it.

'And the phone never seems to stop ringing. I've installed separate phone and fax lines for Abbie's use, but I still get woken up at all sorts of ungodly hours if she's out.' Katharine sighed. 'I sound like a real battleaxe mother, don't I? Maybe I'm being so neurotic because I'm used to living on my own.'

'You know I'd like to change that.'

She took his hand. 'Freddie, darling, you know we wouldn't get on half so well if we lived together. Doesn't this thing with Abbie prove that I'm a crusty old maid who needs to live by herself?'

He shook his head but did not pursue the subject.

'The other trouble,' Katharine went on, 'is that Abbie doesn't know too many people in the industry.'

'Well, we can do something about that,' he said. 'Why don't I give a small party to introduce her to some influential folks? I could invite Charles and Lisa, perhaps some others near her own age.'

That was typical of Freddie, always considering someone else's welfare before his own. She couldn't help comparing him with George. Would George spend five days of frantic organisation to arrange a party for someone else? Probably not. He was far too involved in business and travelling. He seemed to hop off to Europe as easily as others drove to New Jersey. Katharine wished, not for the first time, that she could love Freddie, wished she had the strength to give up George, wished she could stop feeling such a guilty shit.

Even at short notice in late August, and partly because of his closeness to Katharine, Freddie could summon up one of the most stylish gatherings in Manhattan. The guests, routinely booked weeks in advance, made room in their schedule because Freddie was popular, they loved Katharine and they were curious to meet her daughter; attendance at the party, they calculated, would not be a waste of their time.

Freddie's high-ceilinged apartment on Central Park West was part of a national landmark. The airy hallway was filled with a mass of flowers and the doors interconnecting the three reception rooms were open. Air conditioning kept the oppressive ninety degree humidity bearable, but two large French windows were open so guests could drift out on to the large balustraded balcony to admire the view over the park.

Katharine never ceased to be astounded that even in these warm-soup temperatures women would still turn out encased from toe to waist in clinging polyester tights or stockings under their city-chic pastel shift dresses. Only poor white trash went bare-legged, she was told by a fashion icon she had interviewed on the show. The network's phone lines had been promptly jammed with thousands of callers protesting at this politically incorrect statement.

The men, too, maintained a strict dress code. They appeared in long-sleeved shirts and ties, and a variety of pale blue, cream and white cotton suits. The scene resembled a French Impressionist painting against the backdrop of Freddie's rather severe wooden panelling.

Two of New York's foremost columnists were swapping vacation stories with the editors of *Vogue* and *The New Yorker*. The writer of the hottest new movie in town talked tennis with a contender for the White House, while a recently-divorced movie star chatted with Katharine's agent, Buzz Newbold, and a producer who was at that time casting from Long Island for his latest blockbuster. Next to them were long-time friends of Katharine, a couple of famous coast-to-coast anchors who had, unusually, arrived with their wives. Added to the mix was a sprinkling of mid-twenty-somethings, friends of Charles and Lisa, and young executives from Freddie's company.

Lisa had been reluctant to attend. 'I've gotten used to doing things with Katharine and I guess I'm not looking forward to sharing her with Abbie,' she told her father. 'I suppose now that Abbie's in town our lunches and things will stop.'

It was true that Katharine had been in the habit of taking Freddie's family to one or two of the many functions to which she was invited. Since Charles's marriage they had made up a family party to watch football games, attend restaurant openings and museum parties. Over the years Katharine had made a special favourite of Lisa, regarding the easy-natured young woman as a surrogate daughter. They enjoyed shopping and going to fashion shows together and had become close.

Freddie tried to reassure his daughter. 'Katharine will never change towards you, she'll always love you, don't worry. Katharine's never been that close to Abbie. They don't have the same interests like you two do and she finds her quite difficult. Katharine's seen you on a far more regular basis over the last eight years than she has her own daughter. I wouldn't worry. I think you'll find nothing much is going to change.' Lisa seemed unconvinced.

Freddie had also invited Matt Nicolaides, Abbie's agent, thinking rightly that it might be useful for him to meet many of these people. As soon as he arrived, Buzz drew him into a corner to tell him the deep background to the story about their clients in the *National Planet*; it provided a good opportunity to boast about the close relationship he enjoyed with Katharine and her family.

The sight of her agent, balding, avuncular, energetic, filled Katharine with confidence. He was a great asset at a party, for he usually knew the best jokes, the highest-grade gossip. As usual, he was wearing a most expensive tie and a beautifully-cut casual suit. He was the kind of person who hated a gap in his life so he made sure he was talking to somebody at all times, be it a waitress, a client or a garbage collector. Buzz liked to know what they had been watching on TV or in the cinema. He prided himself on being in touch with what the person in the street worried about, what they liked, what they watched.

Buzz's first impressions of Matt were not favourable. He disliked the way he was holding his glass, the way he was chewing, the over-confident stare as he gazed around as though he was part of everything and not the newcomer. In Buzz's world, the signing of one fledgling anchor was not enough to qualify him to join the select group of mega-earning agents who handled the big honchos in this town. Did he realise that he still had to earn his spurs here?

The chemistry between the two men did not improve when Matt's attention was distracted by a waitress bearing a salver of smoked salmon bites. He let out a holler to divert her path back to him and started to chatter about the terrific food. A mite impatiently, Buzz turned away to seek more rewarding pastures.

Freddie made good his promise to introduce Abbie to everybody and Katharine was pleased to see her daughter, confident, pretty and poised on the ascent to a brilliant career, basking in the attention. Katharine had the thought that, as a mother, she must have done something right.

A sharp rap on a crystal glass brought the guests in from the balcony and silenced those in the room.

'Thank you, everyone, for coming here at such short notice. But of course, that's what friends are for,' said Freddie to cheers. 'As you all know, this party is in Abbie's honour.' He raised his glass to Abbie, who was smoothing the skirt of her close-fitting black dress. 'My dear, in this room are the people who are going to make your life as wonderful as it can be in New York. Everyone here is a friend. Don't hesitate to go to them for guidance and wisdom. We all know you'll be a wonderful success, just like your mother. Ladies and gentlemen,' Freddie raised his champagne glass again, 'to our new star, Abbie Lomax.'

Abbie coloured and smiled while her host encouraged her to step forward to respond.

'I'd like to thank you, Freddie, for this wonderful party.

And to all of you for coming,' said Abbie. 'I'm going to do the best I can at my job. My mother's already been a great help and I'm trying to get my father to fly over for the first show.'

This was the first Katharine had heard of the plan and though she was not surprised, she felt a pang that once again she was not support enough for her daughter.

'It can't be bad,' continued Abbie, 'to have two great journalists as parents. Those of you who want to contact me with a story should know that I'm staying in my mother's apartment, but don't worry, Mum, it's only temporary.' There was a ripple of laughter at this. 'I know I'll love living in New York and I thank you all for your good wishes. I appreciate them very much.'

Abbie stepped back to warm applause and noticed that Lisa was standing arm in arm with her mother, idly chatting. They seemed so relaxed with each other that for a second she was suffused with jealousy. Although things were better between them she still watched what she said, alert to avoid any no-go area. The problem was that the past haunted them. Abbie had noticed Katharine's involuntary flinch at the mention of her father. Why couldn't they put guilt, anger, history behind them? Why couldn't she have the relationship her mother obviously enjoyed with Lisa? Maybe she should invite Lisa to lunch. She had so few friends of her own age in New York, what did she have to lose? Perhaps she could learn something from Lisa about handling her own mother.

The eyes, shining high above the streets, seemed to follow her, almost with a life of their own. Abbie's face, measuring fifty by fifty feet, stared down from a poster site high above Madison and East 44th. By day, five halogen lights were switched on which made the whites of her eyes and her row of smiling teeth visible for miles. At dusk an additional fifteen spotlights illuminated the smiling face in

3D relief. Underneath, the legend, in black on white lettering, read: 'Abbie – her mother's best production!! Catch her Sundays 7 p.m. on Globe TV.'

However often Abbie saw the poster, she could not suppress her excitement. And terror.

Finally, after what seemed a lifetime of preparation but was in reality only three weeks, the day had arrived. Sitting in the back of the black Cadillac, Abbie gazed at her reflection in her mirror. Back came the image of a perfect complexion. No dark shadows, no dreaded spot. Nor the giveaway signs of tension, the red ears.

Extreme stress was one of the penalties of the business. Abbie had heard television stars talking about the need for sleeping pills, antibiotics at the first sign of a sore throat, diuretics if they felt bloated, appetite suppressants if they gained a pound or two, uppers if they were over-tired and beta-blockers if they were exceptionally anxious about an impending interview. It sounded crazy. But when sleep refused to come and she began floating around the apartment in the early hours, she ruefully admitted she was beaten. Her producer sent her to the showbiz doctor, whose instant answer to all problems was pills – always, he stressed, within the limits of the law.

Every time Abbie took a tablet she promised herself she would stop as soon as she could take the show in her stride. She fully intended to keep this promise. She had seen too many addicts on uppers then downers to want to follow in their footsteps. As soon as she adapted to the pace she would switch to herbal relaxation pills.

As the car paused at a red light, Abbie inspected another billboard, this time promoting *Here and Now*, her mother's show. 'Stick with the original. Still the best,' it pronounced, below a huge blow-up of Katharine's face. She knew her mother had vetoed the ad agency's first idea, 'Why watch cheap imitations when you can watch the real thing?' thinking it too cruel and aggressive.

Neither Katharine nor Abbie had any idea that this was the slogan the station was using prominently out of town.

Across the country the battle of the hoardings had begun. It was backed up by promos shown regularly on both women's networks and reinforced by radio versions which regularly blasted out their messages across the country.

Katharine's ads, with reels of tape to choose from, featured her meeting great statesmen, top stars and other heroes of the time. Background sound included serious music and words read in a deep and sonorous tone by what the agency called 'the voice of God'. It was all intended to convey gravitas, intelligence, the pursuit of excellence and, above all, trust.

Katharine's team had a superb track record to build on. At seven o'clock every Sunday evening, America sat down to watch *Here and Now.* The series was one of the unifying forces in a multi-cultural country. Its familiar theme tune heralded investigations into such controversial subjects as racism, surrogacy, abortion, the Christian Right and televangelism, mixed up with celebrity soul-baring.

No leader writer, newspaper feature editor or television news editor could afford to miss Katharine's show. It set the agenda for the following day's news bulletins and headlines. She attracted mega-stars from the stage, entertainment and political arenas, and she was adept at knowing the questions that would interest the media. As the saying went in the business, 'Sexton gives good sound bite.'

Katharine's stature set a great challenge for Abbie's team. Her agency used some of the material from her stint in the Chicago newsroom to show her experience and try to combat the doubters who had rushed into print to ask if she was ready to take on a nationwide programme. But without the miles of smiles available to

Katharine's agency, they shot some new footage of Abbie. Her long, lean figure was shown striding across the New York skyline, the bounce of her breasts particularly noticeable. Shots of her eating a chilli dog from a sidewalk stand and laughing with passers-by, roller-blading through Central Park and hailing a yellow cab were supposed to give an impression of youth, friendliness and accessibility. The girl-next-door-and-then-some was the line the advertisements took, all backed by Abbie's own voice so that viewers could get to know her. And love her.

Abbie wished she could have had dry runs in some remote station in Alaska so that tonight's show would be her fourth or even her fifth. There had been several rehearsals in the studio but the 'guests' had been station executives or friends, hardly vigorous tests. Much of the time she lived in a state of euphoria, recognising what this job could lead to. But alongside that the terror was constant, the fear that she would forget some vital fact or do or say something on air that would be an embarrassment.

Her producer was the only person in whom the apprehensive Abbie could confide. Jeri-Ann Hagerty was a young thruster who had been poached from a rival network. She had engineered many private talks with Abbie during which she would offer advice and encouragement.

'Make the most of this fantastic chance you've been given,' she said during one of their sessions. 'Don't analyse it too much. Just make sure you do your homework. I bet Bill Gates has never forgotten the time he was asked by an interviewer about "MS-DOZE" instead of "MS-DOS". Don't let that happen to you. "MS-DOS" is what Bill Gates' whole empire and fortune were built on and you could see he was surprised at the pronunciation.'

'It was just a slip of the tongue.'

'No, Abbie. The researcher should have known that the

interviewer was computer-illiterate. In the Gates context it was really important. So keep at the researchers if you don't get the right stuff. Always ask them for more. Believe me, you could need every last scrap of information. Don't let them put you off. You're up there on the front line. No one puts a caption under your picture saying, "Sorry, my researcher had a bad day so I don't have much interesting stuff to ask."

'And when you're interviewing,' Jeri-Ann went on, 'don't rely only on your belief. Listen hard to the answers, you might find yourself going down some fascinating cul-de-sacs. Above all, enjoy yourself. The great American public out there wants you to succeed, it's on your side and doesn't want to watch you being nervous. So what if some people think you got this because of your mom and it's a great gimmick? Show them why the network took such a chance on an unknown.'

Abbie's first show had three segments; in the first two she would be talking to people who had been propelled into the news that week, but it was the third segment, the celebrity interview, that she was most looking forward to because the choice of guest had been her own.

The limo pulled up in front of the now familiar Globe headquarters on 19th Street. Abbie cradled her head in her hands. This was the moment. She could not ask the driver to go round the block one more time. She had to get out, go up in the elevator and start work on her first show.

Oh God.

As she crossed the sidewalk, she was hailed by a leather-clad delivery boy.

'Hey, it's Abbie, isn't it? Way to go. We're rooting for you.'

A middle-aged couple, overhearing this, paused shyly. 'Do you think we could have your autograph? Your mother signed for us a few years ago.'

'Of course.' Abbie was thankful for the distraction.

It was 4.30 p.m. Two and a half long hours before she went on air. Her mother had warned her not to eat too much before the show. That would not be a problem. Abbie was feeling too anxious even to look at food.

Her dressing room was awash with flowers, like a chapel of rest, she thought irreverently. One particularly splendid array of white roses was from Robert with a card saying, 'You deserve your big break, knock 'em dead. I'll see you *soon*.' Her parents had also sent bouquets with messages of love and luck, her father regretful that he was not able to be with her.

Abbie spent a reassuring half-hour in her office sifting through a shoal of good-luck faxes, cards and a variety of lucky horseshoes. Despite the fond wishes, Abbie could almost hear the knives being sharpened by the likes of Blanche in Chicago.

Like the rest of America, Abbie was aware that her mother had secured the infamous former Mafia boss, Capo de Capo Gino Francetti, for her show tonight, the first in a new series. It was a scoop which ABN knew would make headlines around the world. For the first time, Gino Francetti had been coaxed into breaking his thirty-year self-imposed silence. He would talk about his deals as the head of Crime Inc across America, Europe and Asia. And, more sensationally, he would give details of the secret bargain struck with the FBI to escape a jail sentence. He also intended spilling the secrets of his love life, naming names, especially the women he had shared with an ex-president. Francetti had agreed to be the only guest on Katherine's show to launch his autobiography, which had obtained the largest-ever publishing advance.

Abbie could not compete with the heavy guns of her mother's station. No American agent would risk his star with an untried interviewer opposite the nation's most popular talk show. So her team had had to be more creative and inventive. They had no option. This was where Abbie's British contacts had come in so useful.

The British rock group Caravan was almost unknown in America. Its record had been distributed to DJs only this week and was starting to be played on the youthquake stations from coast to coast. Abbie had kept up with the British music magazines and was aware that the group's continued position at the top of the pop charts and its unashamed use of cocaine and sex had made its young members the bogeymen of British parents. They would, she was sure, be controversial and provocative and would outrage Middle America.

It was a gamble. No one could speculate how their record would sell in the US. Was she interviewing them too early in their American career? And if the viewers were angry with the group, would the audience turn against the untried Abbie and her new show?

Privately many at the network felt it was risky for her programme to go headlong at the youth market but Globe's new research team had spent more time discussing strategy and tactics than they had coming up with names of guests. They realised that their rival *Here and Now* had decided that Francetti was strong enough to hold an audience for the entire show.

The ratings would tell who was right.

Eight blocks away Katharine was soothing the nerves of her guest who had been smuggled in early to avoid the attentions of the waiting press. To keep the unpredictable mafioso happy, the studio had arranged for his favourite pasta to be prepared specially by the chef of New York's top Italian restaurant. With it came two aged bottles of Chianti and a quart of bourbon, all of which had been faithfully reported to the media by his publicist.

Despite, or perhaps because of, his vast experience of

cameras and studios, a testy Gino Francetti was complaining about the lighting, the make-up, his suit, and was still wondering, even at this late stage, whether he was wise to spill so many beans in advance of publication. He debated with himself whether to downgrade his stories, talk a lot and say little, something at which he was practised. When Katharine's producer was told about the ex-gangster's doubts, he set his Exocet missile into overdrive.

Katharine was skilled at soothing doubts in temperamental guests. Half an hour later she walked back into the editorial conference, her relief obvious.

'It's all right,' she said. 'He'll give us what we want.'

'You're a genius,' said Mike O'Brien, the show's long-time producer. 'I thought we were a gonner. You sure he'll spit it all out? All the stuff about the President, the mob, the girls, drugs – and can we use those pictures of them on the boat?'

'Yes, he's cleared it all. He'll be fine.'

'Thank God,' said one of the young, keen researchers. 'Today of all days we've got some opposition and we gotta nuke them.'

The others in the team glared at him. Hadn't he been told that Katharine had insisted no one should mention, let alone bad-mouth, Abbie's show, especially in the jittery hour before the programme?

'Come on, Abbie's no threat to us,' said Mike. 'She's just starting out. Katharine wears the crown. Got that?' The perfidious thought crossed his mind that there would come a time when Katharine would be past it. By then her daughter would have the right kind of experience. That would be the time to work with her.

Suppressing this disloyal notion, he gave his team a broad, confident grin. 'Right now, we've got the best show in town, so get to work! We've all been there, done that, so let's make it a good one, boys and girls.'

★ ★ ★

' "I wanna sleep with you/And tomorrow I wanna sleep with you and your friend/And then you'll never see me again/Snort, baby, snort/Life's too short/And girl, we gotta have fun." ' Abbie looked at the rock star slumped untidily in the guest chair. The interview was not going well. 'What inspired you to write those words?'

He turned to the studio audience and shrugged, which caused a few titters, then stared blankly back at her. She repeated the question. In her earpiece, the producer's urgent voice came through, 'The guy's out of his head. Ask another question quick, for Chrissake.'

But Abbie felt instinctively that the rock star would say something significant if she remained quiet and waited. It was the most expensive silence the station had ever broadcast. It was a technique that made Jeri-Ann nervous, well versed as she was in the demands of impatient audiences, and she had not yet learned to trust her anchor. Despite the increasing volume of instructions being hurled through her earpiece, Abbie held her ground.

Finally, as the cokehead was trying to unscramble his brain, when even Abbie was beginning to think she had made a mistake, she saw his lips moving.

'Well, it's what we guys do – or if we can't, we fantasise about it.'

'Was it a fantasy?'

'Nah. It happened. Happens all the time. I get bored these days with only one chick in the bed so . . .'

Abbie felt a trickle of perspiration coursing down the middle of her spine as she forced herself not to interrupt.

'I like two of them working on me at the same time. Or even three, who's counting?' The pop star began to laugh and made a playful attempt to pat Abbie's knee. Her earpiece almost vibrated with her producer's fury.

'Calm that bum down,' shouted Jeri-Ann. 'This is no

fucking peepshow and stay away from the words of that song, the switchboard is jammed.'

Abbie felt a surge of exhilaration. Her journalistic intuition made her certain that the show was on a roll. It was unlikely that any viewer would switch off now and despite the fears of Jeri-Ann, she fully understood that outrage made good television. Her producer was being panicked by the sheer number of phone calls. Abbie decided to trust her instinct.

'When I first heard your music I thought you and your group were part of a new wave, that you were going to make a difference, like Bob Dylan, make people examine attitudes, maybe even change them. That's why I wanted you on my very first show. But aren't you in a time warp? Your message reminds me of what I read about the sixties, before women's lib, before AIDS, before drugs were so widely available. You're not taking on board the harm your songs could do.'

The dark, brooding eyes which had made him the pin-up of hundreds of teen magazines stared belligerently back at her. 'You have to get their attention first,' he snapped. 'Even Dylan did that.'

'So you'd disagree with all the viewers who have rung in to say you're a mindless punk? Many, like a minister from Ohio, are calling for your records to be banned.'

'Banned. That's quite a good start.' He laughed. 'In any case, those people are not in my constituency.'

'Constituency? Unusual word for a pop star. Ah yes, I was forgetting your degree from Cambridge University.'

'How'd you find out about that?' he asked, his face furious.

'Strangely, it seems to have been left out of your biog but we managed to dig deeper than your press release.' She paused. 'A lot deeper.'

His irritation vanished suddenly and he grinned amiably before lighting his third cigarette.

'I see the no smoking lobby hasn't got to you then.'

He blew a puff of smoke straight into her face.

Abbie coughed. 'How dare you.' Genuinely angry, she allowed her inexperience to show by trying to swipe his cigarette. The star was delighted.

'I've got you going, haven't I? Where's Miss Cool now?'

She took a deep breath and ignored this, flapping the smoke away.

'Attagirl,' said the producer in her earpiece. They were beginning to understand one another.

'You've got brains,' Abbie went on resolutely. 'You know how you're coming across. Does that bother you?'

His grin was insolent. 'You're reading too much into the songs. All I do is try to make people happy.'

'That's your recipe? Drugs, three-in-a-bed?'

'Sounds great to me. Yeah. Those people who've been phoning your show, are they happy? Some of them have screwed up the world, especially that minister. Most of the wars all over the world have been fought in the name of religion.'

'And being peaceful and polite doesn't sell records, does it?' said Abbie.

The star remained defiant as the audience broke into spontaneous applause.

Abbie went in for the kill. 'You give the impression that you think women exist solely for your pleasure.'

He scratched his groin lazily. 'Why not? They never say no to me.'

'That's not quite true. One sixteen-year-old went to the papers saying you raped her.'

'Nah, she was just trying it on 'cos I'm famous.'

'It wasn't just an isolated incident, was it?'

'What you going on about?'

'Have you forgotten the fourteen-year-old who after a sexual encounter with you is still in hospital, traumatised?'

'What fourteen-year-old?'

'This one.' Abbie gestured towards a giant monitor showing a picture of a fresh-faced, smiling teenager.

The rock star exploded. 'Never saw her before in my life. This is another set-up.'

'Really? Then let me introduce you to her father who's on our video link from London. Good evening, Mr Chapman.'

The screen was replaced by a man, uncomfortable at being in the spotlight but clearly determined to tell what had happened to his daughter. The very simplicity of Derek Chapman's words made the story all the more horrifying. He was plainly in great distress as he talked about his young daughter's mental breakdown after her sexual ordeal at the hands of the rock star.

In the middle of his moving description of her plight, the rock star stood up, angrily ripped off his microphone, put his face close to Abbie's ear and snarled quietly but viciously, 'Fuck you,' before storming off the set.

During Abbie's programme, the gallery above the studio, its nerve centre, had kept tabs on the Katherine Sexton show even though they could only watch it mute. One of their researchers took it upon himself to watch *Here and Now* in the next room with the sound turned low so he could relay the highlights at regular intervals. The collective morale sank. Katharine Sexton appeared to have a brilliant television coup.

'Jesus, Gino's just said he and the Prez often screwed the same chick,' shouted the researcher as Ed Dantry walked into the gallery. After a few minutes, the young man returned. 'Gino joined the Mob when he was a teenager and, get this, he says his mother made him do it.'

'Good stuff,' murmured the vision mixer, her eyes firmly fixed on a bank of screens.

The researcher became more excited. 'He ended on a great note. Apparently when he was nineteen he saw two men shot dead, then he picked their pockets. He showed the diamond ring he filched from one of them. He always wears it on his pinkie.'

The Globe team thought this made great television and a groan went round the gallery – just as Abbie walked in, her cheeks flushed and an expectant look on her face. She totally misunderstood their reaction.

'Oh,' she said, crestfallen. 'Was it that bad?'

'Absolutely not.' Jeri-Ann flung her arms round Abbie. 'We were talking about something else. You were terrific, Abbie. We've had masses of calls congratulating you. I wish we'd ditched the other interviews. You done good, kid.'

'I had great research.'

'From your contacts in London. Thanks to that, we were able to track down that first teenager. That was the big breakthrough. Congratulations. How do you feel?'

'A little like a stunned mullet. You know, I felt so sorry for that poor child.'

'We did the right thing. And we've handed our dossier over to the British police. That guy's career just went down the toilet. I hope he spends time where he belongs.'

The researchers milling about showed their approval with wide smiles and Abbie had never seen her boss so animated.

'That was terrific,' said Ed Dantry whose presence in the gallery was a rare honour. 'That'll shock their socks off. You see, we told you it was going to be OK. You were more than OK.'

It needed someone bold to broach the unmentionable to Abbie. Katharine's show.

'Your guy was way more wicked.' Matt Nicolaides, face alight with triumph, had joined the party. 'Who cares about Francetti these days? All the people he hung out with died long before we were born.'

God, this was a weird business, thought Abbie. She

could not get the picture of that young teenager's ordeal out of her mind and all anyone in this room could think about was ratings.

She introduced Matt to all the executives and key people working on her show. Jeri-Ann, still pumped up with adrenalin, was particularly fulsome in her praise of his dark Greek looks. 'I'm into stubby men who can lift me up. Any time he'd like to represent me,' she told Abbie quietly, 'I'm free most evenings after six.'

'Forget it.' Abbie quickly squashed that avenue of thought. 'He's an unusual specimen these days, happily married and trying to be faithful.'

There were muted congratulations from the older hands but some of them were privately sniping. They were irritated that *Tonight*'s target audience was not reflected in their contact books. They were expected to nursemaid this novice who earned three times what they did. In their opinion Abbie had been appointed for the publicity value of who she was and they predicted that her performance would not take a single viewer from her mother. The station should have stuck with the original formula of screening the movie of the week against Katharine Sexton instead of aping her format. Abbie had had a one-off lucky break tonight, they muttered, but the show would probably have a short run until Christmas and then Globe would have to try something else.

But before saying what they thought about the format and Abbie's performance, political animals that they were, they preferred to wait for the overnight viewing numbers before committing themselves.

The figures for Abbie's programme when they came in were good in New York, Chicago and Los Angeles, but metropolitan viewing habits did not always coincide with Middle America's. 'Let's wait and see how she did in Preoria,' said one cynical assistant producer.

When the nation-wide figures were collated, *Tonight*'s

rating was three per cent higher than any previously recorded for Globe for a Sunday night slot. Katharine's show, however, had broken all records. There was unanimity among the media pundits that although both anchors were professional and entertaining, the old-timers, Mom and Gino Francetti, had won hands down.

But across the country, while Katharine had been watched by the parents in the den, teenagers were viewing Abbie in their bedrooms. And they talked about it afterwards. Those young people who had missed her programme would make a point of catching it next week.

Abbie had captured the future.

Chapter Four

The woman was not every man's daydream, but she was attractive enough and she was staring at him. OK, she was frowning but at least she wasn't ignoring him.

Until they discovered he was a showbiz agent most women gave him the frost. Once they found out he could influence producers and maybe get them a slot on television they offered him enough inducements to make him believe he was Tom Cruise. Trouble was, once they realised he couldn't deliver they would start the hassle, bothering him at his office and even threatening to phone his wife.

He and Angela got along fine but it had been ages since he'd had real romping sex. He thought when he moved to New York it would be easy to find it but so far he hadn't had time. His routine hardly varied. He was in the office before 8 a.m. to discuss with his wife the problems she had running the Chicago end. She regularly had problems. By 9 a.m. his rumbling stomach forced him downstairs to the small deli on the ground floor of his mid-town office block. A creature of habit, Matt sat at the same table, reading the trades, ogling the hash browns but ordering the same breakfast, a couple of slices of grilled lean bacon on a low-cal muffin. He had given up eggs-over-easy on the advice of his doctor. At the last medical he had a 7.2 cholesterol rating. Angela had freaked out and ordered him on to a low-fat, low-starch, low-everything diet-awareness programme so he would be around to watch their three sons play for the Chicago Bulls. As if.

Their agency absorbed so much of their time that percentages, gross profit, deals and contracts were mostly all he and his wife discussed these days, in bed and out. Angela hated the separation but she had worked out that he pulled in almost as much with this one client, Abbie Lomax, as the Chicago agency brought in total. Really, Matt should move the family to New York, to where the money was. But Matt was enjoying his new-found freedom and was in no hurry to change his bachelor-like status. Although he was American-born himself, Matt's family was Greek-Cypriot, the men bred to be faithful husbands and devoted fathers, and he was, he was. But oh my God, those New York chicks striding along the sidewalk as though they owned the world made him salivate. Those bouncy, thrusting breasts, the little movement they made swivelling those firm buttocks, the swish of the hair as they passed him by without a second glance – they were enough to drive any man, however well-settled, absolutely crazy. These days, like Jimmy Carter he was faithful to his wife in body while lusting after other women in his mind.

Looking at this woman in the deli he wondered idly what it would be like with her. She had foxy eyes and a curvy little body, outlined in a skimpy white top and a tight black leather mini skirt. It reminded him of that joke about skirts coming in three lengths: five inches above the knee, ten inches above and 'Good morning, Judge'.

His wife teased him that he could double up as that Brit film star Bob Hoskins with hair. And it wouldn't harm him to lose a few pounds. He risked another glance in the woman's direction. God, she was walking straight towards him. Unsmiling, she held out a dollar bill.

'Do you have change? I need to make a call.'

Matt whipped out a mobile. 'Be my guest.'

'No.' Her voice was sharp. 'Just change.'

Matt fumbled in his pocket and handed her some coins. As she walked towards the phone booth at the side of the bar he gazed appreciatively at her retreating legs. Boy, they were up to her armpits. He was glad she wasn't one of those dames who preferred trousers.

A few seconds later he glanced up from his coffee, decaff, no sugar, and saw her heading his way again.

'Could I take you up on that offer of your mobile? Someone's using the booth and I'm in a real hurry.'

'Sure thing.' He hated the over-eagerness in his voice but could not control it. She spoke quietly into the mouthpiece then handed it back. 'Thanks.'

Matt took a deep breath and summoned his courage. 'Buy you a coffee?'

The young woman gave him a withering stare. 'No thanks.' Her voice was curt.

Matt flushed. 'I was only trying to be friendly.'

She paused. 'Do you have any idea how many times I've heard that, bud?'

Matt held up his hands in a supplicatory gesture. 'Gee, sorry. It must be a pain. A good-looking woman like you being pestered all the time. I suppose everyone here has to have an angle. I'm new here and I find this town's a real combat zone.'

Unexpectedly, the woman smiled, wiping out her petulant expression. He caught his breath. She had a great mouth, full, wide, and it wasn't covered by that thick stuff women put all over themselves these days.

'Well, that's different,' she said. ' "Combat zone". I like that.' And she sat down beside him.

It had been a grey drizzly day and Abbie was the first to arrive home. She was in a great mood. Her day had gone well. Great laughs. Great meal. Great sex.

After that spectacular kiss in her apartment, what had

proved impossible to arrange in the whirlwind of her first few weeks in New York had happened effortlessly when Robert visited for a job interview.

'I didn't want to move but, well, there are reasons I need to be in New York,' he told her and she loved the way he looked embarrassed. This was no practised smoothie.

Abbie was not in the frame of mind to search for a husband but she was ripe for an affair. Especially with someone who shared her humour and had the same fascination with the television business. The fair-haired six-footer sitting opposite her scored on both points.

Lunch at the little French bistro had, on one level, been a frothy mixture of reminiscences and laughs, but on another the sexual excitement between them had been so taut, a high-wire artiste could have stepped out with confidence.

Robert was full of indiscreet gossip about Abbie's former colleagues and some of the shenanigans that had gone on since her departure. She laughed at his description of the tricks they had used to convince the boss they were the right people to capture the coveted air time Abbie had vacated. Rumour had it that Blanche Casey was negotiating to join USTV in New York.

'You'd have to have been there to believe it.' Robert pulled a face. 'They were rooting around Svenson like pigs around the trough.'

'Ah well, you know what they say about that,' she countered. 'Never wrestle with a pig. You both get dirty,' she paused, 'and the pig likes it.'

He threw back his head and laughed. Then he rested his hand lightly on hers. 'I'd love to wrestle with you,' he said quietly, trying to look innocent.

After the first kiss in the empty lift of his hotel they could barely restrain themselves. They raced along the corridor, loosening their clothes as soon as they reached his room. Their urgency gave no time for tenderness, but the second time was less frenetic and more inventive, more talk-filled and more satisfying.

'You know,' he said softly, 'I thought you were special the minute I set eyes on you but I didn't get seriously interested until the last couple of weeks. And then you got your new job and I thought I'd lost out before we'd begun. Do you think we'll be able to see each other again?'

Abbie tried to keep her voice light. 'Of course.'

'That's great. I've good feelings about us.'

He was so upfront and honest, it made a refreshing change from the office Lothario. They lay silently in each other's arms until it was time for him to go and catch his plane. If the job interview had gone as well as he hoped, he would transfer to New York. Even so, she would not see him for weeks. He was on duty from Monday until Friday, while her frenetic schedule climaxed over the weekend. Fleetingly she envied people who worked nine to five.

As she stood in front of the fridge in her mother's kitchen, grazing on Conchita's mix of cauliflower, fennel and broccoli slivers, she thought how nice it would be to have a kitchen like this when she found her own home.

To call it her mother's kitchen was not strictly accurate. The only people who cooked in it were Conchita or caterers. Jars of virgin olive oil and vinegars from every part of the world stood in serried ranks on the open shelves of the Shaker blue cabinets. An old solid wood bread board took up much of the centre island, along with jars of dried flowers and wooden salt and pepper grinders. Huge mirrors and antique advertising posters covered the sponged pale blue walls.

In Manhattan eating in was something of a rare event, indulged in by only two categories of people. The poor because they could not afford to dine out and the very rich because it provided privacy and their apartments were large enough to accommodate the staff to prepare and serve meals. It was Mr and Mrs In-The-Middle who patronised the bars, restaurants, bistros, cafés and fast food outlets.

Privacy was expensive, it came with someone like Conchita who magically transformed the low-calorie food they lived on into appetising, palatable meals. She always left bite-sized chunks of crunchy fresh vegetables and fruit in the chill compartment of the giant refrigerator, together with low-fat mousses and spicy dips. Abbie was vaguely aware these took hours to prepare, involving much blending, chopping and grating. But knowing how much weight the camera added, she had disciplined her taste buds over the years not to lead her astray. Sometimes she wondered why Conchita did not help herself to these low-calorie wonders. But the stocky Chilean woman was voluble about the small quantities of food Ms Katharine and Ms Abbie consumed. 'And so much vegetables. It take all fun out of eating,' she would say, shaking her head.

Abbie heard Katharine's key in the lock. She tugged at her slim-fitting navy crepe skirt and hoped her mother would not be able to guess from the creases how she had spent the afternoon.

Katharine was wearing her 'don't recognise me' uniform of fawn trousers, matching turtleneck sweater and pale beige sunglasses.

'If you wore any more of that colour, you'd look like Bambi,' commented Abbie.

Katharine looked at her sharply but was disarmed by her daughter's grin. She must stop looking for hidden meanings in what Abbie said. She was becoming hyper-sensitive.

'Good,' she replied. 'I don't know why this colour works but it does. Nobody recognises me. Try it and see. I got the idea from reading about Marilyn Monroe who was able to melt into the crowd whenever she wanted if she was wearing these sorts of clothes. When she wanted to be noticed, she could flick on an inner switch.'

'How did she manage that?'

'It was to do with the way she held her body, swayed her hips, lifted her chin and stared people in the eye. The star strut, she called it.'

'It also helps if you go out of town and nobody sees you. How was lunch?'

'Good.' Katharine looked away to hide her expression. George had been there and they had left for his new hotel, their old haunt, immediately the food had been cleared away. 'Nina's re-hung the Warhols and they look stunning.'

Several times lately she had been tempted to tell Abbie about George Hemmings but, as she told Nina, 'How can I say I'm having a mid-life lusty affair? Mothers just don't do that. And she likes Freddie. It would complicate things.'

But, like all lovers, Katharine could not resist talking about her new man. 'Nina introduced me to a friend of a friend who owns a small group of hotels, here and abroad.'

'What's he like?'

'He's divorced, a little younger than her, very tall, attractive, simpatico . . .' She stopped, aware she was sounding too enthusiastic, but Abbie's attention was on the contents of the fridge. 'He speaks fluent Italian. One of his hotels is in Rome.'

'OK, we've got the discount,' joked Abbie, liberally spreading cream cheese on a couple of bread sticks.

'I thought you had lunch today.'

'I did,' she answered, handing her mother a carrot stick, 'but I'm still hungry.'

'You would have been fascinated by a woman at Nina's. I couldn't help watching the way she ate. Or rather, didn't eat. She held her knife and fork as though she couldn't bear to touch them, not the primeval way most of us do.

She helped herself to everything on the table but all I saw her put in her mouth was a narrow wedge cut out of a stuffed tomato.'

'God knows we have to watch it,' said Abbie, 'look at all this rabbit food we exist on, but I'd rather miss a meal than do that.' She looked mischievously at her mother.

Katharine returned her smile. The atmosphere between them was definitely more relaxed and she was beginning to be optimistic that old problems might be resolved.

There was a buzz from the doorman downstairs. 'Package for you, Ms Lomax. It's coming right up.'

'Thanks, Joe.'

Each week, staff in the publicity departments at both their networks would send them a compilation of the week's press and television comments. Abbie and Katharine had slipped into the habit of having a post-mortem over a quiet supper every Monday evening and sifting through the cuttings in the bundle.

This week's package contained nothing contentious. They both laughed at the imagination of one paper which had published a story of a long-lost twin brother Abbie was supposed to have in London, complete with photograph.

'Looks nothing like you,' said Katharine.

'As a matter of interest, why didn't you have more children?'

'We tried but four months after you were born, I had a pap smear which showed some abnormalities in the cells of my cervix.'

'I didn't know that. Did it hurt?'

Katharine realised with a start how few personal conversations they'd had. 'Not at all but I had to have a cone biopsy to cut those cells away and years afterwards when I tried to find out why I didn't conceive again, the doctor told me that because of the scarring from that operation, the sperm would have needed hiking boots and crampons to get through.'

Abbie rested her face on her hand. 'Poor you. So now you have only me to concentrate on.'

'Self, self, self,' quipped Katharine. 'You'll get on in television, all right. Oh look, I get eight out of ten for my hairstyle this week in the Atlanta *Courier*, yours is only six.'

'Yes, but they prefer my outfit. Donna will be pleased. And my guests score higher, according to the *Gary Indiana Gazette*,' bragged Abbie.

'Ah, but the folks in the good city of Telluride think you wave your hands too much,' countered her mother. Katharine's smile faded as she scanned a clipping from a widely-syndicated columnist. 'You need to be careful with journalists. I'm sure you didn't say all this stuff about your schooldays.'

'What's that?'

'Oh, that I often missed things like the school play and sports day.'

Abbie shifted uneasily on her chair.

'You know I went whenever I could.'

'Yes, but I hated that school. I did try and understand why you weren't always able to come but it was hard.'

Katharine could not stop a sudden surge of exasperation. 'You have no idea how difficult it was for me after the divorce.'

Abbie shrugged. She had listened to a Greek chorus about the struggle women had to be equal throughout her formative years.

Katharine was stung by her indifference. 'I was only a little older than you are now when your father and I split up. You were seven. I was lucky and success came quickly and, like most people, I have my fair share of ego and selfishness. But I did try to do my best by you although I know I didn't always succeed. How could I? And how often did your father turn up at school events?' Her voice sounded sharper than she intended and she bit her lip.

'Oh, Mum, be fair. His job sent him all over the world.'

Katharine clenched her teeth and said nothing. She had never been able to make Abbie understand how difficult her life had been in those days. In the male-dominated world of television, it was not acceptable to ask for time off because you had a young child to look after. It became easier when more women made their presence felt in the top echelons of business and as she climbed the ladder. In the way of things, her bosses became more accommodating as she became more important to them.

Abbie ran a hand through her hair. 'I'll call Rona and try and straighten it out.'

'No, don't. Don't complain, don't explain. Journalists see that as a weakness.'

In the five weeks since they had been pitted against each other by their respective networks, they had managed to avoid being hurt by the relentless media barrage, good and bad. This was the first time their new-found harmony had been clouded by the coverage but Katharine was all too well aware that the competition would only grow more intense as Abbie continued to hone her skills as an interviewer.

The Alain show was the high spot of the New York fashion collections. Alain was one of the world's most innovative designers and his catwalk had, season after season, offered fireworks. For the last three years he had opted for the first show of the week, 11 a.m. on Monday morning. Hitherto no fashion house had wanted it. The jet-lagged international army of buyers and press might not arrive from Paris, Milan or London in time for a Monday morning show. Only Alain could make it fashionable. 'The others can wait until after me,' he said, referring to the rest of America's designers. 'Plagiarists, all of them. I *am* New York ready-to-wear.'

No one watching the stars turn up in their limousines

to do homage would disagree.

Alain, born Alan Yentovitch, of Brooklyn Heights, loved surprising the fashion cognoscenti and doing things differently. He did not bribe, persuade or cajole. Not for him the old ploys at seducing a glittering front row of the show with a suit hung up in a hotel suite, a piece of jewellery or handbag sent round by hand. His classic stiff white invitations were sent out to home addresses only in the dying days of August. Everyone but everyone would attend, including sports and film stars, pop idols and business tycoons. All of them would squeeze into whichever auditorium the shows were based in that season.

At the back of the catwalk, Alain kept a close eye on the proceedings as supermodels chased their eyebrows with tweezers and hairdressers and make-up artists pulled and prinked them into 'the look': wild manes, deep, smouldering, heavily made-up eyes and ultra-pouting, natural-looking lips. He was young, still in his early thirties, and although he only owned a tiny percentage of the company that made and marketed his clothes, he was already a millionaire.

It was his custom to give everyone who attended his show a gift, something small and perfect, one year a gold-plated key ring, another a linen, hand-edged handkerchief. This year they would be pleased, he thought. A silver picture frame. He always gave the same to the millionaire superstars at the front as to the cub reporters at the back. He was well aware that those in the tiny gilt seats in the boondocks today might merit a perch right up against the catwalk tomorrow.

From the back of the stage, he peeked through the curtain as the murmur from the crowd increased a decibel. It was the entrance of Katharine and Abbie that had caused the stir in the vast white hotel ballroom. He had put them in pride of place in the front row beside the royals from Britain, Monaco and the Middle East. The

TV boys would like that. Abbie was seated next to Jeri-Ann while Katharine was ushered four seats further along next to Freddie's daughter Lisa, her guest. Blanche Casey would not be pleased to be off-centre, he reflected, as she had signed a contract to anchor USTV's talk show, but at least she was in the front.

The show was about to begin. Abbie nodded at Lisa. The lunch had been pleasant enough, but they would never be close friends. As she faced the clicking cameras, Abbie was thankful she had taken Jeri-Ann's advice to visit the studio for a professional make-up. Close proximity to supermodels made her want to look just as polished. Brenda, the make-up supervisor, had been busy tending the wig of one of America's best-loved male news commentators, one of several big-name stars with thinning hair and a large wardrobe of wigs. He often commented how much time he saved by having his hair styled in one room while being made up in another. So Abbie had been directed to Brenda's new assistant, Brooke, who had done a first-class job in very little time; she had even managed to apply the extra-fine eyelashes with skilful speed.

The papers had been full of the so-called war of the anchor women and Alain hoped that his diplomatic seating plans would quell the gossip columnists on this occasion at least; nothing should distract attention from his show.

His hope was misplaced. Abbie was seated immediately opposite the bank of television and press cameras and the pundits counted the number of seconds the cameras lingered on each of the star presenters. Abbie clocked up thirty-nine seconds, Katharine a mere twenty-five. The gossip writers were delighted – plenty of scope there for stories about the Queen Bee losing her place in the hive.

After fifty garments in black, taupe or this season's palest blue had been shown, Alain's individualistic interpretation of a bridal outfit, a vision in armless, backless, nipple-nudging white satin came on. As Alain acknowledged the cheers, his staff distributed three hundred identical packages, each tagged with the name of the recipient in copperplate script.

As Abbie pulled the small silver frame from its elegant velvet drawstring purse, she gazed in bewilderment at the crude postcard stuck behind the glass then pushed it quickly back into the purse.

'Alain seems to have had a lapse of taste,' she whispered to her producer. 'What's in your frame?'

Jeri-Ann held it up. There was nothing but cardboard backing.

'That's strange.' Abbie turned to her neighbours but theirs, too, were blank.

Later, in the safety of her limo, Abbie undid the frame and handed the postcard to Jeri-Ann. It showed a drawing of a naked woman sitting with her legs akimbo, leaving no gynaecological detail to the imagination. Butterfly wings sprouted from her back. The message, typed and pasted to the card, read: 'I intend to clip your wings. Watch out. Fan of Fans.'

'Why would Alain send me this?' asked Abbie, her face troubled.

'I can't believe he was responsible. I'll ask him.'

Alain's excited voice on the car mobile quickly made it clear that he did not know what Jeri-Ann was talking about and she felt it wiser not to go into detail.

As she clicked off the phone, she looked with compassion at Abbie. 'You've had some of the good side of fame, now I'm afraid you have to face up to the downside.'

'I suppose so but what have I done to make anyone send me something so crude?'

'Who knows? It could have been sparked off by anything. They have a fight with their partner, then they see your smiling face on the screen apparently having a better time than they are and boffo, you become the object of their anger. Or their desire.' She added briskly, 'The good thing is they hardly ever persist when they get no reaction from you.'

'But how could they get so close to me? I can understand things being sent to the studio but right there at the fashion show . . .' Her voice trailed off.

'Look, there are literally hundreds of people involved in a show like that. Any one of them could have done it or been asked to do it. These people are wily and you'll probably never find out who was responsible. You have to learn to live with it. Most of us have weird threats at one time or another.'

'What did you do with them?'

'Chucked them in the garbage.'

Abbie toyed with the card, her brow furrowed. 'What's puzzling is that the card is so offensive but it's signed Fan of Fans.'

'I guess he's trying to be ironic.'

'Maybe, but I can't get out of my mind that crazy woman in the Stephen King story. You know the one who kept on saying to the author "I'm your greatest fan" before trying to kill him.'

'Honey,' said Jeri-Ann soothingly, 'that was a novel, not real life. If you worry about it, they've achieved their objective. Try and put it out of your mind.'

Katharine gave her the same advice when Abbie told her about the card. 'But you should tell Matt Nicolaides about it,' she added. 'Let him worry about it for you. That's what agents are for.'

But Matt was out of town and Abbie could not reach him on his mobile. Oh well, she thought, her mother had been subjected to this sort of thing in the past, and if it didn't bother her, she certainly wasn't going to lose any sleep over it.

★ ★ ★

Enveloped in a mist of Laura Biagotti bath oil, Katharine read the magazine interview, her agitation mounting.

> 'Katherine is obsessed with Abbie's programme [the ex-researcher was quoted as saying]. The entire cast is. In the old days, when Katharine came off the set we'd sit around, chew the fat, discuss the show, have a few laughs. The atmosphere was great.
>
> 'Now, the minute her show's over she rushes off to watch the tape of Abbie's programme. She won't listen to anyone else who's seen it, she has to see it for herself. So everyone has to hang around until that's over. And afterwards, there's not a lot of happy faces. Katharine's constantly sounding off about her daughter's hair, what she's wearing, that sort of stuff. There's real bad vibes about it all, none of the old team spirit left, no friendship, just a lot of bad-mouthing about copycat TV. I wouldn't be surprised if I was the first of many to leave.'

Katharine furiously stabbed a taut index finger at a number on the white bathside console.

Her agent picked up his phone in seconds. 'OK,' said Buzz who had read the article and knew what she wanted without her having to say a word except his name. 'I've seen it. Usual place, at noon. We'll talk.'

Katharine arrived at the Babushka on the dot of noon. As the maître d' showed her to Buzz's table, no one paid much attention. The Babushka's sophisticated clientele did not stare at celebrities.

Buzz was already sitting at his customary corner banquette.

'It's infuriating,' Katharine protested as soon as she had sat down. 'It's not just this ridiculous researcher. She was only hired at the beginning of the year but apparently she exaggerated her past experience and Mike soon found out she wasn't up to the job. So she was fired. What I'm upset about are these stories about Abbie and me.' Katharine leaned forward. 'Buzz, we have to put a lid on this right now. I feel completely exposed and unprotected.'

'OK, I'll go see the boss. Mike's a great producer but he's not sensitive to the politics. We can't have people shooting their mouths off like this.'

There was a slight pause. Katharine looked ill at ease. 'The trouble is it's not complete lies. There's the usual tiny grain of truth underneath. I did moan about Abbie's hair but only because the front flops and hides her face. I tell her about it all the time.'

'This gal's twisted it. It's not unknown. Maybe they should think about getting everyone to sign a confidentiality clause,' Buzz suggested.

'Absolutely. If everything I say can be turned round and pitched to the press this way, it'll make work impossible.'

'I'll say all this to Sam. He and Annette have gone away for the weekend but I'll be in there first thing Monday morning. Don't worry, Katie, I'll take care of it.' He gave a swift glance around the restaurant to check out who was there. 'So how's Abbie's agent doing?'

'I've only seen him once since the party but he seems quite sharp. New York's some change after the Windy City but there are sacrifices. He's had to leave his wife behind, she's running the business in Chicago.'

'How do you know that's not a bonus?'

Katharine gave him a playful punch and they were still smiling when the waiter arrived with their order, which rarely varied. For Katharine a baked potato topped with Beluga caviar but no sour cream, no onions, and for Buzz, a small steak, rare, with a large green salad, no fries. Even as an agent you had to look good in this town.

'By the way, I've tried to negotiate an extra two weeks off air a year but Sam's holding out until he sees what the other stations are gonna do.'

Katharine put her knife down with a clatter. 'Other stations? Or are they talking about Globe? Buzz, level with me. Are they more worried about Abbie's show than they let on to me?' Katharine's eyes were challenging.

The basis of their lucrative relationship was that they shared information, good and bad. Straight talking had been the secret of their successful strategy. As one commentator had so neatly summed it up: 'When the car park of television history is littered with burnt-out carcasses, Kate the Great is one of a tiny minority who have sustained a lengthy career.' That ability had gained Katharine an extra five per cent on her last contract.

'All I can tell you, Katie, is what they tell me. Sam loved last Sunday's show. Loved it. All good stuff when we come to re-negotiate.'

'And you're sure he meant it?'

'He wouldn't bullshit me. We've known each other too long.'

'I hope you're right,' said Katharine. 'This mother-daughter feud nonsense is harder than I thought.'

Katharine's apartment, in a pre-war building still with its original cornice and picture rails, was perfect, Abbie thought as she let herself in. Perhaps too perfect. She paused to admire the hallway with its gleaming, elaborately framed Regency mirrors. The hall opened into a circular alcove housing a mahogany table inlaid with marquetry. On it stood an enormous glass vase which was always filled with fronds of greenery and white flowers, whatever the season.

As she walked towards her bedroom she heard the television blaring in the living room. Strange, she had not expected her mother to be home.

'Hey, I'm back,' she called.

If the television had not been switched off abruptly Abbie would have headed straight to her room to change.

As it was, she put her head round the door.

It was an impressive space, two rooms converted into one. Cream and white polka-dot swagged curtains in heavy silk complemented the beige and white cushions on the pair of large, comfortable sofas.

At first Abbie could not see Katharine then she heard rustling paper from the far side of the sofas. There was her mother, on hands and knees, trying to round up a mass of cuttings which covered most of one sofa and spilled on to the pale wooden flooring. There were piles of magazines on the other sofa, on top of which Abbie could see a copy of *People* magazine. Some of its paragraphs had been highlighted in yellow.

'What are you doing?' asked Abbie with an innocent air. As if she didn't know.

'Nothing much,' answered Katharine, flustered, by now attempting to push the mass of cuttings into a large envelope.

Abbie picked up a video case and peered at the title. '*Braveheart*. Are you interviewing Mel Gibson?'

'Um, well, maybe. We don't know really. It was just a thought.'

Ha. Next week's star interview, thought Abbie. No one did that much research if it was just speculative. Her mouth twitched. 'Are you having him on the show or not?'

'He's on our list but . . . no, I doubt it.'

Abbie plumped herself down on one of the deep sofas. She could not resist the temptation to poke fun at her mother's paranoia. 'Oh good. Because if you're not going to get him, I think I will.'

Two red spots appeared on Katharine's cheeks. 'I didn't say we weren't going to have him on. I said I doubted it. That still means we might.'

'But you might not.' Abbie was enjoying herself.

'We're still considering it.'

Abbie began to laugh. 'You should see your face. Relax, Mum. Of course I'm not going to poach. I'm just teasing.'

Katharine paused only a second before throwing a cushion at her daughter. 'You beast. I've been so careful trying to keep things from you.'

'And me from you,' laughed Abbie. 'You caught me on the hop last week. But I don't think you saw me smuggling Iain Banks's new novel into a pile of magazines, did you?'

'No, I didn't.'

'And Jeri-Ann reckons I'm not careful enough.' She imitated the Southern drawl of her producer. ' "Abbie, you're giving yourself extra complications by sharing a place with your mom." '

'Mike thinks the same but I'm sure we can handle it,' said Katharine.

'Of course we can,' said Abbie.

But mentally both of them crossed their fingers.

Katharine was now as full of trepidation as a schoolgirl. Abbie had agreed to accompany her in a foursome with Freddie and Robert for the season's most prestigious charity occasion, the Black and White Ball. Though she was surprised that her daughter had accepted, Katharine was apprehensive that the evening might be filled with tense silences or worse, barbed comments.

Faithful to its prototype, Cecil Beaton's stunning Ascot scene in *My Fair Lady*, the Black and White Ball was held only once every five years. It was organised by the arts-loving septuagenarian billionairess, Cookie Fairweather, who mixed different ages and groups with celebrities she had not seen for years. She had a data base of eleven thousand 'friends' but only her favourites received tickets, all of whom would pay well over the odds to be seen there.

Cookie stipulated a no house-guest or relative rule,

using the excuse that the ball had to keep within fire law limits, but Freddie, one of the first to be sent a ticket – George, as a mere hotel-owner, was not on the list – had asked if Abbie and her partner could attend. Permission was graciously granted and, intrigued by the ball's history, Abbie had persuaded Robert to fly in from Chicago. He was still actively looking for a job in New York and regularly flew in for interviews, which meant extra nights they were able to spend together. Abbie sensed that their burgeoning relationship made him more determined to work in the same city as her.

She had commissioned a gown specially for the evening and was delighted with the results. The fine white silk and the narrow skirt made her feel slinky and sexy. The neckline was lower than she normally wore but she was confident that in such an ultra chic crowd it would go fairly unremarked.

Katharine was resplendent in black guipure lace with a fishtail skirt which outlined her slender frame and frothed out beneath the knee. The dress dipped to her waist at the back and she had filled in the outline with a long string of pearls. But she and Abbie arrived separately not wanting to appear in joint photographs.

The enormous ballroom, ablaze with a line of gold chandeliers, was crowded by the time they made their entrance. It resembled something from a fairy tale. Painted backdrops by top Broadway designers were placed outside the windows to give the feeling of being backstage at a theatre. Trellised walls, decorated with hundreds of the most fragrant white roses, camellias and carnations, were theatrically lit so that people passed in and out of spotlights as they greeted one another. On a central dais, three top bands played continuously, surrounded by huge banks of white hydrangeas. Cookie had sent huge bouquets of the same flowers to all the neighbours so they would not complain about the noise.

As they looked round at the profusion of black and white ensembles, Katharine's eye was drawn to the only spot of colour in the entire room and she nudged Abbie. 'Would you look at Cookie,' she whispered, trying to hold back her laughter. 'Only she would dare to wear scarlet.'

Abbie was admiring. 'I can't wait to get to her age so I can get away with things like that.'

It was a magical evening and Katharine was proud of her daughter, and delighted to be in the company of Freddie and Robert. The four of them meshed well together and Abbie was amusing, light-hearted and relaxed and, as Freddie remarked more than once, she and Robert made a great-looking couple.

When Abbie wanted to freshen up in the cloakroom she asked her mother to accompany her and while they were applying fresh make-up she glanced at Katharine in the mirror. 'What do you think of Robert?'

Good God, thought Katharine, I'm being asked my opinion. This was a first. She kept her voice deliberately light. 'Well, I'm in favour. He's good-looking, funny, attentive and he appears to dote on you.'

Abbie frowned, her blusher brush halted in mid-air. 'I don't want him to get serious too soon. With this new job of mine, I'm not in the right frame of mind for anything heavy.'

Katharine blotted her lips on a tissue. 'I often think that timing is the most important thing in any relationship. But he seems to be very involved in getting a new job so I wouldn't be too worried.'

Her daughter seemed to take that on board. Later, during one of the spirited reels, Katharine found herself swinging from her daughter's arm. Abbie gave her a look of such enjoyment that Katharine experienced a wave of pure affection, something she had not felt for this lovely, spiky, irritating daughter of hers for far too long.

Abbie seemed genuinely to relish being in her mother's company. There was no veneer, no artifice. This was the real Abbie. Why, thought her mother wistfully, couldn't it always be this way?

Chapter Five

Week eight into the new series and Katharine's team was on a war footing. No edict had come from on high, no group meeting had decreed it, but there was a bunker mentality at ABN. The few who had been complacent at the start of Abbie's show were now running around like headless chickens blaming everyone and anyone for the smallest failure. The insecurity was almost tangible. The rest hunkered down and worked longer and harder, trying to second-guess the upstarts at Globe.

Horrified by some of the more malicious press comment, a few of the most trusted associate producers had formed themselves into a kind of kitchen cabinet; they used code names for the guests and disseminated information on a need-to-know basis only. This did nothing for the smooth running of the show. Two people would, unknown to each other, hustle the same agent so much that his client would take umbrage and defect to another programme. Tempers became frayed, rows erupted and the troops became alienated, particularly the new blood. The atmosphere became so fraught that it was re-named the Kate-the-Hate Show. The large bulletin board lost its scattering of jokes and cartoons about the programme and was replaced by a picture of the tranquil Colorado countryside which the corporate shrink had suggested might calm nerves.

The desks at ABN were state of the art, interlocking,

modular, black. The push of a button would release a drawer in which the computer was sited. Matching telephone consoles perched on each work station. The huge room was dominated by a panoramic view of the New York skyline through the wall-to-wall window. Three groupings of beige leather sofas were strategically placed along the length of the window so that three different sets of visitors could be seen at once but enjoy privacy. These touches underlined the fact that this was the number one show. The motto which kept it at number one was framed on the wall: 'NO MATTER WHAT YOU'VE GOT, IT TAKES MORE THAN THAT.'

But in the last couple of weeks, Mike O'Brien, Katharine's producer, had been unable to ignore the mood of uncertainty about the place. A couple of shows had been slightly disappointing, not in terms of ratings but audience appreciation. Focus groups had been unhappy watching a former world champion boxer stare into space, his well-rehearsed lines banished into oblivion, the result of a hundred punches too many. And they were critical of another programme in which the unfortunate parents whose fertility treatment resulted in seven dead babies had become dumbstruck in the limelight. Nothing Katharine could say evoked more than monosyllables from the petrified couple. Commentators too questioned the morality of programmes like *Here and Now* which delved deeply into private grief solely for the delectation of the viewing audience.

Coincidentally, Abbie's interviews on the same Sundays found themselves on the high moral ground. One featured a 25-year-old nun, gang-raped in the Bronx, who forgave her attackers on air. This was followed by a movie star who, on the day he emerged from therapy for his sexual addiction, publicly re-pledged his marriage vows to his wife and begged her to give him one more chance.

These contrasts served merely to make Mike envy his

opposite number on Abbie's show; she had a brash, keen team who were all new, linked by super-glue and the 'Avis Tries Harder' mentality. In his opinion, there was no need for anyone on Katharine's show to feel dispirited. On the last Saturday before a well-earned Thanksgiving holiday, he came in brandishing a fistful of trade magazines, including *Variety*, *Broadcast/Cable Magazine*, *Electronic Media* and *Advertising Age*. He felt a team pep talk was in order.

'Hey, boys and girls, our ratings are holding up great. The publicity, even the bad stuff, has done us no harm. We're still easily number one.'

A cheer went round the office.

He went through the latest figures. *Here and Now* was still Sunday night's top news magazine show; *Tonight* was trailing at number four, behind Fenton TV and USTV. He thought it unhelpful to add that Globe had increased its Sunday night ratings by fifteen per cent since the start of the season, impressive for someone completely new.

'I know some of the stories in the press have got you down and those of us who love Katharine feel in some way we're under threat, under attack. Hell, of course Abbie's doing well, it's in the genes.'

Laughs and nods.

'But I say again, we're still number one. Listen to what Bill Whalen of the *Times* says: "Katharine Sexton's consummate professionalism shines out in a sea of TV disasters this autumn. It says little for the business that her only real challenger is her own daughter but Abbie could still use some matriarchal tips. Katharine's team should relax and enjoy the holidays, they've earned it." '

'But, boss, they keep surprising us,' said one of the newest, keenest recruits. 'You've seen the ad for that stunt Abbie's going to do in Times Square on Saturday morning. Can't we do something like that?'

Mike shook his head. 'Katharine doesn't need stunts.

She isn't a big game hunter. Not with her track record. Do we really want Katharine the Great, friend of presidents and kings, to go bungee jumping?' He was beginning to sound querulous.

'But shouldn't one of us go down to Times Square and check it out?'

'You don't have to go down,' an associate producer remarked wearily. 'Globe is featuring it in all its news bulletins. I've just seen a live chopper view of the scene.'

'OK, guys, let's keep a lid on this.' Mike's tone implied that the discussion was over. 'Our show's in good shape, Katharine knows how hard you're all working and we all appreciate it.'

That appreciation would take on a solid form. Unknown to them, a box of delicacies from Dean and Delucca's food store and a hand-chosen gift from Tiffany had been dispatched to their homes to arrive in time for the Thanksgiving festivities. The network was footing the bill but it had been one of Katharine's treats to make the choice.

Before Mike went into the studio to work out the running order and timings for the show, he switched on his TV. What he saw surprised him. More importantly and for the first time, it shook his confidence.

High above 42nd Street on the bungee-jumping platform, Abbie could not believe how many people had gathered below in Times Square. There were thousands. It could have been New Year's Eve and it was this that had so surprised Katharine's producer. Usually the square was full of tourists but today Abbie's team had reported that it was filled with New Yorkers. The city's pickpockets would be having a field day down there.

Something that had been a half-baked idea in a researcher's mind a few weeks ago had stopped the mid-town traffic today and brought people out in their thousands. It could only happen in New York, Abbie thought, hardly believing they were there to see her. She turned to look at the perfect profile of the latest Hollywood hunk, Luke Forrester, who was attached by a harness to the scaffolding. His make-up was being touched up by Brooke, Brenda's number two. Luke had agreed to take part in the stunt to promote his second film in which he had his first starring role. Within three months they both knew he would never be allowed to front something like this again. His studio and insurance company would not countenance it and, more importantly, he would not need this kind of publicity. He was destined to be big. Monster.

Abbie stomped her feet and clapped her gloved hands together to stave off the crisp coldness of the morning. Her eyes were sparkling, infecting him with her excitement. Silhouetted against the skyline, they stood high above the roaring canyons, their breath making tiny shimmers of mist in the frosty air. Dressed in red suede Globe TV jackets, white sweatshirts, and the inevitable jeans, they had the world at their feet. Literally.

Alongside them were two actors, star-crossed lovers of Globe's top-rated teenage soap, and Abbie and Luke lookalikes. The network's insurers had insisted that the stand-ins do the actual jump.

Down below, families out for pre-holiday shopping were wrapped up in mufflers and woollen hats; pretzel and hot dog stands were doing a lively trade.

'Don't you feel on top of the world?' asked Globe TV's best-known newscaster, sticking the microphone close to Luke's mouth.

The heart-throb gave the lazy grin that would soon earn him his fortune. 'I never thought it would be this much fun. There's a wonderful atmosphere down there, sort of like Mardi Gras.' He leaned over the platform and waved. The action appeared on the three giant television screens around the square. Every woman in the crowd waved back.

The newscaster turned. 'Abbie, what gave you this idea?'

'It was the brain wave of one of our researchers. Her young niece tragically has cerebral palsy and she was trying to find new ways of raising money for research. Then Luke, who's coming on the show tomorrow, heard about it and asked if he could come along. It grew from there.'

Luke put on his sincere expression number two. 'And I was thrilled to join in. There is so much still to be done with children who have this affliction but money can make a difference. So I hope the folks out there, and maybe you folks at home,' he looked straight to camera with his clear, baby-blue eyes, 'can help by giving whatever you can afford.'

'If you want to help this worthy cause by pledging your donation,' said the newscaster, 'here's the number to call right now.' He went on to explain that people wearing the official red Globe sweatshirts would be passing through the crowd with buckets. 'Give all you can spare, folks. I sure hope they'll get filled up quickly.'

Abbie swivelled her head as the camera panned the sun-dappled skyscrapers with their giant metallic water tanks. Here and there the view was interspersed with a rare pocket of green where some intrepid gardener had established a minute roof garden. The few trees, from this height, resembled stalks of broccoli.

Abbie smiled straight to camera. 'There can't be many better places to be than here right now.'

Mike O'Brien stared at his TV monitor in the corner of his office at ABN. Those two up on the bungee jump platform were young, alive, energetic. He was trying to take an outsider's view, dispassionate and uninvolved. He figured that every guy who switched on for the Saturday sports programmes would fall in love with Abbie or, if that way inclined, with Luke. How the hell could you fight that? Best not to try.

He was walking down the corridor when his PA ran to find him.

'Sam Wolfe is on line one and Katharine on line three, boss.'

The decision about which call to take first was easy. 'Tell Katharine I'm in the john and I'll phone her right back,' he snapped, retracing his steps.

'Hi, Sam?'

'What's this cockamamie thing I'm watching on my television?'

Mike felt a surge of relief. The big cheese did not approve. They were not going to have to copy it. 'They only started promoting it this week but I think—'

'Helluvan idea.'

Shit, thought Mike.

'We gotta come up with something that'll put the pressure on, just like they're doing to us. Only better. Let's cut to the chase.'

'You got it, boss. I'll have something on your desk by Monday.' Why did I open my big mouth with the troops? he thought. Please God, let Katharine talk Sam out of it.

Sam, who had the attention span of a newt, had already hopped off to a new subject. 'You got a good line-up tomorrow?'

Mike refreshed his boss's memory with the contents of *Here and Now*.

'Sounds OK. I'll give orders to double the promos between now and tomorrow night. Globe won't have it all their own way.'

'And we've got an even better show for Thanksgiving weekend. We've persuaded Steve Stone to tape an interview with Katharine and you know how long it's been since he's done any TV.'

'You've got Steve Stone, actually in the studio?'

'Yes.'

'That's good, very good. We should think of some stunt around that.'

'OK, but we have to be careful. He hates the press, he keeps well out of the way on that ranch of his. Only Katharine could persuade him to come to New York and it took her months. He's in town just for the interview but I'll think of something. You can count on it, chief.'

Mike put the phone down. He decided not to tell Katharine about Sam's wishes until after the show. She was not a fragile flower but no star about to perform would welcome the idea that her boss was enthusiastic about a stunt her rivals were doing.

He phoned the number she had given; he recognised it as belonging to her hairdresser.

'Mike?' Katharine's voice was sharp. 'Times Square seems to have been taken over. Every set even in this place is switched on to Globe.'

He tried to sound reassuring. 'Two-minute wonder. It'll make no long-term difference to their figures but to be on the safe side I've asked for double the number of promos.'

'Good. But I bet Sam thinks the bungee gimmick is great. I know him.'

'He's probably not even watching,' Mike parried.

'Come on, that football freak? He never moves from his seat on Saturdays until Annette makes him change to go out to dinner. I'll give him a call.'

'I wouldn't trouble trouble until trouble troubles you,' Mike advised swiftly. 'See you later.'

Katharine was nothing if not upfront and she decided to ignore Mike's advice. There was a little time before the one o'clock news, after which the ball game would start. Sam would be off limits then.

'Sam? Have you seen what Globe's up to?'

'Sure, and I was just telling Mike, it's a great stunt. Told him to have some ideas like that ready. Also I just spoke to presentation to double the number of promos for tomorrow night's show, specially in prime time. Don't worry about a thing, it's all being taken care of.' There was a pause. 'Still, how are you on bungee jumping?'

'Not so good but talk trapeze and I'm your woman. I even have the spangled fishnet tights.'

He chortled. 'That's my girl. Have a great show.'

Why had Mike denied speaking to Sam? Why did he feel he could not be open with her? Their whole relationship was based on trust. Or so she had thought. In trying to protect her, he was in danger of opening up a gulf between them.

Katharine pressed a switch on the console neatly concealed in the chinoiserie bamboo bedhead and the thick white cotton curtains lined with pale-blue fabric silently opened. It was raining.

She checked her watch. Seven a.m. God, she felt tired. She had been in the edit suite until after two in the morning and when she had at last gone to bed, a mixture of the trivial and the vital had, infuriatingly, kept her awake during what was left of the night. Half thoughts crowded in . . . Freddie's increasing dependence. He was trying to pin her down for holiday dates but she did not want to commit to that right now. Yet if George should suggest she fly over to help with his problem hotel in Venice, she would be on the way to Kennedy at the shortest possible notice.

Freddie phoned as frequently as George but whereas his were prosaic discussions about where to meet or eat, George's calls made her laugh out loud. His description of some of the conversations with his builders were the stuff of comedy. The hot water came from the cold taps, the sitz bath in suite five had a tidal wave which threatened to drown the resident contessa. Only the paddling pool was a great success for keeping cool. Unfortunately it was sited at one end of the kitchens.

'The trouble is I learned my Italian in America so it's all about getting things done now. They learned Italian in Italy, which has more phrases than you would believe about not getting things done until tomorrow.'

After he had made her laugh, with consummate ease George steered the conversation down a more erotic avenue and the telephone wires between America and Italy vibrated with their verbal lovemaking.

Katharine yawned and stretched over to press another button on the console, a gadget her architect had assured her would save hours of effort. It activated the bath taps. In sixty seconds her bath would be filled to the right depth at the temperature of her choice. She decided that 80 degrees would refresh her for the day ahead.

She glanced away guiltily from the sight of her exercise bicycle, electronic treadmill and chest exerciser in the gym off her bedroom and decided to skip the punishing work-out that she pushed herself through at least three times a week.

Her pre-show Sunday mornings had hardly varied since she had become an established star. First to arrive was the masseur, more often than not a man. Although he had impeccable references and had been employed for years by many of her colleagues, she had thought she might find the first encounter embarrassing and had asked Conchita to be around in the apartment. But the fey young man with thumbs as rigid as iron seemed sexless, kneading her body like a pizza cook working a piece of dough. She did not have a moment of anxiety.

He had learned early that silence was *de rigueur* for most of his clients and Katharine was no exception. She asked him to concentrate on her neck and shoulder muscles, stiffened after many hours hunched over a monitor in the edit suite.

This Sunday Katharine had asked the hairdresser and manicurist to stop by the studio instead of coming to the apartment but she had set aside time for her aromatherapist. A pedicurist was regularly added to this regiment of high-maintenance specialists who visited her home. Nina claimed that the only expert not included was a gynaecologist, to which Katharine quipped that she was working on that.

One shrewd columnist in an article describing Katharine's pampered routine had pointed out that with a face that was recognised in every corner store or downtown mall, Katharine could never slob out. She was the gold card of American television currency. Under these conditions grooming could become a chore. It would also be difficult for a woman like Katharine to enjoy a happy marriage unless the man was in the same business or subservient, preferably both. Katharine thought the article one of the most insightful ever written about her and the few other women in her position.

The aromatherapist arrived precisely forty minutes after the masseur, to give her the ultimate in facials, a massage perfected to rejuvenate, relax and drain the lymphatic glands with a formula so well-guarded that practitioners were required to sign a secrecy clause.

This Sunday, what was ordinarily a delectable experience did not work its magic. As the aromatic oils were gently massaged into her face, Katharine felt unsettled but could not for the life of her fathom why. She began to trawl her mind to try to pinpoint the cause.

Certainly it was not the discussion she would have after the show tonight when she would inform both her network boss and the producer that she was not going to ape some crazy stunt dreamed up by Globe. She was quite confident of winning that one.

Nor did she think it was anything that had happened at yesterday's AIDS Foundation lunch or the first night of *Othello*. There had been a joke or two about the rivalry between her and Abbie on a late-night chat show but they were so common now she hardly paid them any attention.

Ping. She had it. An interview with Abbie in *Boulevard Magazine*. She had skimmed through it but something in it had hit the wrong note. It wasn't the headline, 'The hottest property in TV'. Katharine was proud of the recognition Abbie's talent was attracting. No, it was that little sting in the middle of the eulogy to Abbie's show. The journalist had made a comment, something about viewers liking *Tonight* because they did not need a course in world politics to watch it. Abbie had not replied, according to the interviewer, she had merely laughed it off. That was it. It was a pity Abbie had not slapped him down for that snide criticism. She would have done and the defence would have been included in the article. But Abbie was new to the game.

The therapist was just finishing when Abbie's fresh unmade-up face peered round the bedroom door. Katharine's immediate thought was how hard her own make-up artist would have to work to get the same effect. There were days like this one when she felt every year of her age.

'I'm about to make a pot of tea if you want some,' Abbie said.

When they were seated in the kitchen, Abbie told Katharine how thrilled her team was at the amount of money the bungee jump had raised for the charity.

'I wish you'd told me about yesterday's little stunt,' Katharine said. 'When I first heard about it I was terrified, I actually thought you were going to leap off the platform.'

'Mum, I'm sorry. I just couldn't breathe a word. They were so excited about it. And on the show tonight—'

Abbie clapped her hand to her mouth. 'Sorry. That's another thing I'm not supposed to talk about.' America's First Lady had accepted a last-minute invitation to receive the cheque, a coup the network would announce just before the show.

Katharine laughed. 'All right, but what can we talk about? The weather? Your health?'

'Stormy. Good,' Abbie said brightly.

'I know it's difficult to live together if we're watching every syllable, Abbie, but you have to believe I can be discreet. There has to be some trust between us, doesn't there?'

'Of course there does and I do – trust you, I mean. But the people at work are paranoid about anything getting out. When I spoke to Dad about it he suggested that if I tell nothing to nobody it can't come back to me.'

Ah, always the wise father in the background, she thought. 'In a way, he's right, but it puts a strain on us living together.'

Abbie frowned worriedly. 'Well, would it be easier if I moved out?'

Katharine sucked in her breath. 'No, that would be awful. I wouldn't like that at all.' She had come to enjoy many aspects of having Abbie around, the borrowing of make-up and clothes, the quick snatches of conversation over tea and toast, even listening to the rock music Abbie played so loudly. It was like being young again, a reminder of those pre-marriage flat-sharing days but without the constant stream of young men lying around the sofas talking until the early hours. And she had got used to Abbie's untidiness. 'Besides,' Katharine went on, 'it'll take time to find the right apartment and meanwhile you do find it convenient living here, don't you?'

'Of course I do but we said we wouldn't let all that crazy stuff get to us and I think it's beginning to.'

'It doesn't have to, Abbie.' She thought about that

interview in *Boulevard Magazine* and wondered whether to mention it. Perhaps not. 'Well, I'd better go and get dressed.'

An hour later Katharine emerged from the lobby into the waiting limo. She felt ill at ease with herself and depressed by the sight of the rain-soaked, empty Sunday morning streets. She was beginning to dislike working when everyone else seemed to be involved with family and friends, doing ordinary things like eating Sunday lunch together. God, how long was it since she had done that? If she could spend more leisure with Abbie, maybe they could build up more trust.

Katharine leaned back in the limo, secure in the knowledge that the tinted windows meant she could not be seen. What she described as the car's nightmare of technology – its video viewing machine, fax, two phone lines and battery chargers – was unusually silent this morning, and she savoured the fact.

She began wondering why this mother-daughter story was being kept alive so long. Friends in the television business maintained that journalists, less well paid and less fêted, were jealous. Many of them thought that jobs on camera required nothing more than the ability to read the Autocue, look attractive and show a set of good teeth. Any MAW (model, actress, whatever) could do it. They did not understand that it took experience, stamina and energy to ensure that each take was up to the same standard as the last. And few print journalists could talk to camera, interview a difficult and sometimes hostile subject, take directions from the director through an earpiece and watch the floor manager's timing signals all at the same time.

But what made the top people in television worth the millions they earned was their ability to interact with the lens. It was not possible to judge who had this inexplicable ingredient until they were on screen, but those who did have it could project a charisma which bounded into the living room and evoked positive responses from a wide swathe of viewers. 'If only we could bottle the presence that man has, we could give it to someone else,' Katharine had heard one legendary producer say as he once again had to placate the monster he had created. She was fortunate that she had the magic, that the great American public put her first and, despite everything, she was still top of the ratings.

In sharp contrast to *Here and Now*'s elegant, specially-commissioned designer workplace, the *Tonight* office was shambolic. It had been created hurriedly out of some small offices in the weeks following Globe's discovery that Abbie was Katharine's daughter. Mismatched desks had been brought in from all over the building. Posters and press cuttings were stuck randomly to the wall with Blu-tack, giving the impression of an office in transit.

The accommodation did not worry those who worked there. The median age was under thirty and few of the team had expected to be on such a high-profile series this early in their careers. The comfort of their surroundings was secondary.

'OK, thirty million watched our bungee jump.' Red Skinner, senior producer on Abbie's show, was elated. 'Add the mentions in every newspaper,' he leaned back in his chair and stretched his legs, 'and if only twenty per cent more of them switch on tonight, we've cracked it.'

He leaped up, unable to sit still. The young researchers crowding round his desk watched as he began pacing around them, waving his arms, his flame-coloured hair glinting in the spotlight beams.

'Is the show shit-hot tonight?'

'Yeah,' they chorused at the top of their voices.

'Are we gonna kick ass tonight?'

'You bet,' they shouted.

'Is the new kid gonna make it tonight?'

The response was deafening.

'As always, I want you in there with the studio audience, sitting right there among 'em.' Red was working them into a frenzy. 'I want you to get that audience fizzing, shouting, whooping, calling, applauding. We want noise, we want excitement. Make it a great one, boys and girls. Get to it.'

The production room at Globe quickly emptied, leaving behind the detritus of half-eaten pizzas, ciabatta bread, avocado and tuna sandwiches, bagels and cream cheese and brown paper bags containing the remnants of what the senior editor frequently snarled was the most creative thing they did all day: ordering lunch.

Abbie had been invited for a meal with Jeri-Ann at which she had toyed with some lettuce leaves and a few plump asparagus, conscious as ever of the extra pounds put on by the camera. When she walked into the office just after two o'clock, she was greeted by a spontaneous cheer. She went pink with pleasure. This was the first time she had been applauded by her colleagues and she was gratified. God, how she loved this job, although it terrified her at the same time.

'We're showing the shot of you standing on the bungee platform at the top of the programme,' Red told her with a smile. 'After that we go straight to you in the studio where the First Lady will accept the cheque from you on behalf of the charity.'

The publicity officer for Disco 2000 was anxious.

'You sure Steve Stone will come tonight?'

'As sure as anybody can be with Hollywood stars. My contact's told him you've got the best shit in town, so if he does turn up, keep him supplied.'

'No prob, honey. I owe you one.'

'You owe me more than that. I've got another contact

who works for Globe. She's a researcher on Abbie Lomax's show and on my suggestion she's asking Abbie and her crowd down to the club tonight.'

'Are you serious?' screamed the publicity guy. 'Hey, that's great. Abbie Lomax and Steve Stone together, what a great publicity shot!'

The woman smiled. He was making this easy for her.

Half an hour after the show, Abbie and her team could have bungee-jumped without the aid of elastic. Ed Dantry had phoned from his home in the Hamptons with an upbeat message. 'The show's shit-hot. Abbie's great. I'm gonna give you extra publicity, more promos, more posters, more everything.'

As Dantry was a renowned tight-wad, this sent the team into orbit. Still high on adrenaline, they decided to act on the suggestion of one of the researchers and end the evening at Disco 2000 where the Village met mainstream.

Places where the young congregated to see and be seen reflected a pattern of human behaviour which was centuries old. The French had their boulevardiers and their promenades, the Spanish their ramblas, the Greeks the tavernas, the British flocked to pubs, and in New York they had Disco 2000.

Formerly an old movie house where generations used to smooch in the back stalls, Disco 2000 had been converted into a mammoth dance floor. Every sexual possibility from straight or gay to transsexual, bisexual or hermaphrodite strutted its stuff there, hoping to be noticed, hoping to score with partners or cocaine or both.

Abbie and her team passed the idiosyncratic dress code imposed by the troop of pale, menacing young men who guarded the door. It was impossible to predict what would please them; a group ahead of them who had obviously expected to gain entrance had been unceremoniously barred. The more this ritual was publicised, the more the young (and the trying-to-stay-young) clamoured, paying premium prices, for the honour of being allowed in. The crowd from Globe understood that outfits as straight as theirs, simple unstructured suits for the men, trouser ensembles for most of the women and, in Abbie's case, an aquamarine shift and tight, matching jacket that she had worn for the show, might pose a problem. But her celebrity status opened the door for them.

Inside, what had once been the circle of the cinema was now a mirrored restaurant and bar. It was filled mostly with high-achieving under-thirties and a sprinkling of starlets hoping to catch a director's eye or fading actors hoping for a mention in the gossip columns.

As soon as Abbie was recognised, she was whisked up to the VIP suite in the upper circle, where appetites were satisfied with everything from Diet Coke to the best Bolivian marching powder. Abbie chose her favourite St Clement's cocktail, a mixture of freshly-squeezed orange and lemon juice. She had just taken her first sip when the disco's publicity officer homed in on her.

'Abbie, how wonderful to see you,' he gushed – he had never met her before. 'Welcome to our club. We're so excited at having you here. I want you to meet someone really, really special.'

'No thanks. I'm here for a quiet drink with my friends.' Abbie was firm but polite.

'I think you should come and see who it is. Could be good for all of us,' he whispered.

'I'd rather not.'

Jeri-Ann, well versed in the ways of this publicity-seeking club, intervened. 'Look, I'll come after you in a few minutes if you send word.'

Abbie raised an eyebrow. Being seen with celebrities was part of the job. 'OK, then. Just for a while.'

'Follow me, please, we're so thrilled to have you

here . . .' Abbie pulled a face over her shoulder at Jeri-Ann and allowed herself to be led across the room.

'. . . I'm sure he's dying to meet you.' The cascade of words dried up at last when the publicist came to a halt in front of a face that had smiled down at Abbie from the screen since she started going to the movies.

'Steve Stone, Abbie Lomax.'

Steve Stone stood up lazily, stretching out his long legs. His feet were encased in his trademark cowboy boots.

Abbie was momentarily over-awed. Stone was one of the handful of stars whose name on a billboard could sell tickets all over the world; he was as famous in Shanghai as he was in Beverly Hills. Not only was he a celebrated actor and director, his film festival in New Mexico attracted young independent movie makers every year. Like the one organised by Robert Redford, it provided a platform for artists whose work might not otherwise see the light of day. Several award-winning directors had made emotional speeches on Oscar night thanking him personally for initiating their success.

He was greyer than his screen image but his hazel eyes had the same effect on her as when she saw him on film. As a journalist she was thrilled to see him here. This was not his natural habitat. Between films he led a reclusive life, spending much of his time on his ranch where he discouraged visitors, questions and interviews. Indeed, she could not remember the last time he had spoken to the media. He was one of the few stars big enough not to have to promote his films. They did well enough with just his name above the title.

'I'm surprised to see you all alone,' she said, a touch diffidently. 'I thought stars like you travelled with an entourage.'

He leaned over, exaggerating the lift of his eyebrows, the focus of many a camera angle. 'I'm allowed out on my own now and then.' His cheeks dimpled, making him look far younger than his reported forty-six years.

The publicist was fussing about, asking if there was anything, anything at all, Mr Stone might need. Or Miss Lomax.

'Leave us alone. Please.' The words were soft and the face friendly, but the tone belonged unmistakably to someone used to being obeyed. Instantly. This man had been master of his universe for many years in an industry that outranked television.

Steve patted the banquette beside him and said to Abbie, 'Sit down, won't you?'

Could life get any better? For the second time in a couple of days she asked herself this question. Her boss was putting more money into the show and now one of her great heroes was asking if she would like to spend some time with him. She would try not to be crass but it was difficult to contain her excitement.

'I know you've heard this before but I've seen every one of your films and I love them all.' Abbie was in her best interviewing mode, friendly but not gushing. 'I think what I like about your acting is that you become the character. And that's so unusual for a top movie star.'

'Don't stop.' He made a come-hither gesture with his hands. 'I'm as susceptible to flattery as the next guy.'

'I think you ought to get another Oscar for *The Prodigal*. It was so good I've seen it twice.'

He grinned and made another of those gestures and they both laughed. Abbie was impressed by how unaffected Stone was; he seemed not to want to continue to talk about his career or himself, which was somewhat unusual in a movie star. He was complimentary about her mother's work and said he was sure she would be just as successful one day. Abbie was used to this kind of back-handed compliment but from him it did not sound critical.

He was charming and pleasantly attentive, yet she could

not help noticing that no woman passed him without an appraising glance from him. One or two wore so few clothes that the term 'undressing with the eyes' was superfluous. The procession was constant and Abbie concluded that unless they had weak bladders, they were waiting for her to vacate the slot. Well, she would not. She would try something which never failed to gain attention. Seek advice.

'Steve,' she leaned closer, 'you've been in this business so long, I'm just at the beginning. I don't know how you manage all the madness. I'm finding it really difficult. I'd value some advice on how to cope with it.'

'Never believe in your own publicity is a good start,' he drawled. She waited, and when he noticed her serious expression he took his eyes off the parade of women for a moment. 'I'm no expert but what I've learned is there's a price and don't let anyone tell you otherwise.'

'What kind of price?'

'You have responsibilities that civilians out there can't ever imagine. When my mother was dying I was in Europe making *The Unwanted.* We had another two weeks' shooting and were way behind schedule. With millions of dollars at stake, the insurers would not let me leave. I got an Oscar but I couldn't be with my mother when she really needed me.'

Abbie said nothing and Stone, staring into space, seemed to forget she was there.

'Yes, I can write a cheque for anything necessary but my family and my friends know they can't count on me turning up when it's important. And that's one thing I'd change if I had to do it all again.'

'You'd have different priorities?'

'Don't make that mistake, Abbie. Decide what's important for you. You may not get a second chance.'

This was a different Steve Stone. If only she could entice him to talk like this on her show. There certainly seemed to be a rapport between them. She would not be so gauche as to mention it now but she would get Jeri-Ann on the case in the morning.

Steve shook himself out of his private thoughts and gave a smothered yawn. 'Pardon me, I forget how tiring that flight is from LA.' He turned to face her, smile in place, and Abbie once again felt the full impact of the Stone charisma. She just had to get him on her show.

Stone stood up, towering above her. 'Could you do me a favour? If I leave here on my own, a reporter, somebody, will latch on to me. If you're on my arm they'll get their pictures but I'll be able to shoo them off. What d'you say? Do you mind?'

Photographed with Steve Stone? Would she mind? The hell she would.

'I'd be delighted.'

When they reached the top of the stairs, she was surprised how closely he held her; he had not been at all tactile earlier. He waved away the manager's suggestion that they take the private back exit. Instead, he steered her through the crowded VIP suite and round the dance floor where they were briefly illuminated by the strobe lighting. By the time they made their exit, every photographer had been alerted to their presence and was waiting for them to emerge.

Abbie was baffled. Stone was supposed to loathe paparazzi yet here he was positively courting them. Why hadn't they left by the back door?

At the front entrance twenty cameramen were jostling for position on the sidewalk. As the flashes lit up the night sky, Stone put his arm round Abbie more firmly and whispered into her ear, 'I hate all this, don't you? But give them their picture and they'll leave us alone.' He seemed genuinely pleased that she was with him.

He swooped her into a limo and told the driver to drop her off at her apartment after taking him to his hotel. As the driver drew up at the hotel, he leaned over to kiss her swiftly on the cheek and was gone.

The photograph of the two of them, slapped across five columns of the New York *Post*, the *News* and even the New York *Times*, made it appear as if Steve Stone was nuzzling her neck not just whispering in her ear.

The eligible Mr Stone and the brand new chat star. A romance made in media heaven. The papers loved it.

Chapter Six

In her dreamy half-slumber, Katharine willed herself not to wake up, trying to imagine George was still with her in bed at his penthouse apartment, thinking of the things they had done to each other the night before, remembering his intense concentration, his gentleness, his delicious patience as he brought her to the heights of passion and then shared the tremors of pleasure which had coursed through both their bodies.

They saw each other as often as her schedule and George's business trips allowed. Disguised in a blonde wig and wearing inconspicuous clothes, she was undetected by her adoring public as she and George scavenged among the antique open-air markets dotted around Manhattan, occasionally making a foray to garage sales and small fairs upstate. George's quirky stories entertained her and fellow shoppers who unashamedly eavesdropped. His favourite was the one about the antique hunter who spotted the shop's cat licking milk from a Meissen saucer. Sensing the bargain of his life, he offered to buy the cat and, as an apparent afterthought, said, 'I'd like him to feel at home so I'll take that old saucer he was using as well.'

'Certainly,' said the antique dealer. 'That'll be two dollars for the cat and five thousand for the Meissen.' A pause, then he added, 'It's a great way of getting rid of our cats.'

George had an unerring eye. One of his finds was a pale blue and cream French country-style armoire which Katharine snapped up immediately. It now had pride of place in her bedroom and contained linen and turn-of-the-century pillow cases she had bought many years ago in London's Portobello Road.

Her reverie was rudely interrupted by the phone and her mood abruptly shattered by Mike's anxious voice, 'What the hell is your daughter playing at?'

It was rare for Mike to ring so early on a Monday morning, her precious day off.

'What's she done?'

'I take it you haven't seen the papers. Abbie's in all of them. The *Post*, the *News*, the *Times*.' His voice rose in anger. 'She's hanging on the arm of Steve Stone.'

'*Steve Stone?*'

'He seems to be taking a bite out of her neck.'

'I can't believe it.' Katharine was aghast. All that hard work netting him and he was pictured on the town with the opposition. Her daughter.

'Can you talk to Abbie pronto and find out what's going on? We need to know if we've got anything to worry about.'

'I agree but I also need to talk to Steve. I'll get on to it right away.'

As she hurriedly showered and dressed, Katharine decided it would be best to hear Abbie's version before she tackled Steve. She tapped lightly on her bedroom door. There was no answer and she opened it quietly. Abbie was not there. Katharine looked at her watch. Of course, she would be out jogging. Maybe it was just as well. They were jumping to conclusions; Abbie probably knew nothing about the taping session with Stone.

Katharine clung to the hope all the way to the star's hotel. She phoned his suite from the crowded lobby but there was no reply. An apologetic receptionist explained that the star had left strict instructions he was not to be disturbed until noon.

Katharine toyed with the idea of going up and knocking on the door but instead decided to leave a friendly note saying she would contact him later to arrange a meeting. Before leaving, she ordered a large basket of Mediterranean fruit courtesy of *Here and Now*, to be sent to his suite when he surfaced.

The inevitable television, sound muted, was being played in the concierge's lodge. If Katharine had turned her head thirty-five degrees to the right she would have caught the news flash of her daughter coming out of Disco 2000 arm in arm with the elusive Mr Stone.

Fifteen minutes later Katharine marched into Mike's office, fuming. 'Why was nobody from our team with Steve Stone at the disco? Our office is full of twenty-five-year-olds who would have loved to be his minder.'

'We did what we could, Katharine.'

'I've spent months fixing this up,' she went on. 'I made sure there was champagne and flowers in his suite. I phoned to welcome him. All your lot had to do was babysit him for a few hours.'

'We did. We sent a pretty girl to his hotel – and a pretty boy because you know what I think about Stone. They all had tea together, very pleasant, very civilised, according to them, then he said he was bushed and wanted an early night. What were they to do? Camp in his bedroom?'

'They should have hung around the lobby. We've handled stars before. We know how unpredictable they are.'

'Katharine, if a star wants to creep out the back exit, he will.'

She was silenced but only momentarily. 'Don't we have anyone in places like Disco 2000 who'll tip us off? Didn't he have a gofer with him?'

'Look, I think this guy is into under-aged girls or guys dressed up in ballet frocks. Whatever it is, he's not confiding in anyone. If he's determined to go on night-time wanderings on his own, what can we do about it?'

She sighed. 'Don't these stars realise we don't much mind what they get up to so long as they perform on cue?'

'Yeah, I've become unshockable. I know stars who prefer animals, ones who can't rise to the occasion unless there are three in the bed, even those who like their women dead. But to be photographed with the oppo just before our taping, boy, that's a rough one.'

New Yorkers, reading in their morning newspapers about the wonderful time Steve Stone seemed to be having in their city, would have been dumbfounded at the sight of the star in his hotel suite. The virile-looking heart-throb was leaning against the bathroom door sobbing, his mouth pressed against a thick bath sheet to muffle the sound.

Only a minute ago he had shouted down the phone to his sleepy agent, 'Louis, I've made up my mind. I'm leaving immediately and you can't stop me. I don't care about that frigging TV show.'

'Steve, think what this walkout will do to your career. Think how hard we've worked so that no one would find out about you and Scott. We've built up this image of the straight, outdoors hero type. If you let these guys down, they won't rest till they find out why.'

'I don't give a damn. Scott's just found out. He's got AIDS. I've got to be with him, he needs me.'

'And I'm not saying you shouldn't go. All I'm asking is twenty-four hours. Is that too much to ask? I'll even insist they tape you earlier in the day. Will you wait just a few hours? Will you do that for me, please, Steve?'

'No.'

'Listen, this is really serious, Steve. A bunch of flowers and an apology isn't going to be enough, not this time. Katharine Sexton is a powerful woman and she's relying on you for her Thanksgiving special. If you don't care about that, at least think of me.'

'No, you listen. Scott needs me. Not in twenty-four hours. Now. That's the only thing I care about, the only person I care about. I was talking a little while ago to Abbie Lomax about how I made a mistake in not going to my mother, about priorities. Scott is my priority and I'm going to him.'

'This is the first interview you've done in years. Katharine and I have been setting it up for months. She's devoting the whole hour to you and your films. You can't let her down.'

'Watch me.'

It was one of those bright, brilliant blue November days when running round the reservoir in Central Park seemed effortless. A week or two after arriving in the city Abbie had gravitated towards this green lung which gave the city oxygen, space and freedom to move, as close to most New Yorkers as the next-door deli. Jogging across the loamy soil under wide skies, Abbie had the feeling she was in the country. She had not had more than a few hours' sleep but her energy level today was more than enough to cope with the pace set by the personal trainer she shared with the other fitness fanatic at the network, Jeri-Ann Hagerty.

They had set themselves a future target of two circuits but most days they did not have enough time for more than one. Today Abbie felt she could go on for ever.

'Great pictures, Abbie. Give Steve my best,' called a teenager with a pert, toned body who executed a neat pirouette alongside her before whizzing by on roller blades.

Even in baggy sweatpants and top, bandanna round her head and weights in her hands, Abbie was still recognisable.

A middle-aged jogger, scarlet and sweating heavily under his headband, was more forthright. 'Are you two gonna name the day?' Abbie shook her head and he pulled a face. 'Pity, you look terrific together.'

The good-humoured banter, the compliments from Dantry, the possibility of a Steve Stone interview – life was rosy.

On the way back to the apartment Abbie bought a copy of the *Post*. She was on the front page and it was not a bad picture of her. Steve Stone looked positively hunky. She could see why people thought there was something between them.

There was no sign of Katharine when Abbie returned, glowing, to the apartment. Nor was there a note and Conchita could offer no ideas about where her mother had gone on her day off, except to say she had left early. Perhaps she had escaped the city to visit Nina or gone antique hunting with Freddie.

Abbie put her mother out of her mind and turned to the serious business of the day. She had to go out of town for a 'get'.

In LA, Steve Stone's agent covered his face with his hands. Television people hated last-minute cancellations. The only excuse they would accept was the star's body in a coffin. And then they'd make sure by sticking a pin in it.

Louis Stein stood up and lit a cigar. The TV people would not blame Steve. No, it would be his fault, never the star's. And they would make him pay for it. None of his less well-known clients would be booked for the show for months. The features department of ABN would be a powerful enemy. What could he do?

He stared up at the ceiling. Perhaps he was getting too old for all this.

'Mannie, I need a favour. Right now.' His partner had been dead for nearly three years but Louis still talked to him on a daily basis.

He sat down at his desk and absent-mindedly, without

focusing, lifted the papers in his in tray. Near the top of the pile he found a fax of the front page of the New York *Post*. He saw the glamorous picture of the public image he had worked so hard to foster, finding a special therapist who spent months training Steve Stone to look lustfully at women in public instead of young men, paying off the guys who would otherwise have run to the tabloids. Here was his dream. Steve canoodling with a glamorous young woman. He read her name, remembered that Steve had mentioned talking to her, then raised his eyes heavenwards.

'Thanks, Mannie. I owe you.'

Mike could not settle until he had proof that Abbie was not with Steve Stone in his suite. Only after Katharine had phoned the apartment to be told by Conchita that Abbie was there, under the shower, did he relax.

Two hours remained before the noon deadline when Katharine could contact Steve Stone so they decided to use the time to hone the questions she would put to him on the show, deleting some, substituting others. Finally they were satisfied that the mix was right. Katharine hoped to elicit the information the whole country was curious to know. Why was such an attractive man still uncommitted?

Then they turned to the papers. Boosted by the bungee jump, Abbie's viewing figures had gone up but not by as much as her director, for one, had anticipated. As an older, wiser head could have told him, 'There's no logic to viewing patterns,' for Katharine's rating had also increased, proving the efficacy of all those extra promos. And she had the quiet satisfaction of being proved right about the Globe stunt but she did not say 'I told you so' out loud. She did not have to. Mike received the message loud and clear.

Abbie's show was still at number four but those reading

the runes noticed that the gap between her show and the two sandwiched between hers and her mother's was being whittled away. One influential media pundit predicted it was only a matter of time before Abbie moved up from the number four slot to number three. Although it had been the subject of insider gossip, this was the first time the unthinkable had been put into cold print. The Steve Stone interview would help redress the balance in Katharine's favour.

The phone console on Mike's desk flashed.

'Sorry to disturb you, Mike,' said his PA, 'but it's Steve Stone's agent from LA. I thought you'd want to handle him personally.'

'Good thinking, kid,' said Mike then, holding his hand over the receiver, he mouthed to Katharine, 'A few last-minute demands, I reckon. They're so predictable.' He flicked a switch. 'I'll put it on speaker phone so you can hear.'

Louis' voice came through loud and steady. 'Sorry, Mike. Bad news. We're gonna have to cancel.'

'Cancel?' Mike's eyes nearly popped. 'As in not coming?'

Katharine sat up, white-faced. 'He can't do this to us.'

Louis heard her. 'I'm afraid he can. He already has. I tried reasoning with him, believe me I tried everything—'

'But what about our contract?' Mike's voice was flat as Katharine stared at him, her face a mixture of anger and disbelief.

'Mike, I can't tell you how sorry I am,' said Louis. 'Steve doesn't concern himself with details like contracts. As always, he's left me to sort out the shit.'

'You know we can sue.'

'I told him that. Didn't make any difference. The guy's been a star too long. What can I tell you?'

All of them knew suing was the last thing the network would do; they would only lose face with their rivals and with their public.

Katharine butted in again. 'Let me talk to Steve. I'm sure I can change his mi—'

'No good, Katharine. He's already at the airport. I just settled his hotel bill.'

'But everything was set. Why has he done this to us? What's gone wrong?'

There was a pause. 'I wasn't going to tell you this but I have too much respect for you both to give you any bullshit.' In his office, Louis raised his eyes Mannie-wards. 'As you know, Steve met Abbie Lomax on Sunday night and, well, he's kinda fallen for her.' He took a deep breath. 'To tell the truth, he wants to help her career. That's why he asked me to cancel you out.' He crossed his fingers and lifted his eyes once again towards his dead partner. 'Let me put it to you plainer still. The reason Steve's blown you out is that Abbie asked him to nix your show in favour of hers. And he agreed. It's as simple as that.'

There was silence when the call finished. Katharine sat with her head in her hands. It was not possible that her daughter could have been so underhand. She refused to believe it. But why would a reputable agent risk telling an outright lie? They lived in a media village and it would come back to haunt him soon enough. Perhaps, in her zeal to be the best, Abbie had allowed ambition to outweigh loyalty and scruples. Katharine shied away from the thought. No, Abbie would have an innocent explanation, she was sure of it. All she had to do was ask her.

Then she remembered that Abbie had said she would be leaving town this afternoon. She did not want to quiz her about this over the phone. It would have to wait until they saw each other. When that would be, she wasn't sure. She didn't even know where Abbie had gone. This secrecy about anything connected with work irritated her like hell, not least because she was guilty of it herself.

Mike was the first to speak. 'Katharine, how do you

think Abbie found out about our Special?'

'I've no idea.' She stared at her producer. 'You don't actually believe I told anyone outside this office about Steve, do you?'

For months Mike had not responded to oblique remarks from his team about their star sharing a roof with the enemy. Now his frustration erupted.

'Abbie isn't "anyone", is she?' he retorted. 'You live with her. How else would she find out? I don't know, maybe you left a research note lying around.' Katharine shook her head vehemently and he went on, 'Was it a coincidence she was with him in that disco? I don't think so. Something, someone, must have tipped her off.'

Katharine's hand slapped the desk so hard her palm reddened. 'It wasn't me, Mike. Do you realise how secretive I've had to become? I hide cuttings, I make sure Abbie can't hear me when I'm on the phone, I watch what I say to her all the time. It's a horrible way to live with your own daughter and I hate it but the last thing I'd do is compromise the programme, especially with an exclusive like this. Mike, I know how hard this has hit us, but we've worked together too long for me to be lectured on unprofessional behaviour,' she said, her British accent as ever in times of stress becoming more pronounced. 'How do you think I've survived all these years? By being a blabbermouth?'

'Of course I believe you but why would Stone's agent tell us it was Abbie's doing?'

'And agents never lie, do they?' she said, stung to sarcasm.

'Not about something like this.'

Katharine pressed Auto 1 on her mobile. 'That settles it. I'm going to have it out with Abbie right now. Before I condemn her I want to hear what she has to say.'

There was a trill as the call was being connected but

before the final beep, Mike reached over and jabbed the cancel button.

'No, don't do that,' he said tersely. 'If she realises how spooked we are that's giving them an advantage.'

'Mike, I know it looks bad and Abbie and I may work on rival shows but I'm certain she'd never do anything to harm me, any more than I would want to harm her.'

He looked unconvinced and his scepticism fuelled her anger. But as she stared at his bowed head, she softened. She and Mike had been colleagues for nearly five years. He was the best and they needed each other.

'Good God, we're having our first big row. After all this time.'

'I'm sorry, Katie,' he muttered. 'Of course the leak didn't come from you, I know that.'

She shook herself, her mood now briskly practical. Her show comprised two, sometimes three, different items. Replacing a segment at the last moment was difficult enough, but it happened. Having to scrap an entire show was a disaster.

'I don't think we should waste energy on a witch-hunt. Right now, we've got a more important problem. What the hell are we going to put on the screen?'

In a trailer home in the backwoods of Dakota, Abbie faced a groggy-looking man wearing a vest and shorts, rubbing sleep from his eyes. It was still early on Tuesday morning. In the minute kitchenette his wife was pouring orange juice from a carton.

Glamorous world, television, she thought ruefully. She usually enjoyed meeting people and she adored her job. But here she was, having flown out on her day off, and beginning to feel resentful. The studio was demanding so much of her that it was difficult to have any kind of private life. She and Robert had such difficulty finding time to meet that she worried he would think it was too much trouble. The spotlight was exciting, the invitations which poured in were mostly fun, and so was wearing fabulous clothes on screen, but she could see a time when she would take all these trappings for granted and might prefer to exchange them for a job with more regular hours and a life in which she did not need to worry about the paparazzi and would be able to see Robert as often as she wanted. He was hopeful of transferring to New York, but it seemed to be taking time.

But none of these thoughts showed as she took the proffered orange juice, smiling at the couple.

'The whole nation's rooting for you both,' she said. She turned to the man. 'Someone who has no major sponsor, who designed and built a racing bicycle mostly from washing machine parts, well, that's almost too difficult to believe.'

He was so eager to impress that Abbie had to listen to every step of the traumatic trail towards design perfection, each stage accompanied by numerous original sketches. If he did not win the coming Race of Champions with this revolutionary machine, he stood to lose everything, even the trailer.

'Well, that's what the whole country wants to hear you talk about on my show. The little guy against the Goliaths.'

They were interrupted by a loud knock at the door and a few minutes later the wife appeared carrying a huge bouquet of flowers.

'From USTV,' she announced from behind the blooms. 'Inviting you on their show.'

Abbie licked lips dry with tension. 'I hope you'll decide to come on *Tonight*,' she said quickly. 'We reach the largest number of young people, the kind who'll be inspired by your struggles. I'm not a pushy interviewer and I think you'd feel good about the experience afterwards.'

She could not tell from their expressions whether or not her words had impact.

'We've been sent a teddy bear from Fenton TV,' said the wife, putting the bouquet on the nearest chair.

Her husband nodded. 'Phone calls galore as well.'

Abbie was chastising herself for not bringing a larger basket of fruit when she saw the couple exchange meaningful glances.

'Know what, Abbie?' said the inventor. 'You're the only one who's taken the trouble to make the trip and we truly like your show. We're going to go with you.'

Success could be as random as that, she thought as she reported back to Red Skinner on her way to the airport. His compliments were gratifying. So was Robert's response when she phoned him to say she could be on a flight to Chicago in an hour. Having clinched the major interview for her next show, Red had told her to take a break, as this Sunday's show was in the can, and he would see her after Thanksgiving.

A whole day and night in Chicago with Robert, then a proper Thanksgiving in New York. Abbie hugged herself with pleasure. In the past her colleagues in the busy newsroom in Chicago had been delighted when she offered to work the four days off over Thanksgiving, trading it for a break over Christmas, to which she and her mother, like the majority of British ex-pats, paid more attention. Now they were working in the same city and would be able to celebrate the holiday together. Abbie was looking forward to it.

As the camera panned across the studio audience, Mike, seated in the gallery, heard the laughter through his earpiece.

'Cut to that guy in the fourth row, middle seat,' he shouted. The vision mixer was quick on the uptake and the screen was filled with the shot of a young man rocking with mirth.

Mike began to relax. Not even in his most optimistic

moments had he expected such an enthusiastic reaction to a group of celebrity gossips chewing the fat with Katharine. The past twenty-four hours had been a nightmare of frenetic phone calls, pulling in favours, re-scheduling promos and advertising and trying to minimise the damage to the intricate holiday arrangements of his staff. Arrangements to tape the Steve Stone special a few days before transmission on Sunday night had long been in the planning. He had had no problem asking his staff to work through the night, they had knuckled down cheerfully enough on a diet of strong black coffee and willpower. But he would have had a revolution on his hands if he had asked them to cancel a visit back to the bosom of their families on Thanksgiving Day.

It had been Katharine's idea to invite a small group of movie insiders to reminisce about their off-camera moments, the embarrassing, the candid, the funny and the downright weird. And, boy, were they making the most of the opportunity. The format was a departure for the news-oriented Katharine Sexton but so far it was working brilliantly as a holiday special. And Katharine was handling it like the true pro she was. Not for nothing was she known as 'One-take Sexton' around the network.

At the post-mortem, it was agreed that the wisecrack which evoked the loudest laughter, in a nation plagued by medical bills, was the anecdote attributed to veteran movie star Walter Matthau, 'After my heart attack, my doctor gave me six months to live. When I couldn't pay the bill, he gave me six months more.'

And thunderous roars followed the lesson in sycophancy from a personal aide to legendary producer Darryl Zanuck who, on being asked his highest ambition, replied, 'To die, be cremated then have my ashes scattered on Mr Zanuck's drive so that his car shouldn't skid.'

When the guests had been chauffeured away and the staff began to disperse, exchanging good wishes for a happy holiday, Mike ushered Katharine into his glass-walled office and gave her a bear hug which almost lifted her off her feet.

'That was great, kid. Wasn't the audience reaction fantastic? Maybe we should think about upping our ration of lighter stuff in future.'

'I don't think so, Mike,' said Katharine, keeping her tone casual. 'It was a nice idea for the holidays but we should think hard before we fiddle with the formula. We don't want to be the same as every other damn show.'

'You're right. It was just a thought. What are you doing for Thanksgiving?'

'Oh, the usual. All the trimmings.'

'Don't tell me you're actually going to cook.'

'Me? Cook? Conchita would never allow it. Thank God. I'm sorry you're chickening out. Buzz and Maggie are coming round, so's Nina, Freddie and his family and, oh yes, my accountant David Crozier and his wife – don't make that face, he's good fun.'

'I never hear you talk about Freddie these days. How are things with you two?'

'Fine,' replied Katharine after the briefest of pauses. The truth was she was seeing less of Freddie and more of George. But she did not feel sure enough of him to introduce him to her circle – or to finish with Freddie. She still had not mentioned George to Abbie, or to anyone else. He was being mysterious about where he was spending the holidays and she was too proud to probe.

'And Abbie?' asked Mike blandly. 'Will she be there?'

Katharine's face showed the strain of the past couple of days. 'I'm expecting her,' she said carefully, 'but she's not in New York at the moment.'

'Oh? You sure she hasn't flown to LA to see Steve Stone about coming on her show?'

'No, I've no idea where she's gone but I hope you're wrong,' she said slowly. 'I really hope so.'

Chapter Seven

Katharine regarded Christmas as a British tradition and Thanksgiving, a month earlier, as an excellent rehearsal.

She liked the idea of a country coming together on one special day to thank the Pilgrim Fathers and to celebrate the family. She thought it a unifying force and the epitome of everything good about her adopted land. But just when the occasion should have been perfect, the Steve Stone business had soured it for her.

Abbie had left a warm and friendly message promising she would be back at least an hour before the guests were due. She sounded as if there was nothing wrong. How could her daughter be so insensitive? Surely she realised the enormity of her actions?

Katharine almost wished Abbie would be late so there could be no discussion before the meal. She still clung to the hope that Abbie was entirely innocent, that she had been roller-coastered by less scrupulous colleagues, but the more she had thought about it, the less confident she had become.

Would it be best to have it out as soon as she arrived? That might help to clear the air. Katharine twisted a piece of ivy into a plant pot. Perhaps it would be wisest to wait until the guests had gone. No, she doubted if she could repress her anger that long. If there were going to be fireworks, her guests must not be involved. Only Buzz knew what had happened. And there would be strangers around to help Conchita and it was well known that half the tabloids were supplied by waiters who were as adept at serving morsels of gossip to the media as they were food to the guests.

Katharine stared down at an eerily quiet New York. The sirens were silent, few yellow cabs were cruising the empty streets and except for the occasional Korean-owned fresh fruit and vegetable stall, the shops were shut. America was on vacation. Planes, trains, buses and cars were packed with people travelling from all over the world to be at the Thanksgiving table with their relatives. This was the one time when there could be no excuses for absences. And curiously for America, it was almost non-commercial. No formal invitations were sent out, no one exchanged presents, and however creative the cooking, on this day the ingredients were always the same, turkey, sweet potatoes and marshmallows, the dinner of the Pilgrims sans muskets.

Katharine concentrated on her work in the flower room. When she had bought the twenty-first-floor apartment, she had been fascinated to discover that the previous owners had added this tiny room. It was dedicated solely to flower-arranging. Katharine enjoyed the rare free time she had working with the myriad vases, jugs, buckets, green and white twine, wire and moss. She loved to see her old terracotta pots, which she had had shipped over from London, filled with hyacinth bulbs, box cuttings and agapanthus which relished the New York sun on the secluded balcony garden.

The therapeutic effect of using her hands in this sanctuary did much to calm her but she was still nervous about the forthcoming encounter with Abbie and wondered again if it would be sensible to leave any discussion about work until after the meal. She dismissed that at once. She could not put on an act, not with Abbie.

Katharine sighed and brushed back a wisp of hair from

her forehead. She had three more vases to arrange, for the entrance hall, for the enormous urn that stood at the end of the long corridor, and a centrepiece for the long sideboard. With this Thanksgiving meal in mind, she had spent some of Labor Day on the balcony spraying several of her terracotta plant pots silver. She pressed the white hydrangeas into the damp compost and arranged them so they looked attractive from every angle. The effect was completed by tying a bow of white organza ribbon round the middle of each pot. Later she would tuck a stiff ivory card into the bows and put the pots in front of the place settings.

There was a whooshing noise followed by a thud as the oak apartment door slammed shut, causing the kitchen door to vibrate, then another thud as a bulging suitcase was dropped heavily in the hallway followed by the rustle of mail being sifted then dropped on to the side table. This was followed by a clank as a raincoat buckle banged against the mahogany chair.

And all for a hundred and twenty pounds of vibrant female.

Abbie was home.

Katharine felt herself tense. Carefully, she put down the fountain pen she had been using to write the placement cards.

'Mum? Where are you?'

'In the flower room.' To her own ears her voice sounded strained.

Abbie, eyes shining, appeared holding a large ornamental Chinese-style tureen decorated in the familiar blue and white Willow pattern, a favourite of Katharine's. 'Squillions of white hyacinths are going to pop up out of here by Christmas. They're specially forced ones and the shop promised me they'd bloom in time or I'd get my money back.'

Framed in the doorway, Abbie looked vital, fresh,

bursting with spirited youth. Katharine felt tears prickle her eyelids. She was so proud of her daughter. And so angry. Instead of reaching out for the gift, she found herself involuntarily folding her arms, her body language betraying how incensed she was.

'Did you buy it in Los Angeles, by any chance?' she asked slowly.

Each word reverberated round the room like stones skittering across a frozen pond, immediately puncturing Abbie's *joie de vivre*.

'Los Angeles? No, I was upstate talking to . . .' She stopped, disconcerted. 'Why on earth did you think I was in LA?'

'Isn't that where Steve Stone lives?'

Abbie looked genuinely puzzled then her brow cleared. 'Oh, did you think I went off with him after that stupid photograph in the disco? That was just a publicity stunt. He didn't lay a hand on me, more's the pity.' She gave an ironic shrug. 'And I don't think he ever wanted to, despite what it looked like. God, I'm starving.' She turned and headed for the kitchen. Katharine followed her.

Abbie walked over to the refrigerator where the canapés were being chilled. 'Can I sneak one of these?'

'Have what you like,' said Katharine, trying to make an effort to be pleasant. 'You're sure you haven't been to LA lately?'

Abbie looked up in surprise. 'No, I haven't. What are you going on about?'

'Are you trying to tell me you don't know?'

Abbie shrugged.

Her daughter's offhand response infuriated Katharine. 'Well, I'll tell you what's happened, shall I?' She could not keep the anger out of her voice. 'And then you can tell me your part in it.'

Abbie listened in silence as her mother outlined the

disastrous episode with Steve Stone from its build-up to the debacle.

'And Stone's agent told us it was all your doing, that you persuaded him to cancel so he could do your show.'

Abbie walked to the window, turning her back on her mother.

Katharine relented a little. 'Look, Abbie, I realise people in your station are pushing you but you've got to believe me, this is not the way to succeed. I hoped you and I would never have to stoop to these sorts of tactics, whatever the provocation, whatever the rivalry.'

Abbie wheeled round. 'I'm very, very upset that you think I was involved in this,' she said vehemently, enunciating each word.

There was such emphasis on the word 'you' that Katharine hesitated. 'I know better than anyone, Abbie, how easy it is to get caught up in the excitement of a story and do things you'll regret later.'

'I'm not getting through to you, am I?' shouted Abbie, smacking her forehead in exasperation. 'Why don't you listen to me?'

'Because you're being manipulated and you don't seem to realise it.'

'Manipulated. You're a fine one to talk.'

'What the hell do you mean by that?'

There was a persistent buzz at the door. The silence that followed was filled with the sound of their heavy breathing. A few seconds later Conchita walked in on them carrying an ostentatious arrangement of white roses, lily of the valley, ferns and gypsophila. The card announced that it was a gift from her accountant. He had learned early in his career that the essence of being a perfect guest was to send an arranged bouquet before the event instead of turning up with a bunch of flowers that the busy hostess then had to deal with.

As Katharine and Conchita discussed the best position

for the flowers, Abbie turned on her heel and disappeared to her bedroom.

Conchita's face was downcast. 'Oh, Mizz Katharine, I don't like to hear you two quarrel. It's Thanksgiving. Family time. You go speak to her, you sort it out.'

Katharine shook her head. 'It's going to take a lot to sort this, I'm afraid.' She straightened a cushion. 'I'm going to take a shower. Will you let me know when Mr Freddie arrives?'

As Katharine was applying blusher to highlight the contours of her fine cheekbones, a skill honed by years of watching the best make-up artists in the world work on her face, she could not get the words of Steve Stone's agent out of her mind: '*Abbie asked Steve to nix your show in favour of hers.*'

In a short time fifteen guests would be happily chatting and sipping cocktails in the drawing room. She would have to play the sparkling hostess. What she would far rather do was hide under her bedclothes and have a good cry.

In the bathroom Abbie lay back in the tub battling with a mixture of resentment, anger and hurt. Why was her mother so quick to believe the worst of her? She was certain no one at her network had known Steve Stone was booked for her mother's show. So the Machiavellian theory that she was being manipulated was nonsense.

Manipulated. That word still rankled. She might not have her mother's years in journalism behind her but she was still experienced enough to recognise when people were pulling strings. Stone's agent obviously had his own agenda. Why did her mother believe him and not her own daughter?

Abbie hated confrontation. Listening to her parents quarrelling had made her highly sensitive to argument. She did not admire this part of her character but over the years she had learned to compartmentalise her emotions.

It meant she could be assertive in her job yet retreat from conflict with family and friends.

As she rinsed off the suds, Abbie made two decisions: she would search for a new apartment as soon as possible and she would get away from all this angst and suspicion and fly to London in a month's time to spend Christmas with her father.

Freddie arrived early and realised at once that Katharine was upset. He swept her up in a hug and Katharine leaned her head against his shoulder. It was wide and comforting and part of her wanted to confide in him but she did not want to stir up emotions again and risk spoiling the party for Freddie as well. She fobbed him off by promising to discuss it fully after the guests were gone.

'Sure,' he agreed readily. 'I'll go and sort out the drinks.'

That's what she liked about him. He was so undemanding, never persisted, never gave her any trouble.

Silver salvers holding cut-glass decanters filled with malted whisky, dry sherry and vintage port had been left out in the drawing room ready for Freddie's attentions. He had been in charge of dispensing pre-lunch drinks or cocktails in her household for many years, checking that the ingredients for the iced Martinis were in position, the lemons finely cut or quartered, the ice buckets overflowing.

As Katharine put the finishing touches to her make-up, she could hear him laughing with Conchita. She had refused offers of help in the actual kitchen. 'It's a family day. I don't want to share my oven,' was her reaction before preparing a huge, perfectly-basted golden turkey with all the trimmings.

Katharine emerged from her bedroom, tying the belt of a grey crepe Jasper Conran dress, a favourite she chose for occasions when she wanted to look elegant but feel comfortable. She moved swiftly to one of the huge Regency mirrors in the hall to check her face, smoothing away a runnel of black mascara from underneath an eye.

Freddie was watching her appreciatively from the doorway. He strode over and kissed her cheek. 'Darling, you look perfect. I'm so happy to be sharing this day with you.'

Katharine felt the now familiar pang of remorse whenever she was confronted by the reality of deceiving Freddie. Happily unaware of her feelings, he asked brightly, 'Shall we finalise the seating plan?' He led the way into the dining room.

Katharine looked round the room with satisfaction. The navy and white fabric-covered walls set off the sumptuous table perfectly. The room glowed with Victorian silverware inherited from her grandmother and crystal glasses she had imported from Waterford in Ireland. Since this was Thanksgiving, Abbie, as her only blood relative present, ought to be seated at her right hand. But she did not feel strong enough to keep up hours of polite talk with her daughter in front of guests.

'Put Abbie next to your little granddaughter,' she suggested to Freddie. At the far end of the table. Well away from her.

'Darling.' Nina kissed Katharine warmly on the cheek. They had lunched together only a few days before at one of those smart eateries where the maître d's pondered how anyone could eat so little and spend so much in an hour, but were genuinely pleased to see each other again.

Like Freddie, Nina knew immediately that something was wrong. 'Are you OK?' she asked with concern.

Katharine hesitated for only a second. Part of her wanted to blot out what had happened so it would not overshadow the festivities but Nina would be more adept than Freddie at coaxing Abbie into a better humour, should she sulk. And she would certainly help to deflect any embarrassment if Abbie continued with the quarrel.

Katharine steered Nina into the bedroom and sat down beside her on an elegant chaise longue.

'This ghastly rivalry is doing neither of you any good,' said Nina, after hearing details of the row.

Katharine unclipped an earring and massaged her ear lobe. Nina was right, of course. Was the job really worth all this aggravation between herself and Abbie? The answer was instantaneous and in some ways surprised and relieved her. No, it was not. If she stepped down from her job, maybe there was a chance they could become closer. In any case, it had to be better than what they had now.

Was she capable of such a sacrifice? Suddenly the idea of being out of the limelight became attractive. What did prestige, fame, power mean if she and her daughter were estranged? Financially, she did not need to work again. Perhaps it was time for her to think the unthinkable. She had better not say a word to Buzz about it, it would ruin his Thanksgiving. No, she would trail the idea to Nina and see what her reaction was.

Katharine walked over to the mirror and fiddled with her hair. 'You're right, and I think it's time I tried to evaluate things,' she said carefully.

'What things?'

'Oh, things like giving up my job.'

Nina stood up hurriedly. 'Wow. That's drastic.'

'Maybe it's time for me to do something else.'

'Are you serious?' She stared at Katharine's face. 'Yes, I can see you are.'

'There are plenty of advantages,' Katharine was hurrying her words. 'Abbie and I could be friends and I've enough money now and there are a lot of things I want to do besides interviewing. What do you think?'

'I think I'd be delighted. I need a pal to come with me on what you Brits call "little jollies". We could go to art exhibitions, maybe in Paris, Florence or Venice.'

'Steady on,' said Katharine, laughing but thinking how attractive that kind of life would be. 'I wouldn't disappear completely. I could become a producer, do specials. The big events. Anyway,' she added firmly, 'it's just a thought at the moment.'

'OK, keep me posted.' Nina stood up. 'I hate to change the subject but could I ask where, um, Mr Hemmings is spending today?'

'I don't know. As we're apart for Thanksgiving, I suggested I could arrange to be free for Christmas, and guess what? He says he'll "probably" be abroad on business. Do you think he's lying?'

'Who'll ever know? But I suspect he's a serial bachelor. I wouldn't get too hooked on him before you try dressing him in a straitjacket.'

Katharine smiled. 'Nooo, of course not. Come on, let's go in and give thanks.'

In the event it was Freddie's grandchild, five-year-old Isabel who saved the day. Abbie was charmed by her and as Katharine watched her daughter talking to the child, she felt a wave of longing, remembering Abbie as a baby, a smiling, contented peach of a child. Then at the age of ten baking the lopsided cakes they called the Leaning Towers. If she closed her eyes, Katharine could still recall the squeaks of pleasure from Abbie when she first tried on the flower girl's dress for a friend's wedding. How perfect she had looked in the puff-sleeved confection in palest rose moiré billowing out over candy-pink net petticoats. And the joy on her face as her mother had settled the crown of fresh white roses on her head. And this was the young woman who had not even glanced in her direction during the meal.

When the guests left the table to stretch out on the king-sized sofas in the drawing room for coffee and liqueurs, Katharine noticed Abbie stoop to whisper something to Freddie's granddaughter. The little girl nodded delightedly.

'Would you excuse Isabel and me please?' she asked politely, her eyes still avoiding her mother's. 'We're going to watch a Disney cartoon.' Taking the child's hand, she disappeared into the library for the rest of the afternoon, only emerging briefly when Isabel's parents went home.

Although most of the guests had no inkling from Katharine's behaviour that anything was amiss, there was a dullness in her spirit. Today of all days, when America was celebrating the joys of family life, here she was once again as apart from hers as she ever had been.

Katharine awoke in the early hours feeling depressed and drained. This quarrel had to be quashed before it festered into something really nasty. With a surge of energy she sprang out of bed to make herself a cup of tea. This morning she would indulge herself with the tannin-rich English Breakfast variety.

The hall clock struck eight as her bare feet padded quietly across the parquet floor. To her surprise there were noises coming from Abbie's room and she hesitated, wondering if she should take her some tea.

She tapped softly on the bedroom door and after a few seconds it opened. Abbie was fully dressed and behind her Katharine could see that her room was in disarray. Two suitcases were on the bed, crammed untidily with her belongings.

'What's going on?'

'What do you think's going on? I'm moving out.'

'Abbie, don't, not angry like this. We can work this out. I'm sure we can.'

'No, we can't. We've tried and things have never really been right between us.'

'Look, it was never going to be easy, being in the same

job. And this Stone business—'

'You know what your problem is?' Abbie interrupted brusquely. 'You're running scared. You think everyone's out to get you. The truth is, in our office we hardly ever discuss you. We've stopped taking any notice of what you do.'

Katharine was silent, dazed by this tirade.

'You say we cut corners,' Abbie went on hotly, 'that we take chances and don't do things properly. Well, if it's true, we're only following in your footsteps.'

By now Katharine was fighting to keep her temper. 'I've never stooped so low as to stop another guest from going on a rival show when he was already signed up.'

'You still don't think I'm telling the truth, do you? It's always been the same, you'll believe everyone else, ABN's oinks, your producer, Stone's agent, anyone but me. Can't you see that sometimes you might possibly be wrong? But no. You're Katharine the Great. You think you know it all. You never accept any criticism. Nor any blame. You think you're perfect, far above us mortals.'

Katharine was stung. 'At least I don't involve myself in dirty tricks.'

'How can you say that when it was one of your researchers who slept with Hal Ditzler's agent to get him on the show?'

'And as soon as we found out,' pointed out Katharine, 'she was fired. I don't recall hearing about that kind of discipline on your show.'

'Because no one has gone that far.'

'Oh no?' There was no stopping Katharine now. 'I've heard that your people are using bribery, supplying agents with prostitutes and for all I know drugs as well. You obviously have no idea what's going on out there.'

'That's all rumour. You can't prove a thing because there's nothing to prove.'

'Abbie, you've changed so much you're like a stranger.'

'That's not surprising, is it? We haven't spent much time together. You were so busy you found it convenient to send me away to boarding school when you knew I didn't want to go. And Dad was against it as well.'

'I can't believe you think that. It didn't happen like—'

'You shouldn't have had children,' interrupted Abbie. 'All you've ever been interested in is your career and being in the limelight. You've hated my taking even part of it away from you. That's what's at the bottom of all this Steve Stone business.'

Katharine collapsed on to a chair. 'How could you say such a cruel thing?'

'You don't understand me. You've never once tried to find out what I want, how I feel. Not like Dad. He shows he cares by everything he does.'

'How dare you throw your father in my face?' Katharine spluttered in anger. 'A man who hasn't changed his life one iota for you, who does nothing he doesn't want to do, one of the most selfish men I've ever met.'

'Selfish?' Abbie's tone was scathing. 'That's something else, coming from you.'

Katharine put her hands to her temples, trying to hold back the tears. And in her overwrought state she said the deadly words that would haunt her. 'Do you think you would have got your job if you hadn't been my daughter? You owe your career to me.'

The barb struck home. Abbie exhaled heavily. 'I'm leaving right now. You won't have to bother about me any more, not even at Christmas. I'll spend it with the only parent who does love me.'

With that she picked up her suitcases and left, slamming the front door hard enough to rattle its hinges.

The letting agency's description of the apartment as 'compact yet efficient' was accurate. The decor had obviously been chosen for professional male executives who showered, slept, made a few phone calls and went out again.

The only advantage to the place Abbie could see was that it was closer to Globe's offices than Katharine's apartment was, and she had to admit she liked the bedroom television set which was suspended on the ceiling, descending to eye level at the flick of a switch. The few personal touches she was able to bring to it like the silver-framed photograph of her father did little to alleviate the sterile atmosphere. But over Thanksgiving and at very short notice, this was all Matt had been able to arrange. What a sweetheart he had been to cut short his holiday with his family to come and help her out, and his secretary had promised to produce a list of suitable condominiums at the beginning of next week. Abbie was determined that however busy she was, she would make time to check them out. She did not regret her decision to leave her mother's apartment but she would not stay in this dreary place a moment longer than necessary.

To try to take her mind off her surroundings, she phoned Robert at his parents' house. Her shoulders slumped as she heard the answerphone cut in. She left him her new number and went back to staring morosely at the bare beige walls of her living room.

She still found it difficult to believe that Katharine could accuse her of such a dirty trick. What job could be worth shafting your own mother? She could think of no conceivable situation where she would contemplate it. She could see why those creeps at ABN would believe it. But Katharine? Abbie felt tears welling up. She felt as much alone as when her parents had separated. This was like going through a divorce. From her mother.

Her spirits received another battering the next morning. Her name was all over the tabloids.

'Did Steve Nix Kate For Abbie?' shouted the headlines. 'Abbie In Double-Cross?'

Abbie read the papers with dismay. Who the hell had talked? Somebody had, the information was too accurate. Katharine? She dismissed the thought. No one on her show gained from stories like these.

As soon as Robert read the story he took the first available plane out of Chicago, cutting short his holiday with his family, to be there to cheer her up.

She was glad he was with her, for on Sunday morning the newspaper headlines were even worse. Someone had briefed reporters about her departure from Katharine's apartment. 'Condo Ain't Big Enough For Super Egos' gossip columns trumpeted; 'Duelling Super Diva Flounces Out'.

'Where are they getting this stuff?' Abbie flung the papers on to the kitchen table in disgust. 'I wish I hadn't agreed to that magazine interview tomorrow. They're bound to burrow away at this quarrel.' She gnawed her little finger. 'Maybe I could postpone it.'

'Don't do that,' said Robert. 'You have to face it sometime, so do it head on. That's the only way to deal with unfavourable publicity. Pity Richard Nixon didn't have me on his staff when he was ducking and weaving.'

The electric juicer made a pathetic whimper and Abbie leaned down and whispered to it, 'Don't give up on me.'

'Move aside,' said Robert. 'That machine will never work for a woman.' He pushed, pulled, switched and the juicer started working. His look was triumphant.

Abbie stood on tiptoe and kissed his chin. 'Watch it, you're smirking.'

'I never smirk. Don't stop that,' he muttered, drawing her closer.

For a while Abbie was able to push away the painful memory of her mother's stricken expression before she slammed out of the apartment. She and Katharine had not exchanged a word since then.

After only three months in the job, this was what television was doing to her. To both of them.

When Abbie strode purposefully towards table forty-one at the Café des Peintures on Monday, she was slightly out of breath and fifteen minutes late.

The restaurant was filled with chief executives, directors, producers and publicists and, she was discomfited to see, Blanche Casey, who gave her a glacial stare before whispering to her male companion.

Table forty-one was the restaurant's showcase table. Matt had insisted on it. It was enclosed in a fanciful glass gazebo where celebrities could be seen but not heard.

'You can't sit at a lower rung table,' he explained. 'It'll wreck your standing. If it's good enough for Barbara Walters, it's good enough for you.'

Abbie was shocked. 'You can't mention me in the same breath,' she protested.

'You can't, I can. Give it a few months, everyone else will.'

She was still nervous of the interview but before Robert had left for Chicago, they had rehearsed answers to every possible question that might be put to her. Charlton Perry, *Boulevard Magazine*'s contributing editor, had a formidable reputation for meticulous research.

Abbie greeted him cautiously, trying to cover her nervousness. He quickly put her at ease. As a skilful interviewer herself, Abbie could only admire his technique.

After some preliminary small talk they ordered their meals, asparagus tips and salad for her, Pacific prawns followed by quail for him. Then Charlton Perry took a minute but powerful tape recorder out of his pocket and raised an inquiring eyebrow. As she nodded assent, he pressed the button to record.

He asked about her shows, where the ideas for them

came from, how they were put together, what she found most challenging, securing the interviews or conducting them, all the while leading her towards the nub of his questions in a performance that was seamless. If only television interviews allowed the luxury of a build-up like this, thought Abbie wistfully.

'What's the dark side of success?' he asked. 'What don't you like about it so far?'

Here we go, she thought. But it was a fair question and she gave it an honest answer. 'I don't like the attention from people like you.'

His eyebrow went up.

'I know the situation between my mother and me seems fascinating but I wish the media would give us a break, not examine everything we do or say.' Abbie gave an exasperated sigh.

'Last week some so-called expert in the *Post* compared our body language. They picked a photograph of my mother taken at one of those sedate United Nations receptions, you know how stuffy they can be, and they compared it with one of me taken at a fashion show. Apparently her body language showed she was uptight and lacked warmth, while my stance indicated an outward, friendly, accessible personality. But how do you stand when being introduced to the Equadorial ambassador?'

'Is it true that you've moved out of your mother's apartment?' His voice was tranquil, unconcerned.

'Those headlines were grossly exaggerated,' replied Abbie steadily. Her mission during this interview was to dampen the interest. 'My mother was sorry I left, she'd become used to having me around, but we both knew it was a short-term arrangement until I found a place of my own. I am, after all, twenty-six years old.'

'So there's no truth in the stories that you and your mother had a huge fight over the Steve Stone cancellation.'

Abbie shook her head. '*Tonight* never had any plans to interview Steve. We were not in competition for him.' It was a pity this article would only appear in the magazine in three months' time. She wanted Katharine to read it right now.

'So why did he back out of your mother's show at such short notice?'

'I don't know. It had nothing to do with me.' Would he leave it at that? She hoped he would not ask whether her mother believed this version.

Perry was about to respond when they were interrupted by a red-jacketed waiter.

'I'm sorry to disturb you, Miss Lomax, but I was asked to give this to you right now. The messenger said it was urgent.'

Abbie opened the cheap white envelope. Good God, it was from that nutcase again, the one calling himself 'Fan of Fans'. She scanned the typewritten letter quickly. It read: 'I intend to make you regret the day you went into television. Watch out. Fan of Fans.' She had almost managed to put him out of her mind when there had been no follow-up to the postcard at the fashion show. She folded the letter and put it in her purse.

'Problem?'

She shook her head, trying not to show concern. How the hell had this guy found out where she was lunching? Few people knew she was being interviewed here today. Could it have come from Charlton Perry's office? Had his secretary mentioned her name when she made the reservation to secure the prime table? It could be one of the staff here, perhaps even the waiter bringing them their coffee.

When the interview ended and she was able to leave, Abbie had a word with the restaurant doorman. He told her that the letter had been delivered by a young man wearing sweater and jeans who had refused to leave until he had seen the envelope put into her hands.

When Abbie showed the letter to Matt Nicolaides, he was furious. 'Why didn't I know about this nut? You should've told me about that first message when it happened. If I'm your agent I need to know everything that concerns you.'

'I did try and reach you after the postcard but your office didn't know where you were and your mobile was switched off.'

He cleared his throat. 'Ah yes, must've been my heavy meetings time.'

'Then Jeri-Ann suggested I put it out of my mind so I didn't bother you about it.'

So why had his office not known his whereabouts? thought Abbie. But he looked so uncomfortable she decided not to pursue it. Over the past few weeks Matt had smartened up considerably. Abbie had noticed that his suits were newer and more tailored, he had definitely lost a few pounds, even his nails looked buffed and manicured. This change of image could be due to moving to a more fashion-conscious city, but would she believe that if she were Matt's wife?

'Anyway,' she said, 'this note worries me more. It was well publicised that I was going to be a guest at the fashion show but how many people knew about the magazine interview at the restaurant?'

'Just my office,' replied Matt, 'and I can vouch for everyone working there. What about on your side?'

'Only my producer. It wasn't a secret but I can't imagine she would talk. She's phenomenally discreet.'

'Well, it was an exclusive so I don't suppose Charlton Perry was shouting about it. That leaves the restaurant. They're full of people who get paid by newspapers to tip them off when celebs turn up. I'd go and nose around but there's a danger I might set people yapping and we don't need that. I shall talk to Globe's chief security officer about beefing up your security.'

★ ★ ★

Next morning, Abbie went jogging as usual. When she returned to her rented apartment, she made herself some cinnamon toast and a cup of herbal tea. She wished Robert was still here. She missed him.

She switched on the television. There was an appeal for funds for Public Service Broadcasting by a group of well-known people. They did this fairly regularly and Abbie was about to switch channels when her mother's face appeared on the screen. Katharine's professionalism shone through as she talked warmly about the contribution PBS made to American cultural life. Abbie felt a wave of admiration. She had hoped for so much when she had moved to New York, a new job and a new start to her relationship with her mother, one on a more equal footing. She was damned if she was going to allow media people intent only on printing poison to get in the way.

Still holding the tea, she walked to the phone. She would call her mother but she would not apologise. Why should she? There was nothing to apologise for. What she had to do was make Katharine understand that they were both being exploited by people who had their own agendas, that unless they had a rapprochement their enemies had won.

It was then that Abbie noticed the red light blinking on her answering machine and pressed the playback button.

The voice coming through the machine was low, monotonous and without cadence. She did not recognise it and could not quite make out the short message so she rewound the tape and listened again.

'You can't hide from me. Watch out. Fan of Fans.'

Abbie put the cup down so abruptly the contents splashed all over the floor. Her legs had trouble supporting her frame and she slumped down on to a chair. She had only just moved in here and very few people knew the number so how in God's name did he? Who was this guy and what the hell did he want?

As she wondered whether to ring the station's security office, her agent or Jeri-Ann, she remembered Katharine telling her about being pestered by a fan who had the delusion she was his wife. He had kept up a barrage of calls and letters. Yes, her mother would know what she should do. And maybe this was a better way of repairing bridges than talking about exploitation, which might set them off arguing.

Abbie pressed the recall button for her mother's apartment. 'Hi, Mum, it's me.'

'Oh, hello.' Katharine's voice sound surprised.

Abbie plunged straight in. 'Look, I said some very nasty things to you. I've been thinking about it a lot and I'm truly sorry about what I said.'

There was a short silence then Katharine said quietly, 'So am I. It went much too far.'

'Mum, I think we need to talk. Is there any chance we can meet?'

'I'd like that very much.'

'You couldn't make it today, I suppose?'

'I'm absolutely up to the gunnels but if I rearrange my schedule I'm pretty sure I can get away.'

'Great,' said Abbie. She hesitated. 'I'd like to talk about that freak who sent me that card at Alain's show, remember? I've had a phone call from him here at the new place.'

'How did he get the number?'

'I've no idea. Mum, I badly need some advice. Shall we meet for lunch? I'm supposed to be taping an insert but I'm sure I can sweetheart the producer to reschedule.'

'Yes, that ought to be OK.'

'Luigi's.'

There was a pause. Luigi's was usually so full of media personnel it was almost an extension of the TV boardrooms.

'It's very crowded there, Abbie, we won't get much privacy.'

'I'd rather go somewhere busy like that, I'd feel safer,' said Abbie, then added an afterthought. 'And maybe it'll be good to show people we're still talking.'

'Is that why you want to meet?'

There was an edge to Katharine's voice and Abbie hid her irritation. Damn. Her mother always misunderstood her motives. 'Of course not. I told you, I want your advice.'

They arranged to meet at noon and Abbie then put in a call to Matt who was as unsettled as she was when he heard her news.

'I have no idea how he found out your number,' he said, 'I haven't given it to anyone. Not even my secretary knows it. It's in my computer at home but no one can access the file without the password.'

'Oh, Matt, I've read about this happening to other people, but I never appreciated how sick-making it can be.'

'Right,' said Matt decisively. 'This has got to stop. I'll go in strong again with Globe. We'll put a blanket on your diary, see you have the same driver every day, check your phone calls and change your number. You leave everything to me. I want them to vet everyone who works with you, from top to bottom.'

'Thanks,' said Abbie appreciatively. 'That would make me sleep a little easier. I'm meeting Mum for lunch. She might have some ideas on how to deal with him.'

'Oh? You're talking again, are you?'

'Well, I didn't think we should be at war for ever.'

The phone rang on Abbie's desk an hour before she and Katharine were due to meet. It was answered by a newsroom colleague.

'Katharine Sexton's office here with an urgent message for Ms Lomax,' said the voice. 'She says she's mega sorry but something has cropped up and she can't make lunch.

She apologises for the short notice and she'll phone later.'

'OK. I'll tell her right away.'

Abbie was trying to convince an unimpressed Red Skinner how important it was for her to alter studio schedules for the taping session, without mentioning the reason.

Eventually he agreed but re-assigning times for the vision mixer, floor manager, camera operator, lighting and sound technicians was complicated and it put him in a foul temper. Nevertheless when he had achieved it he put his head round Abbie's door and managed a thumbs-up for his star.

A few minutes later Abbie's PA arrived with the news that her mother could not make lunch. 'Says she'll phone you later.'

Damn. Abbie's disappointment was as keen as if she had been stood up by a lover. How could Katharine have cancelled knowing how worried she was about that creepy Fan of Fans? Lunch would also have provided an ideal chance to put the Steve Stone affair to rest. Abbie was sure Katharine would believe her once she listened to her side of the story calmly and rationally.

As the schedule had been so painstakingly rearranged for her benefit, she would have to disappear from the office as if she was keeping her 'important engagement'. She would ask her PA not to mention to Red that all she was going to do was wander around Bloomingdales.

Katharine glanced impatiently at her watch, trying to ignore the curious glances of her fellow diners at Luigi's. Abbie was not the greatest of time-keepers but this was unforgivable. Katharine could almost hear the onlookers muttering 'Who stood her up?' The place was stiff with people from the industry. It was certain to be in the gossip columns tomorrow. She wished she had not mentioned to the maître d' that she was meeting her daughter.

After thirty minutes and still no sign of Abbie, Katharine pursed her lips and gathered up her belongings. Her daughter would have to have a damned good excuse for standing her up.

She walked to the ladies' cloakroom and called Abbie's office. Her phone was answered by Abbie's assistant who thought she could be honest with Abbie's mother and said, 'Actually, she's gone out shopping.'

Katharine was taken aback. 'Are you sure?'

'Yes, and no one can get hold of her, I'm afraid, she's switched off her mobile.'

Katharine walked slowly over to the washbasin and rinsed her hands. She stared at her reflection without seeing it. It had taken much juggling, inconveniencing several people, to fit in this last-minute lunch. Despite their bitter quarrel, she had been happy to do it because Abbie wanted urgent advice. Now, without the courtesy of informing her, she had changed her mind. Not for anything important but to go shopping.

Fame has changed her, Katharine thought, turned her into someone I don't recognise. Well, she would not contact Abbie. It was up to her to apologise for wasting her time.

Katharine paid for her mineral water and walked quickly towards the exit, gazing firmly into the near distance to avoid any eye contact. Her limo would not arrive for another forty minutes; if she called to summon the driver, by the time he arrived she could be back at the office. She had missed lunch and then to crown the day as she climbed into a yellow cab she snagged her tights and watched as the run travelled up her thigh.

Shit.

Beads of perspiration coursed down Abbie's neck as she turned up the resistance counter on the treadmill.

Abbie still went jogging early in the morning, but she

and Jeri-Ann had been burning up calories at this exclusive gym club a few blocks from the station since Abbie had moved out of Katharine's apartment. So far no one had snitched although they both knew it was only a matter of time before the press found out. Meanwhile they enjoyed the freedom of being able to work out in comparative privacy without the fear of hidden cameras taking pictures angled up the crotch like those infamous shots flashed all over the world of the Princess of Wales.

Her friendship with Jeri-Ann had blossomed; they worked the same hours, talked the same shorthand and shared the same passion for the job.

When she had first arrived in the Big Apple, Abbie had tried to re-connect with some of her old college friends now working in the city. Her mother managed to be friends with 'civilians' – doctors, accountants, financiers – but Abbie found that somehow her schedule and lifestyle made outside friendships impossible. At weekends those people were ready to party but she had to work. On weekdays when she had time off, they would be concentrating on their careers. They were understandably irritated when she had to cancel dates at the last minute and when she talked about some of the celebrities she had to deal with they were either over-awed or thought she was name-dropping. Abbie found herself editing her conversations with them. The loud, funny, warm confidences they had once shared eventually dried up altogether. The only people Abbie could comfortably share experiences with now were the small coterie around her, Robert, Matt to a certain extent, and the people at Globe like the researchers, Brenda and Brooke in make-up, and Jeri-Ann Hagerty.

The small, dark-haired, energetic 32-year-old had a feistiness which appealed to Abbie. She was also best placed to join in Abbie's forages into retail therapy. Jeri-Ann earned good money. She was highly regarded within Globe but her value to Abbie was not only as a producer. Jeri-Ann was unfashionably frank in an industry of sycophants and Abbie found this both refreshing and helpful. Jeri-Ann put her candour down to a solid Irish Catholic heritage. She was also a good listener.

'Why hasn't Katharine phoned?' Abbie puffed. 'It's been several days and not a word of explanation.'

Jeri-Ann shrugged and eased her bra where it had stuck to her shoulder. 'So call her.'

'I thought about it but you know what? I'm tired of being the bad guy. Why can't she believe me? Right at the beginning we agreed we'd hold the faith and, OK, it's been rough but we're both grown up, we ought to fight outsiders not each other.'

'Look at it from her point of view,' countered her friend. 'She's been queen of the ratings for years. She's still number one but when you came on the scene her ratings dipped a couple of points. Imagine how she feels about that? She's not getting any younger and while she still looks terrific, the pressure must be on. You're still new enough to be able to make the occasional mistake and your public will forgive you. You can even afford to experiment a little. But I'm beginning to feel sorry for Katharine because she has to be so goddamn perfect all the time.'

'Maybe you're right, but that's not the point. I'd never do anything to undermine her personally and she ought to take that as read.' Abbie sighed unhappily and jumped off the treadmill, wiping her glistening forehead with a hand towel. She picked up a pair of five-kilo weights. 'Do you think I can lift these?'

'Go for it,' grinned Jeri-Ann, who was proud of being able to manage four circuits with the six-kilo bars. 'Talking about being undermined, did you see that interview with Blanche Casey this morning in the *Post*? Boy, was she bitchy about the two of you.'

'She'll never say a good word about me.' Abbie was philosophical. 'She's told everybody in the world that she would be a better anchor than me. I don't blame her. She's had a lot more experience and, let's face it, I wouldn't be here if it wasn't for my mother.'

'Whoa there. That might have been true at the beginning but not any more. Viewers don't switch on week after week to watch someone's daughter. Most of them don't care about that, according to the latest research. Hey, you're not letting that stuff bug you, right?'

Abbie laughed. 'Not only am I not letting it bug me, I'm going to forget it. I'm spending Christmas with my dad in London. It'll be a real holiday from all the problems here.'

Chapter Eight

The snow-covered roofs of Hampstead looked much as they must have done to Charles Dickens, thought Abbie as she walked briskly up the hill towards her father's mews house. Hollybush Cottage with its distinctive mullioned windows and crooked chimney was one of the most photographed sights in that picturesque area, one which housed many of the capital's intellectuals, media personnel and millionaires.

Abbie took a deep breath of the frost-filled air, feeling a surge of exhilaration. Christmas in London. What a wonderful place to be, if only for a precious ten days while the programme took a break.

In the tiny front garden of the small house in Flask Walk, scarlet berries glowed in the holly bushes and here and there sparrows were pecking greedily at the still-laden pyracanthas. Abbie picked a sprig of holly, enough to decorate a Christmas pudding, and let herself inside, remembering to duck her head to avoid the 400-year-old oak beam straddling the doorway. Her father maintained that the house had been designed for gnomes or drunks on all fours. After some nasty bumps when he first moved in, his six-foot frame now automatically ducked under any of the low beams.

'Perfect timing,' bellowed Milo's voice from his minute study, lodged between the narrow staircase and the pantry. 'I've just faxed the last bit of copy and I'd kill for a pint of bitter. Fancy a stroll across the Heath for a pub lunch?'

'Ready when you are,' said Abbie. 'I haven't even unbuttoned my coat.'

He insisted on lending her one of his ten-foot lambswool scarves, wrapping it several times round her neck so she could only just peep out over the top. They walked briskly over the famous heath with its acres of woodland which had been enjoyed for centuries by highwaymen and more recently by walkers, dog owners and homosexuals cruising for new encounters.

They had picked up the threads of their relationship as easily as if they had been in daily contact. In fact it had been eight months since they had last met in Chicago. Milo was fascinated to hear the minutiae of Abbie's new job and life in the Big Apple.

They skirted Whitestone Pond. In summer this tiny stretch of water was a magnet for single fathers with offspring clutching toy boats. Now it was covered in ice, providing a skating rink for a solitary sliding mallard.

Cheeks aglow, they pushed open the heavy doors of the Duck and Drake. The warmth from a blazing log fire greeted them. The Elizabethan coaching inn was already busy with lunchtime customers; it was a favourite with writers and artists and lovers of real ale. Over individual ramekins of homemade steak and kidney pie Milo showed her how to release the steam by making a slit at the top. 'You want to watch it. You're forgetting your British heritage.'

'Never,' she replied swiftly. 'Sometimes I wish I'd stayed in London. I love my job but things are so complicated.'

His face became serious. 'Look, this problem between you and your mother will blow over if you don't over-react.'

'Dad, she still treats me like a kid, she always seems to think the worst of me. I can't seem to talk to her the way

I can talk to you.' She paused and gazed at him. 'Can I ask you something personal?'

He looked wary. 'I don't promise to answer.'

'Did that affair you had break up the marriage or was it already going wrong so you had an affair?'

He sighed. 'Come on, Abbie. You know it's never as clear cut as that. We married very young and then we grew up. I wasn't around all the time and so your mother concentrated on her career. And she got damn good at it. I suppose we were both too selfish to make a go of it. Our relationship changed. The affair was a good excuse, but your mother knew it meant nothing. It was a sign that the marriage wasn't working so we agreed to separate.'

'Mum says it wasn't only one affair.'

'It was all a long time ago,' he said evasively.

'Are you sorry now?' As she looked at him, she could see how many women would still find him extremely attractive.

He ran his fingers through his thick brown hair, a familiar gesture when he was ill at ease. 'Well, I wish I saw more of you,' he said, sidestepping her question. 'Phone calls aren't good enough. I think I'll suggest to the editor that we up our ratio of White House stories so I can visit more regularly.'

'I'd very much like that. Especially at the moment.'

'Doing the same sort of show at the same time as your mother's was never going to be easy.'

'But what can I do about it? I've bagged one of the plum jobs in television.'

'And is that more important than your relationship with your mother?'

'In an ideal world I wouldn't have to choose.'

'So what do you intend doing about the situation?'

Her father had always asked questions rather than offered solutions. In this way, he had once explained to her, she would learn to think through her own problems and perhaps arrive at the right answers.

'Maybe I should take myself out of the arena, come back and live here. After my experience in America, I'm sure I could get a job.'

'Bit drastic, isn't it, Abbs? And there's a problem. Television here is in a parlous state. I'm not sure you'd be given a proper chance. The BBC is always having budgeting problems and things at the other channels are almost as bad. I'm afraid the good old days when money was thrown at creative people are long gone. The bean-counters have taken over. Of course you could do something else but that seems stupid when you're such a success.'

'I don't feel a success.'

'Of course you are. My advice is to stick with it, at least for now. Show them that you're not a one-season wonder. And if I were you, I would be big and brave and when we get back, give your mother a bell to wish her happy Christmas. Now come on, finish that pie.'

She took his advice but the call, when she made it, was unsatisfactory. There was an irritating echo on the line which prevented all spontaneity. It left Abbie feeling sad. Although she did not know it, it was an emotion shared by her mother.

Over the Christmas holidays Katharine should have received an Academy Award for her performance as the interested guest, happy hostess and concerned companion when all she wanted was George.

Like many single women in New York, she had built up a support system of friends and business acquaintances and she had a ready escort in Freddie. They had taken Lisa for lunch at the Tavern on the Green but the estrangement from her daughter and George's absence increased Katharine's sense of loneliness during what was essentially a family holiday.

She was pleased to hear from Abbie on Christmas Eve although their conversation was very stilted. Abbie told her she was having a wonderful time with her father. What was new? thought Katharine, then bit her lip. She did not want to become embittered. They wished each other a happy Christmas and it was only after she had put the phone down that she realised sadly that although they lived within a few blocks of one another in the same city, they had made no arrangements to meet when Abbie got back from England.

While George was away and the show was having a break, she had had time to think about him a great deal, his teasing humour, his warm smile, the way he reached for her urgently in the night, waking her from a deep sleep to make satisfying love. Apart from a few light, bantering calls which elicited the information that he was spending Christmas Day with some old friends in Rome and would be back a few days afterwards, she had heard nothing. She could not call him because he had not given her a contact number, preferring, as he put it, to ring her.

One thing she had learned early on in their affair was that there was no way George would allow himself to be treated as a fixture in her life. If ever she tried to arrange a date well in advance, he would refuse to be pinned down, pleading travel commitments. So once or twice, although she felt she was punishing herself more than him, she made herself unavailable. It had been quite a successful ploy, but he was way ahead in that game. In all other respects, however, he was an attentive lover.

A week before he left for Europe they had toured the antique shops of the Hamptons looking for china and glass which he wanted as inspiration for copies in one of his hotels. She had admired a small Victorian portrait of a wistful young woman and when she had walked back to the car, he had bought it and presented it to her at lunch. It had been a wonderful, thoughtful surprise. An early

Christmas present, he called it.

They had booked separately into a discreet, exclusive hotel and made passionate love before and after dinner. Their lovemaking seemed to get better and better and at dinner George had been, as ever, a sensitive and interesting companion.

He brought her up to date on the problems he was continuing to encounter with his new hotel in the city. 'I'm not happy with the decor but it's so far behind schedule that I'm having to compromise. And those environmentalists are still giving me a hard time. The building's finished now, you'd think they'd forget the history.' Then, untypically for George, he had looked slightly embarrassed. 'I have a favour to ask, and I find quite suddenly that I'm shy.' He took her hand. 'I don't like presuming on our friendship.'

Friendship? Was that all it was?

'I wondered if you could perform the opening ceremony, darling,' he said hesitantly. 'It's not for several weeks but it would be so good for the hotel. I know we've not been seen in public together and I shall quite understand if you say no . . .'

Why not? Wasn't it time she followed her instincts, said goodbye to Freddie and began to concentrate on George? If the opening ceremony was planned weeks ahead, this augured well for their affair. She could not predict how long their relationship would last but if she didn't try she would never know.

'Of course, I'll do it. Gladly.' She smiled. 'Give me the date when you have it and I'll mention it to a few of my friends. We'll get a really big crowd there.'

He was delighted and she savoured the feeling that he was grateful to her.

Three thousand miles away from her troubles, Abbie was enjoying being with her father and his group of friends, most of whom worked in the British media. Though knowledgeable about American television and interested in it, they weren't involved and she was able to forget her workload, the bitching, the stress of chasing up interviews. Best of all, she did not think about the estrangement with her mother. Or the Fan of Fans.

She was having such a good time that when a last-minute whim made the group decide to travel on *Le Shuttle* to Paris for lunch, she decided to go with them and postpone her return to America. The downside was that she had to switch her booking on a daytime plane to an overnight flight in order to get back to her office on schedule.

The British Airways crew, who were well briefed, made such a fuss of settling her into her seat that she became the focus of all eyes in the first-class compartment. Catching the all-nighter had some compensations. London had been fun but hectic and she was hoping to sleep her way across the Atlantic. She gave instructions to the glamorous stewardess that she would not bother with dinner and asked not to be disturbed.

As she adjusted the straps on her sleep mask, noting with relief that the space next to her was empty, a long, rangy figure slid into the seat and smiled at her.

Abbie was accustomed to this reaction from strange men but this one stared a little longer than was polite, his dancing brown eyes sending out flirtatious signals.

Despite trying to appear unflustered, Abbie found herself pushing the sleep mask surreptitiously under her seat.

'Charm does have its uses.' His voice was mischievous. 'The flight crew wouldn't take money,' he explained, 'so I had to find some other way to get this seat.'

Charm was what he had in abundance, she thought, risking a glance at that handsome profile as he stood up to take off the grey double-breasted jacket that showed all the hallmarks of a Savile Row tailor. His white cotton shirt revealed a muscular back and broad shoulders before he sat down again and began fastening his seat belt.

He was gorgeous. This flight was going to be fun.

'Ah, here's the champagne.' He took a sip. 'Good vintage,' he winked at her over the glass, 'good seat.'

She tried to appear as cool as she was able. This one was dangerous.

'I know exactly who *you* are, Abbie Lomax, so let me introduce myself.' He leaned a little closer and she caught a whiff of exotic aftershave. 'My name's George Hemmings.'

Never had a transatlantic flight passed so speedily. Flying through the night, cocooned in the darkness, the ceiling spotlight illuminating their faces, Abbie felt as though they were in their own time capsule, insulated from other passengers. Her guard dropped and she found herself talking easily to George Hemmings about her job and her life.

Not once during the flight did he mention her mother. This was unusual. Most strangers were curious about the two of them and invariably came up with the same questions: did Katharine mind her daughter anchoring such a similar show to hers? Did they regularly dissect each other's programmes? What did she think of her mother's last interview, whatever it was?

George Hemmings did not conform to this stereotype. He was also outside Abbie's romantic experience. More used to the impatience and unsubtle ardour of younger suitors like Robert she was at ease with this worldly, unhurried stranger, and appreciated his wit and warmth. He evidently did not have much time to watch television because of his hotel business, and he gave every impression of being interested in her as a woman rather than as a media queen.

Still talking, he took her hand, apparently unconsciously, and began playing idly with her fingers. In that moment everything changed.

The sexual charge that ran through her body was as instant and as powerful as being plugged into the national grid. It was not a feeling she had experienced often, if ever. Robert called her 'his slow burner' and she had come to the conclusion that she was a woman who enjoyed sex but was not ruled by it. This feeling was different and the effect George had on her made her wonder whether up until now she had been involved with lovers who were too young.

Her fingers felt burning hot. He was tracing the lines in her palm with a delicate, strumming movement, and the way he was looking at her made her want to rip off his clothes and lie against his naked body under the airline duvet waiting, abandoned, for the consequences.

Gently she extricated her hand and he gave a slow, knowing smile. Abbie blushed. Maybe he could read her mind.

But it was he who raised the subject of lovemaking.

'The problem with most people is the preparation's all wrong,' he said slowly. 'They think about having baths and perfuming themselves and while that's all important, of course, they forget about preparing the most important part of the body, the brain.' He shifted to the edge of his seat so his knee touched hers. Abbie gave an involuntary shiver.

'Many men can jump into bed with anyone. But I need more. I have to have that certain feeling about a person before I make love to them. It's not only physical. I have to be completely relaxed, to be able to laugh in their company. I need to be switched on mentally. It can happen just like that. When all the senses are involved, the woman I make love to will know what I want to do, and if she doesn't, just a touch,' he pushed her fringe away from her eyes, 'will be enough. Don't you find that?'

This would be the time to mention Robert. Strangely, the words went unsaid.

As the undercarriage landed at JFK with a judder, he passed her his business card. She was surprised at how carefully she put it away in the side compartment of her wallet.

George watched Abbie's limo pull away in front of his. Would she mention their meeting to Katharine? If she did, had he done anything to which Katharine could take exception? He did not think so.

He was aware that Katharine and her daughter were barely on speaking terms. Abbie had not mentioned her once during the flight, even when he had provided the opportunity.

He had spotted Abbie at the check-in counter and recognised her immediately. His plan had been to sit next to her to find out how much she knew about him and her mother. When it was obvious from her conversation that she and Katharine led quite separate lives, his intentions had changed.

Still, he had better be circumspect when meeting Katharine in the next day or so. Wait for her to mention that he and her daughter had met on the flight. Katharine was a delightful woman and he was enjoying their affair. So far, unlike many of his lovers, she seemed to accept his comings and goings with good grace. She did not ask what he did or who he met when he was not with her. He appreciated that this was because of Freddie. It was a trade-off. Well, that suited him fine. Because they were never seen in public together none of his other women realised Katharine was taking up so much of his time.

But her daughter. Ah, she was something special. Bright, vulnerable, delicious. Careful, George. She was bound to talk to her mother sometime. With a regretful sigh he made a decision. He had to put Abbie out of his mind.

His resolution soon wavered. After two dates with Katharine and several long phone conversations, she had said nothing about his meeting with Abbie.

A mischievous thought entered his head and would not go away. Enjoy the mother, enjoy the daughter. Without their knowing about each other. The thought was irresistible and he decided to risk sending a reminder of his existence to Abbie, a voucher for the spa at his hotel in New York.

Staff there reported that she had turned up and been told, as instructed, that he was abroad, news she apparently received first with surprise then with obvious disappointment. He felt elated. Her thank you note was brief. She had enjoyed the spa and she would visit it again, the facilities were excellent. She hoped his trip had been successful.

The next time George was with Katharine he mentioned seeing a brief snippet of her daughter's show. Katharine rapidly changed the subject and he deduced they were still not on speaking terms.

During the next few weeks he intensified his campaign, sending Abbie fresh pasta air-freighted from the Cipriani in Venice, then a leather-bound book of paintings of Fiesole in Italy, with the inscription, 'I'd love to show you this one day.'

The presents had the desired effect. Abbie called the private number on his business card. Still, George was cautious.

'I would like to see you one evening,' he began, 'but . . .'

'But what?'

'You probably don't have a moment to spare. So many men must ask you out.'

'They don't actually,' said Abbie. There was a pause. 'I

do have a boyfriend, he lives in Chicago but, well, I think we're having a break from each other. I mean, I don't want to get tied down.'

'Absolutely,' said George smoothly. 'You're still young. I'm sure your mother would approve of that.' He held his breath.

'I wouldn't know.' She gave a short laugh. 'We're not what you'd call close.'

Excellent. George paused for only a second before he asked, 'Are you free this evening?'

Abbie gazed sightlessly at the pastoral scene that dominated the marble fireplace in her new apartment close to the Plaza Hotel. Matt's secretary had fixed the lease for six months and though the original oil paintings had pushed up the price she had been happy to pay to get away in a hurry from her depressing dump. This apartment with its 24-hour security patrol made her feel safer.

Robert was paying her an unexpected visit. He had not said why he was coming to the city but it was probably yet another call-back interview. Whatever, it was an opportunity to straighten out her life. She would tell him she wanted to cool the relationship. He would be arriving shortly and, dreading the moment, she needed to clear her thoughts.

At some stage in her life Abbie wanted a husband and kids. Two kids – unless they were of the same sex, in which case she would probably risk having a third. She had always promised herself that she would not work long hours because she would want to concentrate on being a good wife and mother. Unlike her parents, she would put her marriage first and last. But this was not for now. It was far into the future, six years at least, as she told Jeri-Ann.

She did not want to hurt Robert by going out with

other men but it was difficult having a long-distance affair. They had never discussed the future, yet they regarded themselves as a couple and convention demanded that they were faithful to one another. Young, single and rich, living in one of the world's most exciting cities, Abbie felt she was like a married woman with a husband away most of the time.

Until now it had worked because she had met no one who tempted her to stray. When she went to first-night parties, charity balls or discos, personable and intelligent men often asked for her phone number, but somehow there was never a spark and she could feel herself pulling away, making excuses about how little time she had for a personal life these days, thinking how lucky she was to have Robert in the background.

George Hemmings was different. If she said no to this opportunity she could regret it for the rest of her life. She could learn so much from him, about so many things. Travel. Life. Food.

And George made her insides melt.

She had not been strong enough to refuse his invitation to meet but had postponed the date until tomorrow night because she had to sort things out with Robert first. Jeri-Ann would probably advise her to screw the one and keep the other on the back burner but juggling two men at once was not her scene.

It was complicated. She loved being with Robert. He was a friend, a companion, a lover. But the timing was wrong for a long-term commitment.

Abbie had rehearsed what she would say but now that she was facing Robert rather than the bathroom mirror, she thought her arguments sounded distinctly hollow.

Robert listened impassively and made no attempt to interrupt.

'All I need is a little time to find out what I really want,' she pleaded. 'We have something good, I know that and I don't want to lose you. It's just come too soon, that's all,' she ended lamely.

There was a short silence.

'Is that it?' he asked politely.

She nodded.

'I'm disappointed, Abbie. It's such a pathetic excuse.'

She started to protest.

'Don't.' The vehemence in his voice stopped her short. 'Don't bullshit me. I know what's happened. You've met someone else.'

'It has nothing to do with—'

'You're not sure about him so you want to put me on ice until you decide.'

'It's not like that.'

'Come on, Abbie, it's exactly like that. Well, it's too bad. What we have is good. Very good. But if you can't see that, then perhaps it's as well this has happened. And I agree with you. You're not ready for anything more serious.' Robert's eyes were cool. 'But if you think I'm hanging around on the sidelines while you play the field, forget it.'

'You don't understand . . .'

He stood up. 'I do understand. I wish you'd been more honest. With yourself as well as with me. I think you owed me that.' He turned and walked to the door. 'It doesn't matter now but the reason I came here today was to tell you that I start work at USTV on Monday. In New York.' And with that he left.

Abbie stared at the closed door for several minutes. 'I'm not going to cry,' she told herself. 'I made this happen. It was my decision, I'm in control of my life. Robert's feeling upset now but he'll come round. Of course he will.'

She sank down on to the soft leather sofa and picked up her research notes but she could not concentrate. Seconds later she leapt up to pour some mineral water. Then she switched on CNN but after a few minutes of channel surfing switched off. Why did the image of Robert's hurt face keep on re-surfacing? There was certainly no need for her to feel guilty. Robert would soon realise she was being sensible. He could surely see that both of them had to concentrate on their careers for a while rather than get involved in a serious commitment. And she would have come to this decision whether or not George had appeared on the scene, wouldn't she? Of course.

What she needed now was a light-hearted relationship, which was what George was offering. Abbie had not quite worked him out yet. She had half-expected to bump into him at the spa after the treatments. Instead of her favourite tracksuit, she had chosen a new brown twill Armani, which everyone said was seriously flattering, in case he should appear. There had been no sign of him and she had been surprised at her sense of disappointment.

So far George had wooed her at long distance but tomorrow night she would find out if the magic would survive a dinner date on her home territory rather than in the strangers-in-the-night atmosphere of a transatlantic flight.

The following evening Abbie threw yet another skirt on top of the piles of discarded dresses littering the bedroom carpet. If she did not make a choice soon she would be very late. The pink sheath? Too tarty, might give the wrong impression. The aquamarine? Needed a tan. Finally she settled for an oatmeal shift dress which cast an attractive light on her fair skin. It wasn't wonderful but it would have to do.

George's approving glance as she was shown across the dimly lit restaurant by a black-tailed maître d' made her glad of her choice. His eyes never wavered from her face as he took her hand and drew her gently towards him, brushing her cheek lightly with his lips.

Abbie felt heat coming into her cheeks as she sank down on the padded chair opposite him. Without saying a word this man had the ability to make her feel like a gauche schoolgirl. She fought to control her voice as she looked round nervously at the unfamiliar surroundings.

'I haven't been here before.' She tried to make her voice sound tranquil.

'Best-kept secret in town, this place,' said George, indicating to the waiter that he should open the champagne. 'I didn't think you'd be recognised in here.'

'It's so dark, no one would notice me. Do you bring all your first dates here?' she asked lightly.

He dipped his head and a lock of dark hair fell on to his forehead as he grinned disarmingly. 'I could lie to you and I will. I've never brought anyone here before.'

His chuckle was infectious and so began an evening of non-stop laughter. George seemed to find almost everything Abbie said amusing and indeed, as she gained confidence, she felt that the spin she put on her best anecdotes made them more humorous than usual.

George did not hit a false note. Having thoroughly researched his cuttings file, Abbie was half-expecting this entrepreneur to be too assured, too confident, too practised. But he was none of these. Abbie found him sensitive, warm and extremely likeable. More than that, she had to admit to herself, she wanted him to make love to her. The sexual tension she had felt between them when they had met was still very strong, at least for her. But George gave no sign that he was having the same thoughts. There were no sexual innuendoes, no physical contact after the first brief kiss on the cheek, and yet Abbie was quivering with lust as strongly as if he had been caressing her naked body.

What was it about George that made her want him rather than Robert? Was it simply that she would never be able to tame him, be sure of his affections, the way she was sure of Robert? Why was it she was drawn to men who, any intelligent woman could see, were unreliable Lotharios? She did not know and at the end of the evening, when he suggested that he escort her back to her apartment, she did not care.

As George's uniformed driver settled them into the back seat of the black Mercedes, Abbie rehearsed what she would say as they drew up to her mansion block. Asking him up for a cup of coffee would make her sound like a college grad. But did she have any brandy? And what if it wasn't the right label? Abbie was beginning to feel like a jumped-up Chicago reporter.

George pressed the switch that raised the visibility barrier between them and the driver. She had not quite decided whether she wanted to go to bed with him tonight. This was their first date and she hardly knew him. But her doubts vanished as George put an arm around her shoulders and began kissing her neck sensuously with warm dry lips. Abbie shuddered and gave a quick intake of breath as with what seemed like tantalising slowness he finally reached the corner of her mouth. She turned towards him as his lips searched out hers in a long, lingering kiss. At last she surrendered to the feelings that had enveloped her since she had first set eyes on him.

After many minutes Abbie surfaced to realise the car had stopped in front of her apartment block. George released her gently and kissed the tip of her nose. Before she could summon the composure to invite him up for a nightcap, he said, 'I've had such a wonderful evening, let's do it again. Very soon.'

He climbed out of the car and held out his hand to help her out. Bemused, Abbie gathered up her purse and coat and followed him. It was a frosty evening and, on seeing her, the porter quickly opened the heavy brass-fronted door so she could hurry inside, George's words following her on the night air. 'I'll be in touch.'

A short while later, as she sat pensively in front of the bathroom mirror taking off her make-up, Abbie felt downcast. Weren't those the most inconclusive words in the English language? In her experience, even in these so-called liberated days it often meant a spell of waiting and wondering when or if the man would make that call. It was so irritating, when she knew she could easily invite George to any one of a dozen functions which she could present as being useful for his business, but she would rather die than do that.

Abbie jumped with fright as the bathroom extension trilled and for a moment stared at the white instrument wondering if her tormentor had once again found her unlisted number. But it was George.

'I'm still in the car,' he said softly, 'I can't get you out of my mind.'

Abbie caught her breath and could not think how to respond.

'I need to see you again, Abbie. Are you free tomorrow evening?'

She was not but without hesitation answered, 'Yes.'

And the following night there was no pretence. She had agreed to meet in his penthouse for a drink. There had been no mention of dinner.

George gave her a rapid tour of the impressive five-roomed apartment above his hotel with its open-plan drawing room decorated in five shades of white. She admired the sauna and Jacuzzi which, he told her, needed a specially reinforced floor.

'But this,' he said, 'is the reason I live here.'

Abbie was acutely aware of his touch as he took her elbow to guide her to the balcony window to admire the illuminated skyline. He stood behind her and put his hands on her shoulders to draw her attention to the various landmark buildings. There was a stillness between them for a few seconds and Abbie could sense the heat of his body as he leaned in closer. She felt his breath quickening as he turned her round to face him, his kiss now urgent, demanding.

As they sank on to the softness of the down-filled sofa, Abbie imagined she was looking at herself, marvelling at her lack of inhibition. It was as if she had been with this man many times before; the curve, the fit of him were so familiar she felt not a moment's awkwardness. George interspersed his lovemaking with soft words and such gentle caressing that her nerve-endings shivered. Abbie had never experienced such unhurried pace and such concentration on her pleasure. Surely this was the first time she had really made love?

Chapter Nine

George waited, drumming his fingers, for Katharine to come on the line. He had to play this carefully. Abbie was free today but so was her mother. Over the past few weeks he had alternated between the two but there was a certain frisson in the newer affair. Abbie was as delightful in bed as he had anticipated. Not as experienced as her mother but then he had not expected her to be. Tauter skin, greater stamina and a willingness to learn more than made up for lack of expertise.

For a moment he wallowed in the delicious sensation that he could choose which one to see. Mother or daughter? Neither knew about the other, which made the fruit more forbidden. And tastier.

He had already arranged to meet Katharine for dinner but Abbie was available and at this stage of their relationship he needed to reel her in.

'George?' At last Katharine's assistant had tracked her down.

'Darling, hello. I'm so sorry, I'm going to have to call off dinner.' He sounded regretful. 'That new hotel, more problems, I'm afraid.'

'I see.'

Good God, her voice was chilly. It was obvious she did not believe him. This was only the second time he had cancelled and never at such short notice.

'Hey, Katie, don't be like that. You know if I was free to

choose between a business meeting and you, there would be no contest.'

She said nothing.

'What about tomorrow?' he asked.

'I'm at a charity dinner.'

He would have to make more effort to placate her, not least because his troubled hotel was opening its doors at Easter and he needed her there as guest of honour.

'Darling, I'll call you tomorrow, without fail,' he said. They spoke about generalities for another few minutes but her voice was no warmer when she said goodbye.

He shrugged, certain that he could woo her back.

Katharine's cab dropped her off at the corner of Greene Street, So-Ho, in one of the oldest quarters of New York, where artists like Basquiat, Keith Haring and Warhol had colonised the district, attracting multi-millionaires anxious to rub shoulders with artistic talent to the warehouse-sized buildings. The rich transformed the soaring lofts into palaces with vaulted ceilings and giant plate-glass windows encasing industrial-sized kitchens. The ground floors had metamorphosed into tiny boutiques where artists and designers offered wares ranging from hand-crafted furniture to outlandish pottery.

As Katharine made her way to the gallery where she had arranged to meet Nina, she was energised by the diversity of the people crowding the sidewalks. Puerto Ricans selling bargain-priced gold jewellery jostled with Upper West Side art collectors in search of the newest talent and East Side cognoscenti keen to keep up, up, up. Though she missed London sometimes, Katharine had come to adore this city, the pace, the excitement, even the noise.

Nina was waiting inside the gallery, itself a new find, where she hoped to add to the sculptures she had collected over the years. One or two of her acquisitions had turned out to be an investment but that was incidental. She did not buy to sell.

As they inspected the gallery's current exhibits, it took only a short time for the women to realise that this sculptor's obsession with endless dice and iron bars stuck together in varying positions did not constitute art for them. Katharine was pleased since she was desperate to have Nina's full attention and discuss her unease about George.

Thank God for friends, thought Katharine as Nina ordered two cappuccinos in a quiet coffee house near the gallery. Nina had changed her plans instantly when she heard that George had stood her up, the second time he had cancelled a date in as many weeks. It was possible that he did indeed have some sudden drama at work today but when he phoned she had felt a 'being deceived' buzz under her skin and had wanted to shout, 'You bastard, I know you're lying.'

'Well,' said Nina, practical as always, 'I warned you when you first met that George is wicked. And self-obsessed. He reminds me of a guy whose mirror has love bites.'

'What do you mean?'

'I'd guess he's an expert at deception.' Nina stirred her coffee lazily. 'I recognise it well. I was like that myself after Harry and Jeff.' Harry and Jeff were husbands number one and two. 'I played the field with great enthusiasm. I don't think you realise just how playful I was. I thought of myself as the original Martini woman. Any time. Any place. Anywhere.'

Katharine could not help smiling.

'How many men have said they loved you only to get your pants off?' asked Nina.

'Not as many as I hoped.' Katharine tried to sound facetious, to hide her hurt.

Nina gave her a roguish look. 'They didn't have to

declare undying love to get me. Sometimes they barely had to declare anything. Now I only feel secure with the old and ugly.'

Katharine shook her head at this gross exaggeration. None of Nina's men could be described as ugly although few would see fifty again. Her tall, rangy, model-size figure, kept trim with exercise and liposuction and maintained by a huge fortune, was still a magnet for a certain type of man.

'Katie, can't you stop worrying and enjoy what George is able to give?'

'I'm not sure,' said Katharine. 'I'm annoyed with myself that I give a damn. I still don't know what I want from him. Part of the problem is that we don't spend enough time together. When he's free, I'm not. It's so irritating. We've known each other for eight months and I don't know where he is half the time. He goes away a lot. I have his mobile number and it's supposed to work all over the world but mostly it's switched off.' Katharine shook her head. 'I'm not used to sitting around waiting for a man to phone and I don't like it. But I don't see what I can do. I don't like being too accommodating.'

Nina gave a small shrug. 'You're right. Nothing turns off men like him faster. Hey, you don't think he's making you pay because he's jealous of Freddie, do you?'

'No, I don't. Freddie has never been an issue between us. Perhaps I'm over-reacting because of everything else that's happening.'

'You mean at work?'

'Yes. The trouble is, Globe has stolen the agenda. I agree we have to get it back but not by knee-jerk reaction to hype and newspaper speculation.'

New Year was always a slow time for newspapers, and editors, desperate for stories, filled acres of newsprint with predictions about who would be up and who would be down in the coming season. Many commentators identified Abbie as the face of the future, although none were critical of Katharine's show. *Here and Now* was regarded as a television fixture and out of the range of speculation about newcomers. Nevertheless, Katharine feared that forecasts for the future, space fillers though they might be, would be taken too seriously by her bosses at the station. Certainly, one or two top executives were over-reacting to the hype surrounding Abbie's newer network.

Over the Christmas period ABN had continued its expensive market research which entailed intensive interrogation of focus groups. It gave them evidence of Katharine's rock-solid support as anchor of their show but the research also pointed to worrying signs. Abbie's name was increasingly mentioned during the focus group interviews. She lacked the polish of her mother but many of them mentioned her verve and her youth. They liked her approach and several made a point of videoing her programme while watching her mother. This was borne out by the latest audience figures which placed Abbie's show firmly in the number three slot, ousting the long-standing comedy compendium put out by USTV.

This unsettling information was quickly followed by wall-to-wall promos for Abbie's first worldwide exclusive, the first-ever interview with the future King of Great Britain. At Katharine's network, Mike predicted that the conversation would be the typical anodyne interview given by canny Royals when they were drumming up money for their favourite charity.

Nina's shrewd eyes were watching Katharine intently. 'You've got a lot on your plate right now. Is George worth the hassle?'

Katharine made no reply and Nina patted her arm. 'I remember when you two first met. It was obvious you were going to end the day in bed together.'

'I'd never done anything like that before but I don't regret it. It wasn't all lust. I like him – more than like him.'

'Love?'

'I don't know. When I first knew him I told him I didn't have affairs because I didn't want to burn my fingers. And do you know what he said? "Not me. I have asbestos hands." '

Nina chuckled.

'Maybe I should've taken fright there and then.'

'Nah,' said Nina scornfully. 'Nothing risked, nothing won. By the time you actually discuss having an affair, it's too late. And where, may I ask, is Freddie in all this?'

'The same place he's always been. At arm's length, most of the time. That hasn't changed. I'm very fond of Freddie, you know that.'

' "Fond".' Nina grimaced. 'The kiss of death.'

'No, you're wrong. I need someone like Freddie. *He* is reliable. And he loves coming to events with me, however boring they are. Like this charity thing tonight. What would I do without him?'

Nina had heard all this before. 'Let me tell you Billy Wilder's reply when a fellow actor moaned about Marilyn Monroe being continually late. He said, "Yeah, you're right. I should give the part to my Aunt Ethel. She'd always turn up on time. But who the hell would queue to see my Aunt Ethel?" '

'Meaning?'

'Meaning however much it hurts to do it, you need to cut George a little slack. See what happens. Whatever else he is, he's not Aunt Ethel.'

Despite her best resolve, the prospect of spending the evening with Freddie and three hundred of New York's great and good filled Katharine with gloom. Mechanically she dressed for the glittering occasion.

The charity had booked the Egyptian Room in the Metropolitan Museum and despite herself Katharine was impressed. The round tables shimmered with their dressing of gold tablecloths and seemed almost to drift across the black marble floor. Old friends, new jokes and being the centre of attraction wove their magic too. By the time the evening ended, her spirits were restored. When Freddie suggested he come up for a nightcap, she did not put him off with some excuse about having to be up early. It was only just after ten anyway. The strict hours New Yorkers kept had surprised her when she first arrived in the city. Everything finished so much earlier than in London. The more upmarket the occasion, the more the moguls made a point of leaving long before midnight. The unspoken understanding was that they had to be up early and on the ball for the important deals to be done in the morning.

After a large whisky, Freddie seemed in no hurry to leave. From time to time in the past he had stayed the night but not after Abbie had moved in and Katharine had not encouraged him to start the practice again once her daughter had left.

'I suppose she's too young to risk being shocked,' Freddie used to joke ironically. A little too often.

It was nearly midnight when Katharine collected up the whisky glasses. She was putting them in the kitchen sink when she felt Freddie's arms go round her. Involuntarily she stiffened.

'I have to be up early,' she said automatically, unable to dismiss the memory of how she felt when George's arms encircled her.

'Katharine.' Freddie's voice was pleading.

This man was available, dependable, a rock, Katharine thought. It was she who had changed. She was suddenly overwhelmed with affection and as he kissed her she made an effort to respond. Gradually she succumbed, not to lust or passion but to the comfortable security his presence offered.

The first call of the morning was from the studio to say that Katharine was not needed until noon.

The second was from George.

Katharine had never been good at dissembling and her staccato responses seemed to make George deeply suspicious.

'You're not alone, are you?'

'Yes I am,' she said uncomfortably.

Freddie looked at her curiously from the pillow.

'I want to come round. Now.' George's voice was intense.

'Sorry. Not possible.' Katharine tried to sound businesslike.

'Are you still in bed?'

'Yes.'

'Are you naked?'

'No.'

By now Freddie was taking an obvious interest in the conversation and with a subtle movement she transferred the phone to her other ear and turned away.

'What are you wearing? Describe it to me.'

'Couldn't possibly.'

'Somebody is there. Is it Freddie?'

'Maybe.'

'Ignore him. Imagine what we'd be doing if I was there.'

'I can.'

'Imagine what my hands would be doing.'

'Can I get back to you on this later?'

'No, I want to talk about it now.' When she did not reply he said softly, 'You're not angry about yesterday?'

'Of course not.'

'When can we meet?'

'I'll talk to the studio and get back to you.'

'I love it when you're strict,' he teased. 'Makes me want to put you up against the wall and do it to you hard and fast.'

Katharine caught her breath. 'That sounds . . . interesting,' she said, trying desperately to keep her voice neutral. 'But I have to go now.'

Putting down the receiver, she met Freddie's inquiring eyes.

'These researchers get younger and cheekier every day,' she said as calmly as she could, unable to dispel the delicious thought of what she and George could be doing right now.

'As long as you're sure it wasn't important.'

She looked at him. 'I don't think it was.'

'Good,' he said, and Katharine escaped to the shower.

As the steaming water cascaded down her back, she tried to erase the memory of Freddie's doleful eyes. Last night's experience had taught her that it was impossible to hand out sex like Lady Bountiful.

Over breakfast, she gently explained to him that from now on their relationship had to be on a different plane. 'I'm sorry, Freddie, but the sexual side just doesn't work for me. If we're to continue seeing each other, it has to be as platonic friends.'

He looked upset but accepted the situation gracefully. 'I love you too much, Katharine, not to have you in my life, so if that's the way you want it I'll go along with it. But please remember I'll always want to be with you. That hasn't changed. Nor will it.'

She was grateful to him and pleased to have made the decision. Now all she had to do was try to bring George more into the mainstream of her life.

Abbie stared at herself in the mirror of Globe's make-up room. It was an hour before she had to enter the studio. She half-closed her eyes to enable Brenda to apply mascara. This had to be her best interview ever, a lot was riding on it. Talking to this particular prince would be the opportunity to leapfrog into a different league, to be considered an interviewer of substance. And, more than that, to slip out of her mother's shadow. She was better researched than ever on this one, briefed up to the eyeballs, as Jeri-Ann had put it. She sneaked another look in the mirror. Her face, skilfully contoured, expertly highlighted, did not reflect her inner tensions. Not for the first time she blessed the expert hands of the make-up staff who were able to blend out all frown lines. They were geniuses.

In the event, as always, what mattered was less the quality of her research than Abbie herself. She hit the jackpot by bonding publicly with the young prince. She dispensed with all talk of wildlife and good works and instead discussed the problems of being the product of divorced parents and being isolated at boarding school. The formula worked brilliantly. For most of the interview His Royal Highness and Abbie compared their emotional experiences, for all the world as if they were taking part in a group therapy session. At times the prince appeared genuinely to forget he was in front of television cameras, being watched by millions. He described occasions when he had begged his mother to stop crying and chastised his father for continually making her so unhappy. He talked about the trauma of her death. He mentioned the efforts of his grandparents, the Queen and her consort, to help him.

It was riveting television and the media were hysterical with praise. Rival anchors privately gnashed their teeth and while Katharine could not help being proud, her colleagues at ABN cried into their pillows late into the night.

Ed Dantry, Abbie's mercurial, egotistical boss, called her

personally to offer his congratulations. He had recently realised his ambition and taken over as network president. The raid against the former chief had been seamless. The man had been out-gunned, out-manoeuvred and out of a job within six months of Dantry's arrival in New York. Legend had it that the old boss had barely reached the ground floor exit before his successor's brass plate was being screwed in place. Dantry would joke later that he had had the plate made on his first day in the city.

The hand sifted through the pile of photographs, frenziedly discarding one after another, then paused at a shot, one of a series, of a car crushed like a concertina, the occupant killed by Abbie as surely as if she had driven the vehicle herself.

Yes. Enlarging that segment of the photograph would convey the message. Abbie Lomax would be puzzled but she would never trace it back.

The bitch had gone international. Interviewing foreign royalty. Spreading her fame.

She had to be stopped.

By the end of the month when the ratings were finalised, Katharine's show held steady in the top slot but, in the face of Abbie's success, advertisers who paid top dollar were demanding evidence that their products were reaching target audiences.

So far Katharine had managed to sidestep the more outlandish ideas for promoting the show but Mike's comments at their private post-mortem immediately following her last programme increased her anxieties.

The content had included an interview with a film star whose son had recently been murdered while changing a tyre on the highway and a frank discussion with the head of the Christian Right which had made the phone lines hum.

'Great stuff, kiddo. Considering the circumstances, you did well.'

'Considering the circumstances'? She recognised showbiz-speak for 'adequate but not brilliant'. 'Thanks,' she said laconically.

'We've been going through a rough time lately and, hey, it's only one programme.'

'I thought it went pretty well.'

'Yes, it did. You were wonderful but we've all been under pressure because of this Abbie business and it's bound to show on camera.'

The message was loud and clear. He thought the show had been below par, she looked tired and they would have to do something about it. No comment about the quality of her questioning, based on her journalistic background, the foundation of her career. No, it was all appearance, appearance, appearance.

'Say, how did your holidays go?'

His move away from a sensitive subject was transparent. She ruffled her hair. God, she was getting tired of this wordplay. She wished someone would tell her what they wanted instead of using hints and euphemisms.

Mike requested a conference with Sam Wolfe to discuss the increased ratings Katharine's gossip show had obtained plus the slightly higher approval scores their focus groups had given this lighter-hearted approach. Katharine was not included.

'She may fight it but this says maybe we don't want so much Yasser Arafat and Bosnia stuff,' he told the boss.

'She can't argue with these figures,' said Sam, tapping the pages.

'Yeah, and I'm also going to suggest she zaps up her wardrobe, maybe a new hairstyle . . .'

Sam Wolfe's face showed this was an entirely new train of thought for him and they discussed all aspects of it for at least ten minutes.

When Mike gave Katharine an edited report of his conversation with Sam, omitting to mention that the meeting was at his request, she showed no surprise. Nevertheless she intended to fight her corner.

'Don't tamper with a winning formula, Mike,' she warned. 'We're still number one.'

'But to stay there, Katharine, we need to move with the times. Do things our audiences may not expect, like getting some psychics on the show, ghost busters. That kind of thing.'

Mike talked about the research into literacy and educational levels in the modern Western audience, ending with the not-too-surprising conclusion that Katharine's celebrity gossip show pointed the way to greater success in the ratings. What he wanted, she thought gloomily, was part of the dumbing of America. By making her show more lightweight, more like their rivals', they would attract a younger segment of the audience. But there was a danger in this and she could see it clearly. Why couldn't they? By going downmarket they would lose their core audience along with their distinctive voice. Generally those viewers who wanted substance as well as froth had higher incomes and therefore more clout with advertisers. Why were they not considering this important fact?

She listened in silence as Mike went on to outline his ideas about softening her on-camera appearance. She had learned long ago not to react instantly to ideas she found unacceptable. Mike was, after all, her fourth producer. If necessary, he could be replaced. Instead she sought the wise counsel of her agent.

'For God's sake, am I my own person or what?'

Knowing his client well, Buzz waited until she came to the point.

'It's the old standby,' she fumed. 'They think they need something different and they always begin by changing the set. Well, they've just done that. Now they're starting on the anchor. Mike said I should have a bloody makeover.' Her tone hardened. 'He thought I should look a little different. "Zap up your wardrobe" – he actually said that. And then he suggested I go to a different hairdresser, perhaps have a lighter colour. What are they trying to do, Buzz? Turn me into an older version of my daughter? I'm really unhappy about all this.'

After the slightest of pauses, Buzz took a line she was least expecting. 'I think Mike's right.'

'What?'

'Listen, Katie, television's playing hardball now. You've already got one direct competitor in your slot and I hear USTV are thinking of doing their version of your show at the same time too.'

'That's crazy scheduling.'

'It may be, but suddenly that audience seems to command top dollar and ABN is not going to sit back and let the others cherry-pick. So you get a different wardrobe, you look a little different, and audiences sit up and say, hey, look at her. That means more people switch on, which means higher ratings, which means more money from advertisers, which means your network's happy. And all you have to do is spend their money, look even more wonderful and do the job you know so well and do so brilliantly.'

She paused to consider. 'What you say makes sense but I suppose I feel this is only the beginning. When they've finished "zapping up" the set and my appearance, before you know it I'll be headlining Miss Universe and talking to her about her plans for charity work. If they want me to continue to get world-class interviews what sort of climate does that create?'

'Katie, you're one of the best interviewers I've ever seen on television. They'd be crazy if they watered that down. But what they're aiming for, in my opinion, is more light and shade.'

'I'm already doing my share of the triumph-over-tragedy stuff.'

'My advice, for what it's worth, is to hold your fire. So far all they want you to do is splash their money over your clothes and hair. This you hate?'

Katharine laughed. 'I know it sounds stupid, but I have a certain style.'

'What are they going to do? Make you wear PVC? No, they're going to experiment with colours you haven't worn before. That kind of thing. This isn't so crazy. Katie, I'll fight to the death on your behalf if they try to make you change the content of the show against your wishes. But don't let's dig our toes in over this peripheral stuff.'

She exhaled. 'All right, if that's what you think, I'll go along with it. But Buzz, I can smell hypocrisy in the air.'

The changes required of Katharine were minimal compared with those that affected her production team over the next few weeks. Many of the older researchers were replaced by trendies from the music press, the universities and bookers from populist talk shows. Katharine insisted on keeping several of her tried and tested lieutenants but the remaining staff were placed on short-term contracts. Morale nose-dived. Most felt obliged to put in even longer hours. No one took renewal of their contracts for granted and some spent precious time during the day surreptitiously applying for other jobs. Down on the production floor, the effect was to rock the confidence of what had been for so long a well-honed, top quality band of television professionals.

Katharine felt as unsettled as everybody else but she hid her turmoil under a cloak of professionalism. Discouraging disloyal talk, she concentrated on welcoming the new staff, at the same time sympathising with the old and using her contacts to help them find other work. In a surprisingly short time she knitted the new team together, earning the gratitude of Mike who quickly appreciated that her abilities would reflect well on him.

She drove herself harder than ever. Always a perfectionist, she tinkered endlessly in the editing suite, to the annoyance of some staff who did not appreciate finishing their shifts well after midnight. Mike had to field complaints about how hard it was to keep up with her these days. 'Tough shit,' was his reply. 'She has to do what she has to do. Kate doesn't compromise. Why do you think she's been on top all these years? If you can't keep up, get back to the kitchen,' he told one outraged feminist.

Her first coup under this new regime was to follow her hunch that she could, once again, persuade Steve Stone to give her an exclusive interview. He had not appeared on Abbie's show and Katharine, knowing how difficult he could be, assumed that negotiations had broken down.

She flew to Los Angeles to lunch Stone's agent and found him full of contrition and apologies for his client's peremptory cancellation. Her policy of never having badmouthed Stone proved an invaluable asset. Louis Stein had been both impressed by and grateful for Katharine's restraint in the face of the last-minute cancellation, and the fictitious reason for it. What had seemed at the time to be heaven-sent inspiration had made him feel distinctly uncomfortable in the days that followed. Prodded by a guilty conscience, he welcomed the opportunity to make amends.

Two weeks later, Steve Stone appeared on Katharine's show and confessed that his whole life had been a sham. And during a fair but tough interview, he broke down, describing the loss from AIDS of his long-term partner.

When he had composed himself, Katharine took hold of his hand and said, 'Steve, your public is out there listening to you now, what do you want to say to them?'

He looked directly into the camera and into millions of American homes. 'I'm sorry. I've lied to you from the beginning and I beg for your forgiveness. But I have suffered and will suffer for the rest of my life.'

'Why are you telling us now?' Katharine was at her most compassionate.

The star took a deep breath and hesitated for a moment, as if making a decision. 'I guess it'll be public knowledge soon so I may as well tell you. I've also developed AIDS.'

Katharine's sensitive handling of this fragile man and his courage so impressed the nation that it defused any homophobic talk, as the following day's shocked callers to radio stations, even the right-wing ones, testified.

Only Sam Wolfe struck a sour note. He described AIDS as a 'sleazy' subject and made it clear he feared a backlash from advertisers.

But Katharine was robust in defence of her questioning. 'I would do it all over again,' she said. 'You have to take risks now and again, even triple-jumps-from-the-trapeze risks. What's the point of this job if all I ever do is play it safe?'

He was wrong. Katharine's ratings sky-rocketed and for a glorious week or two she was fêted by her colleagues, lauded by the critics and congratulated by advertisers who jostled for last-minute spots.

The euphoria was short-lived. The ratings put *Here and Now* still at number one but Abbie's show had jumped to number two, the direct result of her interview with the prince.

The young pup was nudging at her mother's heels.

Chapter Ten

Abbie's major interview that night with Hollywood's newest teen tycoon had veered between non-stop laughter, scurrilous observations and amazement at the figures being written into his deals. At 22 he had signed a three-movie contract which had stunned even the sensation-seekers of tinsel town. While Jeri-Ann, in the gallery, was satisfied that the show had maintained its ratings, news of Steve Stone's revelations on *Here and Now* had been filtering through all evening, taking the gloss off Abbie's excitement. Immediately the cameras were switched off, she went to watch a video of Katharine's interview in Jeri-Ann's office.

The producer skipped through the credits of Katharine's show and the introductions then said, 'Here's the good stuff.'

'I can't believe what I'm hearing,' said Abbie after a few minutes. 'Usually you can guess if a guy's gay but I was this close—' indicating with her hands how near she had been sitting to him – 'and I can tell you the man reeked of testosterone. And he was ogling all the women passing by. He put up a great pretence.'

Jeri-Ann shook her head dolefully. 'What a waste.'

Abbie rubbed her ear lobe thoughtfully. 'That man caused so much trouble between me and my mother. I'd love to know the real reason why he cancelled her show. Maybe our talk about the priorities in life had something to do with it.'

'Nah,' scoffed Jeri-Ann, 'it could be millions of reasons. Stars are crazy. That's why they're stars. You can bet he didn't plan to tell his adoring public that macho man swings on the other side of the street unless—' she paused for a second – 'unless he thought it was going to come out anyway. My guess is that his doctor's given him a few months to live.'

'Oh God, how awful,' said Abbie. Then after a moment's hesitation she asked, 'Do you think Steve'll let me off the hook with Mum, explain what really happened?'

'Forget that. Stars never explain. These monsters only concern themselves with number one. Especially when they're dying. In any case, don't kid yourself, I hear from all quarters that Katharine and her team are hivey about us. If you ask me, one missed interview shouldn't have had this kind of fall-out. It's got to be more than that.'

'Perhaps you're right.' Abbie looked thoughtful. 'She was always going on about the way we went after our interviews, dirty tricks she called it.'

'Look, there's no one I admire more, professionally, than your mother,' said Jeri-Ann carefully. 'But she's never been under threat before. And you're young and smart. The problem is you're also her daughter, that's difficult to cope with. I'd give her some time, she'll come round.'

Abbie switched off the set. 'You've got to hand it to Mum, she's a great interviewer. It was seamless, he hardly realised how much he was telling.'

'She's been doing it a long time, but you're well on the way to being as good as she is.'

Abbie gave a self-deprecatory shrug.

'Hey, fancy hitting the town later on?' asked Jeri-Ann.

Abbie hesitated. 'No, I think I'll have an early night.'

Jeri-Ann looked surprised and Abbie felt a pang of remorse. This was the first time she had lied to her friend.

That was the only thing that bothered her about the affair with George. He refused to meet any of her friends, saying teasingly that he did not want to share her. So, as they would inevitably bump into people who would recognise her if they went out, they spent most of their time in George's apartment watching movies, playing backgammon and making love.

But in a way, keeping George a secret suited Abbie. It avoided all that endless speculation in the press about whether or not they would get married. Also, the Fan of Fans stuff had given her a jolt. She had been advised by security to be more circumspect about giving out information on her movements, whether to journalists or friends. It was a pity, because she preferred being frank whenever possible. One more thing to blame on fame, as Jeri-Ann put it.

The affair with George was light-hearted, fun and did not involve discussions about the future. Quite different from how it had been with Robert. But if Abbie was completely honest, she did miss her old lover and sometimes was nostalgic for the way he was integrated into her life, fascinated with every nuance of her job, while George did not seem to be overly interested in it.

George was volatile and unpredictable and she was mesmerised by him. In her previous relationships she had usually been the dominant partner, as in her college days, or, as with Robert, been regarded as an equal. George was not so crass as to spell it out but she had the distinct impression that he was in charge, especially when they were in bed. Their affair was so high voltage it probably would not last but she was enjoying it, for now.

The woman was a show-stopper, a real looker, and when she bared her pearly-white teeth at him, Buzz was fascinated. He gazed at her with enjoyment. Great tits, he thought. What was Sam Wolfe doing employing her as his secretary? With that body, that smile, she should be fronting one of his quiz shows. Prime time.

He was examining some of the awards lining the walls of Sam's office, many of them publicly attributed to Katharine, when the secretary spoke again.

'I'm so very sorry, Mr Newbold.' Her voice was throaty and alluring. 'I'm afraid Mr Wolfe's caught up in an emergency and he's going to be at least ten minutes more. He apologises profusely and hopes you're able to spare the time to wait a little longer. May I get you something to drink?'

'Yeah, sure.'

'Decaff, latte, double espresso, or tea? English, herb, mint, jasmine? We also have some wonderful no-calorie muffins that Mr Wolfe just loves.' She gave him a beseeching gaze as if her very job depended on his willingness to wait. Knowing Sam, he thought, it might do.

'Just straight, regular coffee,' he said evenly although his brain was shouting, 'Tell that asshole to hurry up. I won't wait much longer.'

The television business had a reputation for keeping agents hanging about to soften them up before negotiations. But this had not happened to him for some years, not since ABN had snapped Katharine up on a seven-million-dollar contract after a fierce bidding war among rival networks. But that was then and this was now. Sam's call had put the seal on a week that had begun badly. The ratings for Abbie's show seemed to have lit the flame of hysteria at ABN. Buzz had detected a note of panic when he had last spoken to Mike. The agent had tried to calm the atmosphere by pointing out that surveys showed Abbie was known to only 59 per cent of Americans while Katharine's 'familiar score' was a robust 84 per cent. Mike had not been comforted. 'But her score is static while Abbie's is climbing,' was his comment.

Katharine had not been unduly alarmed by the figures.

She accepted that with the growing number of other competitors in the field now, the cake had to be cut into more slices. But lately, she had confided, she was finding it harder and harder to psych herself up before the show. Prospects were being courted by so many rivals that it was no longer a certainty, as had been the case for several years, that her programme would land the week's major news interview.

Lately many of the serious big-name interviewees had begun demanding to know with whom they would be appearing. Not all of them felt happy about appearing with a murderer, for example. Some millionaire businessmen and statesmen who did not have to rely on the oxygen of publicity had accepted invitations from less prime-time, more news-orientated programmes transmitted during the week.

One of the clauses in Katharine's last contract stated that she did not have to make personal visits to reel in a catch. ABN had willingly accepted the restriction since her name and reputation had been enough in the past to entice major personalities exclusively on to *Here and Now*. With more aggressive competition, however, that was changing and Katharine was expending more and more effort to persuade potential guests to appear on the show. Indeed, these days she did not have time for anything much other than work. When researchers failed to persuade a reluctant guest they often implored Katharine to try to assure them that though the programme had flipped into slightly lighter mode, her style had not changed. The topics they would discuss would be taken as seriously as they had been before.

But in trying to obtain youthquake guests Katharine frequently had to admit defeat. Her reputation as an interviewer famed for discussing complex subjects daunted young pop stars and sometimes frightened subjects suddenly projected into the news. Occasionally her failures popped up talking happily on the *Tonight* show. The constant comparison between anchors was wearing Katharine's team down. Abbie's confidence in front of the cameras meant there was no more talk about new pretenders, they had to take her seriously.

Buzz had been worried when Sam's office had rung to make this appointment. Normally they communicated informally by phone and met face to face only when Katharine's contract negotiations were due. But that would not start for another fourteen months.

'Mr Wolfe will see you now.' The secretary's relief was apparent and Buzz wondered how far she would have gone to keep him here. But he was getting old. He did not play those games any more.

His first glimpse of Sam made him revise his suspicions. He seemed genuinely apologetic for the delay.

'I'm sorry, Buzz. Those goddamn attorneys wait for nobody. And nor do slander writs. Can I get you anything? Coffee, orange juice?'

Buzz smilingly refused and, taking his cue from Sam's friendly manner, began to relax. Maybe this was nothing much to worry about.

'You know how happy I am about Katharine's work.'

Uh-oh, thought Buzz.

'She's such a great asset to the station. And we're very, very pleased with the way things are going.'

This was not going to be so good after all.

'Of course we've got more competition, we have to look at what the others are doing but Kate the Great's not called that for nothing, right? She's streets ahead of anyone else.'

Buzz kept his relaxed expression intact, but every nerve in his body was straining for Sam to get to the point.

'And when I say she's number one, we're going to keep her at number one.'

'Right,' said Buzz impassively.

'Globe's nurtured the Abbie Lomax show into a real ratings beauty. They've hit number two for the last three weeks, they're on a run but that's where it's gonna stop or I'm not called Wolfe. By name and nature.' He laughed.

Here it comes, thought Buzz.

'How old is Katharine? Forty-five, forty-six?'

'Forty-four,' said Buzz, automatically deducting two years. So this was what it was all about.

'Hmm, forty-four,' repeated Sam slowly. 'We have to remember who we must keep happiest of all. Advertisers. Two nights ago I was in Scottsdale at the home, the very palatial home,' he gave Buzz a knowing glance, 'of Bill Riley.' Bill Riley was a big player who had a lot of advertising clout with the network. 'Now, like us, he adores Katharine. His wife adores Katharine. His daughters adore Katharine. But,' Sam leaned forward, 'his sons, young, intelligent men, exactly the type Bill wants to buy his products, they watch Abbie.'

'Well, we can't please all the folks all the time,' said Buzz mildly.

'We know we've got the middle-aged women and we've also grabbed their daughters but if, like Bill, you're about to launch a million-dollar fashion range for young dandies, you want the guys as well. Especially when you're planning two spots a night.'

Mentally Buzz whistled. Each thirty-second spot could cost up to half a million dollars.

'Bill confided that he felt that Katharine, wonderful as she is, is looking . . . how can I put it? A tad tired, a little jaded.'

Buzz was indignant. 'I hope you didn't let him get away with that.'

'Of course not, though I had to pacify him, naturally. Well, after thinking about it, I came up with what I believe is a perfect compromise. He was pretty pleased about it. It's why we're here now, Buzz.'

At last.

'Katharine should have a break, a vacation, on us. And while she's having this vacation, she could have an eye tuck, a chin tuck, whatever. Tidy up those little areas that are beginning to droop. I personally think she could do with something in the breast area too, make them . . . you know.' With his hands, Sam graphically demonstrated what he meant. 'And anything else she feels she needs. I think Katharine will be pleased, don't you? She'll thank me at the end.'

'She'll never do it,' Buzz exploded.

'Katharine's not stupid. She knows there's a time for surgery. Buzz, this is the time.'

'I've handled Katharine for eight years and let me tell you, she doesn't appreciate being told to do something she's not ready for.' Buzz emphasised each word with a stamp of his hand on the sofa.

'Before you get on your high horse, take a look at this.' Sam slid a piece of paper across his desk.

It was a memo from the show's producer. Buzz read it with dismay. It said: 'As instructed, I have changed the lighting for Katharine's personal camera. When you see the run-through perhaps you would give me your input about whether the results are softer and more flattering. But there is only so much we can do because we can't have her lighting too different from that of the guests.'

Sam was watching him. 'Katharine needs a whole new image and I'm sure you agree with me,' he said.

'No, definitely not.' Buzz sounded firmer than he felt. 'I don't think there's anything the matter with her current image.'

'Wrong. She needs to look younger, smarter, more zippy. That's the combination that'll keep her at the top.'

'I'll put it to her . . .' Buzz shook his head.

'There's a lot at stake here, Buzz, and you may have got

the wrong impression.' Sam paused. 'This is not a request.'

Buzz looked at him levelly. 'In that case I warn you she may want to walk.'

'If she does, we'll sue. And we'll ask millions.' Sam reached into a drawer of his heavy mahogany desk and took out a copy of Katharine's contract. 'I've highlighted the relevant section,' he said smoothly. 'Our lawyers have been all over this. It's totally kosher. They say we're entirely within our rights to ask for changes in her appearance.'

Buzz frowned. The yellow-marked paragraph was standard throughout the industry for presenters. It said that the star agreed to do 'whatever the network deemed necessary' to improve the ratings of the show. This was always taken to mean doing promotional work or co-operating with the publicity department. Never, as far as Buzz knew, had it been interpreted to include going under the surgeon's knife, for God's sake. He could hardly contain his fury.

'Buzz, we don't want a fight. What's a little cosmetic surgery? It'll elongate her career. She'll earn a great salary for much longer. Is that good for us? Definitely. Is that good for her? You bet.'

Buzz said nothing.

'I've discussed the timing with Mike. During the Easter break would be best. We'll send her to Brescia in Rio de Janeiro, he's the best in the world. Big bucks, of course, but we'll pay.' Sam stood up. The meeting was over. 'I can see this has taken you by surprise but she'll accept it from you. She loves you.'

For how long? Buzz wondered.

Buzz had had a lifetime's experience of being the harbinger of bad news. The entire entertainment industry invariably used an agent to deliver the dirt when a contract was not going to be renewed or an option not picked up. Good news they gave direct to the client.

But this bombshell kept Buzz awake. How could he tell an attractive, successful professional that her job now depended on having a gob of skin removed from her eyes and jowls and her breasts pumped up? She was his friend, for Christ's sake, as well as his client. She would reject it out of hand, he was sure of it. Katharine had always made it clear that what mattered was journalistic skill, not a film star profile. And over eight successful years she had proved her point. Sure, she was an attractive woman and that had not hindered her. And of course some interviews succeeded as well as they did because of her looks. She accepted that part of her appeal was her appearance. But the reason her salary always went up was because she crossed sex barriers. Her tough but fair questioning and her empathy with her guests appealed to male and female viewers alike. Buzz could not imagine Sam Wolfe ordering any of his male anchors to get their jowls tightened. It was so goddamn unfair. OK, Abbie was younger and her ratings were creeping up but it was hardly surprising given the rubbish Globe had been putting out before in that time slot.

Buzz was realistic about Katharine's value to his agency. He had never regarded her simply as a cash cow but the truth was she did generate the major slice of his income. He accepted that she would not go on for ever but they both agreed she had a good few years of high-earning capacity left and she was younger than he was so he took it for granted that she would be on top until his retirement.

Katharine's views on cosmetic surgery were well-known to him. While never dismissing the possibility that it might be necessary in such an image-conscious profession, she considered it as an option for the future, though most other stars on view to the public thought about surgery from day one. In British culture, she would say, cosmetic surgery was something to think about later rather than sooner. And she would joke that except for having Abbie she had never been hospitalised, and that she was too cowardly to submit to the knife voluntarily.

In an effort to buy more time he phoned Sam the following day for a stay of execution. The network boss was charming, jovial but intransigent.

After fifteen hours tussling with the problem Buzz had to face the fact that however he tried to sweeten the pill, Katharine would see it for exactly what it was. Besides, he did not want to jeopardise the trust they had built up over the years. Grimly he decided his only option was to be frank.

'I won't do it. I just won't.' The usually melodic voice was discordant. 'How dare he? The coward. He didn't have the balls to tell me himself.'

'Katie, I know how you—'

'I'm not against having cosmetic surgery, far from it. Virtually every woman my age in our circle has done it. But it's quite another thing to be ordered to have a breast enlargement and then only because my daughter is well-endowed. That's outrageous. I'll be damned if I'm going to be dictated to because they're in a panic. I'll walk.'

'I told Sam this would be your reaction. He pointed out that technically you'd be in breach of your contract.' Would she castigate him for not being smart enough to predict problems in that clause? Buzz held his breath, then relaxed with relief at her next words.

'So I'm in breach. Big deal.'

'Knowing him, I think he'd sue. Big.'

'Let him.'

'But then you'd be tied up in the courts for God knows how long, you wouldn't appear on screen and you wouldn't get paid.' Neither, of course, would Buzz.

'I don't care.' Katharine was firm. 'If I cave in over this, what control will I have over anything in future?' She shook her head then pushed her chair away from the table and began pacing the room. 'My entire career has been based on journalism, not the shape of my nose. In my opinion they're ruining the reputation of the show with their short-term obsession with ratings. They keep steering me into softer interviews, less contentious subjects. And now this insulting order.'

'Katharine, steady. Don't make hasty decisions.'

'Buzz, you've always told me my timing was impeccable. Well, now it's time to make a decision. I have enough money invested to give me freedom. And it's not only this ridiculousness. I'm not happy with the way the industry's going. Principles and friendships are being thrown out of the window to clinch big stories. I heard just last week that Norm Thompson had to give up newscasting to go on the road to chase after "gets" – on the orders of some young buck producer half his age. Next it'll be my turn.'

'I'd never let that happen.'

'You won't be able to stop it, Buzz. Anyway, the work's harder, it takes a lot of high-powered courting to get the big interview. And damn advisers like lawyers, relatives or friends are often on a power trip themselves. If they don't agree with every comma in the deal, they threaten to persuade the client to go with somebody else. No, better to leave with dignity before being pushed out.'

Buzz tried to speak but she had not finished.

'It's different for Abbie. These things are happening to her at the beginning of her career, she's resilient enough to cope. Abbie's never known "the good old days". And you know what?' She wheeled round to face him. 'I see many positives in leaving the job. This business with Abbie has been destroying me, destroying us both. If I step out of the arena, my only child and I can stop being rivals. I may be learning all this a little late but it might, just might, be possible for Abbie and me to become friends. It's a good thought. And before you tell me again that I'm being hasty, this isn't the first time I've thought about it.'

'You could regret doing this,' said Buzz, shaking his head. 'Are you sure it's wise to make such a big sacrifice?'

'What sacrifice? I've been earning big bucks for years and my accountant's been telling me that with my portfolio I can live at this standard,' she waved her hand round the apartment, 'for the rest of my life. I'll go and see him and sort it all out.'

His face froze with dread and she leaned forward to pat his hand. 'I'm sorry, Buzz, but as we British say, you and I have had a jolly good innings.'

'I never thought you'd back off from such a plum contract, Katie. Please, promise me you won't do anything just yet. Let me talk to Sam again.'

'I'll talk to Sam myself.'

'No. Don't. Let me deal with him. I'm sure I can come up with a plan.'

But Katharine would not give way. When Buzz was cornered, he always tried to play for time. It was clear he had no plan, no strategy for dealing with Sam other than to comply with his wishes.

'Sam's influenced by the ad kings of Madison Avenue who think youth is the answer,' Katharine said matter-of-factly. 'It isn't, but because of my daughter's success, he wants to change me. Of course they can make me appear younger. I'm lucky enough to be one of the first generation of women who can take advantage of modern knowledge. Look at me,' she was warming to her subject, 'I eat right, exercise till it hurts, and I'm lucky to have a certain build and an arrangement of features that mean I can appear youthful for many more years yet. And then if the plastic surgeon steps in he can do further miracles – fix my eyes, my nose, my breasts. But Buzz, just because science can do all this nowadays doesn't make it right. Doesn't it worry you that this affects the basic order of things? OK, Abbie and I don't get along right now, but at least I'm not trying to ape her, to recapture my youth and be her age again.'

Katharine stood up. She had not realised how passionately she felt about this.

'I've never tried to be her sister. I'm her mother, for God's sake. And what do you think will happen in the future when gravity catches up with my body? It'll be liposuction this, skin peeling that, on and on. I'll die looking like a young woman on the outside with more scars on my body than railway lines in Grand Central Station. This is my health, my life that Sam Wolfe's playing with and I will not have it.'

Buzz could only stare. She was magnificent.

'Well, Sam has made me confront my future. Maybe I wouldn't have chosen today to decide to bow out but it's been rumbling around my mind since that terrible row at Thanksgiving. I know this is the right thing to do.'

'Don't make up your mind finally, not until—'

'No, Buzz. I have made it up. I could switch to being a producer. I think I'd be happier behind the camera, making my own programmes. I could even do some specials and sell them to Sam.' There was a mischievous glint in her eye. 'You could still be my agent. You may not make so much money but I'll last longer. Nobody cares if a producer has wrinkles.'

And she laughed for the first time that afternoon.

Katharine felt a surge of exhilaration as she stepped out of the shower. Buzz had urged her to sleep on her decision. Well, she had. And she felt great about it. She could see a new chapter in her life opening up. Her anger at Sam's controlling behaviour was contributing to a burst of vigour.

She would not confront him. Indeed, she regarded his order as the catalyst she had needed to kick-start her into a new way of life. Discussing her changed circumstances with her accountant would be the first step in the process of parting company with ABN.

Rubbing herself vigorously with a thickly-woven bath sheet the size of a tablecloth, Katharine found herself excited at the prospect of becoming a help-meet to her daughter. After the session with David Crozier, she would track Abbie down and fix another lunch. This time, she would make her daughter understand that she had a life-changing decision to discuss with her.

As she glanced at herself in the bathroom mirror she thought there were other advantages in vanishing from the screen.

Cheesecake.

How long was it since she had been able to eat a whole slice? Not to mention chocolate, Danish pastries, chilli dogs, milk in coffee, French bread . . . and butter, glorious, fattening, yellow butter. And shopping. Freed from the constraints of her show, choosing clothes would not be a chore to be undergone with the wardrobe supervisor. For the first time for years she could strobe or clash with the background to her heart's delight, she could stay up as late as she liked, be Queen of the Black-Circle-Under-The-Eyes Society. Who would care?

She decided to test her news on the three people closest to her.

Freddie's reaction gave her an inkling of how the wider world would react.

'Darling, you cannot be serious.' He sounded unhappy as well as incredulous. 'I don't think that's a good idea at all. You'd miss it so much.'

'Maybe, but I want to do other things and I need Abbie to think of me not as the competition but as her mum.'

He seemed not to hear. 'Let's face it, you've become

used to being on the A list. And in this town you'd get demoted pretty quickly.'

Katharine was upset by his response but she held her tongue. What was bothering him was that he would not be able to enjoy the fruits of her fame. Certainly it would be a change, but one that she could probably cope with better than he could. Freddie positively gloated each time a coveted invitation was displayed on her mantelpiece. He preened when they were snapped at premieres and appeared in the glossies. His secretary kept a scrapbook, for God's sake. It was a side of Freddie's character that had always irked her but because there were so many advantages in having him around she had tolerated it. Now she gave a small frown. Those advantages were diminishing by the minute.

George's reaction to the news was unexpected.

'Do what makes you happy, my darling,' was all she could get him to say. 'It's your life.'

While she was pleased his response was the opposite of Freddie's, she realised with a pang that he remained as uncommitted as ever. She was due to open his new hotel at Easter and briefly she wondered if her departure from the spotlight of *Here and Now* would matter.

Nina's pleasure was wholehearted. 'That's terrific,' she said at once. 'You'll be able to come out and play more. I can't wait.'

Thank God for Nina, Katharine thought, not for the first time.

She was feeling very positive when she strode into the offices of Crozier, Smith and Barrell, one of New York's top accounting firms. She and David Crozier went back a long way. When she had first started to earn serious money, a colleague had advised her to do what he did and put her money into property tax shelters. When she stared at him uncomprehendingly he had introduced her to his 'shit-hot' accountant.

David Crozier had set up a limited partnership with Katharine and her colleague, investing two million dollars of their joint money in a retirement housing project in Florida. Under David's day-to-day management, the partnership had prospered. Two years later a delighted Katharine appointed him her personal financial adviser, handing the supervision of her entire income over to him, relying on his expertise completely. And her confidence had been repaid. He had been rock solid even through the bad days of recession.

When her colleague had died unexpectedly, his son joined her in the partnership but because he lived in San Francisco, he had no involvement in the running of the business. In any case, this was not arduous. Apart from signing documents at quarterly meetings, Katharine had little to do. Occasionally David would call on her to sign letting agreements but they had kept the paperwork to a minimum and the few discussions that were necessary often took place on the telephone.

In the midst of a ferocious work schedule, Katharine was pleased that this part of her life, at least, was being handled with efficiency, probity and, according to the accounts, flair. She regarded the top fees David charged as another sound investment in her future.

David's office reflected his success and his seniority. He had a coveted corner suite with a spectacular two-sided panorama of Manhattan's wondrous skyline and a toy-town view of the famous ice-skating rink with its pirouetting figures.

'Katie, you look marvellous.' She was wearing a superbly-cut tweed trouser suit teamed with a white cashmere crew-necked sweater. It threw a light on her face which accentuated her lavender eyes. She exuded an air of well-being and sheer *joie de vivre*.

'Thank you. I feel it.'

'No, really, have you just inherited a million dollars?'

'In a way,' she said happily, moving to the window. The sun, low in the sky, gave out a typically bright Manhattan glow which lit up the room like a stage. Without taking her eyes from the view she said, 'Isn't this a wonderful day to be in New York?'

He laughed. 'I don't know what you're on but whatever it is I want some.' He perched on the arm of the brown leather sofa. 'Are you going to sit down while we talk or stand there radiating good will?'

'Well, I am excited but send for some of your famous decaff and I'll tell all. No, make that real coffee. I'm in a mood for danger.'

As calmly as she could, Katharine recounted the reasons leading up to her decision to quit her presenting career. She did not expect David to enthuse over her determination to opt out. Like Buzz, he had earned millions over the years out of their association. It would be a big bite out of his turnover but he had a great reputation and would surely have no trouble attracting other clients in her place. She was sure that in a few months he would have made up any shortfall her decision might cost him.

It was impossible to detect from David's expression how he was taking the news so she plunged ahead.

'I know this is going to be a blow to you but I don't want you to try and dissuade me,' she said firmly. 'I've thought it all out very carefully and this is how I want my life to develop. Leaving my job will be good not only for me but also for Abbie. It isn't as if I need to keep earning at the same rate. You've seen to that.' She beamed at him.

It was David's turn to walk to the window.

'David? Say something. At least tell me I'm a fool.'

He stared into the distance. When finally he turned round, Katharine was taken aback by what she saw in his face. Gone was the bonhomie and the jovial manner of a few minutes ago. Now his eyes were wary and his demeanour formal.

'I cannot emphasise this enough, Katharine,' he said carefully. 'I advise you most strongly not to give up your job.'

He called her Katharine, not Katie. 'Why not?'

'There's a great deal of money at stake here. You're in your peak earning years. That's a hell of a thing to give up. In my view, it would be foolhardy and I urge you not to do this.'

Katharine was disappointed by his reaction. She had hoped that he would be pleased for her, if not as a professional adviser then as a friend. But accountants were by nature prudent creatures and she supposed he was right to adopt a cautious attitude.

'You're probably right but I've made up my mind, David, I'm going to leave. I can't go on for ever. Why should I bash my brains out and put myself through hoops just for money? I've enjoyed the fame and prestige but I want to do something different with my life now. And, thank God, I have the financial freedom to do that.'

'What would you say if I asked you to carry on for another six months?'

'I'd say no. Why should I?'

'Because the timing's not right. In about six months I'll be able to sort out the accounts, finalise payments, get everything in good order.'

'David, you're a great accountant but you haven't been listening. If I stayed, even for the short time you suggest, Sam would insist that I have that cosmetic surgery and I'm damned if I'm going to do what he wants. He wouldn't wait six months, and neither will I.' There was an edge to her voice. 'I hope I make myself clear.'

'You have to consider all the implications and it's my duty to make you do so. You will lose a great deal of money if you cash in everything now. Fiscally it's not the right time of year. These things need careful consideration, the ground needs to be prepared.'

'So how much would I lose? And how much do I need anyway? I have all the clothes I'll ever want and I can actually save money if I'm not working because I won't have to be the grande dame any more. I can cut back on expenses like clothes and beauty treatments.'

There was a long pause while David examined his fingernails. 'Look, I didn't want to do this but I'm going to have to tell you something you'll find hard to understand. I can't do what you want because . . . the money's not there.'

Katharine's eyes widened in disbelief. 'Not there? What do you mean?'

'Now don't get excited,' he said hurriedly. 'It hasn't been lost, not for ever anyway. It's just not available, temporarily.'

'Explain how my money can disappear "temporarily"? Either it's there or it's not. Give it to me straight.'

Katharine reined in her impatience. Though her instinct was to bombard him with pertinent questions, from experience she realised it would be quicker to allow David time to tell his story. Like all people who understood figures better than words, he needed to explain the facts in logical sequence and could not be hurried.

He began with a plea. 'I want you to know that over all these years I've operated your accounts in your best interests although it may not appear so.' He mopped his brow with a white silk handkerchief. 'This is so difficult for me . . .'

Katharine waited.

Slowly and painfully he told her how he had lost their money. As his words sunk in, Katharine clenched her fists so hard her nails imprinted themselves on her palms. She could hardly believe what this smooth operator, this upmarket accountant, a partner in one of the most prestigious New York firms, was saying.

David's difficulties had started when one of his personal

investments collapsed. To shore it up he approached a high-profile property developer for a loan of five hundred thousand dollars. The developer offered what he described as an ingenious solution. Having just completed a commercial development which was not fully let, he wanted to make a quick sale to finance another development nearby. The proposition was that if David found a cash buyer quickly he would receive enough commission to cover his losses.

The solution was simple. David had access to Katharine's portfolio of investments and they offered a temptation he could not resist.

'You took my money? Without my permission?'

'Just as a loan,' he said quickly, 'a temporary measure, that's all.' He could not meet her stern gaze.

'So what went wrong?'

'The first thing was that the developer needed more money and insisted I should throw in my commission as well as a substantial bank loan, which I did.' David paused and Katharine thought he was on the edge of tears. 'But that still wasn't enough and I had to clinch the deal. I was in too deep by that stage.'

'So?'

He took a deep breath. 'Then I mentioned that I was your financial adviser and they said the deal was as good as done if . . .'

'If what? Tell me?'

'If you would stand guarantor for the debts. Katharine, I had no choice. It was the only thing that made them agree.'

'Go on.' Her voice was dangerously calm.

'I had to get you to sign the documents.'

'When did I do that?'

'You signed anything I put in front of you.'

'Because I *trusted* you.' Her emphasis made him flinch and he bit his lip.

'I thought I'd make a killing for us. And I still might.

The money's tied up but as soon as—'

'Might? You've got a nerve to say that to me now.' She stood up. 'I never thought you'd do anything underhand, especially using my name and my reputation.' She fixed him with a furious gaze. 'David, understand me. I want my money now. All of it. I want it now, damn you.' She made her way round his desk and began opening drawers. 'I don't care how you get it. Where's your cheque book?'

He caught her wrist roughly, his fingers pressing so tightly she gasped. 'I won't waste your time. It would bounce anyway. Katharine, there's no money, and if the development company discovers its major guarantor is giving up a substantial income, it will foreclose on the loan. But I promise you—'

She put her hands over her ears. 'I don't want to hear any more.' She lowered her hands again. 'You swindler. Why should I have to pay for your mistakes? Why can't you sell your house, and that fancy car – everything?'

He shook his head sadly. 'There's nothing to sell, no insurance, nothing. I'm mortgaged to the hilt, we're having to move to a rented condo. I don't have anything,' he whispered.

'Well, if I have to sue you for it, I will,' she said angrily, making for the door. 'I intend to consult my lawyer right away.'

'Just a minute, Katharine. I'm afraid you can't walk away from this as easily as that.'

She stopped and turned round.

This time David was far more succinct. 'If you blow the whistle on me now, yes, I'll go to prison. For fraud. But I'll drag you down with me.'

Katharine sat down again, thinking that he was exaggerating to gain her co-operation. One glance at his face told her he was not.

He explained that, to secure the valuation at a high

enough level, he had given the impression that the building was fully rented and generating lucrative letting income by drawing up fictitious leases for non-existent companies. Leases to which ostensibly she had been party.

At last she found her voice. 'You've made fraudulent and criminal representations to get a loan?'

'Yes, Katharine.' He paused. 'And so have you.'

Katharine was aware that her ignorance would be no defence in law, however clever the attorney. Nor would it help to say she did not know what she was signing. She would be regarded as a fool. Exactly what she had been.

She stared at him with hostility. 'You got me into this mess. How are you going to get me out of it?'

David's face was as white as his handkerchief. 'I'm in just as much of a financial predicament as you are but it's not all bleak. I think we might be able to get a legitimate let for the building,' he said eagerly, his words tumbling over each other, 'only the conglomerate negotiating with me need about six months before they relocate. They won't sign anything before they need to but it's copper-bottomed.'

'Copper-bottomed.' She repeated his words scornfully.

'Yes, and when it goes through we can rely on those funds to repay the debt and get our – I mean your money back. You might even make a profit.'

Why should she believe him? How could she ever rely on him again?

He saw her hesitation and plunged on. 'I know I shouldn't ask for anything, Katharine. I've been lucky enough to have your friendship and that's obviously at an end now. I'm more sorry about this than I can say but you would never have known about it if you hadn't given me this ultimatum today.'

'Exactly. On the surface you like to appear the respected adviser, all probity and caution. Underneath you're rotten, in cahoots with anyone to make a fast buck.'

'I can't blame you for thinking that but I beg you to do nothing. Give me time to complete the deal. Otherwise we're both in trouble. All I'm asking is that you keep on working a little longer.'

'For six months, you said.'

He hesitated. 'Maybe nine months. A year tops.'

A year.

She stood up, the joyous mood long gone. Suddenly the sun was not shining so brightly. She recognised clearly that she was trapped.

Trapped into the rivalry with Abbie.

Trapped into the relentless workload.

And, for all her brave words, trapped into obeying Sam Wolfe's orders.

Oh God.

Chapter Eleven

Abbie peered into the small oven. Surely that Yorkshire pudding should have risen more by now? And why hadn't it turned brown?

Dinner at her apartment, cooked with her own hands, had been her way of repaying George for weeks of costly wining and dining.

'I think it's time you tasted some real British food,' she had joked.

'OK, I'll get Chef to make some.'

'No. I want to cook it.'

He seemed amused. 'Why?'

'Because you won't let me pay at a restaurant, not that we go anywhere but your penthouse.'

'Best service in town.'

'Anyway, most women cook, some of them do it every day so I want to try. It would be a challenge.'

It would have been cheaper for her to take him to the best restaurant in town. The ingredients had cost a fortune, particularly air freighting Dublin Bay prawns from Ireland – not strictly British, she thought, but close enough. Her 'homemade' apple pie had been prepared for baking by the wife of the press attaché at the British Embassy, a contact who had become a friend after a recent interview. For the main course, there was no contest; she would serve roast beef and all the trimmings.

George, clutching a corsage of freesias and a bottle of

claret, arrived punctually. Abbie was by then flushed, harassed and looking less than glamorous. Her experience of cooking extended no further than simple student fare and she had not appreciated that even professionals found the timing involved in cooking the main course tricky. George's lips twitched when she rushed him to the table because everything was ready. 'The vegetables are a little overdone,' she apologised. In truth, they looked exhausted, as did the hunk of beef which was by now the colour of roof slate while the pale, flat Yorkshire pudding had never recovered from the shafts of cold air she had allowed into the oven on her frequent inspections.

Abbie rested her head in her hands and looked grumpily across the table. 'Damn everything.'

'Come here,' said George softly.

He sat her on his lap and gently kissed her until she began to smile.

'What's going on in that lively brain of yours?' he asked teasingly.

'I'm so disappointed. I wanted to cook you a really wonderful meal. I thought it was easy. And look at this rubbish. A child could have done better. I wanted to feed you up so you'd relax your guard.'

He looked amused. 'I didn't know I had one.'

'Oh, come on, George, you put up barriers whenever I ask you any personal questions. You like being mysterious.'

'No I don't.'

'Yes you do.'

'Try me. What do you want to know?'

'About your past.'

'That's easy. I was trained for hotel management in London, Paris and Geneva and then—'

'No, no, nothing about your business. I mean things like where you were born and,' she hesitated, 'you know, why you've never married, that type of thing.'

His eyes glittered with enjoyment. 'OK. As you can see, I was born and then I grew up into this wonderful human being you see before you. And no, I've never found anyone special enough to want to spend my life with them.' He twirled her hair round his fingers. 'So far.'

Abbie coloured. Why had she asked that question? He was looking at her so intently, she did not know what to say. George was a flirt, and she wasn't vain enough to think he was considering any kind of commitment to her. But where exactly did she want this relationship to go?

George tried to control his smile. Eventually they all brought up the subject of marriage. Sometimes he invented an Italian wife and sometimes he said he was endlessly searching for the right mate. It depended on the circumstances. But this woman was definitely maintaining his interest. Every time he looked at that luminous skin he wanted to touch it. She had so little artifice compared with older women. Her mother for instance. Not that that detracted from Katharine's charms, she stimulated him mentally and physically. But there was something appealing about teaching a younger woman the delights of eroticism. If only they could be cloned together, the combination would constitute his perfect woman. What a delicious situation this was for a man to enjoy; he hoped to make it last as long as he could.

Of course it was not easy, he had to be careful. It had been foolish to cancel Katharine at such short notice. Her pride had been wounded and he had to make amends or she might blow him out of the water. She was in a vulnerable state right now. Apparently there were problems with her career, though he did not know the details. It was a principle of his not to involve himself in the minutiae of his women's business worries. That way lay madness. In the past he had been accused of not recognising the concept of guilt and he could not quarrel with that. If women became too complicated, he simply moved on.

But he was not ready to let Katharine go just yet, at least not until the hotel was safely launched at Easter. He was as certain as he could be that one of his special phone calls would lure her back.

Now what was he going to do about sweet Abbie and her inedible meal? Simple. He would make it clear that he was hungry for something else.

Three weeks after Buzz relayed to Sam Wolfe that Katharine had, without explanation, caved in and would agree to his demands, Dr Roberto Brescia, the famed plastic surgeon, flew in under conditions of great secrecy for a private consultation with ABN's anxious star. In his hotel suite he illustrated how he could change the shape of her eyes. Gazing at the computer-generated images of her face, Katharine marvelled at how easy it seemed on screen.

In spite of her parlous financial state, she had almost walked out when she discovered that Mike O'Brien was to sit in on her interview with the doctor.

'This is utterly humiliating,' she protested and was only partly mollified when Mike pointed out that the station was spending a substantial amount of its money and he was merely acting as watchdog to ensure it was properly used.

Katharine was not sure that this guardianship of the finances was his only reason. Her suspicions were proved correct when she observed that the doctor appeared to pay as much attention to Mike's views on what was needed as he did to those of his patient. What she did not know was that the network had already sent videos and photographs of a rival anchor, her daughter Abbie Lomax, to the good doctor – 'To give you an idea of what we're aiming for,' as Mike brutally put it to the doctor when he talked earlier by phone.

While Katharine was resigned to accepting some work on the area around her eyes, she was taken aback when Mike and the doctor pushed for a more radical lift involving a major tightening of her jaw line and entire neck area.

'It will give you such firmness, it will take ten years off your appearance. I guarantee it,' said Dr Brescia. 'I have been studying the videos of your show and I have to say your appearance is good, very good.' The doctor leaned closer. 'But I can make you look much younger.' Once again he turned to his computer and illustrated how he would do it.

Katharine watched in silence. Her peers in the business regarded cosmetic surgery no more seriously than a trip to the dentist for cap work. It was a modern adjunct to their armoury. She supposed it was her British background that made her so wary, so reluctant.

And the doctor had not once mentioned the four-letter word that, according to Nina, surgeons never used.

'Pain,' said Nina, one of cosmetic surgery's most fervent adherents, 'is a concept that they hardly ever discuss. If you bring it up, even the best of them will say something like "everyone's different, but my patients tell me they experience discomfort more than anything else". That's horseshit. It hurts like hell.'

Katharine decided to put Nina's cynicism to the test.

'Is all this going to be very painful?'

Dr Brescia gave her an understanding nod. 'Everyone's different, my dear, but most of my patients say it's more uncomfortable than anything else, being unable to eat solids for a few days, a certain lack of mobility, that kind of thing.'

'I see.' Clearly, Nina knew what she was talking about. Katharine glanced at her computer image. 'It all looks very good on your screen here but I've met too many women who resemble stretched skeletons after surgery.'

The doctor threw his hands theatrically into the air. 'Vandals, vandals. You'd never get that with me. I, Roberto Brescia, promise you that.' He went on to describe an intricate procedure involving the latest laser treatment, which had excellent results and involved a much shorter recovery period. He assured her she would regain full mobility of her face after five or six days. 'And while you're under the anaesthetic, why don't I give you an extra inch or two on your bosom?'

'No, I told you I don't want—'

'It makes sense to have everything done at once,' interrupted Mike, 'so that you have only one absence from the studio.'

'Mike, I really don't want anything extra. I'm not ready for it.'

Mike appealed to Dr Brescia. 'Isn't this exactly the right time? When she still looks great and before things are actually necessary?'

'Definitely.' The surgeon nodded so vigorously Katharine surmised that he and Mike had agreed all this in advance. 'The longer you wait, the less elasticity there is to work with. In my experience, the sooner the better.' He switched off the computer and swivelled round to face her.

'So many patients come to me afterwards and say they wish they had been braver, had more skin taken out here,' and he prodded the smooth surface under his eyes, 'and more, much more put in up here,' he cupped his chest area. 'Take my advice, have it all done now and you will be very happy.'

The doctor turned back to his computer, swiftly bringing on to the screen a computer graphic showing the outline of a woman's body which Katharine imagined had been drawn using her measurements. He moved the mouse to zoom in on the breasts.

'Look at this,' he tapped the screen with his finger. 'I propose to augment this area by just one inch, no more. This will have the effect of lifting your own breast tissue and will give a rounder and firmer appearance.'

Nina had urged Katharine to have breast implants. 'I've never regretted having them done. Look at these. They've changed my shape and given me more confidence to take off my clothes.'

Sensing that his patient's resolve was weakening, Dr Brescia described the soya-based material he would use. This, he informed her, behaved in a more natural fashion. 'For instance, when you're lying down, they won't stick up like mountain peaks as silicone implants do. But they do have one drawback. If you go skiing, they react to extreme cold so they might need massaging.' He wriggled his eyebrows at her roguishly. 'I'm sure you will have someone who could do that for you.'

Katharine found herself agreeing a date when she would fly to Rio de Janeiro, at the beginning of the Easter break. This would give her time to recover before starting work on the next run of shows. In the meantime, she and Mike agreed she would record several interviews which would be used during the time she would spend at the clinic.

When the doctor escorted her and Mike to the door, he patted her arm. 'Courage, my dear Miss Sexton. Put your faith in me. I am the best and I guarantee you will be delighted with my work. You will look younger, more beautiful and, dare I say it, even more desirable.'

Katharine returned his smile. She had to admit he was quite endearing and he was not, after all, to blame for her predicament.

Damn that crooked accountant. Damn Sam Wolfe. And damn television for its double standards whereby men could survive with baggy eyes, greying hair, wrinkles and a pot belly while women had to appear everlastingly young, slim and unblemished.

★ ★ ★

The carmine varnish gleamed as it caught the light of the dressing-table mirror. Brenda's assistant was applying the final coat of fixative to Abbie's nails as Jeri-Ann walked through the door.

The assistant, Brooke, was very talented. If it would not have caused serious political fall-out, Abbie would have liked her to do her make-up instead of the less innovative supervisor.

'That colour's very exotic,' commented Jeri-Ann. She leaned against the make-up counter as Brooke gathered up her things and left. 'It makes you look vampish. It's a man, right? I've seen that little smile when you think no one's looking and you've been positively glowing lately. Been going out with him what, about a month?'

'Six weeks,' said Abbie, blowing on her nails. 'Next Tuesday.'

Jeri-Ann admired Abbie's ability to attract men but did not appear to be envious, though she openly wished for a Robert in her life. So far Jeri-Ann had been looking for love in all the wrong places. She had not met Mr Right though liaisons with Mr Definitely-Wrong, Mr Totally-Inferior and Mr Downright-Disaster had not put her off the hunt. Now, she wasted no time on finesse. 'So spill.'

'Not much to tell.' Jeri-Ann was discreet but Abbie did not want to jinx things. 'I met him on the plane back from London.'

'Married?'

'No.'

'Gay?'

'Definitely not.'

'Neurotic? Psychotic? Psychic? Don't laugh, there's always something wrong. He could be a secret Nazi. Or worse,' she shivered theatrically, 'have a mother. My advice is to stay alert.'

'Thanks for the warning.'

'What's he look like?'

'Umm, warm, dark and handsome.'

'Lucky woman.'

'He's also sophisticated, well-travelled, speaks four languages, and,' Abbie groaned, 'he has beautiful hands.'

'Ah, yes. Hands. Part of the good things in life. Like a dog.'

'But you know the best thing about him? He's not psyched by this fame junk. He's so sorted out.'

'Go for it. What I'd give for one of those. The only guys I seem to meet are toxic bachelors.'

'Toxic what?'

'You know, committo-phobes, those slippery eels who say they're in love but practise serial monogamy.'

'Maybe that's George. It seems strange he isn't married.'

Jeri-Ann was philosophical. 'He might be lying. You'll find out soon enough. In the meantime, enjoy. Hey, I hope your nails are dry, I promised Mrs Stern we'd see her in exactly twenty-five minutes.'

Abbie raced towards the elevators. 'Come on, we can't be late after all the trouble we took to reel her in.'

Adele Stern was the distraught mother of a young man who had walked calmly into a fast food restaurant a few days earlier, taken out a gun, and shot dead six teenagers who were there to celebrate a birthday. Then he had turned the gun on himself.

The other talk shows had gone after the grieving families of the victims but Abbie had homed in on the assassin's mother, a widow from North Carolina who had sensibly gone into hiding. It had taken intensive detective work to track her down and a great deal of sympathetic persuasion to win her round. Abbie had clinched the deal by pointing out to Mrs Stern that she would have to hide permanently until she told her story to somebody at some time. Besieged through her attorney by every newshound in the business, Abbie's words struck home.

In the middle of the madness, to Mrs Stern Abbie appeared to be the most sympathetic. The grieving mother had already rejected an enormous birthday cake her lawyer had sent her, bearing the frosted message, 'USTV: We're on YOUR side.' One of Abbie's researchers told her that the sender of the cake had boasted that basically she tried to be as ingratiating as she could without actually vomiting. The cynicism showed.

Now, after agreeing to appear on Abbie's show, Mrs Stern was holed up in an uptown hotel waiting to talk to Abbie, whom she regarded as a friend, someone who would protect her against the worst vagaries of a voracious media and who would give her the opportunity to present her own point of view. She felt her son was as much a victim as those he had killed.

Abbie was greeted warmly by the hotel's doorman. It was one of the things she loved about America. Ordinary people genuinely pleased by success. The hotel receptionist, too, was welcoming.

'Hello, Miss Lomax,' she said with a friendly smile. 'I thought you must be coming in because I have a letter here waiting for you. It was dropped off about thirty minutes ago.'

Abbie and Jeri-Ann exchanged alarmed glances. This was supposed to be a highly secret operation. Few people knew about their movements. Several hard-hitting promos a few hours before transmission would alert viewers to their exclusive soon enough. The inevitable response from cranks, anti-gun lobbyists and religious zealots who would complain about the air time being given to a 'woman who spawned a devil' would add to the publicity. In the meantime, Abbie had told Mrs Stern that she should use an assumed name which was known only to her and Jeri-Ann. It was not necessary to warn the widow from Carolina not to venture from her suite under any circumstances. She had been trembling with fear ever since the massacre.

The receptionist, mistaking the discomfort on Abbie's face for anxiety about the contents of the large cardboard-backed envelope, was quick to reassure her. 'Don't worry, Miss Lomax. This has been through our X-ray machine. Whatever's inside is harmless.'

Abbie took the envelope over to a quiet corner of the lobby. 'Who the hell knew we were coming here?' she said worriedly, more to herself than to Jeri-Ann. She ripped the envelope open then stared in horror at a photograph of a car so mangled it was unrecognisable.

'It's from that bloody crazy,' she said shakily, passing the photo to Jeri-Ann. A typewritten message stuck to the bottom said, 'This death was your fault, you bitch. Watch out. Fan of Fans.'

'These nuts often blame celebrities if something bad happens in their life,' said Jeri-Ann slowly. 'What I don't understand is how the hell he knew you'd be here.'

'He wants me to know that I'm not safe anywhere. This is getting scary,' said Abbie, white-faced. 'Somehow he has access to my movements. And the security people think vetting my mail and sending a car for me is enough protection.' She put her head in her hands. 'Just when I think he's gone away I get another message. I'm beginning to suspect everybody around me. It's an awful thing to live with. Do you think it's anyone in the office?'

'No, I don't,' answered Jeri-Ann firmly. 'I'm sure nobody there bears you a grudge.' She glanced at Abbie's frightened face. 'OK, here's what we're going to do. I'll go see the chief of security and tighten the thumb screws on the bastard to get you twenty-four-hour protection. It's tedious but we'll have to do it until this guy gets fed up. These sad sacks often do. The main thing is, don't let it take over your life.'

'That's what everyone tells me but it's easier said than

done. I keep on asking myself, why does he want to frighten me? What's he get out of it?'

'There's usually no logic to the actions of this kind of nutter, but it wouldn't do any harm to trawl through your back interviews in Chicago to see if you've rattled any cages. In the meantime, let's find out if the receptionist saw who brought this letter in.'

But the receptionist explained that there were so many deliveries, it would be impossible to single out who had brought in what. There was a squiggle in the delivery book but it was illegible. The identity of the sender would have to be put aside; they needed to talk to Mrs Stern.

It required all Abbie's concentration to keep her mind on the job in hand, which was to try to prepare the apprehensive woman for her forthcoming interview. Later, when Abbie returned to the office, her first thought was to talk to George. He could put things into perspective for her, make her laugh away her gloom.

As usual he was not at home, just that damn answering machine. Hurriedly Abbie replaced the receiver and tried his mobile. It was switched off. Finally, she managed to get hold of his assistant but, as always, the woman stonewalled. He was in a meeting and had left instructions not to be disturbed.

'Would you like to leave a message, Miss Lomax?'

No, she would not.

Needing to talk to somebody, Abbie pressed Auto 2 on her phone. Matt was always available when she called.

She recounted the events of the afternoon and repeated her fears that she was being hounded. 'Matt, I'm feeling freaked out. Tell me, am I making too much of this?'

'No, I don't think so.'

'Did you tell anyone I was going to be at the hotel?'

'I'm trying to think but I'm pretty sure I didn't.'

'There has to be a leak.'

'It's not from my office, I'm sure of that.'

'Do you think it's someone from another television station?' she asked carefully.

'You mean on *Here and Now*? Could be, I suppose, though it seems a bit extreme.'

'Can we meet, Matt? Where are you now?' she asked.

'Having a massage.'

Matt looked with gratification at the naked woman stretched languorously beside him in his bed. She never seemed to mind that he kept her away from fashionable restaurants.

Abbie was his most lucrative client but she could wait a little. 'Give me an hour,' he told her.

It was the first time he had not given Abbie priority but he could not get enough of this incredible woman. God knew why she had picked him but since that meeting in the bar she had made herself available for him night and day. 'You're the planner, the thinker, the dreamer I've been searching for,' she told him. 'Whatever it is I need to turn me on, you have it for me, baby.'

At first he had not believed her and had been on his guard. Surely she would ask him to speak to this producer or that director on her behalf? But no, though she loved to hear him talking about his work, she seemed to have no interest in a career in acting, modelling or television. On the dawn plane from Chicago on Monday mornings he hurried straight to her apartment to find her waiting for him, compliant, eager and interested in only one thing. What a lucky guy he was.

This woman made him feel he was the world's best lover, and when he was with her, he could be. He often speculated that his wife would be amazed at his imagination though he did worry that Angela might be getting suspicious. However, he was careful to ensure that his new-found sexual knowledge did not transfer to Chicago. Once or twice she had questioned him rather too closely about where he had been on a particular night. And last weekend she had again pointed out that he made as much from one client in New York as the entire agency in Chicago. Would it not be sensible, she asked, to consider moving the family to New York where they could expand the agency with more profitable clients?

Matt had to perform some nifty footwork to squash that logical vision of their future. Didn't Angela realise they needed both offices to be profitable before getting someone in to do her job? And there was no telling how long Abbie's career would last. Television was a fickle business. No one, least of all Matt, could predict whether Globe would renew her option. It was much too early to talk of decanting with the boys to New York. Angela had accepted this.

True to his word, an hour later Matt was in Jeri-Ann's office with Abbie and the producer.

'We gave this interview top security rating,' Jeri-Ann said. 'Only six people know we are going to do the programme, and only four of those knew we were going to meet at the hotel – Abbie, me, Matt and the mother herself.' She looked at Abbie levelly.

'I've gone through every minute of my day and I'm absolutely certain that I spoke to no one about Abbie's programme,' said Matt. 'I had a big session with my accountant and it was all figures, figures, figures. I didn't talk about Abbie at all. To anyone.' Nor had he.

'I doubt it's from within the office,' said Jeri-Ann. 'We've never had a leak like this before and my assistant and secretary have been with me for years. They followed me from my last job. If they were going to start being indiscreet, I sure as hell don't think they would start with this, especially my secretary. She was the one who helped sew up the interview.'

'Maybe the leak came through me,' said Abbie. 'I could have been overheard while I was making phone calls in the conference room or even at my desk.'

'What about the mother?' said Matt.

Abbie squashed that at once. 'Mrs Stern is very nervous about doing the programme. For God's sake, she's had death threats. She wouldn't take any unnecessary risks.'

'I'm stumped,' said Jeri-Ann.

'Shall we call in the police?'

'No,' said Matt and the producer simultaneously.

'We don't want any publicity on this,' Jeri-Ann asserted. 'The police have a hot line to most news desks. What this gook probably craves above all is recognition that you're frightened, that we're taking notice of him. However difficult it is, my advice for us all is to stay cool and then this will probably fizzle out. In the past we've found that the police anyway have very little expertise that our security boys can't match.'

'And so far the guy's no more guilty than hundreds of other sickos,' Matt said. 'A pornographic card, a phone call, a picture of a car crash. I can understand how creepy they make you feel but what can the police do when he's made no real threats?'

They were right, Abbie thought gloomily. She wished she could discuss it with Katharine and ask her for advice. But they had not spoken since Christmas and she could still hear the cruel insult she had flung at her before she left her apartment: 'You shouldn't have had children.' Would her mother ever forgive her?

In the days that followed Abbie lived in a state of high alert, tensing each time the telephone rang at home. Once a passer-by tried to block her path and she recoiled, only to realise it was just an autograph hunter. Outside her apartment block she would wait in the limo until the porter spotted her and came from behind his desk to open the door, something he did not do for other residents. When one of them complained, he rashly told them that he had been asked to provide extra security; he did not say why, he did not know the details, but this snippet quickly hit the gossip columns, which made Abbie even more nervous. The Fan of Fans was probably rubbing his hands with glee at this public confirmation that he was getting through to her.

Matt spoke informally to his police contact and reported back to Abbie. 'We were right not to involve them,' he told her. 'He says that until a crime has been committed, their hands are tied.'

'So until someone throws acid in my face, they won't do anything? Great.'

'We won't let it come to that, Abbie.'

After that it became a habit for her to run between the car taking her to Globe and the comfort of the revolving doors to her building. Although she tried not to allow the Fan of Fans to dominate her thoughts and prevent her leading a normal life, she found herself mentally checking faces whenever she was in a crowd.

She was puzzled by George's attitude to her problem. He seemed to take a rather phlegmatic approach to it.

'But you must have received other hate mail,' he said.

'Not like this. Why, do you think I shouldn't take this so seriously?'

'I didn't say that. Of course it isn't pleasant but I shouldn't let it rule your life.'

'Easy to say,' she grumbled.

She noticed that a red-haired jogger had been running near her apartment every morning that week. He had made no attempt to approach her but it bothered her. When she told George about the jogger he made sympathetic sounds but did not suggest she move into his penthouse with him temporarily as she had hoped he might. Perhaps he felt it wasn't practical as he was constantly flitting between Washington, Paris and Rome.

And he had been strangely embarrassed about telling her that Katharine was to perform the opening ceremony at his new hotel on Thursday next week, the day before Good Friday. Abbie was unconcerned about that. George would not discuss her with Katharine. Television celebrities were asked to functions constantly, it was part of the job. And George told her the invitation had been arranged through his press office long before he had met Abbie. She did not think it odd that he did not invite her to the ceremony. Aware of the estrangement with her mother, he would not want to embarrass her. It showed sensitivity on his part, she thought.

Their affair was passionate but unfettered by reality. His behaviour was unlike that of any man she had ever known. Although he was attentive and phoned often, he did not make himself available every time she was free. She idly accused him one day of keeping their affair away from public gaze because he had another woman. The ardour of his lovemaking that night convinced her this could not be true.

'Why would I need anyone else when I have you?' he asked.

While George's elusiveness might be unsettling and the attentions of the Fan of Fans worrying, Abbie's career continued to flourish. The interview with Mrs Stern, the last before the Easter break, was a triumph. According to Jeri-Ann, an experienced hand in gauging audience mood and changes, the programme catapulted *Tonight* into a different arena, away from the safety harness of showbiz material and into the minefield of current affairs, with its unpredictable but potentially rewarding agenda.

Mrs Stern began by trying to put the killing into the context of her son's upbringing. It was only after gentle but insistent probing from Abbie that she blurted out the story that would make banner headlines the next day.

'What did your son mean when, before pulling the trigger, he said, "Sleep is good, death is better"?' Abbie asked. A contact in the police department had given her this piece of information; it had not been reported anywhere.

There was a long silence as Mrs Stern struggled to control her emotions. She said, 'That was what his father's suicide note said.' She faltered and Abbie waited for her to regain her composure. 'It's a quote from Heinrich Heine – my husband was German, you know. He liked to read the German philosophers. Heine said, "Sleep is good, death is better; but of course the best thing would be never to be born at all." ' Tears coursed down Mrs Stern's cheeks. 'I blame myself,' she sobbed. 'My son was the one who found his father. It was a terrible shock to him, he was so young. I tried to talk to him about it but he would never open up and I was full of my own grief. I should have sent him for counselling back then. I should have insisted. If only I had, this . . . thing would not have happened.'

Then, hesitating, she puckered her forehead and said sorrowfully, 'Abbie, I want to tell those poor parents that for the rest of my life I will share their grief . . .'

There had been an unprecedented response from viewers, a great percentage of them, Abbie was pleased to learn, sympathetic to Mrs Stern.

The studio director told her afterwards that the interview had generated one of the most highly-charged atmospheres he had ever experienced in his career. 'You created the moment,' he said. 'You seized the chance and knew when to shut up and let her do the talking. It was great, great television.'

Matt, too, was jubilant, and not just about the success of the show. The week before, Abbie's Q rating, the top-secret measure carried out by the networks to assess a personality's appeal to viewers, had risen to twenty. Though Katharine boasted a Q rating of twenty-seven, the difference was the smallest recorded between them since *Tonight* had started. When Matt had discovered this he had insisted on a top-level meeting with the station boss to renegotiate Abbie's contract and he had just been told that his efforts to get his star client a mouth-smacking rise had been successful.

He caught up with Abbie straight after the show and told her the good news. 'Of course, you know why they've agreed. Your programme costs less than half a million dollars to produce. If you weren't there they'd have to go for drama or comedy which could run to two million and your show earns nearly as much as a drama would in advertising income.' Abbie had heard Matt sound off on this subject before. 'So you can see why they're eager to keep you happy. I've also arranged a new clause, that the network picks up all bills for any extra security you might need.'

Abbie gave him a round of applause.

Matt preened. 'Lucky there was an option in your contract that we could renegotiate after six months.'

She smiled fondly at him.

'Luck had nothing to do with it,' they said in unison.

'This calls for a celebration,' said Abbie, more relaxed than he had seen her for weeks. 'Why don't we get in some drinks to say thank you to the boys and girls?'

'Good tactics,' said Matt. 'I'll go get some champagne. We'll make a night of it.'

'I wish I was on speaking terms with my mother then I could invite her.'

'Just as well you aren't,' retorted Matt. 'It would inhibit your gang and the bosses here wouldn't be too keen on fraternising with the enemy.'

The enemy. Abbie had to admit that this severe indictment of her mother and ABN was an accurate gauge of the prevailing atmosphere within Globe. Though the madness of the media coverage had abated, there were still days when columnists searching for inspiration wrote a few hundred mocking words bristling with comparisons between their shows. Much was made, too, of the fact that the two women never surfaced at the same functions. It was rumoured that hosts understood that one of them would be a no-show if the other's name featured on the guest list.

In the midst of the laughter, clinking of glasses and the buzz of conversation, Abbie felt exhilarated. Researchers, secretaries, cameramen, vision mixers and executives were milling around in an atmosphere of excitement, good humour and camaraderie. She felt part of a successful team. Even the usually lugubrious sound guy was smiling and when Jeri-Ann suggested a quiet supper with a few of her colleagues, Abbie happily agreed.

The party began to disperse and Abbie excused herself to return to her dressing room, reserved exclusively for her on Saturdays when she was rehearsing and on Sundays when the show was being produced. On other days it was occupied by Globe's mid-week presenters, though a thoughtful management had allocated a lock-up drawer to each of them.

When she had the room to herself, Abbie tended to spread herself, subscribing to the old adage, 'Boring women have tidy homes.' The disorder in her bedroom at home was replicated now in this dressing room. It was difficult to ascertain the colour of her make-up counter, covered as it was with every conceivable brand of cosmetics in tubes, jars and packets, all of them separated from their tops.

Abbie noticed a couple of notes stuck to the dressing-table mirror. She peeled them off to read them. The first one was a reminder from the duty studio manager that the next day's taping had been put back one hour. She scrumpled it up and tossed it in the general direction of the overflowing wastepaper basket.

As she read the next note, which was typewritten, the colour drained from her face and she sat down heavily.

Jeri-Ann came through the door leafing through some schedules for the following week. 'Did you see the times for the taping tomorrow? Why can't they check with me first? Are they OK for you?'

She became aware that Abbie was sitting motionless, her distress evident. 'What's up?'

With trembling fingers Abbie handed her the note.

Jeri-Ann read the word-processed text out loud. ' "I've left a little surprise inside your fridge. I'm not finished with you yet. Watch out. Fan of Fans." Oh God, not him again. What d'you think he means this time?'

'There's only one way to find out,' said Abbie firmly and she went over to the small cabinet tucked neatly beneath a work surface.

'No, Abbie, let me,' said Jeri-Ann quickly.

Reluctantly Abbie stood aside while Jeri-Ann crouched down and slowly opened the fridge door.

She reeled back, a look of distaste on her face. 'Oh shit,' she exclaimed. 'This man's sick.'

'What is it?' said Abbie, peering over her shoulder.

'He's put a condom here.' Jeri-Ann paused. 'After he's used it. It's on top of one of your publicity pictures.'

Abbie clutched her mouth, feeling sick. The thought of some kink masturbating, fantasising about what he was doing to her, was repellent.

Jeri-Ann pushed her gently away and closed the fridge door. 'We'd better not disturb anything in case there are fingerprints.'

'I'm going to nail this bastard,' said Abbie fiercely. She grabbed the note and ran to the door. She thrust the piece of paper at the security guard on duty in the corridor.

His eyes flickered briefly across the note and swiftly he went into the dressing room. He glanced round the room and then began opening and closing closet doors.

Abbie, pale-faced, watched silently until, satisfied there was no one hiding, he fished out his mobile and spoke urgently to his boss then left the room.

A few minutes later there was a tap on the door and Brenda's concerned face peered round.

'No, no. Come in,' said Abbie.

The make-up supervisor, followed by Brooke, had been alerted by the guard that the star was in distress, though they were not told the cause.

Jeri-Ann explained what had been found in the fridge and Brooke grimaced in disgust. Brenda said, 'Is there anything you want, anything at all?'

Abbie shook her head.

'Well, if there is, we'll be in the make-up room,' and she patted Abbie's arm as they left.

Abbie felt an urgent need to be surrounded by familiar faces. 'Jeri-Ann, could you get hold of my mother, please? She's probably at the studio. And we'd better get Matt up here.'

Jeri-Ann got short shrift from ABN. Katharine was out of the country, was not expected back for a couple of weeks and, no, they were not able to get a message to her. Faced with this intransigence, Jeri-Ann did not explain the situation.

Abbie then phoned her father in London. Milo Lomax did not waste words. He would fly out on the first plane to New York.

Matt exploded when he heard what had happened. 'That's it. It's time we took advice from the best security firm in America instead of those dumb bastards at your station. From now on, the guy's gonna have to be faster than a weasel up a trouser leg to get to you.'

Chapter Twelve

After six hours on the red-eye from Los Angeles, Nick Toshiba looked as fresh as if he had just strolled across the park. His quiet air of authority reflected his formidable reputation as a specialist in identifying and dealing with fans whose interest in a celebrity strayed beyond the acceptable. Stalkers, blackmailers, tormentors.

In tinsel town the star culture had proved a magnet for this modern menace. Toshiba had made a mountain of dollars in his chosen field. His family was mainly involved with computer companies; he had no interest in this area but shared his family's commercial skills.

After eleven years in the Los Angeles Police Department, Toshiba had left to set up an independent specialist anti-stalking unit. In a short time, his expertise and that of his team had become well known and Toshiba Incorporated was now consulted by police forces throughout the world.

When Matt had approached him, his first request had been for a letter of authorisation to the human resources director at Globe TV to allow him to scrutinise its data banks. Exactly how he was going to circumvent the data protection legislation to gain access to this highly confidential information was not explained and considering the hefty fee he was charging Matt felt they had bought the right not to be involved. Next, Toshiba asked Matt to send him all the Fan of Fans' messages. Luckily, Abbie still had the postcard she had received at Alain's fashion show. She had not taken it very seriously then, but some instinct had made her hang on to it, just in case there were repercussions.

Now, Nick Toshiba was ready to meet his client. Short and stocky, he had a powerful build which with a few more pounds and intensive training could have made him a contender for a heavyweight boxing championship. He was alert and agile, and somehow his bulk gave clients added confidence. He was a formal, dignified man who regarded himself as an equal, however great the name of his client.

'Of course the perpetrator is usually a man but let's start with an open mind, shall we?' he told Abbie and Matt in Matt's office downtown.

'But is he an obsessed fan or someone from my past that I've slighted in some way?' Abbie had gone over and over this in her mind.

'I'll be going through your address book and checking out all possibilities. He hasn't asked for money so it's not blackmail. He's putting pressure on you because for some reason he believes he has a real grudge against you, Miss Lomax.'

'I've been racking my memory but I haven't come up with anyone who might feel so full of hate and anger towards me.'

'Presumably the phone message didn't give you any clues.'

'None at all. I couldn't even tell whether it was a man or a woman.'

Toshiba nodded. 'Anyone can buy a voice changer over the counter from a shop selling security devices. You set a level on the microphone inside the receiver and this has the ability to alter a voice so that it is unrecognisable in tone, pitch, and even gender.'

'What I can't understand is how he seems to know so

much about me,' said Abbie. 'That's what I find so scary.'

Toshiba glanced down at his notes. 'Well, discovering where you lunch or putting a postcard in a present clearly labelled with your name isn't so difficult. But locating your private phone number is some way further along the road. And we have to assume that he has an accomplice who has access here.' Toshiba took off his glasses. 'I shall be frank with you. It won't do you any good, Miss Lomax, if I underplay the dangers you could face.'

He pulled out a sheet of paper from his briefcase. 'I've done some groundwork. The messages have all been typed on a word processor. I sent them to a behavioural analyst who states that he cannot detect particularly violent characteristics in the phrases used in the first message on the postcard. Although the words "Watch out" are repeated later, he believes they are used as a kind of mantra, not with the specific intent of doing you harm. The photograph of a smashed car is a different matter, however. I'll read you what the analyst says about that. "The sender blames your client for having caused the death of the driver. The implication is that your client must suffer a similar fate, something underlined in the short message left on the answer machine." ' Toshiba looked up at their worried faces. 'While precautions must obviously be taken, he adds that in his experience physical danger does not come from stalkers who announce their intentions in advance.'

'That's cheering,' said Matt.

'The condom found in your dressing room puts a sexual spin on events, although the true fantasist uses his own sperm on these occasions. In this case, the condom contained only a well-known spermicidal jelly, according to Globe's security people.'

Abbie shuddered at the memory. 'What's the significance of that?'

'It could be several things. He could be impotent or

afraid that we have his DNA on record. Or it could be a woman.' Toshiba put the report back into the briefcase. 'The perpetrator is not conforming to a typical pattern. But we've only just started our inquiries. It's early days yet.'

'Why d'you think he's doing these things?' asked Matt.

'An educated guess? It could be revenge for something that's happened for which he blames you, Miss Lomax, because you're in the public eye. He'll want you to do something and part of his personality wants to keep you in suspense so you're more compliant when that request comes, whatever it is.' Toshiba leaned forward, elbows on his knees. 'I know what a worrying time this is for you, Miss Lomax. The way I operate is to be as frank and straightforward as I can. There's nothing the perpetrator can do that I haven't seen before. I've only one priority, that you come to no harm, either mentally or physically.'

'How are you going to ensure that?' asked Matt.

'The first thing we have to do is to throw a blanket of security around you. Up until now I believe your network has tried to be discreet about this but I want this guy to see that you're being protected,' replied Toshiba. 'That's important, but I have to tell you there's a problem with it. It will show him that you're anxious and that could feed his delusions. We've tried it both ways, but in your case being subtle is by now too risky. In my view, we need to indicate that you are heavily guarded at all times. I have a team of highly-trained operatives, men and women, and from now on wherever you go, one of them will be with you and that includes the john.'

Abbie frowned and he gave her a hard stare. 'From today I want you to cancel all personal appearances and stop sending out autographed pictures.'

'What's the harm in that?' asked Matt.

'If you were setting up a shrine, you would need photographs.'

'I don't know how publicity will take that,' said Abbie.

'You let me handle them, Miss Lomax,' Toshiba suggested politely.

Abbie was beginning to dread what all this security would involve, thinking of her meetings with George. 'It'll be so awkward having someone shadowing me, going everywhere with me, and I mean everywhere. Is all this really necessary?'

'Sorry, Miss Lomax, my contacts in the police and security departments could give you a list of stars who said the same thing at first. Candice Bergen. Rod Stewart. Sandra Bullock. Julia Roberts. Even Sylvester Stallone. They all discovered in the end that it was a necessary precaution.' He stared at her, his eyes unblinking. 'And it will end. That I promise you.'

Toshiba exuded such an air of confidence that Abbie began to relax.

'Ninety per cent of these creeps just want attention, Miss Lomax. Once they achieve their fifteen minutes of fame, they fade away. But if our stalker is part of the other ten per cent, and so far that doesn't seem to be the case, I know how to handle him. Any time he slips and commits a recognised offence – trespass, say, or carrying an illegal firearm – we can pounce.'

Firearm. This was the first time anyone had mentioned that this guy might be armed. Abbie felt her stomach knot.

'And if he keeps going long enough, we can build up an overall picture of a "credible threat" and prosecute him under a stalking statute.'

Abbie and Matt exchanged dismayed glances.

'If he keeps going long enough? What does that mean?' asked Abbie warily.

'Well, the longer he operates, the greater our chances of nailing him.'

Toshiba insisted that one of the station's security guards

escort his new client back to the studio and see her safely ensconced with the producer. Then, accompanied by Matt, Toshiba went to the network's financial department where he signed a contract. At the same time a weekly direct debit to Toshiba Inc. was authorised via the network's bank.

Formalities dealt with, Matt suggested they repair to a local bar, one of the many that had proliferated around the network's headquarters. He had some questions to ask Toshiba and he hoped the security specialist would answer them with a frankness he would not have allowed himself with Abbie.

'So tell me,' said Matt when they had their drinks, 'what are we up against?'

Toshiba stared thoughtfully into his glass of bourbon. 'There are three different types of stalkers. First there's the pest who's mentally deranged, then we have what's known as erotomania, the love-turns-sour syndrome,' he peered over his spectacles at Matt, 'but I think Miss Lomax's stalker fits into the third category, the obsessional. And they're often the most dangerous.'

'Why?'

'They tend to be so fixed on their mission, whatever it is, that they take incredible chances. There's no discernible pattern so it's more difficult to catch them.' Toshiba took a swig of his drink. 'But we do, in the end.'

'Abbie swears there's nobody in her past who's capable of doing this.'

'It's often the most unlikely person. That's why Miss Lomax will never be without a guard from now on. We'll try to be discreet but she won't be out of sight, even on private functions.'

'That's going to play hell with her sex life,' joked Matt.

Toshiba disregarded the comment. 'I'm off to investigate the background of everybody who has been in contact with Miss Lomax since the programme started.'

He rose to his feet and folded away his spectacles. 'And that includes you.'

Matt understood at once that Nick Toshiba was not joking.

As good as his word, Milo Lomax was on the first plane out of Heathrow after the call from his distressed daughter. He landed the following day and Abbie was there to pick him up.

He took her into his arms. It was several minutes before she could speak.

'Dad,' she said through her tears, 'I can't tell you how glad I am you're here. Thanks for coming.'

'I'll always be here when you need me, sweetheart. You know that. Come on, I'm in urgent need of a stiff drink and a steaming bath, in that order.'

On the way back to her apartment, driven by Toshiba's security guard, Abbie outlined what had been happening to her. Talking it over with her father made her already feel calmer. His very presence was comforting and took her back to the days when she believed he could solve all her problems, however insurmountable they appeared. In a strange kind of way she still half believed that.

She offered to swap her bedroom for the small box room she used as a spare wardrobe but he would not hear of it.

'I'm an old war reporter,' he grinned at her. 'I once used a pile of mud as a pillow and I slept as soundly as on a feather mattress.'

Although the apartment was designed for bachelor living, Abbie enjoyed having her father around. Hearing the noises he called singing when under the shower, seeing him make endless phone calls and watching him wrestle with the ice cube tray delighted her.

They decided to eat the cuisine of every country except Britain and America while he was in New York. They began that evening with Chinese ordered from a four-star emporium at the end of the block. While they ate, she told him there had been no reconciliation with her mother.

'It's a very difficult situation, Abbs, you two being in the same business and living in the same small media village. Even so, I think you should tell her what's happening to you. I tried to contact her as soon as I heard what happened but couldn't get hold of her.'

'Neither could I. It's all very mysterious. Apparently she's out of the country and they won't give us the number. And now, well, I don't want to bother her. I've got you here and Matt's organising proper security . . .' Abbie shrugged and her father looked at her with compassion.

'Still, it'd be rude, Abbs, if I didn't try to talk to her as I'm over here. Do you know where she is? I'm sure I could get her contact number.'

Abbie shook her head. 'My producer phoned Mum's agent and he mentioned something about Brazil but says she's not contactable until the week after next at the earliest. God knows who she's tracking down there but it must be someone important because Sunday's show was pre-recorded.'

'Well, I hope to be around for at least a week. I think you need a strong dose of TLC but I'll have to go back after that. Wouldn't it be a good idea to give your mother a call when she returns from wherever she's been?'

'Dad, you didn't hear some of the things we said to each other. And I did try, as you know, but she stood me up at that lunch. In any case, what could she do? She'd only interfere and now you're here I don't need her.'

Milo made a face. 'Darling, you don't mean that. You can't go through your life not talking to your mother.'

'I haven't told you everything. I didn't want to spoil our Christmas.' Briefly she recounted the Steve Stone incident.

'She was judge and jury and I was found guilty. She wouldn't listen to my side of things.'

Her father shook his head. 'Sounds familiar.'

'Steve didn't appear on *Tonight* but he did, in the end, appear on her show. She must know now that I didn't have anything to do with his original cancellation but she hasn't even had the courtesy to contact me and apologise. No, for the time being I think it would be best for us to have as little to do with each other as possible.'

Katharine had scheduled her operation during the show's Easter break, two days after she was due to perform the opening ceremony at George's controversial hotel. But less than a week before the ceremony, she had to cancel. An international statesman required Dr Brescia's services in a clinic in his own country. Reorganising the doctor's crammed diary meant Katharine had to fly to Brazil on the last Sunday before Easter. Saturday was spent recording the last of her interviews to cover her absence. When she left work that day, her 'working holiday' officially began, although her flight wasn't until Sunday evening.

For someone so adept at cancellations himself, George was less than gracious when she apologetically told him she would be abroad on his big night. His irritation turned what had been a glorious afternoon with him rather sour.

'It's very short notice,' he snapped. 'Couldn't you postpone your trip a couple of days?' It was a reasonable enough request but she could not tell him the truth. She had no intention of telling George of her humiliation.

'No, it's impossible, I'm afraid. It's out of my hands. I'm so sorry about it,' she said, genuinely upset to let him down.

'Well, I guess if you can't, you can't,' he said stiffly.

'Is there any way I can help?' she asked. 'I could write a letter for you to read out, saying I'd hoped to be there.'

She paused but he said nothing. 'It's better than nothing.'

'No, it isn't.'

'George, I really can't do anything about this. It's work. You understand that surely.' Again, he did not speak. 'Anyway, I have no doubt the opening will be a smash,' she said warmly but he refused to be mollified and left soon afterwards.

This was something else for which she bitterly blamed Sam Wolfe.

So far, the network had been completely successful in covering Katharine's tracks. The media reptiles had not stumbled across any hint of her impending surgery and her colleagues accepted the story that she was going abroad to persuade some world-famous luminary to appear on the programme. Who the quarry could be was the subject of much inter-office speculation.

Katharine's arrival at the back entrance of Dr Brescia's clinic was a model of discretion. The staff were well-used to dealing with celebrity clients who were variously reported to be 'on a trip to Sri Lanka communing with their guru' or 'motoring around Europe' or 'walking the Great Wall of China'. Among the many subtleties they had perfected to maintain secrecy was a postal service that involved sending mail to sister clinics in foreign outposts for franking if a client so requested. They were also celebrated for their ability to satisfy the most idiosyncratic of appetites, on one fabled occasion sending to Harrod's of London for a particular brand of British sausage for a woman so famous that even her initials would have disclosed her identity.

On a whim, Katharine had registered under her mother's maiden name, Palmer, which only her daughter and ex-husband would recognise.

Her home for the next two weeks was a large but sparse suite which contained a television video recorder plus all the latest movies, and a library of bestsellers and glossy magazines. It was bare of all frippery, apart from a multicoloured cushion on the white leather sofa. The cushion had been embroidered in petit point by a grateful patient with the motto, 'Gravity with gravitas.'

Dr Brescia's eminent clientele regarded him as the da Vinci of the scalpel. Indeed they said of him that he was equally skilful with words.

'You have the most beautiful eyes, Miss Sexton. Stunning. But I will give you perfection,' he had declared.

Katharine had reiterated to Dr Brescia almost to the point of rudeness that she did not want anything too dramatic to happen to her appearance. Colleagues and her public should think she had been away on an undemanding assignment which she had combined with a holiday.

The surgeon had lifted his hand and said, 'My dear, I think I have the message.' He laughed. 'A woman of your grace and charm would not want to look as if she has had cosmetic surgery. But then you would not be with me if you did.'

His reputation rested on his light, deft touch at the temples, behind the ear for the jaw line and under the chin. He would also make a neat incision for the implants under Katharine's 36B breasts to ensure they looked perky even after their droop-by date.

It was only on the third day after surgery that Katharine felt strong enough to make the effort to contact Nina from her large, cool room, its wooden shutters tightly closed against the noonday sun. Carefully positioning the phone to avoid putting pressure on the tiny clips which were clamping the incision behind her ear, her breasts tightly bandaged, she tried to convey to her friend, without moving her jaw too much, that Dr Brescia had been wrong and she, Nina, had been right. What she was experiencing was not discomfort but stupefying, wincing, flinching, dominating pain. She was only half joking.

'I'm told it's like childbirth,' said Nina. 'I gather you forget that pretty soon, and this is the same. Once the bandages come off you admire the effect and don't remember all the agony.'

The bruising at first rather obscured the benefits of the surgery, but after a few days Katharine was forced to admit that Dr Brescia had done a good job.

This did not lessen her fury with her accountant and she daydreamed frequently about how she could torture David Crozier very, very slowly, physically as well as mentally, and not get caught. Her feelings towards Sam Wolfe were none too warm either.

She had time to speculate about George and what he could be up to. Her mental picture of him making passionate love, as only George could, to another woman was so vivid she experienced a stab of jealous pain sharper than any from her surgery. She would try and rectify the bad feeling between them on her return and wondered why she was so flawed that she could not accept a man who loved her but needed to pursue one who did not. Perhaps it was because she found George a challenge. He discouraged all talk about his background but somewhere beneath the veneer of confidence and charm and the ability to make her feel she was the only person in the world who mattered, there had to be a crack in his armour. When she found the real man beneath the veneer, maybe then she would find out whether she could love him.

Toshiba called a council of war at the Globe building the day after his meeting in Matt's office. Apart from Abbie, those invited were Matt, Chuck Dempsey, Dantry's deputy and spy with over-all responsibility for security, and Jeri-Ann.

Toshiba started by thanking Dempsey for his co-operation. 'With my specialist knowledge and your organisation, I think we can nail the perpetrator.'

Clever tactics, thought Abbie, who had made no secret of her criticisms of the station's security arrangements, to Toshiba, to Matt and to her father. Dempsey remained stony-faced. Toshiba would need to do much more wooing.

'We know the person we're searching for works right here in this building,' Toshiba said. 'Or has an accomplice working here.'

'That's fucking obvious, if you don't mind my saying so,' said Dempsey.

Toshiba stared at him impassively. 'Forgive me if I do state the obvious. I've found that recounting all the facts sometimes triggers off an idea or a memory that can be helpful.'

Dempsey did not respond. Typical, thought Abbie. Call in an expert then spend time rubbishing what he says. She felt resentful that Dempsey had paid only lip-service to her problems.

Toshiba quickly ran through the list of incidents that had built up to the planting of the condom in the refrigerator, ticking off each one on his fingers. 'Our guy's not sticking to any discernible pattern. He seems to want to unnerve Miss Lomax by proving he can get access to her anywhere, any time.'

Dempsey gave an impatient sigh. 'Any idea what's behind all this?'

'My theory is the motive is jealousy. I've discussed with Miss Lomax and her agent who might want to destabilise her and although there are no obvious suspects we have to consider several people in the Globe building.'

Toshiba scanned his list of suspects. Unlikely as he felt some of them were, all had to be checked out. He had grouped them into three areas of her life. First, her small circle of friends, which included Robert Bridges and George Hemmings. Next, Globe colleagues like Jeri-Ann Hagerty, Red Skinner, researchers, technicians, make-up and wardrobe staff, particularly part-timers and temporaries, and her agent Matt Nicolaides. Finally, her rivals, like Blanche Casey at USTV.

'And we can't rule out that our suspect might be at ABN, the rival network employing Miss Lomax's mother,' Toshiba added. 'He might have recruited an accomplice here.'

Abbie shook her head. 'I don't want to believe that.'

'Misguided loyalty can drive people to extremes. Who has the most to gain if your energies are diverted away from your show?'

None of them answered.

'Embarrassing and painful as it is,' he said, 'we can't afford to dismiss anyone from our inquiries.' Toshiba stood up and began pacing behind the chairs. 'I want to talk to everyone who knows you personally. Mr George Hemmings, for example.'

The extent to which her family and friends were going to be dragged into this suddenly hit Abbie. 'That's ridiculous,' she said hotly. 'He wasn't even in New York when the condom turned up, he was in Paris. I spoke to him there. I'm sure George has nothing to do with this.'

'And Mr Bridges? Perhaps he is trying to make you unhappy because your relationship ended when you met Mr Hemmings.'

'Robert is busy building a new career. I would stake my life on him not being involved.'

'Then what was he doing having lunch in the hotel just after Alain's fashion show?' asked Matt swiftly. 'I saw him there.'

'You were there too, Mr Nicolaides,' said Toshiba.

'What are you trying to imply?'

'That everyone's under suspicion,' he turned to face Abbie, 'including you, Miss Lomax.'

Matt snorted. 'Are you saying she's sending condoms to herself?'

'It wouldn't be the first time somebody's used this tactic to attract publicity for themselves. For what it's worth, I don't think that's true in this case. All I'm trying to do is ensure that you don't close your minds to any possibilities, however far-fetched they might seem now,' Toshiba said evenly.

'I appreciate that,' said Abbie, 'but this is very difficult for me. I want to shield those close to me from unnecessary embarrassment as far as possible.'

Dempsey could not contain his irritation. 'Look, guys, do you need me any more?'

'No, Mr Dempsey, we're at the end of this briefing.' Toshiba looked round the room. 'You've been given the gist of the problem and all I ask is that I receive full co-operation from everyone.'

'Done,' said Dempsey before walking from the room. Matt and Jeri-Ann followed but Toshiba asked Abbie for a few moments in private.

'I hope by now you understand that I will always act in your best interests and sometimes I might have to be very direct,' he told her when they were alone.

'Go ahead.'

'How important is George Hemmings in your life?'

Abbie flushed. 'I'm not sure. We've only known each other since Christmas. I met him on the plane coming back from London.' She watched him write this down in his ever-present notebook. 'But with my schedule and his business commitments we haven't been able to spend much time together.'

'Is it special between you?' he persisted.

'My instinct is that it might develop into something special but we're not near the stage where we talk about the future.'

Again he made a note. 'You said he was in Paris when the condom turned up. Are you sure about that?'

Abbie was beginning to get irritated. 'You can't possibly

think he was connected with that filth,' she said sharply. 'I'll prove it. I'll damn well ask him right now.'

Toshiba was noncommittal. 'Good idea.'

Abbie fished out her mobile and pressed Auto 4. She did not recognise the voice that answered the phone. 'Is Shelley there, please? It's Abbie Lomax. Oh, you're covering for a few days? OK, I wonder if you could do me a favour? Could you give me Mr Hemmings' number in Paris? I've stupidly mislaid it.' The truth was she had never had the number. George always phoned her when he was out of town.

Abbie listened, then, 'Oh, I thought . . . I must have been mistaken. When will he be back?' A pause. 'I see.' She gave an embarrassed laugh. 'I can never keep up with his movements. Sorry to have bothered you.'

Toshiba watched her intently and to cover her confusion she bent her head over the phone as she switched off the power. 'There are a dozen reasons why he could have cancelled his trip without mentioning it to me,' she said a touch defiantly.

'Sure,' said Toshiba evenly.

He waited till Abbie had left the room and then rang George's office himself. When he explained his business, George came on the line and reluctantly agreed to meet him next morning in his office.

Well used to the type of man he was dealing with, Toshiba had his opening gambit prepared.

'Mr Hemmings, I don't want to take up too much of your time and I give you my word that whatever you say will go no further, unless it is relevant to my investigation. But I should point out that in my experience evasions of the truth always surface, sooner or later.'

George shifted slightly in his chair. 'What did Abbie tell you?'

'Only that you were friends, very close friends.'

'Then you know that I would never do anything to jeopardise that.'

'This is just a formality. We need to check out everyone she knows.'

'The idea that I could be a suspect is ludicrous but,' he leaned back, 'on the basis of strict confidentiality, go ahead.'

'You were supposed to be in Paris but you cancelled the trip, correct?'

'Er, no. No trip was scheduled.'

'You told Miss Lomax—'

'I lead a complicated life, Mr Toshiba. There are times when I prefer people to think I'm abroad.'

'I see. Would you mind telling me where you were last Sunday?'

'For much of the time I was here in the office, working. Unfortunately my business does not grind to a halt at weekends.'

'And the rest of the time?'

A pause. 'I was out having lunch.'

'Can you be a little more precise?'

George sat quietly, gazing at his fingers.

'I need to know how long you were out.'

'I left about two and returned to the office around six.'

'And you were with?'

George stared out of the window. 'I was with a woman friend.'

'Ah. A friend. Is she a friend in the way that Miss Lomax is a friend?'

'Yes.'

'Would she verify that she was with you?'

George sat up abruptly. 'I absolutely forbid you to approach her.'

Toshiba raised his eyebrows. 'You were away for four hours, Mr Hemmings. Enough time to have planted that condom.'

'Don't be ridiculous. Do I look like someone who would do a crazy thing like that? I wasn't even near the Globe building.'

'Where were you?'

'In this woman's apartment.'

'Anyone see you there?'

'The doorman.'

'Does he know you?'

'No.'

'So you don't go there often?'

'No.'

'I'd like the name of this woman.' When George did not answer he added, 'I would be most tactful when speaking to her.'

George swivelled his chair to face Toshiba. 'OK,' he said harshly, 'I'll tell you where I was on condition you keep away from her. You can check out the story with the doorman. You don't need to involve her. And you won't tell the doorman what this is all about.'

Toshiba nodded slowly and opened his notebook. 'Agreed.'

'I was with Katharine Sexton.'

'Miss Lomax's mother?' Toshiba's face was impassive but George flushed with annoyance.

'My private life is my business, no one else's. I can do without that holy Joe attitude. Now get out and see you stick to the deal.'

Toshiba closed his notebook. 'Thank you for your time,' he said courteously and rose to his feet.

The doorman, shown a photograph of George, confirmed that he had stayed in the apartment block all afternoon. A pity, thought Toshiba. A reason to go back and press George Hemmings a little harder would have been very satisfying. He crossed his name off the list of suspects and wished he could warn his client that her boyfriend was a sleazeball.

★ ★ ★

Katharine peered closer into the bulb-ringed mirror in her bathroom. The bruising had faded but her face still felt stiff and slightly tender. She viewed her appearance with the objectivity of a stranger, having spent many years looking at herself in monitors or on videos, dispassionately searching for flaws or unattractive mannerisms then trying to alter them. Her camera persona had become the model that television trainers pointed to as the one to imitate.

Buzz had been fulsome with praise when she stepped off the plane from Brazil. 'You look like the person I first met all those years ago,' he had said.

Buzz was the first person who knew her well to see the results of Dr Brescia's work but she did not trust his judgement; it was in his interest to boost her morale. In fact his effusive compliments alarmed her since she did not want to be too different from the Katharine who had flown off to Rio. But perhaps he was right. For a minute or two tonight, in this light, she looked more like a sister than a mother to Abbie. She had fought against having her shoulder-length hair cropped and sun-streaked but her stylist had been adamant. She was glad now. It did suit her. The change of hairstyle, the surgery and losing five pounds had cropped years off her age.

In the two days since she had been back in the office her colleagues had complimented her on how well she looked, seemingly satisfied with her bland explanation that she had been able to add fullness to her breasts over her 'working holiday' by using weights.

This story was leaked to the press and for a week or two every downtown gymnasium was over-booked by matrons hoping to achieve the same miracle. Though the press gossiped for several days, and one journalist did make a call to several well-known clinics about the possibilities of Katharine having had cosmetic surgery, the story died when, in spite of intensive efforts, no hard evidence to support the speculation emerged.

'We don't want it to get out,' said Mike, 'or it'll add fuel to the reports that we're worried about Abbie's show.'

'But we're not worried, are we?'

'Damn right we're not,' replied Mike, sounding a tad too hearty to Katharine's ear. She was about to pursue the subject but they were interrupted by a call for a team briefing.

Sam Wolfe, like many men in positions of authority, assumed full credit for her improved appearance when he saw her. 'You see, I was right. You look great. I bet now you're pleased I insisted.'

She graciously acknowledged his compliments but mentally she screamed at him, 'If ever I get real power in this business, the first thing I'll do, slug-face, is fire you for being too fat!'

This satisfying thought had created such a glow that when she smiled, the impact had lifted Sam to his feet and he had actually escorted her to the door.

Katharine turned away from her critical inspection in the bathroom mirror and went to her wardrobe. What should she wear tonight? Indecisiveness about what to wear was unlike her but she was nervous and excited about Nina's party. George would be there. Freddie was on a business trip to Rotterdam so she was going alone.

Freddie, too, had commented on how terrific she looked when he had called round to welcome her home with a large bunch of white roses, but then he always was generous with his compliments. It was George's reaction that mattered. She had spoken to him briefly on her return – for once his mobile had been switched on – and it was clear he had not recovered from his fury over her cancelling her appearance at the launch of his Manhattan hotel. He did not suggest a meeting – her punishment, she supposed, for letting him down.

She looked through a rail of skimpy dresses for the second time. The dresses, all of them designed to be worn bra-less, had been sent round by her assistant and were on loan from boutiques in Fifth Avenue, which, like many in the south of France and London's Knightsbridge, were off limits to women over size 10. Finally she selected a white one teamed with a bolero which she would wear during cocktails then take off at dinner.

When Katharine walked into Nina's crowded party forty-five minutes late, there were extravagant greetings from many familiar faces. But no George. Extricating herself as soon as was polite from a producer who insisted on telling her what seemed to an impatient Katharine the entire plot of his new film, she made her way into the dining room which was set up for a buffet supper. Unoccupied.

Finally she found George in the library, his attention completely absorbed by a leggy, limber blonde who appeared to have him on heat. They had distanced themselves from everyone else in the room and were sitting on a sofa at the far end. His body was in profile, leaning close to the young woman, an effective barrier against anyone who might want to join them. George's fingers were trailing languorously up and down her bare arm, a gesture that Katharine, devoured by jealousy, recognised well.

Turning her back on the engrossed couple, she retreated swiftly to the drawing room. It took her only seconds to get into lively conversation with the best-looking man she could find, determined not to allow her hurt and dismay to show. How ironic that on a night when she felt her most attractive for years, George should choose to ignore her.

George had choreographed the whole scene, selecting the young blonde as perfect for his purpose, guiding her towards the sofa then waiting for Katharine to discover them. Long before she knew it, he had been aware she was standing there watching them. He had turned up the heat, pleased she was observing his performance. He wanted to hurt her as badly as she had hurt his hotel launch.

At the short notice she had given him, no crowd-pulling substitute was available. He had implored Abbie to cancel her television industry dinner but she was due to give the keynote speech and even he had understood eventually that she could not snub the influential organisers.

His hotel was supposed to attract the kind of clientele who would have been there on opening night, celebrities, millionaires, opinion-formers. Katharine's absence had turned the whole event into an embarrassing disaster. The last-minute cancellations of A-list guests when they learned that Katharine was abroad meant he and his staff had almost had to pull in passers-by from the sidewalks so that the banqueting hall would look full. The positive publicity that a high-grade turnout would have generated would have done much to overcome its very high prices which building delays caused by those heritage nuts had necessitated. As it was, bookings were thin and the hotel continued to be a massive drain on his resources.

Well, his little game between mother and daughter was over. He would never forgive Katharine. And he was going to tell her that.

They acted like strangers throughout the meal and it was only after coffee was served in the drawing room that Katharine was aware that George had turned his attention towards her at last. She felt a firm grasp on her elbow.

'Let's get out of here,' he said gruffly. 'I need to talk to you.'

He steered her into Nina's lush, palm-filled conservatory with its profusion of powerfully-scented orchids and gardenias. The beauty of the flowers was wasted on them.

His gaze was insolent as his eyes travelled slowly over her body. 'You look . . . quite rested.'

Katharine ignored the half-hearted compliment and took his arm. 'I've missed you,' she said. With an almost irritable movement he moved his arm away. 'What's the matter? You're not still angry with me, are you?'

'And why shouldn't I be? You set my hotel back six months, the hotel I've had trouble with every step of the way from planning to completion.'

'George, I told you as soon as I could. I was so sorry to let you down but it was unavoidable. You know I would have been there if it had been at all possible.'

His expression was unyielding and Katharine saw a different side from the ardent lover who had wooed her all these months.

'Can you imagine what it was like for me that night?' he said harshly. 'I felt a complete fool.'

'I'm sorry. How often can I go on saying it? George, I'm not sure you can blame me for everything.'

'Oh, but I do. You didn't have to tell all your famous friends that you weren't going to make it. Once they knew that, they fell away like flies.'

'You're wrong. I didn't tell anyone anything.'

'I don't believe you. Why else didn't they turn up?'

'Are you calling me a liar?' Katharine was outraged. 'Is that what all that nonsense with the blonde was about?'

'It wasn't nonsense. I was enjoying the company of a woman who cares about more than just her own career.'

Katharine took a deep breath. 'How dare you? I've shown how much I care for you. But right from the start of our affair I've never been able to rely on you. I never know where you are half the time.'

'We're always interested in what the star wants. What the star wants, she must have,' he said sarcastically.

'I think this has gone far enough, don't you? If that's

how you feel, I think it's best if we don't meet again.' Katharine found herself issuing the ultimatum instinctively, half hoping, half expecting that he would brush it aside and revert to the George she had known and desired, still wanted.

His response was chilling. 'That's fine by me.' He shrugged his shoulders with indifference and turned to leave.

Involuntarily, Katharine put out a hand to draw him back. It caught his elbow and he glanced at her over his shoulder. 'The fact is, darling, like most of America I've already switched to the newer, younger model.'

'What on earth do you mean?'

'Ask Abbie.'

'Abbie? My Abbie?'

'No, not your Abbie. Mine. Mine for the last few months actually, as often as we can manage it.'

She stared at him, stunned. 'I – I don't believe you,' she managed to stammer.

'You don't? Well, what can I do to convince you? Let me think. I know. Does this sound familiar? Go back to your last fight with her when she, just like me, walked out on you. "You owe your entire career to me", that's what you told her. Wow, was she angry. And what was it she shouted at you? Oh yes. That you were so busy with your career you should never have had children, something like that.'

Katharine stepped back as if he had slapped her.

'And darling, there's something else,' he drawled. 'Abbie knows all about you and me. She finds the whole situation highly amusing. We both do.'

And with that he walked out of the door.

Chapter Thirteen

Abbie flung open the glass doors to the balcony and took a deep breath, revelling in the greenness of Hyde Park in the early spring morning. It was one of those cloudless English days when it was impossible to imagine grey skies.

It had been dark when she had booked in the previous night. The Gladstone was one of London's most desirable locations. Overlooking the rows of chestnuts edging a lake, it traded on its coveted reputation as the country retreat in the heart of town. Its Georgian façade masked the latest technological wizardry available to architects and designers to create luxury, convenience and efficiency. The stately-home grandeur of the Gladstone was why the hotel was able to charge a premium from those wealthy enough to afford its prices.

The frock-coated receptionist had offered Abbie the choice of two suites, one immediately above the other. 'Both have an excellent view of the flamingos in Buckingham Palace garden,' he said. 'One has been allocated to you, the other,' he examined the register, 'to Katharine Sexton. As you've arrived first, you may take your choice. May I recommend the Horatio Nelson Suite? I think the balcony is just a touch wider than the one in the Winston Churchill Suite.'

Abbie stretched again, jet lag gone, and began to relax, the fear of the Fan of Fans receding now she was out of America. Murphy's Law decreed that the minute an extremely expensive security outfit had been hired to protect her with guards at the ready, that would be the time the menace took a holiday. Perhaps the pest had taken fright at the stringent security and had decided further harassment was not worth the risk. She hoped so.

It was a pity George had pulled out of the trip. Initially he had agreed to commemorate the fifth-month anniversary of their meeting by coming with her to London. She had been elated at the prospect of being seen with him in public. And, as she told him, he would be a great support when she met her mother after months of not speaking. Unfortunately, something so urgent had cropped up that George had been forced to cancel his trip.

Abbie had shown her anger, accusing him of not making the same effort as she did. 'Why is it that you never change your plans for me, not once?' He had blustered and tried to soothe her, managing, as always, to assuage her doubts. 'I'm successful because I focus on what I need to do,' he told her. 'I allow nothing to get in the way of that, not even you, my darling. And you can't say I didn't make that clear when we first met.'

She was too proud to let him know that she wanted more from him, she wanted to be a part of his life. She understood now how Robert must have felt. But perhaps George did want a change in their relationship. Behind her in the suite was a magnificent bouquet of flowers, their sweet scent filling every corner of the connecting rooms. The card simply said, 'From an admirer' but according to the receptionist the sender was from New York and had faxed specific instructions to the manager of the hotel, a personal friend. The sender was a Mr Hemmings. It was too early to phone him, she would talk to him later.

It had been a last-minute invitation to come over to be a presenter at the prestigious International Television Awards Commission held this year in London. Unlike the

Oscars, the panel of judges for the ITAC awards was drawn from top TV personnel in five continents. The awards were not given for emotional reasons, there were no still-alive prizes or sorry-you-missed-out-last-time accolades; the recipients were all masters of their craft. It was said in Los Angeles that an ITAC award put a nought at the end of anyone's salary cheque.

ITAC's original choice as presenter had fallen ill and for a comparative newcomer like Abbie to be selected was an indication that the industry took her seriously. And as it was being held mid-week and she would be away only three days, her show would not suffer. She would be back in plenty of time to anchor the next one.

The only cloud on the horizon was meeting Katharine. That would be tricky. They were at war and it had spilled over in public yet again. In an article published only last week, Katharine had been quoted as saying, 'Young interviewers often make the mistake of not listening to the answers. It can make them appear, well, somewhat self-centred, a little selfish perhaps. Qualities,' she had laughed, 'more apparent in private.' Though she had made clear this was a general observation, not a criticism of her daughter, Abbie had taken it personally.

So when she was contacted for a quote she was ready: 'I think it's time the industry realised that young people dislike television that is bland or part of the establishment. It switches off audience and interviewer alike. Judging by our ratings, viewers seem to be responding to shows that are upfront, gutsy and have an attitude.'

It was all part of the hype surrounding speculation that the ultimate honour was about to be conferred on Kate the Great, the first woman, and the first broadcaster for many years, to be nominated for an ITAC Lifetime Achievement Award. Matt had done his best to get Abbie into another hotel but he had been told that as the ceremony was being televised from the Gladstone, ITAC preferred participants to be close to hand.

When Ed Dantry had heard from the organisers that Abbie was wanted as one of the presenters, budgets were forgotten in the excitement of a fledgling network's being accepted by their peers in this way.

'Honey, this is worldwide coverage. It's worth millions to us – and to you.' He promptly authorised the drafting in of two more freelance researchers to garner material in readiness for Abbie's return, and signed the cheque for the Gladstone Hotel without demur. At his suggestion, Globe made contact with an independent television company in London to assist in producing material that could be included in later shows. The plan was for Abbie to interview some of the world-famous celebrities who were due to attend.

Initially Abbie had been startled but pleased when Matt said he would accompany her, though he would not, of course, be staying at 'that pricey joint they picked for you'. 'All the movers and shakers in television will be there in one place,' he added. 'It won't do any harm to be seen around them. And, boy, will it put up your price when I renegotiate your contract.'

The butler designated to her suite appeared on the balcony carrying an impeccably dressed tray bearing hot croissants and freshly-squeezed orange juice. He set it down on the decorative, wrought-iron table. As Abbie darted inside to fetch her newspaper, she heard a whirring of wings and a loud squawk as an impudent pigeon swooped in and pecked at the croissants. With a laugh, Abbie shredded the remainder and threw it over the railings, watching in amusement as the bird was joined by a dozen more screeching scavengers.

Oh well, she thought, it was probably for the best. The designer of the outfit she was wearing for the awards ceremony had warned her to be very careful about her food intake if she was going to do justice to the little crimson sheath he had moulded to her body. 'No underwear, please, darling. Every line will show on camera.'

Abbie checked the time. Matt would be waiting for her in the foyer. They were going to do a spot of sightseeing before her rehearsal this afternoon.

As soon as the lift doors parted, she heard his indignant voice from the direction of a boutique. 'Look, lady, I've been all over the world and nobody's ever refused my credit card.'

The stylish sales assistant was apologetic but firm. 'I am sorry, sir, but unless you are staying here, you'll have to pay cash. I realise it's inconvenient, but it is hotel policy.'

Abbie went to his rescue. 'Take heart, Matt, you're in good company. They won't even accept credit cards, from the likes of the Murdochs and the Turners unless they're resident. What are you buying?' She peered over his shoulder at some red lingerie lying on the counter. 'My compliments to your wife, she has you well-trained.'

Matt seemed embarrassed. 'Oh, it doesn't matter,' he shrugged. 'Angela only said to bring her something delicious from London. I could buy her a cake.'

'No, no,' said Abbie firmly. 'Husbands like you need to be encouraged.' She smiled at the sales assistant. 'I'm in the Nelson Suite. Please put whatever this gentleman wants on my bill.'

'It's not important,' Matt protested, waving his hand at the assistant. 'Forget it.'

Abbie picked up a wispy suspender belt. 'They *are* for your wife, aren't they?'

'Of course! When would I have time to chase after other dames?' He took her arm and steered her out of the shop, through the busy foyer and into a taxi. Abbie had promised to show him Covent Garden.

Abbie's face was not known in Britain and as they sipped flutes of chilled Desmoiselle champagne at a pavement café beside the cobbled centre known as the

Piazza, she was undisturbed by autograph hunters. Matt pulled his gaze from the bustle and chatter of the poseurs strolling ostentatiously through the square and noticed that she was staring reflectively into her glass.

'What's up?'

'Oh, I'm dreading meeting my mother and when I do the vultures are going to be out there watching for any sign of the feud.'

'I know you're unhappy about the press but don't knock that feud,' said Matt, his eye caught by a busker in a leopard-skin leotard who had locked himself in chains for the benefit of a circle of sightseers. 'It's electrified Sunday-night viewing and given your show a real buzz.' He sipped his champagne. 'Terrific for ratings.'

Abbie slammed her glass down. 'I know television's a cynical industry but I never thought I'd hear you say something quite so stupid, so . . . insensitive. Goddammit, Matt, my mother and I haven't talked for months. She's booked into the suite right above mine and I'm nervous about seeing her. My own mother. And you talk about ratings!' She jumped up. 'I'll see you back at the hotel.'

'Aw, Abbie, don't take it like that. I'm sorry, my mouth runs away with me sometimes . . .'

She didn't stop to listen. Matt was still fumbling for his money to pay the bill when a double-decker tourist coach rumbled to a stop on the cobbled street. Agitated banging on the windows made Abbie look up and she saw with dismay that the coach passengers, obviously tourists from America, had recognised her and were trying to catch her attention, some attempting to photograph her through the glass.

Whoosh. The pneumatically-operated doors opened and a phalanx of passengers rushed down the steps. Stumbling over the cobbles, about twenty of them began running towards Abbie, shouting her name and waving.

Like a stag at bay she stood motionless until Matt charged in. He grabbed her hand and pulled her down the road at a run. After a few seconds, conscious of the curious stares of passing office workers, Abbie panted, 'Have they given up?'

Without slowing his pace, Matt looked over his shoulder. 'All but one of the fittest pensioners you ever saw.'

Abbie started giggling.

'Come on, step on it. He's catching up.'

'No, wait.' Abbie came to a halt and narrowly avoided colliding with the elderly man. 'You win,' she told her fan, holding her aching side. 'I can't compete.'

'You didn't have a chance, young lady,' he agreed. 'I ran for the Olympics in 1956. The marathon.'

'Oh,' gasped Abbie.

'Yup, I'm seventy years old and I still run every day. Now, your autograph, if you please.'

Abbie gave it willingly, then asked for his address. He might be an interesting person to come on her show.

Matt noticed that the rest of the passengers had spotted their idol talking to one of their number and were moving towards her. He raced towards the coach driver. They had a brief conversation and then the driver suddenly blew a whistle, loud and sharp. The group stopped, turned, looked at the driver urgently beckoning them towards him. Obediently the pack turned and in a few minutes had reboarded the coach which slowly drove off down the road.

'How did you do that?'

'Told him the truth. You didn't want to be bothered right now so could he get 'em back on board and circle the block.'

'You see, that's the British for you,' said Abbie, walking towards the Savoy Hotel where she was reasonably confident they would find a taxi. 'It's the war spirit, you know. The instinct lives on, makes them sum up the situation fast. Someone needs help, they give help.'

'Yeah, you're right,' said Matt. 'Musta been the war spirit.' He raised a hand to hail a cruising taxi. 'But the twenty pounds I gave him sure didn't hurt.'

She laughed as she climbed into the cab. Matt followed, a wary expression on his face.

'About what I said back there, I'm sorry. OK?' She nodded. 'Friends?'

'Friends with an agent?' She smiled. 'Don't push your luck.'

The digital display at the front of London-bound Concorde registered Mach 2. They were flying above the speed of sound but Katharine paid no attention to it or to the sumptuous feast offered by British Airways. Nor could she concentrate on learning the acceptance speech which might or might not be needed the next day. She was cocooned in a world of pain, not physical as her cosmetic surgery had been, but emotional and therefore harder to bear.

There had been a choice of two Concorde flights to London that day. Katharine had chosen the less convenient one, certain that most of those attending the ceremony would have flown earlier. She could not face bright, intelligent conversations all the way across the Atlantic.

She was dreading the next couple of days. It was ironic that she should be feeling so miserable when she was in the running to be the first lady of her profession. Only one other broadcaster, Walter Cronkite, had walked away with ITAC's Lifetime Achievement prize, and it had never been given to a woman.

She briefly considered turning down the invitation but the organisers had persuaded her to attend. They understood, as did Katharine and everyone else, that without an impressive presence of American heavyweights an international awards ceremony would not be representative of the world's television industry.

She already had a display cabinet crammed with prizes, two Emmys for top news anchor and miscellaneous plaques gained for her work on programmes achieving the highest viewing figures. But the ITAC accolade was regarded in the industry as the big one, putting the recipient into a tiny group of television near-immortals. The commercial benefits that winning the award would bring her would be more than welcome in her present financial circumstances. Ever realistic, however, Katharine appreciated that though she was the only nominee from the States in her category, there were several other candidates, notably from the UK and Canada.

When she learned that Abbie had been asked to be a presenter, her first instinct had been to cancel her flight to London. But what possible reason could she give, not just to the ITAC organisers but to Buzz and Sam Wolfe? ABN had a stake in this too, after all. And the gossip columnists would have a field day. Their appetites were already aroused by the fact that both mother and daughter had been invited to the ceremony.

Since George's shocking revelation, Katharine had found her will to concentrate on work taxed to its limit. She could not rid her mind of the image of George and Abbie together. At first she had told herself that he was lying, he was just hitting out at her. On several occasions she had started to phone Abbie but each time she picked up the receiver George's words would echo and re-echo in her brain: 'She knows all about you . . . finds the whole situation highly amusing . . . we both do,' and she would slam the instrument down savagely. No. George would not dare lie about something she could so easily check. He had to be telling the truth. How else could he know the actual words of their bitter quarrel?

Abbie. Her daughter.

They had talked about her in bed. *They had laughed about her.*

How the hell had she and Abbie got to this point in their lives? It had never for a moment occurred to Katharine that a lover would ever come between them. Abbie's father, money, the job, yes. But not this.

George had taken such pleasure in imparting the cruel news and undoubtedly he would have relayed details of their row to Abbie by now. Abbie was not presenting the award for her category yet at some stage they would have to acknowledge each other. Somewhere she would have to find the strength to stand alongside her daughter and aim a rictus grin at the cameras. She would have to set her inner dial on autopilot, keep emotion under strict control and discipline her body language. Never once must she allow anyone, least of all Abbie, to glimpse for one second how utterly humiliated she felt.

Her dark thoughts were interrupted by the flight stewardess offering her a glass of chilled champagne. Katharine waved it away but could not resist the Beluga caviar spread liberally on a piece of Melba toast.

She could understand how Abbie had fallen for George, but where had the two of them met? George had said the affair had been going on for months. For some men, and clearly George was one of them, bedding a mother and daughter would be a terrific coup, particularly when they were both media celebrities. Had he ever gone straight from her bed to Abbie's? Once again Katharine tried to close her mind to the mental picture of George making love to Abbie but the killer question persisted: *had he preferred her daughter's firm young body?*

Why hadn't she suspected that he was seeing another woman? Pieces of the appalling jigsaw began to mesh. The cancelled dates when he had to 'go out of town' at the last moment, his vagueness about his movements, his excuses when he had not been in touch. He probably saw lots of other women – in Rome, Paris, wherever he owned hotels, no doubt. But never, never, did she suspect her own daughter. God, she had been such a fool.

And not just with George but with other men. Her duplicitous accountant. Her boss. If only she could walk away from her job, her fame, her old life. David Crozier had stolen more than her financial stability, he had stolen her independence. She no longer controlled her own destiny, Sam Wolfe did. Those who said money did not matter were naive optimists. A hefty bank balance enabled anyone to snub the likes of this entire Concorde passenger list and parachute out of the difficulties of life.

They were due to land in forty minutes and Katharine decided to do a 'Joan Collins'; she would repair to the lavatory to change her outfit and regain some sort of tranquillity.

The smiling stewardess retrieved her red crepe two-piece from the aircraft's ample hanging space. Most passengers travelled with hand luggage only so they did not have to wait at baggage carousels. One of the make-up staff at the network had organised a collection of miniature lotions and potions for her, everything she would need to cleanse, revitalise and apply a fresh image. The British press kept a soft spot for her somewhere in their suits of armour, as they did for all ex-pats who had done well abroad; they would be out in force at the airport and the hotel.

Despite her misery Katharine felt some pleasure at the thought of returning to her old haunts. She was coming home. London had been swinging in her youth and apparently it was swinging again. Pity she had missed it both times, the first because she was too young to take part in the nightly fiestas around Soho and now because she would only be there for a couple of days.

As Katharine left the baggage collection area she found

a uniformed chauffeur holding up a placard bearing her name. Her greeting was followed by blinding flashes from photographers gathered to record her arrival and she rushed through, smile fixed in place, grateful that the driver's colleague was waiting in the car, engine idling, ready for a swift getaway to her hotel.

For London she had to put on a brave face.

Abbie was lying on the pillows purring down the phone.

'George . . . oh,' she groaned. 'That's naughty. And so cruel when I'm three thousand miles away.' She wriggled. 'No, no, that's a waste . . .' She gave a half-stifled laugh. 'I'd rather wait till I get my hands on you in person. And I hope this line isn't—. Blast, someone's knocking on the door. Don't go, I'll get rid of them.'

The slender mustachioed young man in the doorway was holding a basket of hairdressing accoutrements.

'Oh, of course. Come in. Sorry, I thought you were coming later.'

As the hairdresser entered, a tentative smile on his face, Abbie raced back to the telephone. 'George, sorry, it's someone to do my hair,' she said in a low voice. 'This telephonic congress will have to be postponed for a few hours.' She blew a kiss down the receiver, ''Bye till then,' and turned to the hairdresser.

'Sorry, I'm not quite ready. I'll just have a very quick shower and wash my hair. I won't be long.' Then she paused. It was lovely not to have a guard with her in London and there was no reason to suspect this young man but she had promised Toshiba she would not take any chances.

'Do you have any identification?'

He pointed to his lapel which bore a name badge and the hotel's logo. 'I've got this,' he said, 'or you could phone the salon downstairs.'

'No, it's OK. I'll only be a few minutes.'

Less than ten minutes later Abbie seated herself at the dressing table. She had brought a publicity shot of herself which she showed the hairdresser and asked him to duplicate the hairstyle. He was obviously a man of few words and as the mirror did not extend further than the top of her head and reflected only his capable hands, she felt no necessity to make small talk.

It was such a pity her father was out of the country. There were aspects of her relationship with George that she would have liked to discuss with him. She was relieved that she was not being paraded on George's arm like a trophy. But, why did he insist on keeping their relationship such a secret? Perhaps her father could come up with an explanation. Regular phone calls kept Milo up-to-date with what she was doing and who she met. They stopped well short of exchanging details about their respective sex lives, but she would have welcomed her father's advice on dealing with a sophisticated older man. Wouldn't you know it, just when she was in London he had to fly out to Cape Town.

'Spray, madam?' the hairdresser interrupted softly.

'No, thank you, I'll do that just before I go out.'

She tipped him when he left and then laid out her black silk tights on the bed and checked through her evening bag. Her dress, encased in cellophane, was hanging in the wardrobe. At the second fitting, the seamstress had pinned the satisfyingly heavy crepe in folds so the material clung like a second skin, supporting and lifting her cleavage. Rarely had she felt so sexy. Abbie hoped it would give her the confidence she would need to face such a critical, glittering audience, one that included her mother.

She was about to take the dress out when the phone rang. It was Matt.

'I'm with the head of current affairs at BBC Television,' he explained. 'Could you spare a few minutes to come down and meet him?'

'Now? I'm getting ready for the ceremony.'

Matt had warned her that he was trying to arrange a meeting. The BBC executive thought her British background and American experience ideal for an upcoming series of interviews which they planned to target at both UK and US audiences.

'I know you have to get ready but there won't be time after the awards and he's leaving for Johannesburg early in the morning. It won't take long.'

Abbie wanted the experience of working with the BBC. It would mean spending time in London and she would be able to see more of her father. She stepped into a navy-blue coat dress, taking care not to disarray her hair or smudge her make-up, and went downstairs.

The promised short meeting extended to half an hour and Abbie fairly ran back to her suite to get dressed. She doubted if anything would happen with the BBC quickly but she had promised to fax some ideas for interview subjects.

She hurried through the door, switched on the lights, and walked into the dressing room. She sat down on the stool in front of the mirror to touch up her make-up and fix the false lashes she had not had time to apply earlier. Then she got up and went to the wardrobe. She took out her dress and carefully pulled off the cellophane. It took only a second or two before she absorbed what had happened.

Jagged slashes had ripped the thick material from bodice to hem. Her dress, her beautiful dress, was ruined. Unwearable.

'Oh my God.' Abbie sank to her knees, aghast. 'I can't believe it. I just can't believe it,' she mumbled out loud, fighting back the tears. Who could have done this? Why?

Then the panic started. She felt a wrenching in her stomach, like the grip of an internal fist. What if the slasher was still here in the suite, next door in the bedroom or in the bathroom? She edged her way stealthily to the door and rushed out into the corridor straight into the butler. Quickly she told him what had happened. He went into her suite immediately to search it thoroughly while she waited outside, trembling. The butler found no sign of anybody. Abbie asked him to phone Matt and within minutes he was with her.

Abbie was inconsolable. 'Who could have done this?' she wept. 'It couldn't be an ordinary burglar, nothing else seems to have been taken. Look, here's my money, still intact.' She opened a large, flat wallet. 'Here's the jewellery I'm supposed to be wearing tonight. Why didn't they take that?' She gazed at him, her face streaked with dribbles of grey mascara. 'Why would somebody do this? What have I done to make a person hate me so much?'

Matt put his arm firmly round her shoulder and sat her down on the sofa. 'I've asked the butler to get hold of hotel security. They'll be here soon. And I'm going to phone Toshiba but we've got to stay calm and think this out.'

'Calm!' The tears began welling up again. 'It must have happened when I was downstairs with you. Nobody's been here except the hotel hairdresser. Matt, think if I'd been here, this maniac might have attacked me instead of my dress. And it's ruined. What am I going to wear now?' Abbie began to nibble her nails, something she had not done since she was a teenager.

'Shit, Abbie, looks to me like somebody's trying to destabilise you, maybe even trying to stop you going to that ceremony tonight.'

'But who?'

Matt hesitated. 'I don't like saying this, kid, but who has most to gain if you're not there?'

She stared at him uncomprehendingly.

'Your mother's network,' he said harshly. 'Don't look at me like that. I can't help thinking that someone in her station has to be involved somehow.'

Abbie was so taken aback she stopped crying.

'Think about it,' he went on. 'All those things that have happened. It's got to be her people behind this. And if it is them, your mother must know what they're up to.'

'My mother? You can't be serious.'

'Look at the facts. You two haven't spoken for months. You have no idea what poison they're pouring into her. According to Jeri-Ann those people are vicious about you when they're in competition for interviews. They're desperate to stay at number one. I don't see how your mother could stay aloof from all that.'

Abbie made an enormous effort to gain control of her racing thoughts and said abruptly, 'I can't believe it but there's only one way to find out.' She grabbed the slashed dress and ran wildly along the corridor, too impatient to wait for the lift.

Matt raced after her. 'Wait, wait. Let me go with you.'

'No,' she threw over her shoulder. 'This is something I must sort out myself.'

So intent was she on confronting her mother that she had no recollection of racing up the stairs. All she was conscious of was bashing her fist against the door of the Winston Churchill Suite.

Katharine's face registered shock when she saw her distraught daughter. Abbie pushed brusquely past then wheeled round and flourished the dress.

'This is the dress I'm supposed to be wearing tonight,' she screamed. 'Look at it, just look. It's been ruined.' And she flung it on to the carpet.

Katharine bent over to examine the ripped dress, an expression of mounting anxiety on her face.

Abbie gave a swift look around the living room and then ran into the bedroom. After inspecting the dressing-table top, she began opening and closing drawers, scrabbling through the contents.

'Would you mind telling me what you're looking for?' Katharine asked sharply from the bedroom door.

'Scissors, a knife, anything that can cut,' replied Abbie tensely. She was on her knees searching under the valance of the four-poster bed.

Katharine's eyes glittered angrily. 'You think I'd do this?' she shouted, holding the dress aloft by its shoulder strap. 'To my own daughter? That's pretty rich coming from you after what *you've* done to *me*.'

Abbie flashed her a belligerent look. 'You're not still going on about that bloody Steve Stone business, are you?'

'I'm not talking about him.'

'Then what?'

'You can't think of anything else you've done against me?'

'No.'

'Are you saying you don't remember fucking my lover?'

'Freddie?' Abbie's voice was incredulous.

'You know damn well it's not him,' said Katharine venomously.

The two women faced each other like gladiatorial combatants squaring up in an arena.

'He's the only boyfriend I know about,' said Abbie finally.

'Don't pretend with me.'

'Who the hell are you talking about?'

'George Hemmings.'

Abbie gaped at her. George? *George and her mother?* It wasn't possible.

'Don't try denying it. He told me himself.'

'I've no intention of denying that I've been having an affair with George Hemmings,' retorted Abbie. 'Why should I? I'm not married and neither is he. But you've been going out with Freddie as long as I and anyone else can remem . . .' Abbie's voice faltered and died as she realised what Katharine had said. 'What do you mean he told you himself?'

Every line of Katharine's body was tense. 'I've been having an affair with him since last summer.'

'You're making this up. I don't believe you,' Abbie gasped.

'I've been to his penthouse for dinner dozens of times. Mario's the name of his chef and Wendy, the housekeeper, is the one who brings a glass of vintage champagne once she's taken the coats.' Katharine saw the colour drain from Abbie's face. 'He drives a Mercedes coupé, his bedroom is painted royal blue, he uses Versace aftershave. Shall I go on?'

Abbie was speechless.

'There's no point in denying you knew he was having an affair with me at the same time. He told me you didn't mind. He even quoted what we said to each other in that row we had before you left my apartment.'

Eventually Abbie found her voice. 'Do you really think that I,' and she put great emphasis on the word, 'would want to have anything to do with a man who was screwing my own mother?' Tears of anger and anguish welled up. She turned her back so Katharine would not see her distress. Her mother was so obviously speaking the truth. Katharine was not playing games.

George, the man she loved, was having an affair with her mother.

'If you were looking for a way to hurt me, you've succeeded.' Katharine's voice was also tearful. 'I don't understand you. I never did. You seem capable of anything these days.'

Abbie turned on her. 'You always believe the worst of me,' she shouted through her tears. 'You never give me the benefit of the doubt.'

Katharine was so taken aback by her anguish she began to have doubts. 'He told me you knew all about me but you didn't care.' Katharine's eyes registered the hurt she was feeling. 'And he said you were both amused by the situation, laughed about it.'

'How could you believe such a thing? It's all lies. I knew nothing about you, nothing at all. *Oh God.*' Abbie slumped on to the bed and put her head in her hands.

Katharine came and sat beside her. Tentatively she put a hand on Abbie's arm. 'I believe you, Abbie.'

Abbie raised her tear-streaked face and looked at her mother. 'I thought I was in love with him. He was . . . so different from my other boyfriends, the opposite of Robert, and he was a challenge, I could never pin him down . . . Oh Mum, I'm so sorry for everything. He's made such a fool of me.'

'Of both of us. And I'm sorry too. I wish I'd had the guts to confront you about what he said but I thought I'd just be making an even bigger idiot of myself.'

Abbie took both her mother's hands in hers. 'George could never have got away with this if we'd been speaking to each other.'

'I agree. As soon as he realised we had no contact, there was no danger of him being found out. And we were never seen together. That was my doing. I didn't want to hurt Freddie. He doesn't know about George.' Katharine paused. 'Freddie's still a dear friend but we're no longer lovers.'

Abbie looked pensive. 'George and I were never seen together either. He told me he wanted to keep me all to himself in the penthouse. Now I know why. God, he's a shit. I never want to set eyes on him again.' She was silent for a moment. 'What on earth made him tell you all those lies?'

'He was angry with me because I had to pull out of the launch for his new hotel.'

'Good God,' said Abbie, 'so he said those terrible things to you just because he didn't get his own way for once. And we made it so easy for him.' She sighed heavily. 'Look where this rivalry has got us. For a few minutes I actually thought my own mother had something to do with my dress getting slashed. Matt said you and your people were the only ones to gain from it and I leapt to the wrong conclusion.'

Katharine showed her anger. 'What an irresponsible thing for him to suggest. My station might fight hard to win in the workplace but to imagine I'd be party to anything so malicious, that's outrageous.'

'I think it was the shock of seeing the state of the dress and I suppose he's influenced by this propaganda war.'

The phone shrilled and both women jumped.

'My nerves are shot to hell,' said Abbie as Katharine took the call.

'It's Matt.' She handed the receiver to her daughter who quickly informed him that they needed to find another culprit.

'That fits in with what I've just heard,' he told her. 'Will you please apologise to your mother on my behalf. I guess I went a little crazy. I'm coming up now.'

Matt had astonishing news. The young man who had so skilfully styled Abbie's hair was unknown at the hotel's beauty salon. Her appointment with them had been cancelled earlier that afternoon by someone claiming to be her personal assistant.

'So who on earth was he?' Abbie asked. 'He was wearing a hotel name badge.'

'Easy enough to forge,' said Matt, 'though it's more likely he filched it from the salon. Thank God he only went for your dress,' he added fervently.

'He must have done it when I went for a quick shower. He arrived earlier than the appointment time. Maybe he thought I wouldn't be there. But how the hell did he find out I was having my hair done in my room?'

That was the first thing Matt had checked out. Abbie

had been interviewing visiting celebrities for her show and he had discovered that her schedule had been photocopied for many of the crew. He also told her the salon's appointment book lay open on the desk for anyone to see. 'And now, on top of everything else, I've had four British papers on to me already.'

'I'm not surprised,' said Katharine. 'The British tabloids have a formidable net of informants, this hotel's probably riddled with them. So is the police force.'

'I'm rushing out a short statement,' said Matt, 'but I advise you to say nothing, absolutely nix. There's no way reporters can get to you inside the hotel but they'll be camped out front. At some point the police will want to talk to you, of course. At the moment they're downstairs in your suite looking for fingerprints which they will cross-check with those of the hotel staff but they're not very hopeful this will give them anything useful. I've been in touch with Toshiba and brought him up to date. He'll probably call you later.' With that, Matt left them to give the hotel's security staff a hard time.

Abbie began to pace the floor relentlessly. 'When I think of what that freak could have done I get goose bumps. He was touching my hair, for God's sake. He had scissors in his basket. If I hadn't taken a shower while he was there, he wouldn't have been able to slash the dress, so what alternatives did he have up his sleeve – still has?' Abbie stopped pacing and sat down on the bed. 'I'm really not looking forward to going out in front of all those people. He might still be hovering around and when he sees the ruined dress hasn't stopped me going to the ceremony, God knows what he'll do.'

'Look, the slashed dress was scare tactics,' said Katharine. 'If he had meant to harm you he had plenty of opportunity. I promise not to leave your side all night, and I think it would be a good idea if you came up here and shared this suite.'

Abbie gratefully accepted the offer. Both of them were well aware that there was much still to settle between them but now was not the time.

The maids and butlers on both floors helped carry up Abbie's clothes and hang them in the spare wardrobe in her mother's bedroom. Abbie's valuables, her make-up and other bits and pieces were handed over in silver-rimmed antique glass bowls by the butler.

Katharine checked her watch. 'We haven't much time before the ceremony begins.'

'What the hell am I going to wear, Mum?'

'How about this?' Katharine held up a black silk sheath dress.

Abbie was certain she had intended to wear it herself; it had been hanging on the outside of the wardrobe. 'I can't take that,' she protested.

'Oh yes you can. I brought my favourite little emerald number along as insurance and I'll be just as happy in that.'

'But you wore it for the Oscars. You don't want to wear it again.'

Katharine smiled. 'That dress did me no harm then, did it?' Indeed it had been the subject of a headline in *Women's Wear Daily*: 'Katie Comes Out On Top'. They had voted her décolletage the most 'outstanding of the night'. On that occasion her breasts had been lifted by a platform of foam padding. This time, thanks to Dr Brescia, that would not be needed.

'Well, that's very generous of you,' said Abbie. 'I really appreciate it.'

'Now how can I help you get ready?'

'If you could just lay everything out, I'll re-do my eyes.' Abbie reached into the bowl containing her make-up. As she rummaged around for eye drops she spotted a florist's card with a typewritten message on it. She was about to put it away safely so she could write a thank you note later when the signature jumped out at her and she let out a scream.

'What's the matter,' asked Katharine, alarmed.

Ashen-faced, Abbie held out the card. It read: 'The dress was too good for a bitch like you. Watch out. Fan of Fans.'

'Oh my God. That's the weirdo who sent you the drawing at the fashion show. He's followed you to London?'

'I've had a series of messages from him,' said Abbie, her voice shaking.

Katharine was appalled when she heard how the Fan of Fans had been disrupting her daughter's life. 'Why didn't you let me know, at least when it got serious enough to call in Nick Toshiba?'

'You were away and Dad flew over. I don't know what I'd have done without him.'

Katharine took her daughter's hand. 'I'm sorry I wasn't there for you. All I can say is that I intend to be from now on.'

'Thanks, because I'm really scared.'

'We must let the police have this and sort out security,' said Katharine briskly. 'We know this bastard wants you to miss the ceremony,' she went on. 'Well, you're not going to. So you finish getting ready and I'll get on to the police and then the ITAC organisers to say you'll be slightly late. And we'll go down together. I don't want you to be left alone, not for one second.'

As the two women stepped down the curving staircase with camera lenses protruding between the marbled balustrades, there was a barrage of shouts from the paparazzi and a frenzy of clicking and flashes. The photographers were quick to recognise the news value of a picture of the warring TV queens in the same frame.

The story was that these two had not been speaking to each other but here they were, smiling, arms linked, apparently on very friendly terms. If it was an act, it was a good one. The old hands suspected a publicity cover-up but, like their rivals, they pleaded for 'just one more, please . . . Abbie, a little closer, thank you. Turn to me, to me . . . just one more, please?'

As Abbie and Katharine stood there, posing for the photographers, not even these trained observers could discern any trace of their turmoil. Beaming broadly for the cameras, Abbie murmured, 'Do you think that bastard is one of them?'

'Whoever he is,' said Katharine, sounding more confident than she felt, 'we'll get him. Don't worry.'

The three camera crews elected to represent the hundreds of organisations that had applied for filming rights snaked their way through the crowds. Outside, lines of mounted police and security guards had been drafted in to control thousands of eager fans struggling to see the celebrities. Television buyers from as far afield as Malaysia, Uzbekistan and Beijing were vying with each other to clinch deals on syndicated material the West had been enjoying for years. Katharine's series was already being bought by eight English-speaking countries worldwide and Abbie's was fast catching up with five companies committed to purchase so far.

The superb meal before the presentation was a gourmet's delight but Katharine, moving the food around her plate, passed the time in a daze. She found herself unable to make small talk and her fellow diners attributed her silence to pre-award nervousness. Looking across frequently to the table on the right where her daughter was seated, she saw that Abbie's posture was rigid and her smile tight. She, too, kept turning her head, as if searching. Katharine was overcome with compassion. Abbie seemed so vulnerable. She would have given anything to be the target of this enmity rather than let her daughter be the victim.

Abbie showed no sign of her inner turmoil when, poised and smiling, she presented one of the evening's prizes, watched by her mother.

Katharine felt her arm being shaken gently and started with fright.

'Sorry, Katharine,' said her neighbour, the European head of ABN. 'I thought you hadn't realised it's nearly your turn. They're about to read out the nominations. Good luck.'

On the podium the spotlight was on the chairman of the judging panel. 'The field this year was exceptionally strong,' he said, 'but I am happy to tell you that the decision was unanimous. The winner of the ITAC award for Lifetime Achievement in Television is,' and he paused theatrically, 'a woman whose poise and authority lends credence to every report she presents.'

Her neighbour was already giving Katharine a nudge.

'Ladies and gentlemen, Miss Katharine Sexton.'

The room erupted with genuine delight. Katharine was a popular choice with her colleagues and the cameras captured a delighted daughter leading the standing ovation.

As Katharine passed Abbie on the way back to her table, she offered the bronze winged figurine for inspection, whispering, 'One day this will be yours.'

The pleasure on Abbie's face would have delighted any editor in search of a front page cover but it was a picture that the cameras missed.

Mother and daughter slipped away as early as was decent and Katharine, having eaten nothing, ordered mushroom omelettes from room service.

'We must be able to work out between us who your tormentor is,' she said, unzipping her dress and putting on a towelling robe.

'Don't think I haven't spent many sleepless hours going over and over it,' said Abbie. 'It has to be someone who knows me well and at one time or another I've suspected everyone around me. He seems to be able to get near me at will, even here. There's no hiding place. Presumably he hired that hairdresser.'

Katharine walked to the window and stared out at the glittering skyline. 'I hate to say this and you're not going to like it but there's only one person I keep coming back to. One who knows everything about you. Your movements, your phone numbers, where you live and who you lunch with. Matt Nicolaides.'

Abbie laughed out loud. 'Mum, he has more to lose than I have if I crack up. There's no logic in that. What could possibly be his motive?'

'Logic doesn't come into motive, not if he has an obsession about you. Who knows why people do these things? You can't deny he's the only person who knows as much about your movements as you do.'

'But Matt's been supportive every step of the way, bullying me into doing things even when I don't want to,' Abbie replied, 'suggesting I go to receptions to see and be seen, insisting I do interviews when I can't be bothered. He's into raising my off-screen profile all the time. Hardly the actions of someone who wants me to fail.' She leaned back, exhaustion threatening to take over.

'There's something else in his favour,' she continued wearily. 'Toshiba and his staff have checked and re-checked everybody on the show in New York and that includes Matt and his staff, in Chicago as well as in New York. They've all been given a clean bill of health.'

'Well, I can't argue with that but whoever's doing this knows a damn lot about you, that's all I can say. I wish I'd known about this ghastly mess earlier.'

'I was desperate to tell you about it. That's why I asked you to lunch. It was such a shame you had to cancel.'

'I didn't cancel. It was the other way round. I'd been sitting at the restaurant table half an hour when I realised you weren't coming. I was furious. I thought you'd left it rather late to stand me up. And then to put the lid on things, I was told you'd gone shopping.'

'I only went shopping because . . .' She paused. 'That's strange, we had to reschedule all the recordings so I could meet you and then just before I was going to leave for the restaurant I got a message that you couldn't make it. I was angry and upset with you because I'd told you I wanted to discuss this lunatic. And then when you didn't phone I was so hurt.'

'We were set up,' said Katharine. 'And whoever wanted to keep us at loggerheads succeeded. Who gains by that?'

'I don't know. Certainly not Matt, though he does believe your station will do anything to do us down.'

'We can play tough, I'll acknowledge that. But as far as I'm concerned, never dirty.'

'Like I'm supposed to have done in the Steve Stone business?'

A wary look passed over Katharine's face but Abbie plunged on.

'Now you have to hear me out on this.'

Carefully she explained what had taken her to Disco 2000 and exactly what had happened at the club and afterwards.

'So you see, I had nothing to do with Steve pulling out of your show.'

Katharine took this on board and then said slowly, 'It's true we only had the agent's word for it and I didn't ask him about you because he was too keen to make amends. At that stage I was anxious to get Steve on screen. But why would he make up such a desperate lie? I've known him for years.'

'I don't know. Maybe Steve pulled out originally because something happened to his partner and he needed to be with him. It was something we talked about at the time, that when someone close to him needed him, he'd go.'

'You could be right,' said Katharine. 'Whatever the reason, I'm very sorry that I doubted you and that I took his word rather than yours.'

'Thank you for that,' said Abbie quietly. 'I suppose we'd been fed so much bile to drive up the hype, we were ready to believe almost anything. The problem is, you end up trusting no one.'

'Do you feel you can trust me now?'

'Of course.' Abbie blinked back tears. 'In an odd way I'm almost glad my dress was slashed because otherwise I don't think we'd be sitting here sorting all this out. I'm so sorry for everything that's happened between us.'

For a moment Katharine caught a glimpse of the daughter she had known in childhood, gentle, sweet-natured and brave enough to show her vulnerability.

'What a lot we have to make up, Abbie. So many missed moments, so many lost memories. I blame myself. I could have – should have – been there more, done more to start the healing. I've been putting too much energy behind the wrong priorities. I know that now.'

Abbie chewed her lip. 'No, I have to admit it wasn't always your fault. I deliberately misunderstood you sometimes. I behaved like a pig.'

Gratified that Abbie accepted some responsibility for their difficulties, Katharine chose her next words carefully. So often in the past she had been misinterpreted. 'I wanted to contact you many times over the last few months. But I held back because ever since you were a teenager we haven't been the best of friends.'

Abbie nodded. 'I suppose I felt that sometimes you didn't understand what I was going through.'

'Well, I thought I did but obviously I didn't communicate that to you. My long hours didn't help and whenever I did try to make amends, somehow it didn't come out right and we ended up misunderstanding each other.'

'I knew you were reaching out,' said Abbie, 'but I was so angry with you, for such a long time. I suppose I felt that I wasn't important enough to you. Holding back was the only way I could punish you.'

'Abbie, if you had the impression you weren't the most important person in my life, then I don't blame you for how you behaved. If it's any consolation to you, I've punished myself, believe me.'

Abbie put her arms round her mother. 'Oh Mum, there've been times when I've missed you so much.'

Katharine returned the hug and kissed her. 'So have I,' she said, the tears clinging to her lashes. 'From now on, you're not going to face problems alone. There is one good thing that's come out of all this madness. It's helped me get my priorities straight. I'm trying to get out of my contract. I want to quit my job.'

Abbie was aghast. 'That's crazy talk. You're still the best, you shouldn't leave. Why on earth would you want to? Because of us?'

'Well, mostly. I did think that if I took myself out of the equation you would see me not as a television rival but as a mum again. But it was also because the network ordered me to have cosmetic surgery.'

'They ordered you?' Abbie was perplexed.

Katharine nodded. ' "Kate the Great" doesn't even have control over her own body.'

'I can understand why you resent being told to do it but is it so bad? Everybody I meet these days seems to have something or other done.'

'That's not the point, Abbie. I probably wouldn't have minded having some nips and tucks. But this wasn't my choice. Not the timing, not anything.'

'Except that I think you look fabulous. However much it cost . . .'

'Plenty.'

'. . . Whatever you went through . . .'

'Plenty.'

'It was worth it. They'll take you for my sister.'

Yes, that was the trouble, thought Katharine.

'So why didn't you walk if you felt so strongly about it?'

'I couldn't afford to.'

'But you've earned top dollar for years. You must be rolling in money.'

'Huh.' Katharine gave a bitter laugh. 'That's another area of my life I didn't pay enough attention to. I've been swindled, Abbie.' She gave Abbie a succinct résumé of David Crozier's disastrous gamble with her capital. 'Learn from my mistakes, Abbie. Keep control of your life.' She went to the dressing table and sat down.

'That sounds good in theory,' said Abbie as Katharine took a dollop of make-up remover from a jar and began applying it liberally to her face and neck. 'But I have no control over what the Fan of Fans will do next.'

'You could have,' Katharine swivelled round to face her, 'if instead of waiting for him to strike, we go after him.'

'How could we do that? I don't want to sound defeatist but if Toshiba and the station's security people haven't tracked him down, what chance have we?'

'We could try to work out his agenda.'

'How?'

'I have an advantage over the security staff, and Mr Toshiba for that matter,' said Katharine. 'I'm a woman. I bet I'll be able to help you remember details about all this business that you've forgotten. And if it is a loose cannon at my station, surely I'm best placed to help?'

'OK, I'm willing,' said Abbie.

'Right, let's take the hairdresser. Start from the beginning, the minute you opened the door of your suite and saw him standing there.'

Carefully Katharine went over the ground with Abbie, using as much skill as on her most withdrawn interview subjects. In this way she elicited precise information about the hairdresser's appearance and the phraseology of the few words he did say.

Katharine stretched wearily. 'I haven't come up with anything that strikes me – yet.' She yawned, easing her bra strap across her shoulder. 'God, I'm tired.'

Abbie sat up. 'Do that again.'

'Do what?'

'What you did with your bra.'

Katharine twanged the strap again. 'This?'

'That's it. The hairdresser did that. That's a very feminine gesture, isn't it?'

'Maybe he's a transvestite.'

'But what transvestite lifts a bra strap instinctively, with such a natural gesture?' Abbie asked hurriedly. 'That comes from years of wearing the damn things.'

Katharine seemed doubtful.

'Don't you see, Mum? We've been assuming all along that the Fan of Fans is a man. What if it's a woman? It all makes more sense.'

'But what about the condom?'

'If you wanted to disguise your gender you might do that. It was filled with jelly, not the real thing, so it could have been a woman. Toshiba pointed that out.'

'Then think who it could be. Who have you upset so much that she has a grudge?'

Abbie hesitated only for a second. 'The obvious one is Blanche Casey. She had her nose pushed firmly out of joint when I moved to New York.'

'But she isn't in London,' said Katharine.

'She could have hired the hairdresser.'

'Risky,' replied Katharine. 'She'd be putting herself in a very vulnerable spot. Also, Blanche is doing well at present. Why should she bother? No, the more I think about it, if the hairdresser is a woman, she must be your Fan of Fans. One and the same person.'

'I'll go through the security files on Globe employees again when I get home. I ought to be able to spot anyone who looks like the hairdresser. And I think we should tell Toshiba about this now. What time is it in New York?'

But when Abbie phoned him, he was not overly impressed. 'You're basing your supposition on a very tenuous premise,' he said. 'Until there's some definite evidence, I'm keeping an open mind, although I agree there must be a connection between the person who's writing these notes and the phoney hairdresser. News of your vandalised dress has made all the afternoon's news bulletins here,' he went on, 'so you're in for a tough time when you get back, I'm afraid. I'm sure I don't have to remind you both that silence is our best weapon at this time.'

'Absolutely.'

'We'll have people at Kennedy to see you home tomorrow.'

Abbie confirmed her arrival time and replaced the receiver. She began to get ready for bed.

'We must be brave and lay all our ghosts,' Katharine said softly. 'We have to talk about George.'

Abbie flinched. 'I suppose you're right.'

The experience was not as harrowing as they had expected. They began with comparing notes about the circumstances under which each had met him. They were not surprised at how similar the encounters had been, George employing the same chat-up techniques with both of them. How ingenious he had been in persuading them to keep the affair secret. But mother and daughter skirted around the minefield of how he had wooed them into bed. That was a subject they would probably never be able to discuss.

'I wish we could pay him back somehow,' said Abbie eventually.

'My sentiments exactly. The trouble is whatever we do,

we have to be very careful. That wolf in cheat's clothing—' she gave a half smile – 'could blackmail us for life.'

Abbie looked alarmed. 'I hadn't thought of that.'

Both women were silent for a moment then Katharine gave a little grin. 'Abbie, what's the thing he loves above all else?'

'Easy. His penis.'

'Exactly.' Katharine took a sideways glance at her daughter. 'He's good, isn't he?'

'The best.'

They both smiled.

'I interviewed a scientist once,' Katharine said, 'who told me, off air unfortunately, that he was giving up some new tablets he was taking for high blood pressure because they had disastrous repercussions on his love life. A choice between death and dishonour, he called it, because they made him impotent.'

Abbie's eyes lit up. 'Will they work on anyone?'

'Quite dramatically, according to the scientist.'

'But not permanently, I hope. I mean, much as I'd like to see George hung, drawn and quartered, I wouldn't wish a permanent droop on him.'

'Neither would I,' said Katharine. 'No, there are no ill effects at all, apparently – other than temporary impotency. My tame pharmacist will let me have the right dose.'

'So how do we get George to take his medicine?'

'The tablets work best, for our purposes, if they're crushed and enter the bloodstream quickly. In champagne, for example. All we have to do is make sure he has a glass or three and then, when he's ready for action, he'll discover . . . he isn't.'

'Doesn't that mean going to bed with him? I couldn't bear that now.'

'We don't actually have to do the deed – he won't be

able to anyway. All we do is give the impression that we intend to.'

'But you had such a row with him, how are you going to make a date?'

'Flattery should do it. He's very vain, as you know. I'll tell him I miss him so much, nothing matters as long as I can see him, blah blah. I think, too, that he might feel I can still be of use to him to boost his hotel – it's still not doing well. So could you, of course, but my ITAC award and all the publicity about it might work in my favour. It was his self-esteem as much as his pocket that was hurt when the hotel launch fell flat. At any rate, it's worth a try, isn't it?'

'Damn right it is,' said Abbie. 'And I think we might actually pull it off.' She laughed and then said slowly, 'But there's a problem. He'll have seen the coverage of the awards ceremony. We looked pretty friendly. Won't he assume we've discussed him?'

'Not if we tell him that it was all an act put on for the cameras. My wanting to come back to him will make him think we're still at war.'

'You think he'll believe us?'

'Why shouldn't he? You know he has an ego the size of Denver. He won't dig too deeply. The important thing, Abbie, is to be very understanding when he can't get it up.'

'What's the fun in that? I'd rather gloat.'

'Try not to. We should both find a way of appearing sympathetic but with a little barb. He is getting on a bit, after all, so I could say something like, "Darling, you've got to expect this sort of thing at your age." '

'Yes,' said Abbie, entering into the spirit of things. 'I could stroke his brow and say something similar, that I've heard this is a common problem with men of his age.'

'That ought to do it. He might suspect we're in cahoots but how can he prove it? And that, my darling daughter, will be our revenge. I'll ring him as soon as I get back. Once I'm finished with him, he'll probably be desperate to prove his virility with you.'

Katharine held out her hand. 'Game?'

'Definitely.'

They shook hands and the deal was sealed.

Chapter Fourteen

At Kennedy airport Abbie moved, smiled and struggled through the pack of shouting, snapping press photographers, flanked by camera wagons and satellite dishes. Toshiba's protective guard quickly shepherded her into the forecourt and off towards the limo without her having to do more than look pleasant. Katharine, besieged in the same way, emerged a few minutes later. They arrived separately at her Fifth Avenue apartment, where Toshiba's people had kept the entrance clear of the press.

Although the slashing of Abbie's dress had made the front pages, journalists could not take the story further. Globe had been inundated with requests for interviews but all entreaties had been stonewalled by the publicity office with the standard response that the incident was being investigated by the British police. Until there were further developments, no more statements would be made.

The press, deprived of new fodder and without even a quote from Abbie, decided that her return merited only a re-run of the stories in British newspapers. The incident was attributed to a 'British vandal'. One enterprising tabloid had offered a reward for information about the mysterious hairdresser but so far it had elicited no response.

What Abbie found most satisfying was that there had been no leaks from the *Tonight* office. Globe's staff had been called to an emergency meeting where Jeri-Ann had stressed how important secrecy was to the successful completion of the investigation. So far no one had broken ranks. Journalists knew nothing about the condom or the link between the incidents in New York and London.

Abbie was buoyed up by the reception she was given by her colleagues and by Ed Dantry in particular. No one could recall him sending anybody else such an over-the-top basket of roses as now dwarfed her desk.

On Tuesday morning she was going through that week's script when her assistant called over to her softly, 'Abbie, line three. Your Mister Wonderful.'

Her first instinct was to refuse George's call but she had made a firm pact with her mother. Chastising herself for being a coward, Abbie felt her body tense as she picked up the receiver.

George was in ebullient mood. 'Darling, you looked magnificent at the ceremony. I saw the photo in the papers, that dress was terrific, it showed every gorgeous curve of you.'

Despite her best intentions, the sound of his voice made her tremble.

'Did you miss me?' he went on, not waiting for a reply. 'When are you free? Tonight, I hope. I've great plans for us and, believe me,' he gave a low chuckle, 'they don't include eating dinner. Darling, I can't wait to get my hands on you. Can you get away? I'd like to come round right now to take you out of there.'

His words tumbled out without pausing for her response. Had he always been so egocentric?

Abbie remained silent while he rambled on. Revenge would be all the sweeter for allowing him to dig a deeper pit. Abbie closed her eyes. As clearly as if he was lying next to her she could feel the strength of him, his breath on hers, his hands bringing her body alive. If only it was easy to switch off that electric chemistry between them.

She was furious with herself. How could she think of him this way, knowing what the bastard had been up to? She listened in a daze as he went on describing what games they would play, how he would bring her to ecstasy again and again and again. He had perfected the art of telephone seduction and slowly she felt her resolve weakening.

'Oh Abbie, darling, I want you. I need you.'

If he were to confess, plead forgiveness, renounce all other women, swear to be faithful, maybe . . .

'You're the only woman for me,' he was saying.

That brought her abruptly back to reality.

The only woman? Liar. How she longed to shriek the word at him.

Now she knew the truth about him she could hear him condemn himself with every word. She had hoped that he found her exciting because of her personality or her sense of humour. But no, obsessed by the physical side of their relationship, all he appeared to miss was her body. What a laugh.

At last he noticed her silence.

'Darling? Are you still there?'

'Yes, I am,' said Abbie coldly.

'What's the matter? You sound upset with me. You knew I couldn't come to the airport so—'

'No, I'm not upset, just a little tired. Darling, I'll be there at six with a wonderful bottle of French champagne I bought for you in London. Krug eighty-nine, it's supposed to be one of the best years ever.'

When the call ended, Abbie still felt tense. She picked up the phone again and rang her mother.

'Mum. I thought you might like to know, my turn has come.' She heard Katharine chuckle and suddenly felt better.

'What did I tell you? The man's like putty in our hands – in more ways than one.'

Abbie was still smiling as she carefully picked out a dress to wear for George that evening.

Much later, as an empty bottle of champagne rested upside down in the silver bucket, Abbie put her hand on the bedroom doorknob, ready to leave George's bedroom, an expression of concern on her face.

'Darling, I'm sorry I have to get back. I've such an early call tomorrow.'

George lay back on the white linen pillows, eyes closed.

Abbie glanced at the empty bottle and suppressed her amusement. So far, events pretty well matched Katharine's account of what had happened three days ago. Her mother had told George, 'You have to expect it, darling. After all, we're not getting any younger. These things happen.' At this, Katharine said, he had retorted, 'Not to me,' and buried his face in the pillow.

Now Abbie took a deep breath and said the killer sentence she had been rehearsing. 'Don't worry, darling, I've heard this is a common problem with men of your age.'

George's eyes flew open. 'Don't be ridiculous, I'm in my prime,' he snapped.

Abbie turned her face away quickly so he could not see her delighted smile. 'I'll be in touch soon,' she called gaily over her shoulder as she let herself out of his penthouse.

George phoned her a couple of days later.

'That little problem I had the other night? I must have been tired. And I'm definitely giving up champagne from now on. Darling, I want to celebrate. Are you free later on?'

'It's going to be difficult.'

'Do try. I'm aching for you.'

'George,' she said brusquely, 'I don't see any point in pretending. I know you've been having an affair with my mother.' She heard a sharp intake of breath.

'Darling, that's history. I can explain everything.'

'It wasn't history until very recently, was it? You were seeing both of us, making the same promises, saying the same words and enjoying every second of your double-dealing. As to whether you can explain everything, I doubt that very much.'

'Look, it was difficult. Once I met you I wanted to give her up but I didn't want to hurt her.'

'Let's just examine that truly sensitive statement, shall we? You and I have been having an affair since Christmas. During that time you were also sleeping with my mother. Just how long were you planning to wait before you gave her up? Six months? A year?' She did not give him the chance to answer. It was wonderful to feel in control of her emotions. 'George, listen to me,' she said coldly, emphasising each word. 'I am never going to see you again.'

There was silence and then George laughed. 'I don't blame you. Either of you. But, boy, was it fun for me while it lasted. And you have to admit, you didn't do badly out of it. You're a much better lover now than you were when I met you.'

Abbie slammed down the receiver. The shit was right. Damn him.

The package in the first post of the morning was marked 'Private and Confidential' but Ed Dantry's personal assistant ignored that. Nor, when she opened it, did she express surprise at seeing the unlabelled video inside. One of her duties was to arrange private viewing sessions of video films which could never be aired on prime time television.

It was the contents of the accompanying letter that caused the unflappable assistant a frisson of anxiety. In the normal course of events she passed anonymous mail straight to security but after the incident of the ripped dress in London, her boss had given orders that anything even remotely suspicious-looking connected to Abbie Lomax should be seen by him personally.

He was on his way up to the office. Because she disliked being caught unawares she had instituted an early warning system to alert her the moment he entered the building. It was so effective he had nicknamed her 'Radar' after the character in MASH. She was standing at the door when Ed Dantry burst in.

Like many men who had immense power, Dantry hated wasting a second. The atmosphere was instantly galvanised as if fuelled by his exceptional energy.

'Put my nine o'clock on hold and get me advertising. We've got big problems.'

'Before you do that I suggest you take a look at this,' she said, holding out the letter. 'You may feel it should take priority.'

As he walked into his office reading the letter, she followed him, the video in her hand.

'Holy shit. What's all this about?'

'Well, here's the video that came with it. Shall I put it on?'

'Yes, and get me Dempsey pronto. And the legal boys.'

Dantry pressed the remote control button and the wall-sized flat-screened television set flickered into life.

Abbie was called out of the Friday afternoon conference to take Matt's call. The security guard on duty outside her office raised his eyebrows.

'No, Luke. Just a phone call. I'm not leaving,' Abbie told him.

Matt's interruption had to be an emergency as the last full briefing before transmission involved the entire team and was regarded as the most vital of the week.

'I've had a call from on high,' Matt said. 'He wants to see us now, right away.'

'What's up?'

'Don't know. Can't be the contract, not at this stage. I usually go to first base with someone else.'

'What else could it be?'

'Trouble.' Matt disliked worrying Abbie but he knew how seismic it was for Ed Dantry to summon an agent and his star to his inner sanctum without warning. He arranged to pick up Abbie from her office so they could go together to the thirty-eighth floor.

A row of stern faces greeted them as they were shown into Dantry's palatial office. Abbie hesitated at the doorway. There were no words of welcome and this unsmiling, serious reception was so contrary to Ed Dantry's usual effusive greeting, Abbie was unnerved. What could have swung her away from being the network's sweetheart? It looked as if she was about to be subjected to one of Dantry's notorious rants. What on earth had she done?

'Abbie, thanks for coming. Please sit down. Our most senior lawyer,' he indicated a tall figure in the corner, 'has insisted that we follow this procedure.' He gave an apologetic shrug. 'I am advised that we shouldn't talk until we've viewed this video.'

Bewildered, Abbie watched Dantry activate the video machine. The screen went from black to a shot of a Parisian loft which had in reality been filmed in the Boston docks. She relaxed. Although it was years since she had last seen it, Abbie recognised the film at once. For God's sake, was this what they were getting so worked up about?

It had been made as a student production for the degree finals of her art course and had won a gold medal, with particular plaudits for the moody opening shots of the high-ceilinged room with its *fin de siècle* furniture and fabric-covered walls. The director was her then boyfriend Ben Kempinski who had dreamed of becoming America's answer to the Italian film genius Michelangelo Antonioni;

Ben would spend hours behind the projector analysing the themes of the cinematic master, often when he should have been studying something else.

This last film before graduation was to be Ben's masterpiece; he had boasted to the small production team that like Steven Spielberg's first efforts, which had caught the attention of a major studio, their work, too, could make history.

The thirty-minute movie described the life of a sensuous, voluptuous courtesan played by Abbie, who for the duration of the film wore very little clothing. One particular sequence showed her and a lover pretending to make love. It lasted less than sixty seconds in the half-hour video. Ben had argued that it was essential that his star do the scene in the nude to maintain the integrity of the story. He had promised that he would make only one copy which he would keep safely and use only with her consent. The only other person to see the film would be his examining tutor. Eventually they had reached a compromise. Abbie would wear minuscule flesh-coloured panties and a flesh-coloured bandanna to cover her breasts.

Caught up in Ben's excitement, she had quite enjoyed the filming experience. True to his word, he had not asked her to do anything unsavoury and had directed the lovemaking scene with a delicate skill, covering her apparent nudity with shots of the other actor's body. The result had been tasteful, evocative and pleasing.

Here it comes, she thought, aware that Matt was shifting in his seat beside her. This must be what all the drama is about.

The camera lingered over the lean figure of Abbie stretched languorously on the four-poster, her body outlined under a satin sheet, an inviting smile on her lips, her hand lifted, fingers beckoning to a naked man in the foreground.

What was this? Abbie straightened in her chair and her mouth opened in astonishment. The muscular young man began to lick the female's body, first the nipples then slowly travelling downwards. Abbie's embarrassment turned to incredulity as the camera panned to a female pudenda that filled the entire screen.

The naked man began to make slow, sensuous love to the responsive body on the bed.

Abbie caught the eye of the station's chief security officer whose lascivious face showed obvious enjoyment. Dempsey stared at her with an insolence that chilled her.

'That's not me.' Her voice was high with indignation. 'I don't know who it is but it's definitely not me.'

Not one of the men said a word. Their eyes remained fixed to the screen.

The back of the actor's head obscured most of the woman's features. His mouth slowly travelled down the woman's body, then she performed the same service for him, turning her face away from the camera. God, that does look like my body, thought Abbie nervously. She tried to catch Matt's eye, but he steadfastly gazed at the screen.

Matt could already see the headlines. All his career he had had to manage the presentation of unpalatable facts. He hated the description 'spin doctor' and saw himself more as a media psychologist, offering a benign interpretation of even the most damaging information about his clients. An abortion became a wisdom tooth operation, time off for a detox or drug rehabilitation was translated into a trip to search for spiritual enlightenment.

Matt had spotted Abbie's potential as soon as she hit the little screen in Chicago but he had been left in no doubt during the initial negotiations for the New York job that she had got her big chance because of who her mother was.

And she had done well. In a sleaze-ridden age she had captured the public imagination from the start, being pigeon-holed as the clean living but beautiful girl next door type. No court cases, not even a ticket for a traffic offence. A nation used to fallen heroes was delighted to find that, like her mother, Abbie appeared to have no dark secrets. She did not snort cocaine at parties, was not promiscuous, did not depend on alcohol to lessen the tensions of her high-powered job. Even better, from Matt's point of view, was that the press loved her. OK, there was the much-publicised feud with her mother but they seemed to be taking Abbie's side in that. And it was great for ratings.

But being filmed on a bed with a man not her husband and going down on him? Even in these sensation-ridden days, viewers would surf away and switch off in droves. The backlash would be all the more fierce because her fans would feel cheated. They would think her image was phoney. As Matt well knew, no other nation on earth could go small-town and stand on its moral high horse as quickly as America. Would anybody of any stature agree to being interviewed by Abbie once this video was seen out there?

He could see his bank balance dwindling and a swift return to Chicago and his dull private life if his star client lost her show. Abbie was protesting that the buck naked woman on that screen was not her. Jeez, he could swear it was.

Matt was aware which way the wind was blowing by the expression on Dantry's face. Bringing the network into disrepute was the gravest sin. Even so, Matt was not yet prepared to think the unthinkable, that the station might terminate Abbie's contract.

He was sorry for Abbie. She could have had a great career, no question. But Ed Dantry was one of the most ruthless operators in television. He ran a network worth billions. OK, Abbie's show was a hit. But it was a mere hour a week, a fly-dropping on Ed's schedule. Abbie was good and what a publicity coup her being Kate the Great's daughter. But they had milked all the publicity they could from that angle and there were many thousands of other hopefuls out there.

He would not be able to protest if they invoked the moral turpitude clause. But he would put up a damn good fight for Abbie's career before he wrote her off. He owed her that.

'Stop the film. Now.' Abbie's voice was rising. 'I'm telling you that's not me up there. I don't want to see any more.'

'You're saying it's a fake?' Dantry's face was hard to read. Abbie was one of the few lucky ones on the payroll never to have witnessed the dark side of his character. Leaving the financial negotiations to others, her dealings with him had been conducted in an atmosphere of flattery, enthusiasm and charm, however phoney.

'That's exactly what I'm saying.'

'Let me get this straight. It's you on the bed, correct?' Abbie nodded. 'But it's not you doing the porn stuff.'

'Absolutely not.'

Dantry snapped his fingers at Chuck Dempsey. 'Rewind to when she goes down on him. Yeah, there. Freeze the frame.'

The screen flickered with the image of the woman bending over the man's body, performing oral sex. Her hair hid her face. For a few seconds they all stared at the static picture.

'It sure as hell looks like you,' Dantry said finally.

'Yes, it may do. But it's not me in that frame. They obviously used a double.' Despite trying to appear calm, Abbie felt tears of frustration welling up. They all doubted her word and, by his expression, so did Matt. Why had he not said anything in her defence?

'Ed, you have to take my word for it. Someone has tampered with that video. Yes, I did take part in a student art film for our finals at college and some of it's there at the beginning but the sex has been added later.'

Chuck Dempsey still had that sneer on his face.

'If you rewind you'll see I have a sheet over me at that stage. Then I sit up and you see my back is naked. When that scene was shot, I was covered up in front and had panties on. But in the next shot, there, the woman is completely naked. That's when the new stuff has been added. The entire episode was quite innocent and only lasted maybe thirty or forty seconds. Not this ten minutes of filth. All I had to do was lie there under the sheet. I didn't do anything specific.'

'It looked mighty specific to me,' said Dempsey.

Stung by the sarcasm in his voice, Abbie fought to contain her anger. She was not going to win this one by losing control. Momentarily she considered asking for a private word with Matt but dismissed it instantly. That would be taken as a sign of guilt.

'Do you ever see my face? All you see is a woman who resembles me. Her hair always hides her features when she's not being filmed from the back.'

No one spoke.

'I'm not in the habit of lying,' she was proud that her voice did not quiver, 'and I would ask you to take my word on this.'

The silence was broken only by the sound of clearing throats and shifting seats. Finally, Matt spoke.

'Who sent this to you, Ed?'

It was the lawyer who answered. 'It was that crazy who's been hounding Abbie for months. The Fan of Fans.'

Oh God, thought Abbie, not again. 'Hounding is right,' she said, her face pale. 'Doesn't that tell you anything?' She turned to Dantry. 'I don't understand how you can question what I say about a filthy video sent to you anonymously by someone whose mind is obviously sick.'

Again the lawyer spoke. 'We had the video checked out as soon as we saw what was on it.'

Dantry nodded. 'That's right, and it shows no sign of having been tampered with. If it's a fake, it would have involved two different shoots and we all know how difficult it is to match those up. But it's perfect. Everything on that video is exactly the same. We've checked colour grading and types of film used. We've compared the positions of the bed drapes, the way the sheets have been folded – things only skilled professionals would notice. Our guy in the lab couldn't find any disparity.'

'Your guy is wrong.' Abbie thumped the arm of the chair with her fist. 'I tell you once more, the porn stuff in that film is fake. Of course you can't see the cuts and joins because it's a copy. Probably second, maybe even third generation. We don't know. To examine the video properly you'd need to compare it with the master film.'

'We know that.' Dantry was dismissive. 'We took that into account but our guy is ninety-nine per cent convinced this video is for real.'

Globe's hard-nosed veterans knew every camera trick in the business. They were familiar with techniques like substituting locations, people and dialogue on film and if they had tested for all of those and were still convinced that it was not a fake, Abbie was about to lose the battle.

She was under no illusions about what it would mean if she could not convince the powerful suits in this room that it wasn't her in the pornographic section. She was fighting for her career.

'I don't know what's going on here,' she said tersely. 'Maybe the director carried on filming that same day after I'd left using some woman who resembled me. I'd never do that stuff and he knew it.'

Dantry stood up, picked a letter off his desk and handed it to Abbie. 'Well, it's expertly done, but this nut means business. We've got big trouble.'

The lawyer murmured to Matt, 'I'm afraid the evidence against your client seems very strong.'

'Here's a copy for you, Matt,' said Dantry. 'Chuck is having the original checked for fingerprints and Toshiba is on the case too.'

Abbie read the words with mounting distress.

'This is from the Fan of Fans. Abbie Lomax is a porn star. Here is my evidence. I have sworn statements to prove this film is not a fake. If she does not read out the following statement on her show this Sunday I will send copies of the film to every media outlet in the city at noon on Monday: "I have decided to leave my job in television because I have harmed too many people. They know who they are and I apologise sincerely to them. This is my last appearance and I will not under any circumstances make a further statement." '

'That's outrageous. It's blackmail. I won't do it.' Abbie could not sit any longer and began pacing the floor.

'The way I see it, Abbie, we have no choice.' Dantry was curt. 'None of us likes a gun at our head but this isn't the time to mess around. I don't have to remind you that it's Friday afternoon and we've a show to prepare for Sunday.'

Abbie felt an explosion of rage. Not one of these bastards had admitted the possibility that she could be right. She glared at him. 'Ed, can't you see this is what this nutter has been working towards all these months? He, or she, wants to destroy my career. You're just going to sit there and let that happen?'

'Of course not, Abbie. We're doing this to *save* your career. We need to play along with this crazy and give ourselves time to smoke him out. Please, see it our way.' For the first time Ed Dantry showed some semblance of humanity. 'Our loyalty is to you. But I can't deny that we have to look at this from another perspective. You may be able to persuade us that you didn't star in a porn movie, but advertisers, they're a different breed altogether. They demand no smut, no scandal, and they believe that where there's smoke there's fire. If this nutcase goes public, I don't need to spell out how much revenue we're going to lose. It'll ruin your show because we wouldn't be able to fund it. You see our problem? That's why we need to go along with this for the moment.' He paused. 'What do you say, Abbie?'

If she held out, they would pull the show. If she appeared to go along with all of this, she would buy time. Whatever happened, she was not going to quit on air.

She said carefully, 'I see I have no choice.'

Dantry gave a relieved smile. 'Good. No one is to mention the video outside this room. Understood?' He got up. 'That's settled.'

When Abbie and Matt had left, the network boss turned to the others in the room.

'The way I figure it, we can't lose here,' he said. 'We'll get millions of dollars of free publicity when the reptiles find out what's behind that little speech. And let's face it, after that, Abbie's reputation as Miss Clean will be shot to hell. So, OK, we have to let her go.'

'We'll get her on the morals clause,' the lawyer interjected quickly.

Dantry nodded. 'Then we pull in someone else. Abbie's built the audience, done her job. While I think of it, ring that agent of what's her name?' He clicked his finger. 'Blanche Casey. See how wedded she is to that channel of hers.'

Katharine was appalled when she heard about the doctored video.

'Mum, you can't imagine how awful it was. I was so embarrassed sitting in the same room with those men mentally licking their lips and God knows what else as this nude woman cavorted on the screen. She did look like me and she was stark naked. You could see everything in anatomical detail. In the original version you couldn't see a damn thing, it was very discreet.'

'I'm sure it was. I remember how shy you were about showing your body when you were young.'

'The video sent to the station was not Ben's.' Abbie's pale face showed the strain of the last few hours.

Toshiba had told her it was a waste of time trying to locate the video houses that could have handled the fake. There were six thousand in the city at the last count and those were the ones paying taxes and, as he pointed out, it could have been copied anywhere in America. It was also likely that their suspect would have used a false name and paid in cash.

Abbie passed a copy of the letter to her mother whose face registered increasing outrage as she read it. 'And Dantry's taking notice of this?'

'He didn't give me the impression he was on my side.'

'I can't believe it. The man must have his own agenda. Nobody gives in to this kind of blackmail. You can't do it. If you did, we'd all be run by every crank who crawled out of the woodwork.' She tossed the letter on to the table. 'And Matt agreed to your doing this?'

'He thinks we have no alternative. But Mum, I know Dantry. If the press finds out about the video, I'm out, and they'll invoke the morals clause. And then they'll get someone else to anchor the show.'

'What's Toshiba doing about tracking down this Fan of Fans?'

'He thinks we may be wrong about it being a woman and that it could be Ben Kempinski. But I know Ben wouldn't do that to me and I've told Toshiba so. He's not the type to terrify or blackmail me.'

'People change,' Katharine said gently. 'Tell me, when did you last see him?'

'Not since college.'

'After that last quarrel?'

'Yes. He was upset that I wanted us to cool it for a while and you know how it is when you get a new job, especially when it was so exciting being an intern at Globe's station in Boston.' Abbie's voice was strained. 'The last time I spoke to him he said he was finding it difficult to cope not being part of a couple any more but I was working all hours, weekends, holidays. And when I was transferred to Chicago I just didn't have the time for him and eventually we grew apart.' She shrugged. 'That kind of thing is inevitable, it doesn't mean he'd harm me.'

Katharine's shrewd eyes did not waver from her face. 'Could he have a grudge against you?'

'I don't see why. We were young. Break-ups happen.'

Her mother stood up. 'Well, he'll have the master film so at least when we get hold of it we can prove you were telling the truth.'

'Toshiba's trying to track him down now through the college. He wants me to try and think of any little thing I can remember about him, his family, friends, anything. And he's checking out the three others who helped produce the film.' Abbie chewed her lip. 'If Toshiba doesn't come up with something quick I'm going to have to make a fool of myself on Sunday night. That gives me less than two days to go. But Mum, I'm not going down without a bloody good fight.'

It was after ten but the frightening events of the past day had set them on an adrenaline high. Katharine and Abbie decided there could be no sleep until they had news from Toshiba's Boston visit. Katharine suggested that they go to Abbie's apartment and check on the contents of her college trunk which was stored in the box room; it might yield clues. She made the suggestion more to occupy her daughter's mind than in the hope of finding anything helpful.

Katharine stared at the jumble of diaries, mementos and snapshots that made up her daughter's past. It resembled the mess that was Abbie's bedroom.

'Right, we need to be logical,' she said. 'Let's sort through all the diaries first. I suppose we don't need to worry about anything that happened before the video filming.'

Abbie's diaries were sparse, containing only the briefest mentions of family birthdays and cryptic messages which were unintelligible now even to her.

Her mother opened a small jewel case. 'Who gave this to you?' she asked, holding up a sorority pin.

Abbie thought for a moment then shook her head. 'Nope, I'm ashamed to say I can't remember. College was fun but so many exciting things have happened since I left, those days have sort of faded. The film was the last big thing I was involved in with Ben. We worked eighteen-hour days and we all had many different jobs to do, there was no time for temperamental egos. But Ben was thrilled with the result. Oh look, I've found this picture of him taken at the end of filming. God, he looks tired. We all felt like that.'

A young Ben Kempinski smiled out at them. Even from such a small picture it was possible to see that he had inherited many of the distinctive features of his Slav background. A shock of dark hair fell over his forehead; he had high cheekbones, a wide jaw and what looked like perfect teeth but a slightly misshapen nose.

'That picture was taken a few months after he broke his nose in a football game,' said Abbie. 'Does he look like the type of man who'd be obsessive? Or spiteful? He's just not that kind of person. Why would he need to be? He could just pick up the phone and talk to me. Nothing will convince me he was responsible for any of this.'

Toshiba phoned to say the college in Boston had supplied him with a photograph and Kempinski's last known address. Ben had moved from Boston . . . to Chicago. Toshiba was on his way there now. Ben in the same city without contacting her? That was strange.

'I think we've done all we can for tonight,' said Katharine. 'Let's go back to my apartment and try and get some sleep.'

Abbie reluctantly agreed. It was now after midnight; Toshiba was unlikely to have any more news tonight.

It was late morning before Toshiba's eagerly-awaited call came.

'Our chief suspect is out of the frame.'

'I knew it,' said Abbie triumphantly. 'It was totally out of character for Ben. He denied it, right?'

'Ben Kempinski is dead,' said the detective.

Katharine reached forward as Abbie's face contorted with shock.

'Oh God, how terrible.' She turned to her mother. 'Ben's dead.' Katharine walked to the extension and listened in as Abbie asked what had happened.

'He crashed his car.'

'Poor Ben. He was the same age as me. I can't believe he's gone.'

'I've spoken to a few contacts in the police department and the coroner's office,' Toshiba said briskly in an authoritative, unemotional tone. Police training had long since established that sympathy was rarely the best way to deal with victims of grief. It was liable to release such a torrent of emotion that the recipient was unable to absorb information. 'There seems to be an idea that it could have been suicide.'

'Suicide? I don't buy that. Ben wasn't the type,' said Abbie. 'He was so talented, he had so much to live for. Why would he take his life? It must have been an accident.'

'You could be right. There was no note. But from the tyre marks it seems he drove straight into a tree, no attempt to swerve.'

'But that's such a messy way to end a life. Ben was so precise, so meticulous. I don't believe he'd do that. How about his friends, what do they say?'

'He didn't appear to have friends, or none that I could find, but neighbours said he was depressed, out of a job and into drugs. There was a substantial amount of crack cocaine found in his blood at the post-mortem.'

'God, how awful. What a waste. If only I'd stayed in touch with him. I wish he'd contacted me, I might have been able to help.'

'I doubt if you'd have been able to do much. Even his parents weren't able to help him. I've tracked them down and they say they hadn't seen him for a couple of years before he died, not since he moved in with a woman.'

Katharine quietly replaced the receiver and crossed the room, putting a comforting arm round her daughter's shoulders.

Abbie could hear Toshiba flicking through his note-book.

'Name's Cheryl Haskell. Do you know her?'

'Yes, I do,' Abbie's voice lifted in surprise, 'or rather, I did. She used to hang around with us at college, though I didn't think she was that close to Ben afterwards. Have you spoken to her?'

'Not yet, but I'd sure like to. She and Kempinski took an apartment in Elm Drive but she left after the funeral and hasn't been seen since.'

'She was involved in the video,' Abbie said. 'Cheryl was the gofer, making coffee, going on errands, that kind of stuff.'

'What's her story?'

'She wasn't a student. She used to be a part-time waitress at the college cafeteria and because she always looked after our table we got to know her well. After a while she started turning up at parties and football games. Everyone knew she had a soft spot for Ben and I used to kid him about his faithful puppy. But we thought he was more sorry for her than anything else. He felt she didn't have our advantages. We all thought that, come to think of it. That was why we included her in everything. During the day she was training at the nearby school of hair and beauty.' As she spoke the words, she caught her mother's astonished gaze.

'The hairdresser.'

They spoke the words simultaneously and Abbie continued excitedly down the phone, 'Remember our theory about that hairdresser in London being a woman? It could have been her.'

Abbie's elation suddenly subsided. 'No. I would have recognised her. It couldn't have been Cheryl. She was fatter and shorter than the person who came to do my hair. And her colouring was quite different. Cheryl always looked quite flushed.'

'People can change their appearance, Miss Lomax, and this is the strongest lead we have, though I don't know how she could have done all this Fan of Fans stuff without you spotting her, and until we find her we can't answer that. Unfortunately she seems to have disappeared into the ether.'

The one nugget Toshiba had managed to extract from a tenant in Cheryl's previous apartment block was that she was always urging Ben to go to New York to raise money for his films. She was convinced he was a cinema genius. 'According to the neighbour, she would have walked on broken glass for him. Something bad was bothering him and he took it out on her. He was a pig but she never whined. Not once.'

'Believe me, there's nobody around me who looks remotely like Cheryl.' Abbie was adamant. 'I can't make it out. If she ended up getting the guy, why would she resent me?'

'I've said all along that the Fan of Fans' actions are so inexplicable, it has to be personal,' was Toshiba's reply. 'These people are irrational and logic doesn't come into it. Cheryl Haskell must be the major suspect. Your trouble started shortly after Ben's death, which points directly to this woman.'

Abbie had hoped that her tormentor would turn out to be a deranged stranger, a misfit in a lonely one-room apartment, fixated by a face on television. In a way it was a relief to put a face to the shadow that had haunted her for months but at the same time it was chilling to think it was someone she knew, someone from her past, someone with whom she had shared laughter, fun, endless cups of coffee. And all the time Cheryl, if it really was her, had been consumed with envy and resentment, so full of hate that she would take a pair of scissors to slash a dress belonging to her 'rival'. Abbie shivered. If Cheryl blamed her for Ben's death, what else was she capable of?

'We're still trying to identify that vehicle in the crash photograph sent to you,' Toshiba went on. 'I'd bet next month's pay cheque that it's Kempinski's car.'

Abbie registered the comforting sounds of Katharine clattering about in the kitchen and managed a smile. It was so unusual. Saturdays were usually busy but she and Jeri-Ann had agreed to liaise by fax. Toshiba had stressed how important it was to keep clear of the office. Thank God she had her mother to run to. She felt so much more secure in this comfortable apartment, especially with a guard permanently on duty outside.

The atmosphere now between the two of them was so relaxed she had given her mother a hug this morning, quite spontaneously. It was something she had done often as a child and Abbie was surprised at how natural it still felt. Katharine had seemed delighted by this small gesture and had responded warmly. It was as if they had retreated in time, wiping out all the intervening misunderstandings, problems and arguments, able to discuss anything.

Except George. Once they had carried out their plan to humiliate him (which she had told no one about, not even Jeri-Ann), his name was off their agenda.

Abbie sighed. He was a bastard but though she hated to admit it, she missed his spontaneity, the way he would surprise her by whisking her to one of the hotels in his chain when she least expected it. She coloured; it was such a cliché that women preferred rogues. She hoped she had the sense to learn from this devastating experience and grow up to appreciate men like Robert. She wondered how he was getting on in his new job.

In the kitchen, Katharine's mobile chirped. It was Freddie – they were leaving the main line free in case Toshiba called.

'Freddie, it's lovely of you to want to help but at the moment we're in the hands of this specialist. Yes, she's holding up pretty well, thank you.'

'I'm sure you're helping all you can, which is good of you, darling, after everything that's happened between you.' Freddie's voice was solicitous.

Katharine lodged the phone under her ear and sipped her coffee reflectively. 'It's an amazing thing, but all that seems to have slipped into the past. This business has focused our attention on something other than ourselves. You know what happened this morning? Abbie actually hugged me. I was so taken aback.' Her voice faltered. 'Isn't it silly that something other people take so much for granted should make me fill up?'

'You sound upset. Shall I come over?'

'No, no. I'm fine,' she said quietly. Freddie and she had seen little of each other for a while and she did not want to reactivate the relationship. 'I'm just happy that Abbie and I seem to be back on track. We're waiting for Toshiba to make contact then I'll get in touch with you.'

There were four short jabs to the bell of Matt's apartment.

He flung open the door and pulled the young woman roughly into his arms, kicking the door shut with his foot. He nuzzled her slender neck and began fumbling with the buttons on the sleek-fitting jacket.

'Oh, baby. Thanks for coming round. Make me forget what's going on.'

Abbie walked into the kitchen waving a photograph triumphantly. 'Look what I found, a photograph of all of us who worked on Ben's film. This one here is Cheryl Haskell. I'll have to fax it to Toshiba.'

Katharine took the photo and scrutinised the face of the woman they strongly suspected was Abbie's pursuer. 'In this she doesn't conform to, shall we say, the standard idea of attractiveness, does she?' she said. 'That would add to the jealousy, the thought that she couldn't compete with you?'

'I suppose so.' Abbie was staring into the distance. 'You know the worst thing, Mum? It gives me the heebie-jeebies to think I could be seeing her every day. Talking to her. Smiling at her. God. How could I not recognise her?'

'Well, if you look at photographs of me ten years ago, I look completely different. There are things you can do to change your appearance and I'm sure a trained beautician would have learned better than most.' Katharine looked again at the image of a smiling Cheryl. 'She looks tubby in this picture. Shedding fifteen or twenty pounds would completely transform her shape, especially the face. She could alter the colour of her hair, modify that flushed complexion you described. I've seen our make-up people use a special green powder for that. And high heels would make her appear taller. She could even adjust the timbre of her voice. Margaret Thatcher lowered hers by two octaves.'

Abbie nodded thoughtfully.

'You haven't seen this Cheryl for years,' Katharine went on. 'I reckon it'd be perfectly possible for her to look and sound so different that even you'd be fooled. And remember that's exactly what she set out to do. I'm sure we're on the right track.'

'It seems so extreme,' said Abbie. 'I've done nothing to Cheryl. I haven't been in touch with Ben since we left college. I don't see how she can blame me for his death.'

'Bereavement does odd things to people.'

'Well, unless we can flush her out soon, my career's over, kaput. I don't suppose I could even go back to a small station in the back of beyond.' Abbie looked disconsolate. 'I have to prove that video's a fake, Mum. And there's so little time. It's hopeless.'

'No it's not.' Katharine's voice was energetic and strong. 'I've had an idea buzzing about in here,' she tapped her forehead and stood up. 'Time for an injection of caffeine. I'll put the kettle on, you bring your contacts book and fax machine in here.'

After she had poured them both a cup of freshly-brewed coffee, Katharine sat in the chair by the window and faced her daughter, arms folded.

'This . . . person isn't going to win. You know what we're going to do?' She took her daughter's hand in hers. 'We're going to join forces and fight her. We have a lot in our armoury. Ask yourself, why are we at the top? I'll tell you why. Because we're fighters. We're not scared of competition, we're not scared of criticism, we spend our lives trying to be better than anyone else. And you know what our best weapons are? Our minds. Don't tell me that two women like us can't defeat someone whose actions are governed by spite, who's feeding off a misplaced grudge and who's seeking revenge in the most cowardly way, anonymously.' She paused, an expression on her face that Abbie recognised as her into-battle mode. 'She doesn't know what she's unleashed. You and I haven't started fighting back yet, not until now.'

What a formidable woman. Abbie had never admired her mother more and felt a surge of optimism.

'If you're in a tight corner like this, it's best to attack first.'

'What do you mean?'

'The more I think about it, the more I feel you shouldn't do what Dantry wants. Don't apologise. Don't say goodbye to your career on air.'

'I don't see how I can avoid it. What's the alternative?'

'I have a suggestion.'

Abbie listened with increasing excitement as her mother sketched the outlines of her idea.

'God,' she said, 'that's nerve-racking. Do you really think it could work?'

'Well, we need to sew up all the details and, yes, it is risky. You may not be in full control at every, or indeed any, stage so you'll need to be fast on your feet but with a little luck I think it could work. Are you up for it?'

Abbie did not hesitate. 'Absolutely. I hated myself for sitting back and letting Ed Dantry run all over me. Let's face it, he's not concerned about me. All he's paid to worry about is revenue. I can't rely on him to think about my career.'

'Exactly,' said Katharine.

'Hell, Mum, I'm glad you're on my side.'

'Better now than never, kid.'

They began to work out the details of the plan, juggling the times, discarding impracticalities, refining ideas. 'We must make use of this woman's state of mind, the fact she worshipped Ben, to flush her out,' said Katharine.

They were interrupted by a call from Toshiba who was about to catch a flight back to New York. He said that his people had been checking on all the students involved in the production of Ben's film and none of them had any helpful information. They had cast-iron alibis for the time of the London trip and for all the other incidents. Nor did they have any idea what had happened to Ben's original film.

But he did have one vital piece of information. Another neighbour had told him that Cheryl went to New York three days after Ben's funeral. Before she left she gave the neighbour her prized camellia, a favourite of her lover's, so the woman assumed the move was permanent.

'Mr Toshiba, you're worth every cent of your bill.'

It was the only time Abbie had heard him laugh.

'That's another piece of the puzzle in place,' she said to Katharine, and they went back to work. At one stage Abbie went round the apartment collecting letters which Katharine tied up with a length of brightly-coloured ribbon.

Over a long night and countless phone calls pulling in impossible favours, the plan did at last begin to seem feasible.

Chapter Fifteen

It was Sunday morning and at ABN's *Here and Now* offices Katharine was trying to compose herself after a heated editorial conference with Mike. She had told him everything and he had been full of sympathy for her daughter until the moment she confessed that she had given away the exclusive centrepiece of next week's programme.

His bellow of anguish could be heard all down the corridor. When he was finally able to speak, he said with real feeling, 'You didn't have the right to do that.'

'It was my idea and my contact.'

'Yes, but you're working for ABN, not Globe.'

'Look, I'm sorry, Mike. But this person seems to be capable of anything. Her actions have been getting more extreme. Abbie's life could be in danger.'

'But she's guarded.' Mike was not giving an inch.

'You don't know what we're dealing with here. The woman seems to be able to move at will. She knows Abbie's every movement. We've increased security but she's still getting through. This was the only way I could think of helping Abbie in the time left. Trust me, Mike, I'll make it up to you.'

'How can you be sure it'll work?'

'I can't.'

Now it was show time.

Matt was in the studio audience; he had promised to sit

through what he thought was her last show. Ed Dantry had made it clear that should any mention of the porn video leak to the media, Abbie was finished. In Matt's view there was not a hope in hell that it would stay secret. Before she went out on to the studio floor, he had hugged her, squeezed her hand and wished her luck so effusively that she had looked apprehensive.

An hour before the signature tune announced the start of *Tonight*, Abbie was swathed in a pink nylon garment, having her face made up. She stared at her reflection in the mirror, gratified at how calm she appeared despite being dry-mouthed with nerves.

'I think I'll put on extra blusher today.' Brenda was being her typically pragmatic self, reaching between baskets of brushes, cosmetics and hair rollers as she began her task of erasing all traces of strain from Abbie's face.

'Brooke,' she called to her number two. 'Do you have blusher number nine over there?'

The young assistant rummaged around her box and brought it over.

'I've got a bit of a gap at the moment,' she said. 'Is there anything I can do?'

'Sure thing. I'd kill for a cup of herb tea.'

'What about you, Miss Lomax?'

'No, thanks,' replied Abbie absently. She checked the time. The helicopter should have left by now. At least the weather conditions were in their favour. Still, it was going to be a close-run thing.

She went over the show's running order in her mind. The links would be on Autocue but she liked to learn them almost by heart. Once in Chicago the machine had broken down and she had never forgotten her terror. She would never again rely totally on that inanimate object. The first two interviews had been recorded earlier that afternoon. Her producer had insisted that Abbie would be in no fit state to do live interviews on the night; Abbie was grateful to have Jeri-Ann on her side.

'That's it,' said Brenda, 'you're done.' She touched Abbie's shoulder. 'Abbie, we all know what you're going through and we're so sorry and I wish I could . . .' She was unable to continue, she looked near to tears.

Abbie patted her hand. 'I know, Brenda,' she said, 'I know.'

The tension in the gallery affected everyone on the studio floor, even those not privy to the unfolding drama. There was a heightened sense of expectation, greater than the customary fever that accompanied the run-up to every show.

Up in the gallery, the external phone buzzed again.

Jeri-Ann listened for a second or two then put her head in her hands. 'Oh God,' she said to no one in particular. 'What the hell else can happen tonight?'

During the first commercial break, she raced across the studio floor to Abbie who was checking through her notes. There was no time for finesse.

'We have a problem. I don't think McLeod is going to make it.'

'What? I can't believe it.' Abbie tried to control her panic. This was the only eventuality she and her mother had not anticipated. He was crucial to the plan. What could she do if he did not turn up?

Jeri-Ann said soothingly, 'I'm sorry, but these things happen. Don't worry. We're digging out the Helliwell interview in case of no-show. Be ready for a change of links.'

'Where is McLeod?'

'The fuckwit of a driver went to the wrong heliport and our star's grabbed a cab but traffic's not moving.'

Martin McLeod was America's newest literary icon. The 28-year-old had been on the New York *Times* best-seller list for the past ten weeks and he had struck a chord with readers because of the way he reflected the humour, life and attitudes of the young. It was his story that had given Katharine the idea to trap Cheryl.

Katharine had been first to interview him six years ago with his debut novel. She was one of the few who knew that his so-called writer's block since then was due to heroin addiction. She had kept in touch with him and had introduced him to a formidable drug expert who had eventually succeeded in helping him overcome his addiction. For her efforts she had received a personally inscribed copy of his much-acclaimed second novel which was optioned for millions by a film studio: 'Without your help this would not have been written. Your grateful friend, Martin.'

At first McLeod had been adamant that he could never go public about his former drug addiction. 'It would destroy my cred,' he told Katharine from his hideaway in Cape Cod. 'I would have helped if I could. But my publishers would be upset and I think my family would prefer it if I didn't.'

Katharine was in a class of her own when it came to persuading reluctant celebrities to appear on a talk show. She had dealt with far tougher cases than Martin McLeod and when she pointed out to him that his reading public would be enlarged to the power of ten by this one frank admission, his attention switched to whether or not his lover could accompany him in the helicopter.

And after all that effort it looked as if he would not get to the studio in time.

Through Abbie's earpiece the floor manager's voice was as calm as ever. 'Forty seconds . . . thirty-nine . . . thirty-eight . . .'

The Helliwell interview was already in the machine awaiting the attentions of the vision mixer. The star had come into the studio to record an interview to publicise his new film, due to be screened the following Sunday.

The producer would have to apologise to his film distributors for putting out the recording a week earlier than promised.

The Autocue operator was substituting a new link as Jeri-Ann told Abbie that Martin McLeod's interview would definitely have to be killed.

Her chance to trap Cheryl Haskell was slipping away.

'. . . thirty-one . . . thirty . . .'

Think. Think.

Jeri-Ann interrupted her inner turbulence. 'I've kept Matt up to date with what's happening. Abbie, I hate you having to do this but get through it the best you can, kiddo. We're all rooting for you.' She bit her lip. 'This is a shitty way to go out. Dantry's being a prize prick.'

Abbie smiled at her friend, grateful for her support. Her mind was whirling furiously as Katharine's words came back to her, 'Be prepared for any eventuality.' Yes, but did that include a no-show?

'. . . twenty-six . . . twenty-five . . .'

Think. Think.

Her mother had warned her that she should do what was best and act instinctively. Well, there was something . . .

Only twenty seconds left . . . nineteen . . . eighteen . . .

No time for refinements. No time to confer with her producer or warn the director, the vision mixer, the floor guys. None of them had a clue what she was going to do within the next few seconds; all their meticulous forward planning would go haywire. But she had to do it. Her career would end tonight if she did not. And she would have to be quick because the camera operator would expect to stand down during the recorded item.

As the last few seconds of the signature tune for the Diet Coke commercial faded, she ran through the key words she planned to use, took a deep breath and readied herself.

In the gallery the director murmured to the vision mixer, 'Camera one to Abbie, roll Autocue and . . . cue Abbie.'

The floor manager gave her the signal and she turned to the central camera whose red light indicated it was the functioning lens.

'Ladies and gentlemen, we were going to show you an interview I did with Brad Helliwell earlier today but I've decided not to do that. My career is on the line tonight, maybe my life too, so I thought I would tell you about it. None of the people who direct this show was aware that I would talk to you about my private problems. But I've decided to confide in you because I need your help.'

It took a moment before the director registered that the words coming out of Abbie's mouth did not match the introduction on the Autocue. 'She's not sticking to the script,' he shouted furiously to his colleagues. And to Abbie he yelled through his radio link, 'What the fuck are you up to?'

Abbie ignored the screaming cacophony in her earpiece and kept her voice steady. She forced herself to concentrate on one thing only. Keeping the attention of the audience at home. It was rare to be cut off mid-sentence in television but her story would need to be riveting.

As a news reporter in Chicago she had all too often been called upon to ad-lib and give a graphic summary of some incident she had just witnessed. No rehearsals, no time to rewrite, just straight to camera, sometimes with hair uncombed and only the merest hint of lipstick. And if her words were not dramatic or exciting enough, she would later receive a tongue-lashing from her editor.

'I'm taking a lot of flak from the director up there.' Abbie gestured in the direction of the gallery. 'They want to know why I'm not sticking to the script.'

She pulled out her earpiece and let it dangle over her

shoulder. Then she focused directly into the black eye of the lens. She forgot about the audience, her colleagues, the millions at home. She was addressing Cheryl Haskell and her alone.

The phone by her side buzzed shrilly.

'We'll ignore that, shall we?' Abbie gave her most dazzling smile. She picked it up and laid the receiver on the desk. Now there was no contact at all between her and the control room. If they switched her off now she was finished anyway.

Upstairs the director looked helplessly towards the producer. 'Shall I pull the plug?' he asked her.

At that moment the phone rang. Ed Dantry's furious squawks were heard throughout the gallery.

'I want her off. Now!' he commanded.

Everyone turned to their immediate boss, Jeri-Ann Hagerty, ready to comply with her orders instantly. As she hesitated, a breathless researcher shouted, 'Martin McLeod's in the building.'

'Get him up to Abbie quick,' snapped Jeri-Ann, rising from her chair. 'I'm coming down and I'll brief him.'

Abbie's face was tense as she braced herself to tell her secret to the watching millions. 'Someone's blackmailing me. They have a porn movie featuring me as the star.'

There was a shocked gasp from the studio audience.

Abbie instinctively raised a hand. 'It's not what you think. That movie is a fake, but such a clever one it's going to be hard for me to prove it.'

The studio audience was silent now. She had them. Upstairs would not switch her off.

Jeri-Ann was rushing to the podium, propelling an anxious-looking Martin McLeod towards the spotlight surrounding Abbie. He walked hesitantly up the steps, offering his hand.

Startled, Abbie took it. 'Oh, you've made it,' she said with a smile. She turned to the audience, 'Ladies and gentlemen, the Pulitzer prize-winning author, Martin McLeod.'

The writer sat down in the guest's chair.

'Don't stop, Abbie. I want to hear about this porn movie and I'm sure these folks can't wait either.'

Thunderous applause greeted his words. That should sell a few books, thought McLeod. It sure as hell wouldn't do his sales any good if he butted in now. This was good television, it would work in his favour.

'The movie was sent to my boss, Martin, can you imagine?' Abbie was saying. 'The trouble is some shots are from a movie I helped make with a friend at college. It's so well spliced with fake inserts that not even our technical guys could see the join on the copy. Nobody's going to believe it's not me performing on that bed.'

McLeod sat back in his chair. 'Well, Abbie, I'd like to help you tell your story. I guess I'll have to take over your role and interview you.' He turned to camera. 'This is for real. Stick with us.'

To Abbie he said, 'Tell us about the man who made the college movie.'

Ben Kempinski came alive for America that night. Abbie described the young man she had loved and how he had thrown away his talent, his family and finally his life because of his drug habit.

'That's why I agreed to come on the show tonight,' McLeod told the audience, 'to tell my readers and their parents that the same thing nearly happened to me. I called it writer's block but it was a cover-up for my heroin addiction. I could easily have ended up like Ben.'

Abbie looked at him gratefully. 'Thanks for that.'

Then, as they had planned, she delved into a drawer of the leather-upholstered desk and pulled out a bundle of letters tied with bright blue ribbon.

'These letters contain Ben's innermost thoughts about what was important in his life, his vision, his plans for his future and for the children he hoped to have.' She held them aloft. 'These are his monument and I am privileged to have them. I keep them with me always in my dressing room to remind me of how fragile life can be. This has come home to me with great force over the last few months. I've been subject to psychological torture by someone who blames me for Ben's death.'

'Why would you be blamed?' asked McLeod.

'Because the stalker thinks that if it hadn't been for my callousness, Ben would be alive today. So this person is taking revenge on me in the only way they know how, by making my life hell. It's all part of some plot to break me.'

'Have you any idea who it is?'

'No, that's the trouble. But the instructions with the video were quite clear. This show was supposed to be my last. I was meant to say goodbye not only to this show but to a television career.' She looked straight into camera. 'And I was also supposed to apologise for the harm I'm accused of doing to Ben. If I was in any way to blame for his death, I am deeply sorry.'

Abbie stood up slowly to give the camera time to track her movements.

'But you know what? I'm not going to say goodbye. I'm not going to give up my job, not while you, my viewers, still want me here.'

A thunderclap hit the studio as the audience rose. Martin McLeod stood up with them and, smiling broadly, joined in the shouting, stamping, cheering.

Abbie stood motionless on the podium, the spotlight on her tearful face. After thirty seconds, she raised her arms, gesturing for silence.

'Thank you. That's all I needed to know.'

The switchboard was ablaze with lights as hundreds of viewers bombarded the station with congratulatory calls.

'She made me cry for my wasted youth, my lost opportunities.'

'Abbie was brilliant.'

'It was wonderful television.'

'You must be very proud of her.'

She won the approbation not only of the American Feminist Society but the Daughters of the Pilgrims as well. Her appreciation rating nearly went off the charts at 97.4 per cent, the highest ever recorded by the network.

Faced with these statistics, Ed Dantry gave Abbie his full public backing for her brave stand and was quoted in the following day's newspapers as being 'completely convinced that the video is a fake. We were behind her every step of the way.'

'Far behind,' said Katharine caustically when she read it.

Immediately after her show, Katharine dashed over to the Globe studio to be with her daughter. She was in time to witness Abbie being hugged by a delighted Jeri-Ann and surrounded by what seemed to be the entire production crew of cameramen, lighting engineers, make-up, wardrobe, scene-shifters and the editorial team. Her watchful guard was by her side.

As Katharine made her way across the vast floor, the crowd, recognising her, parted for this rare visitor from a rival planet. Putting her arms round Abbie, she said, 'Well done. I'm proud of you.' There was applause and she whispered in Abbie's ear, 'Remember, we must make our exit as public as possible.'

Abbie's nod was imperceptible. Loudly she said, 'I'm going to take Katharine away and open the biggest bottle of champagne we can find.'

Many from the studio audience were waiting on the sidewalk for autographs and showed their pleasure at being able to capture two stars at once. Cameras flashed like disco strobe lights and a smattering of applause followed the women as the limo driver leapt out and ushered them into the sleek black car while Abbie's personal guard slipped into the front seat.

Leaning back against the soft leather upholstery, an exhausted Abbie turned to Katharine. 'Public enough for you?'

Katharine nodded. 'Are the letters in your drawer?'

'Yes, securely locked.'

'You must have freaked out when Martin didn't turn up. Without him there it would have been a lot harder to get into the drug abuse and wasted lives story.'

'Don't remind me, Mum. I never want to go through that again. Thank God the viewers liked it. Jeri-Ann would have been sacked as well.'

'You couldn't have handled it better,' said her mother. 'Your spontaneity could well turn out to be more effective.'

The driver obeyed their instructions to drive round the block and return them to the back entrance of the studio, where a surprised security guard let them in with a 'Forgotten something, Miss Lomax? May I get it for you?'

'No, it's all right, Charlie.'

Abbie and Katharine, followed by the bodyguard, took the service lift down to the now silent studio floor in the basement then made their way up the internal staircase to the gallery where Abbie's show was produced. Only half an hour ago her face had been seen by millions across the nation. Now the power for the air conditioning, the switches, dials, meters and activating buttons had been turned off and the place was in semi-darkness, deserted. The bin overflowed with abandoned scripts and dozens of plastic cartons, half filled with Diet Coke, coffee and Tab. That and pens and yellow stickers lying on the console were the only evidence of previous frenetic activity.

In the faint glow from a security monitor they could

make out the reassuring bulk of Toshiba sitting on the floor, out of view of the glass panel in the soundproofed door. They crouched down beside him. The guard stationed himself at the end of the corridor.

'The line feed's working well,' whispered Abbie, pointing to a playback monitor which showed the interior of her dressing room. The camera, fitted with a night-light lens, had been positioned on the wall with an extension arm high up in the ceiling.

Katharine could see that the lens spanned the door and most of the room, including the mirror and the rows of bottles of make-up and perfume ranged untidily underneath.

Abbie fiddled with the camera controls until the lens was centred on a side drawer fitted into the worktop. 'When there's action, throw that switch,' she instructed her mother, pointing to a lever on the console.

Katharine nodded. 'I'm ready.'

From then on the anxious group sat in silence in the stuffy, overheated gallery, their eyes fixed on the small monitor, waiting for some sign of movement in the dressing room. Never had time dragged by so slowly.

'I'm not sure if I can keep this position much longer.' Katharine began massaging her cramped legs. 'My calves are killing me.'

'It's been nearly two hours,' whispered Abbie to Toshiba. 'Do you think anything's going to happen?'

Toshiba glanced at his watch. 'Let's give it another fifteen minutes.'

Abbie was beginning to have doubts. Would the trap work? Sitting round the kitchen table organising the payment of technicians to install camera equipment in her dressing room and persuading a dubious Toshiba that it would work had been the easy part.

Toshiba grabbed Abbie's arm and pointed to the monitor. The dressing-room door was slowly opening.

They stared transfixed.

An indistinct figure came into shot. The figure was wearing an anorak with the hood pulled forward over the face, making it impossible to tell whether it was a man or a woman. It paused before shutting the door and appeared to be waiting. For half a minute the figure stood motionless.

The watchers hardly dared breathe, although there was little danger of the intruder hearing noises from the gallery.

A gloved hand, holding a key, reached over towards the drawer.

Katharine jabbed at her daughter's arm. 'Where did that key come from?' she hissed.

Abbie shrugged her shoulders expressively, without taking her eyes off the screen.

Slowly the drawer opened and the hand began sifting carefully through the contents. It lifted out Abbie's desk diary and what looked like a large folder. Then the hand emerged holding the bundle of 'Ben's letters' that Abbie had flourished earlier in front of the cameras.

Abbie pointed excitedly towards the power switch and Katharine gave the lever a firm pull, activating thousands of kilowatts of electricity.

The dressing room was immediately flooded with blinding white light which caused the automatic iris in the camera lens to kick in. While the lens adjusted down to the correct light level, the screen blanked out. They held their breath, fearing that the camera had died, but after a second the image returned.

The figure had wheeled round, startled, and the movement had dislodged the hood. Now in mid-shot, it was directly in line with the lens.

'Quick, an ECU,' hissed Katharine.

Abbie pushed the remote control to activate the zoom on the dressing-room camera for an extreme close-up.

Without taking her eyes off the monitor, Abbie leaned over to mobilise the bank of screens. She switched the vision mixer control panel and the wall of small screens in the gallery flickered into life.

Abbie gazed in shocked disbelief at the face, frozen in terror, that filled row after row of monitor screens.

Once more the hooded figure filled the screen, this time on the giant television set in the library of Katharine's apartment as they relived their moment of triumph the next day. Toshiba had been called round for the post-mortem and Matt was expected at any moment.

After the viewing, the detective turned to the two women.

'I have to compliment you two, you beat the professionals fairly and squarely.'

'No, no, Mr Toshiba,' said Abbie quickly, 'it was a team effort.'

Katharine nodded. 'Yes, it was crucial to know about Cheryl's obsession with Ben and you dug that up. That gave us the idea for the trap.'

They were in Katharine's sitting room, after a late breakfast and a good night's sleep. Toshiba had brought along a copy of the video tape of Abbie's dressing room and the image of her tormentor flickered on the television set.

'She won't worry you again,' Toshiba assured Abbie. Cheryl Marylou Haskell was currently being held in police custody until the preliminary court hearing scheduled for next month. Bail had been refused. 'I was with her for a while before the police took her off. She told me Ben Kempinski talked about you constantly and compared her unfavourably with you. You were the perfect woman and she was someone he used. He couldn't have sex with her unless he was watching a video of you. At first the video was made up of snips from your Chicago news reporting items. Later he needed more stimulation and dug out his student film with supplementary raunchy footage which he shot on the same day using a woman with the same figure and colouring. He intended to make an entire porn version as his show reel. But he started taking drugs and never got round to more than the fifteen-minute version.

'Poor woman, I feel sorry for her.' Abbie sank back on to the sofa cushions. 'I never thought I'd say that.'

'Someone more sane would've left the guy instead of taking it out on you,' said Katharine.

'What set her off? Ben's death?' Abbie asked.

'I think it started before that.'

Rifling through his notes, Toshiba told them the turning point seemed to have been triggered by a letter Kempinski wrote to Abbie at Globe TV while she was away in the south of France. 'He asked you for an introduction to a television producer on your station and when your studio sent him the standard "I remember" letter, he took it as a brush-off. After that his drug intake increased, which caused his fatal accident. Cheryl Haskell thinks he was trying to kill himself. Having read the accident reports, I tend to agree.'

'Oh God, how awful,' said Abbie. 'I didn't know anything about his letter.' She looked at her mother. 'If only I'd kept in touch with him. Maybe if I had, he would still be alive.'

'I don't agree with that at all,' said Katharine. 'You can't take responsibility for someone else's life. For God's sake, he had all the advantages, looks, talent, education, the lot. It's his fault that he didn't make use of them, not yours.' She turned to Toshiba. 'I can understand why Abbie didn't recognise the woman. She must have lost what? Twenty-five pounds, maybe more. And that short blonde hair changes her face completely.' Katharine turned off the video and the screen went blank.

Abbie nodded. 'She was dark-haired and smooth as the hairdresser – a wig, presumably. And she must have been wearing coloured contact lenses because when she turned up in my hotel suite I swear her eyes were brown. She's a talented actress as well as a very skilful make-up artist. But what I can't understand is how she got herself to London without being missed from the studio. You checked everybody's movements.'

'I've looked up my notes,' replied Toshiba. 'She called in sick with a sprained wrist. But she provided the medical back-up and we accepted that. Of course I now have to assume that note was forged. It's one of the things the police will investigate.'

'I can't see how she'd know I was going to Disco 2000. Unless, she suggested it to one of the researchers. But how on earth did she get hold of my home phone number? Or find out where we'd stashed Mrs Stern?'

'She was one of your inner circle,' Katharine pointed out. 'She was working in the studio right under your nose and she had access to your dressing room.'

'But she couldn't access that kind of information. Very few could and she wasn't one of them,' said Abbie firmly.

'Then there is only one explanation,' said Toshiba. 'She must have an accomplice.'

'But who?'

'I don't know. Yet.'

The intercom buzzed from the porter's desk to announce Matt's arrival.

'What a relief,' he said excitedly as he joined them. 'I hear you nabbed the stalker.' He turned to Toshiba. 'Who is she?'

'Her name's Cheryl Haskell.'

'Never heard of her.'

'You wouldn't,' said Abbie. 'She worked in the studio. You never met her.'

'Did you find out why she did it?'

'It's all history, she knew me from our college days.'

'And she's borne you a grudge ever since, eh?' He shook his head. 'These weirdos. Where is she now?'

'In police custody.'

'Congratulations, Mr Toshiba. You said you'd do it and you have.'

'I'm afraid you're complimenting the wrong person. It was Miss Lomax and her mother who devised the trap.'

'Trap?'

'Watch this.' Katharine picked up the remote control and rewound the video.

'This is it, Matt,' said Abbie. 'Look at this. She'll turn round in a second, the hood falls back and you get a great view of her face. Here it comes.'

There was a choking sound from Matt and Abbie turned anxiously towards him. 'Matt? Are you OK?'

He was transfixed, his face ashen as he stared at the screen, oblivious of her question.

She took his arm and tugged at his sleeve. 'Matt. What on earth's the matter?'

Katharine switched off the video. 'Get him some water, he looks dreadful.'

'No, don't,' said Matt. He took out a handkerchief and wiped his brow.

Toshiba looked at him sternly. 'You know this woman.' It was not a question.

Matt nodded and pointed to the now blank screen. 'Yes. She works as a freelance hairdresser going to people's homes. But she had nothing to do with your stalker. She couldn't have done those things. There's some mistake.'

'Then why did she break into my dressing room and try to steal those letters?' demanded Abbie.

'I – I have no idea,' stuttered Matt. He stared from one to the other. 'You've got hold of the wrong person, I tell you. I mean, her name isn't Cheryl.'

'Yes, it is. She was born Cheryl Haskell,' said Abbie. 'But when she managed to get a job in our make-up department she changed her name to Brooke Adams.'

Matt appeared to shrink physically as he absorbed this information. 'My God.' He sat with his head in his hands. 'What have I done?'

'What are you talking about?' asked Abbie, puzzled.

'I've been such a fool. She's been using me . . .'

'Matt, will you explain?'

'Oh, Abbie, I'm really sorry.'

'I don't understand what you're talking about,' said Abbie, shouting in frustration.

Matt looked up, his face miserable. 'I met her soon after I came to New York. We've been having an affair for months. That's how she must have found out all those details about you.'

Toshiba nodded in satisfaction. The last piece of the jigsaw was in place.

Matt groaned. 'I've been taken for a sucker. Oh, she was clever, I'll give her that. She never asked a single question about you, Abbie. She didn't seem to be interested in the television business, that's what I liked about her.' He groaned again. 'I was so crazy about her. I paid for her to come to London just to spend a few hours with me. Oh, Abbie, it's my fault she was able to get to you. I can only apologise.' His voice trailed off.

Katharine and Abbie looked at each other, stunned, then at Matt's hunched figure. Eventually the silence was broken by Abbie.

'You're not the first person to be deceived by a good-looking face and a manipulative character.' She and Katharine exchanged a quick glance. 'We've all been fooled by her, Matt. She used to sit next to me painting my nails, for God's sake, and making up my face. Smiling at me. It makes me sick to think of it.'

Matt seemed not to hear. 'I know I didn't tell her

anything,' he went on, talking almost to himself. 'But God knows she had the run of the apartment often enough. She must have hacked into my computer, gone through my diaries, everything.' He stared at his client and apologised abjectly once more.

'I don't blame you, Matt,' said Abbie. 'I really don't. You couldn't know.'

'What's going to happen to her, Mr Toshiba?' asked Katharine.

'She'll be sent for psychiatric evaluation,' he replied. 'Then the police will decide whether to treat this as a criminal action or a case of diminished responsibility.'

'I don't want to press charges,' said Abbie, 'and I don't think the network is keen on this going to court.'

'No, in my opinion she's likely to end up in a psychiatric unit.'

Matt sat up suddenly. 'Angela won't have to know about this, will she?'

'It's too soon to say,' Toshiba told him. 'You might be needed as a witness.'

'Oh God. She'll never forgive me.'

Chapter Sixteen

Ed Dantry walked round his desk and greeted Abbie with open arms.

'Abbeeee, my little star. I knew you'd think of something. What did I say to everyone?' He nodded in the direction of an uncomfortable Dempsey who had just received a bollocking for his inept handling of the station's security. 'Look at all this publicity.' Dantry gestured to his desk and the sheaf of newspapers full of stories about the stalker using an Abbie lookalike in a porn movie. 'We have twenty front-page mentions of the company. You can't buy that stuff. From now on, we're gonna push out the boat for you. You want it, just ask. An interview with the Pope in Rome? You got it first class. More promos? You have my word on that.'

Abbie watched his antics with a detached expression. Eventually she said quietly, 'Thank you,' barely able to contain her anger. Asshole, she thought. All smarmy smiles and smug self-satisfaction. Not a hint of an apology. No word of regret for making a mistake of monumental, catastrophic, Empire-State-like proportions.

A disgusted press officer had earlier leaked to her the draft of Dantry's statement prepared before Sunday's broadcast that he was 'invoking the morals clause' to cancel her contract.

So, salivate all you want over the publicity, bud, thought Abbie, you'll never have my loyalty again, nor my respect and definitely not my gratitude.

She turned and walked towards the door.

'Hey, where you off to?' asked a disconcerted Dantry. 'We have some French champagne on ice here.'

Abbie turned round slowly. 'Sorry, I have an urgent appointment. With my mother.'

Sam Wolfe had seldom looked so concerned, his bald head tilted to one side, his face squeezed into an expression of sorrow.

'Katie,' his voice dropped an octave, 'if only I'd known what you and Abbie were going through. I would have done anything to help. You know I'm always here for you.'

Katharine looked at him dispassionately as he rifled through the newspapers on his desk, his face now smiling. 'This publicity's gold dust, fabulous. You must be very happy.'

She shrugged. She had worked for him for the best part of ten years and he had no idea what she thought, what she felt about anything.

Sam sat down beside her on his leather sofa and took her hand in his. 'Now what can I do for you? More promos? Bigger budget? Today's the day to ask,' he chortled.

She paused, extracting her hand. This was the man who had had no compunction about overruling her objections and ordering her to undergo cosmetic surgery. OK, she could have resigned, but her crooked accountant had put paid to that. Sam Wolfe and David Crozier were now both linked together in her mind.

'There is only one thing I want from you,' she said, deliberately pitching her voice low so that he had to lean forward in a supplicatory stance. 'I want out from my contract. Today.'

He started back. 'Katie, what's the matter? Are you ill?'

She raised her voice. 'Never felt better in my life.'

'Are you going to Fenton TV?' he asked harshly.

'I'm not going anywhere. I want out. Completely.'

'What's up? You're top of the tree. Why do you want to quit?'

'Because I need to be in charge of my life. Me. Not you.'

He rubbed his brow. 'Let's not be hasty. Let me discuss this with Buzz. More money's no problem.'

'Sam, you don't understand. It's not money. It's freedom.'

His bonhomie vanished and his mouth tightened until his lips almost disappeared. 'Walk out and I'll sue.'

Ah, this was the real Sam Wolfe. That didn't take long.

Katharine gathered up her briefcase and made for the door. She turned to look at him, a smile on her face. 'Do that.'

Mother and daughter met in a mid-town champagne bar where Abbie was testing a bottle of vintage Louis Crystal.

'How did you get on?' Abbie asked as Katharine sat down at the small marble table. 'That triumphant look gives me a small clue.' She nodded to the waiter who filled both their glasses.

'I wish you'd been there,' crowed Katharine, 'you would have loved it. I was word perfect and Sam played the part as if we'd rehearsed it. He actually said he would sue if I walked.'

'Wonderful, just what you wanted.'

'He was so predictable. When he said those words, do you know what I did? I strolled coolly to the door, turned, collected myself for a second, then shot him. "Do that," I said and swept out.'

Abbie chuckled. 'So he has no idea about the libel settlement?'

'Obviously not,' replied her mother, her face alight.

'Have you told Brad and Verity? After all, it was their villa that provided the setting for the reptiles' shots of us "smooching in the sun".'

'It seems so long ago, doesn't it?' said Katharine. 'So much has happened since then, so much has changed. But to answer your question, yes, I have, and they've invited us to celebrate with them at their villa this summer.'

Abbie was delighted. 'Great. The story's sure to leak tomorrow. You can't keep quiet about an award of seven million bucks, tax free.'

'Oh, to see Sam's face when he realises I don't need him or his company.'

'Those poor suckers on the *Planet* must be feeling sick today.'

'Well, I hope it'll teach them to check their facts. I hear the editor's for the high jump. Apparently they call him the "Brit shit". Mine was the third writ he had to settle. He'll never know how grateful I am to him. He's got me off the hook and made me decide what I'm going to do.'

'And what are you going to do?'

'From now on I intend to be my own boss. I'm starting my own production company. I've even thought of the name, "Double Kiss Films".'

Abbie was quick on the uptake. 'Ah, the X in SeXton and LomaX are the kisses. That's neat. Good for you, Mum.'

Katharine shrugged off her black linen jacket. 'Nina's put some money into it – but first she and I are going on an art tour of Venice. What about you? What happened when you saw Dantry?'

'Just as you predicted,' smiled Abbie. 'He oiled all over me but no apology, of course, no "I'm sorry I was throwing you on the shit heap", nothing like that. He thinks money is the answer to everything.'

'They all do,' said Katharine. 'Mind you,' she said with a smile, 'it often is.'

'There's nothing I can't have, nothing he won't do for me. You can picture him, can't you? He was so baffled when I said I had to leave to meet you, couldn't believe it.'

'I bet he couldn't.' She sipped her drink. 'What time's your appointment with Fenton TV?'

'Six, at the apartment. They said it was better to meet somewhere private.'

Katharine nodded. 'You can't expect Ted Fenton himself to be seen with a prospect before she's signed up. But if the big cheese is coming, that new anchor job must be in the bag.'

'I hope so. Going mid-week's going to be a challenge.'

'But you can do it. And they know it so I hope Matt's going to go in tough. He is doing the contract negotiations, isn't he?'

'Yes, although he sent me a formal letter of resignation. He feels he's let me down but I tore it up. I reckon he's getting enough hassle from Angela. I don't think she'll leave him but she'll certainly make him pay.'

'Their marriage seems strong enough to cope. Hey, I hope your contract will leave you time to work for "Double Kiss" now and then. I'm already talking to the BBC about supplying segments for one of their current affairs programmes.'

Abbie was impressed. 'You don't hang around.'

Katharine smiled and toyed with her glass. At Abbie's signal the waiter topped up their champagne.

Abbie raised her glass. 'A toast,' she said. 'To freedom.'

They touched glasses and drank.

'And to gal pals?' said Katharine, with a mischievous glint.

'And the *National Planet*.'

'Guess what?' said Katharine. 'Nina's heard that George has completely given up champagne. Won't touch the stuff. Thinks it's bad for his health.'

This set them off into such peals of laughter that all around the bar heads turned.

Lowering her voice, Katharine added, 'The word is he's set up base in Monaco. And,' she placed heavy emphasis on the word, 'he's applying for citizenship.'

'What on earth for?'

'With George it would be for money or sex. In this case it's both. Apparently he thinks this'll make him a more suitable consort for one of the royal princesses.'

Abbie shook her head. 'Wow, did we have a lucky escape.'

'All my men get over me very quickly,' said Katharine, waving an expansive hand. 'Freddie hasn't spent much time mourning either. I saw a picture of him yesterday at the Harlequin Ball. And who was he with? None other than your good friend and mine, Blanche Casey.'

'I'm sorry about that,' said Abbie. 'He's much too nice for her. I hope he doesn't take long to find that out.'

'Talking of former lovers, have you spoken to Robert lately?'

Abbie rummaged around in her handbag and pulled out a piece of headed notepaper from USTV.

Katharine read it quickly. 'That sounds promising. He wouldn't have bothered to write if he was still angry.'

'He doesn't say anything significant, Mum, just how pleased he is that I'm OK.'

'Why not call him?'

Abbie thought for a moment. 'I think I will.'

'You taking my advice?'

'Yup.'

'Hold on,' said Katharine, putting her hands over her eyes. 'Everything's going black.'

Abbie gave her mother an impish smile and Katharine leaned back, relishing the moment. She had a strong feeling that the more trusting, honest, happier alliance she now enjoyed with her daughter would last. She and Abbie would be a unit yet independent, mother and daughter yet equals.

But best of all they would be friends.